BLURB TK

Balls

Gorman Bechard

A PLUME BOOK

PLUME
Published by the Penguin Group
Penguin Books USA Inc., 375 Hudson Street,
New York, New York 10014, U.S.A.
Penguin Books Ltd, 27 Wrights Lane, London W8 5TZ, England
Penguin Books Australia Ltd, Ringwood, Victoria, Australia
Penguin Books Canada Ltd, 10 Alcorn Avenue,
Toronto, Ontario, Canada M4V 3B2
Penguin Books (N.Z.) Ltd, 182–190 Wairau Road,
Auckland 10, New Zealand

Penguin Books Ltd, Registered Offices:
Harmondsworth, Middlesex, England

First published by Plume, an imprint of Dutton Signet,
a division of Penguin Books USA Inc.

First Printing, March, 1995
10 9 8 7 6 5 4 3 2 1

 REGISTERED TRADEMARK—MARCA REGISTRADA

LIBRARY OF CONGRESS CATALOGING-IN-PUBLICATION DATA:

Printed in the United States of America
Set in Baskerville

PUBLISHER'S NOTE
This is a work of fiction. Although real people appear in their natural settings,
none of the events depicted in the story really happened and are entirely ficti-
tious. Any actions, motivations, or opinions attributed to or about real people in
the book are purely fiction and are presented solely as entertainment.

BOOKS ARE AVAILABLE AT QUANTITY DISCOUNTS WHEN USED TO PROMOTE PRODUCTS OR
SERVICES. FOR INFORMATION PLEASE WRITE TO PREMIUM MARKETING DIVISION, PENGUIN
BOOKS USA INC., 375 HUDSON STREET, NEW YORK, NY 10014.

for Kristine

Acknowledgments to: Bob Dixon *(for stats, slang, 'n' stuff),* my agents Matt Bialer & Mike Sheresky *(for really pushing the book),* my editor Danielle Perez *(for really wanting to publish it),* producers David Kirschner & Christine Rothman *(for really wanting to make it into a movie),* Shane Lambert (for the *Tombstone* artwork), Kathy Milani *(for all the continued support, feedback, & cool dust jacket photos),* Laurie Scheer *(also for the support, despite the fact she detests baseball),* Deanna Matz *(for her always inspiring comments & suggestions),* the 1993 New York Mets (for forcing my hand), and lastly to my scriptwriting partner Steve Manzi *(who likes seeing his name on the acknowledgment page).*

CONTENTS

Overnight with Howie   0

PART ONE: BATTING PRACTICE

1. In the Wink of an Eye   0
2. The Grandfather, the Chief Justice, & the I-Man   0
3. Bart Giamatti Is Spinning in His Grave   0
4. Enquiring Minds Want to Know   0
The Baseball Beat   0
5. Moses Speaks   0
6. What Do You Want on Your Tombstone?   0
7. It Ain't the Four Point Six Ounce–Size, Smooth Mint
   Gel Crest Toothpaste Pump Dispenser, It's the Motion   0
8. Magnetized   0
Overnight with Howie   0

PART TWO: PLAY BALL

Manhattan Meteorites 2000 Season Schedule   0
Manhattan Meteorites 2000 Promotion Dates   0
9. Ready   0

10. Through Wind, Rain, Sleet, or Snow   0
11. Clichés, Lineups, & Paperbacks   0
12. Private Conversations   0
13. Slumpin'   0
14. The Family That Jeers Together . . .   0
Overnight with Howie   0

PART THREE: THE ALL-STAR BREAK

2000 Midseason Standings   0
15. Purgatory   0
The Baseball Beat   0
16. Pizza 'n' Roses   0
17. Commercial Breaks   0
Overnight with Howie   0

PART FOUR: THE SECOND HALF

18. Through Wind, Rain, Sleet, or Snow Revisited   0
19. Streakin'   0
20. Everybody Was Kung Fu Fighting   0
21. About That Rain Check . . .   0
22. Reciprocation   0
The Baseball Beat   0
Overnight with Howie   0

PART FIVE: THE RACE FOR THE PENNANT

23. Sleeping with the Enemy   0
24. Meant to Be Broken   0
25. The Appreciative Fan   0
26. Guns Don't Shoot Ballplayers, Fans Do   0
27. Success & Bullets   0
28. Let's Go to the Videotape   0
29. Vincent Van Tombstone   0
30. No Excuses   0
2000 Final Standings   0
Manhattan Meteorites Team Statistics   0
Overnight with Howie   0

PART SIX: THE POST SEASON

31. Late   0
32. Biblical Proportions   0
The Baseball Beat   0
National League Championship Series Line & Box Scores:
  Game One   0
  Game Two   0
  Game Three   0
  Game Four   0
  Game Five   0
  Game Six   0
33. Have a Drink on Me   0
National League Championship Series Line & Box Scores:
  Game Seven   0
Overnight with Howie   0

PART SEVEN: THE WORLD SERIES

34. No Simple Answers   0
35. Fly Me to the Moon   0
Epilogue   0

Overnight with Howie

"Let's go to the phones. We've got Joey from Bensonhurst. Go ahead, Joey. You're overnight with Howie Rose on the FAN."

"Hey, Howie. First off, let me say that I'm an L-T-L-F-T-C."

"A longtime listener, first-time caller."

"You got it. I'm a very big fan of your show in particular. I've been listening to you since the days of the first installment of 'Mets Extra,' and let me tell you, you really know your stuff."

"Well, thank you. Do you have a question?"

"It's more of a comment really. And I'd kinda like to hear your thoughts on it."

"Shoot."

"It's about the Mediocres. . . ."

"Cute."

"Thought you'd appreciate that. Remember you heard it first here."

"So noted."

"Anyway. It's about their first-base problem. Seems everybody's got something to say, and I'd like to toss my two cents in."

"I don't know if problem is an appropriate word, but go on."

"It ain't right, Howie. I mean, c'mon, really. It just ain't right. This Matt Stern guy is ruining the national pastime. It's like blaspheme."

"Don't get religious on me. It's baseball. And it's Matt Stern's baseball team. It's his team, Joey. You've got to remember that."

"I'm trying, man. But I'm so pissed off I can't see straight."

"Let's look at it this way. What do you do for a living, Joey?"

"Auto repair."

"All right. Answer me this. If your boss hired someone new. Let's say someone who specializes in transmissions."

"We could use someone like that."

"Okay. If the person was a crack mechanic, would it matter to you if they were black or white?"

"No. But this ain't a black or white thing."

"Would it matter to you if they were male or female?"

"I don't know. I guess not. Not if they could do the job. But this ain't a garage. This is baseball. And people shouldn't screw around with baseball. Y'know the saying, If it ain't broke, don't fix it."

"But Joey, baseball's in dire need of some fixing. Has been for years."

"But this ain't the way to fix it."

"That's a matter of opinion, right? It's all a matter of opinion and it's only a game. But, look, we've got to cut this short and take a commercial break. When we come back, we'll be speaking with WFAN's legal consultant, John Starks, to get his take on the implications of tomorrow's Supreme Court–sanctioned game between the expansion Manhattan Meteorites and the world champion Atlanta Braves. The first baseball game of this new century."

 PART ONE

Batting Practice

*Kids are always chasing rainbows, but baseball is a
world where you can catch them.*
                              —Johnny Vander Meer

In the Wink of an Eye

One step. Her first step out of the on-deck circle that had been stepped on only once before, and that by a batter who just struck out looking. It was all so new, the on-deck circle, the uniform, the stadium, the grass, the freshly painted lines—foul and otherwise.

Another step. A deep breath. The air, chilly, but not that chilly for February in New York. It was loud. Very, very loud. But what were they saying? What were the now-standing 38,710 curiosity seekers chanting? Was that her name? She didn't think so. Well, maybe. Or were they booing, hissing, screaming for the pitcher to knock her on her ass? Some of the noise had to be support. It had to be. She believed that. If only it weren't so goddamn loud.

Another step. She looked around. The colors. The milk chocolaty brown of the dirt, the greens, the home whites and away grays. The big man in black. The bricks and neons and ivy and advertising. And the banners. There were lots of banners and signs. One read: Go, Gehrig, Go! Another read: What's in Your Cup, Louise? Another: Three Cheers for the Babe Gehrig! While another: Stay in the Kitchen, Where You Belong! Then one read: Matt Stern Sucks! Another: Baseball Diamonds Are a

Girl's Best Friend! And yet another: Where's George Steinbrenner When You Need Him Most? And there was even the old standby: John 3:3.

But it was a sign that read Real Ballplayers Don't Wear Panties! that caught Louise Kathleen Gehrig's eye as she took yet another step, this one into the batter's box. She had to smile at that one, smile and even laugh a little to herself, all the while thinking, Says who?

Ⓦ   Ⓦ   Ⓦ

Number four took her position, checked, then double-checked, just in case. It was there, in her back pants pocket. A little good luck charm. A prevention, a cure, a guarantee that there were no lost causes, at least not on this ball field.

She glanced first into the Meteorites' dugout—her own dugout—and caught a quick handful of go-ahead nods, you-can-do-it glares, and even an encouraging thumbs-up from Meteorites catcher Bob Dixon, then looked back at the umpire, a massive tower of fat and oil dressed appropriately in black. She gave a quick look at the opposing team's catcher, Pete Sacker, then turned to face down the pitcher.

Left-handed hurler Rocky Goetz—winner of last year's Cy Young Award and MVP of the 1999 World Series—had had his fastball clocked at 103 miles per hour. He had a curveball that almost always curved, a dead fish backdoor slider that left even the most proficient batters swinging to the wind, and a change-up and split-fingered fastball that weren't too shabby either.

Rocky spit out a wad of well-chewed tobacco, adjusted his cup, then got in position. He glared at Louise, then smiled a shit-eating, tobacco juice–stained grin.

The crowd exploded into cheers of "Louise! Louise! Louise!" which were met by chants of "Rocky! Rocky! Rocky!"

Louise, her thirty-six-ounce bat resting an inch or two off her left shoulder, tuned out the noise, all of it, and smiled back. What an ugly son of a bitch, she thought.

Rocky was thinking just the opposite. Now that's a real pretty smile, swirled around in head, pissing him off that he wasn't able to control such thoughts, that he was forced to block them out with others, like, You won't be smiling when I get through with you, babe!

Pete sent Rocky the appropriate sign—a fastball, right down the middle. But as Rocky lowered his arms to the set position, Louise winked. What the fuck! the pitcher thought, shaking his head. Normally a cute girl winking in his direction would set some blood rushing south, but this just pissed him off more. Really! Who the hell does this Louise Gehrig think she is anyway? was the question he asked himself as he delivered the first pitch.

"Strike one!" the ump yelled.

The crowd went ballistic and the chanting increased in both tempo and volume.

Yeah, I'll take that, Rocky thought. Blow the bitch away with three pitches. He glared in at his catcher, who was calling for a curveball, low and outside. Rocky shook him off. A fastball, I want to kill her with speed.

Louise stayed calm. It was the fastest, hardest pitch she had ever seen. Right down the middle, but traveling at the speed of light. She always took the first pitch. *Always.* She was a patient batter—enough TV sports commentators had taught her that lesson early on. See what the pitcher's throwing, read, calculate, then adjust.

Rocky finally procured the fastball sign. Moving into position, he wound up and let it fly.

Louise began her swing the moment the ball left Rocky's outstretched fingers. It was a mighty swing, smooth, controlled, but when it was over, the ball was smothered in Pete's mitt, and the ump was yelling, "Strike two!"

"Yes," Rocky muttered, "I'll show you where to stick that number four."

Late, Louise thought, just a little late.

Too close for comfort was what was running through Pete's mind. He had the best view of the batting situation, and he knew better than anyone that if Louise had begun that swing a millisecond earlier, that ball would have been out of the park and bouncing off the garbage that littered the East River.

She plays like a girl, Rocky thought, laughing a little to himself. Rocky had some pretty strong opinions as to what women were good for, and playing baseball was nowhere to be found on his short list.

Go ahead, smile, Louise thought, I'll show you who plays like a girl. Smile, you asshole. Smile.

Rocky glared in yet again at his catcher. The crowd noise had become unbearable, even to him, but he knew that the calls of "Rocky!" were now eclipsing the murmurs of "Louise!"

A curve, low and away, was what Pete called for. Rocky shook him off, once, twice, a third time, then again, causing the catcher to hustle out to the mound for a little one-on-one with the star pitcher.

"Another fastball," Rocky said.

"The last one was too close for comfort," Pete insisted.

"Bullshit! She can't hit."

"She's gotta be doing something right. Otherwise we wouldn't be here."

"Fastball."

"Listen to me. Curve, low and away."

"Fastball, right down the middle."

"It's your ass."

"Ain't no bitch on this planet that can hit my fastball." Rocky spit. "Trust me."

Pete hardly trusted any pitcher, let alone Rocky Goetz—"The size of his salary is only surpassed by the size of his ego," many an anonymous teammate had been known to declare. But if Rocky wanted to throw the heater, then let him.

All three players took their respective positions. Louise adjusted her stance just a little, digging in her left foot. Pete gave the universal sign for a fastball—one finger, his middle—and swallowed hard as the star pitcher began his windup. The ball shot out of Rocky's hand—a pitch clocked at 101 miles per hour by the ubiquitous man with the radar gun—but Louise had already begun her swing.

Crack!

Thirty-eight thousand, seven hundred and ten fans, as well a number of players, fell silent for a moment, then rose to their feet in a collective cheer.

"Shit!" Rocky screamed, watching the clean line drive sail to the warning track in right field. The Braves had been playing her in—figuring Ms. Gehrig could hardly hit someone like Rocky Goetz for power—and Louise was rounding first base by the time right fielder Shane Brown retrieved the ball under the 353-foot marker. She made it to second with a stand-up double and a smile. Rocky Goetz wouldn't look at her. He wouldn't give her *that* satisfaction. Instead, he stared down his catcher, who shrugged I told you so and smiled just slightly behind his catcher's mask.

⑪ ⑪ ⑪

Heading into the bottom of the fourth inning, the Meteorites were leading the Braves 1–0. The one run was scored in the first, when, after making it to second, Louise stole third on Rocky's very next pitch, then made it home when short stop Jesus "That's *Jee-zus,* as in the Son of God" Maldonado hit a sac fly to deep center field.

She had been greeted in the dugout by a series of high fives, but not one solitary pat to her behind—a tradition in baseball which, though admittedly peculiar, was one tradition that Louise was, well, looking forward to.

I'll have to do something about that, she had thought at the time, taking a seat on the bench between second baseman Elvis Jones and catcher Dixon. I'll definitely have to fix that.

She was scheduled to lead off the fourth inning, and as she made her way to the batter's box, the crowd at South Field jumped to its collective feet and chanted her name. No one yelled for Rocky Goetz—not a one. A fact that he was more than well aware off.

Pete Sacker began by calling for a curve, low and away—though he knew better.

Not a chance, Rocky thought, glaring at the girl who had made him feel such a fool three innings back. He was throwing fastballs, and only fastballs—he was going to kill her with his motherfucking fastball, or at least that's what he told Sacker in the dugout. Where was the fastball call?

Louise took her stance, Pete gave his pitcher the call he so desperately needed, then Rocky set, wound up, and delivered.

"Ball!" the ump yelled.

It was so high out of the strike zone that Pete had to leap to catch it. He tossed it back to the mound, then shrugged, wondering, What the hell? Mr. Cy Young Award was not known for being wild.

"Ball!" the ump yelled again after the second pitch, which was in the dirt, then again after the third—high and away.

Pete tossed the ball back, gave Rocky the fastball sign, then sighed. If the double and subsequent stolen base had rattled the pitcher, he couldn't help but wonder what this walk was going to do.

Rocky set, wound up, and delivered. But this time the ball hit the dirt and bounced over Pete's head, and Louise Gehrig was on first with a walk and nobody out.

The fans went wild. Rocky Goetz just glared, not at his catcher, but at a cackling old man seated just behind the Meteorites' dugout. The old geezer was hooting and hollering up a storm. Where have I seen that face before? Rocky thought to himself, not recognizing that the smiling, laughing, happy face belonged to Supreme Court chief justice Norven Dougherty. It was the face that had placed Rocky in his current predicament. It was a face Rocky would never forgive.

Rocky's very next pitch—his first of this inning to Jesus Maldonado—was so far over Pete's head that the catcher didn't have a chance at catching it. Not a chance in hell. Rocky Goetz, who hadn't thrown one wild pitch during the entire previous season, threw his first of the day, and Louise was now on second base, with her eye on stealing third.

It's going to be a long inning, Pete Sacker thought, subconsciously adding, and I'll enjoy every blasted minute of it.

The Meteorites scored four runs during the bottom of the fourth inning. With Louise on second, Rocky walked Jesus Maldonado; then, during a called third strike to cleanup hitter Jeff Carter—former right fielder for the Kansas City Royals who hit over twenty homers a year, seven seasons running, and whose career batting average hovered at the .300 mark—the two base runners pulled off a successful double steal, and the Meteorites had runners on second and third with only one out. Left fielder Sandy Downs—a former Astro who had batted .326 the previous season—unfortunately popped up in shallow left, leaving no chance for Louise to make it home.

With two outs, Rocky started feeling confident, as if he could get out of the inning without further harm. At the plate stood Elvis Jones, the Meteorites' second baseman, a lifetime American Leaguer, as well as a lifetime .290 hitter who was nonetheless clueless when facing strong lefties—and Rocky Goetz was as strong as lefties came.

The first pitch was just outside.

Damn Sacker and his fucking *curveballs, low and away*, Rocky thought.

Next pitch.

"Strike one!" the ump yelled.

That's more like it, Rocky thought.

But the next two were balls, both just out of the strike zone, fastballs both—just high.

With the count three-one, Rocky slipped in a backdoor slider that had Elvis fanning away at all the baseball enthusiasts seated on the right side of the infield.

Full count.

Another fastball, right down the middle, Rocky figured, and he'd be out of the inning. He set, wound up, and delivered.

"Ball four!"

Just low.

The bases were loaded, and up to the plate stepped catcher Bob Dixon. At thirty-six and with a bum knee, Dixon probably should have called it a career—a probable Hall of Fame career with 395 homers, number twenty-eight on the all-time list. He should have taken his millions from the lackluster seasons with the Philadelphia Phillies, the six moderately successful seasons with the Mets, and those four remarkably victorious seasons with the Boston Red Sox (winners of three of the last four World Series, they had released him, claiming they needed to make room for a minor league catching phenom, when in actuality they wanted to trim their operating expenses) and opened up the Greenwich Village jazz club of his dreams, spending the rest of his days listening to riffs from Blue Note legends. But the man could still hit for power—he had thirty-one dingers for Boston in '99—and he knew the ins and outs, the faults and weaknesses, of virtually every hitter in baseball. He could call a convincing game and hold a pitching staff together. And though his bones tended to creak a little too loudly at times, he could still throw out a runner stealing second at least 50 percent of the time. Not bad for an old man.

Rocky had always had problems with Bob. He had lost the first game of the World Series to him when the then Red Sox catcher belted a solo home run in the bottom of the ninth to end a scoreless tie. Things of course had turned around, and Rocky had gone on to win not only game four, but also to pitch a one-hitter during the seventh and decisive game.

Pete respected Bob not only as a catcher—a Gold Glove winner eight years running—but as a hitter. He knew Bob could make contact with a curve and send it out of the park, and that fastballs were his weakness—he had problems hitting them. Slow bat speed was the culprit. But since Rocky was definitely in his heater mode, Bob presented little to no threat at all.

Which was exactly what Rocky was thinking—Crunch this, motherfucker—as he nodded to Pete's one-finger sign, set, wound up, and delivered.

"Strike one!" the ump yelled.

A fastball, down the middle.

"Strike two!"

Again.

Bob stepped out of the batter's box, placed the tip of his bat against the ground, and leaned the other end against his thigh. He glanced up the line toward third base. Louise was hunched over, eternally in position. Her baby blues flashed his way, then the thumb of her right hand jerked itself upward—a you-can-do-it and a smile. Bob nodded his appreciation; then, taking a deep breath, he wiped his sweating palms against the sides of his uniform, gripped the bat, and stepped back in.

If Rocky Goetz had one problem area that he wished he could magically correct, it would be the fact that on occasion his fastball curved. His mind said throw a fastball, his arm wanted to throw a fastball, even his fingers and wrist had *fastball* written all over them. But when the ball shot out of his hand, it wasn't fast and it wasn't straight. Such was the case with his third pitch to the Meteorites' catcher. A fastball that was neither fast nor straight—that is, until Bob hit it, and it traveled fast and straight, right out of the park.

Braves skipper Keith Hernandez had attempted to pull Rocky Goetz from the game after the conclusion of the fifth inning. "Sorry, Keith," Rocky had said. "Not this time." He had other things in mind, and when Louise came to bat in the bottom of the sixth inning with her team leading 5–1, it was time to put them in play.

Pete had seen the evil gleam before—at least three times last season—so he took a quick trip out to the mound to try to calm Rocky down.

"Don't," he said.

"Don't what?"

"Hit her."

"Would I hit a girl?"

"Right now I think you'd kill *that* girl, given the opportunity."

Rocky smiled, then spit a glob of tobacco out the side of his mouth. "Don't worry about it."

"I am worried."

"Well, don't," the pitcher said. "Just get your ass behind plate and fucking catch, like you're supposed to."

"Fuck you," Pete said.

"No"—Rocky spit again—"fuck you."

Pete took his position behind the plate. He called for a fastball, right down the middle. Rocky shook him off. Okay, Pete thought, a curve, low and away. Rocky shook his head. A backdoor slider? No. Try the fastball again. No. Hmmm. The curve, high and inside? Rocky nodded and smiled and moved into the set position.

"Watch out," Pete whispered.

But it was too late. Rocky had already completed his windup and had let loose with a pitch seemingly aimed at Louise's head. She jerked back—her reflexes taking over—and the ball only grazed her right bicep. But grazing or not, getting hit by a baseball as hard as stone traveling in excess of ninety miles per hour hurts like hell.

Louise turned and glared at the pitcher. She mouthed the word *asshole.* He smiled and spit. Pete stood and said, "You okay?" She nodded and took a step in the direction of first base, never taking her eyes off the man on the mound. But with every subsequent step, the tension in South Field doubled. Rocky started mouthing off in her direction, taunting her to rush the mound. But Louise never stepped out of line—she just kept glaring and heading toward first.

His teammates would claim that it was Rocky yelling something about "pussy" that finally drove Bob Dixon over the edge. The same teammates would later claim they had never seen the catcher run so fast. But run he did, like the proverbial bat out of hell, out of the dugout toward the mound, where he plowed headfirst into the chest of the Rocky Goetz, sending him sprawling and coughing up blood.

The benches cleared, with but one exception, for what some sportswriters dubbed "The Brawl to End All," and the game was interrupted for close to twenty minutes. Nine players got ejected, including Bob, Jesus Maldonado, Jeff Carter, third base coach Sam Cox, Meteorites manager Lefty Johnston, and four Braves. Louise might have been among them if she hadn't been tackled by first base coach and hitting instructor Gary Tomlin on her way into the melee—tackled and ordered to "Stay put! You got something to prove," he had screamed, "do it with your bat!"

Rocky Goetz also left the game. But he was unaware of it, unconscious and carried away, as he was on a stretcher, to the nearest hospital emergency room.

The Meteorites' starting pitcher and the ace of the new staff, Reggie Borders, got himself into trouble in the top of the ninth. Still leading 5–1, he walked the Braves' leadoff hitter, then gave up a clean line-drive single to the next batter. There were runners on the corners and no outs. And while baseball experts would argue that for a pitcher to deliver eight solid innings before spring training was nothing short of miraculous, especially in these days of setup men and highly paid closers, for Borders it was all in a day's work. The man was a workhorse. The highest paid player on the Meteorites—he had a three-year, $33 million contract—he had gone 21–11 with a 2.43 ERA with 19 complete games for the California Angels the previous season. When the Angels could no longer afford his services, Matt Stern could.

Pitching coach Tim Waddle, acting as manager after Lefty Johnston's ejection, stepped out of the dugout and strolled to the mound. The team's relief pitching ace, P.J. Strykes, had been warming up just in case. And, in Waddle's mind, it was time to shut these suckers down for good.

Reggie tossed his coach the ball and said, "Sorry."

"What are you talking about?" Waddle asked. "You pitched one hell of a game."

Reggie nodded sadly. "But it wasn't good enough," he said, walking head down toward the dugout.

The coach removed his cap and scratched behind his left ear. "Jesus Christ," he muttered to himself. "What's his problem?"

P.J. ran out from the bullpen. Waddle handed him the ball and the instructions, "Destroy 'em."

P.J. nodded, and waited for Waddle to get back to the dugout before unloading his first pitch: a sinking fastball—it was the only pitch he threw. It was the only pitch he needed. One hundred thirty-one saves in three seasons for the Seattle Mariners proved that. But, as with the Angels and Reggie Borders, the Mariners could no longer afford to keep P.J. on the roster. Enter Matt Stern.

The first Braves batter to face P.J. was catcher Pete Sacker. Being a lifetime National Leaguer, he had only heard rumors of the relief pitcher's stuff. Now he got to experience it up close and personal.

P.J. set, wound up, and delivered.

"Strike one!" the ump yelled.

What the hell was that? Pete wondered.

Again.

"Strike two!"

Pete figured he'd better at least attempt a swing.

"Strike three!"

Shit, he thought to himself, this is going to be a long season.

It took seven additional pitches for P.J. to strike out the side and for this Supreme Court–sanctioned exhibition game to be added to the history books.

FINAL LINE SCORE					
Atlanta	001 000 000	1	3	1
Manhattan	100 400 00x	5	9	0

The Braves slipped away into the safety of the visitors' dugout while the Meteorites gathered on the field to congratulate one another. All eyes turned toward first base as Louise made her way toward the area in front of the mound where P.J., Reggie, Elvis, Coach Waddle, and a host of second-string players were high-fiving and slapping one another's behinds.

Louise walked over directly to P.J., her left hand met his in a loud clap head high, and then, as he turned to accept congrats from another teammate, she nonchalantly patted his tush. A lot of thoughts immediately rushed through P.J.'s head, the most prevalent being, *I liked that*. But as he turned to watch the Meteorites first baseperson deliver high fives and pats to the rest of the team, and even receive a few in return from the more adventurous sorts, he couldn't help but wonder what it was going to be like playing 162 games with this gutsy rookie at first base.

"What're you thinking?" Bob Dixon asked as the relief pitcher stepped into the dugout.

A shrug and a smile. "I guess we're stuck with her."

"Yeah," the catcher said. "Thank God for small favors."

"Thank Norven Dougherty."

As Louise and her teammates left the field after that very first outing, there were many fans of the game, both at South Field and watching at home or in bars on TV, who felt elation as they had never known the feeling to exist. The chills and goose bumps had done their part, but now it was something more. History? Perhaps. But more likely the future. They had seen into a crystal ball and the forecast was enthralling, the forecast was sunny with not a cloud in the sky, highs of eighty-two and zero percent humidity.

But for others, also fans of the game, the crystal ball had cracked in half, had split wide open and unleashed demons and gremlins and hatred and bile. The ball predicted hurricanes and tornadoes and tidal waves of intolerance. The ball predicted pain and heartbreak. The ball predicted death. The ball predicted that Louise Gehrig would never make it in the world of major league baseball, that October would never come. And there were many fans of the game who would make sure that prediction came true, even if it meant taking matters into their own hands.

◎ **2** ◎

The Grandfather, the Chief Justice, & the I-Man

She was born on October 14, 1976. Two weeks premature, exactly as her grandfather Joe Gehrig had predicted on his deathbed:

"No grandchild of mine is going to miss a World Series game," he had whispered at the time, through a series of coughs and wheezes that would have had the Vicks VapoRub running for cover. "He'll pop out in no time at all," Joe promised his unmarried yet eight-month-pregnant daughter, Margaret Marie. "No time at all." Another cough. Then another. "But just promise me one thing."

"Sure, Dad," she said, sniffling back the tears. "Anything."

"Name the little bugger after the greatest baseball player who ever lived."

"But," she said, searching for words, wondering how her father could think of baseball at a time like this, then figuring that maybe it was the least painful thing to think about. "But, Dad, what if it's a girl?"

The old man laughed. "A girl! Ha! It won't be a girl. Can't be," he said, the laughter mutating into a coughing fit that racked his once mighty, once towering frame.

Margaret sat quietly, not thinking about names and babies,

and the mess that had gotten her in that condition in the first place. The pain of seeing her father so disabled had long ago numbed the thought process. The fear had dislodged all reason. The longing—longing that her dad could be okay—had taken on presidential proportions. "I promise," she said softly, then raising her voice over the phlegm-filled *yack-yack-yack,* "I promise, Dad. I promise."

The fit subsided. The wave of terror passed, at least for a moment. Joe smiled and squeezed his daughter's hand. "A boy," he whispered. "Early." He coughed again—once, violently. A drop of blood escaped his left nostril. A gasp escaped Margaret's throat as she closed her eyes and began to sob.

Joe patted her hand soothingly, gave her one last loving look that Margaret would never see, could never remember and hold on to, and then, also closing his eyes, he said, "One hell of a ballplayer."

Margaret could only cry harder.

As for Joe, he took one last breath, then died. But even on his deathbed, even in that condition, Joe Gehrig would have been the first to admit that two out of three wasn't bad.

"The Mets!" Joe Gehrig screamed at his then nine-year-old daughter. "Damn it! Margaret Marie Gehrig. You're lucky your mother's not alive to hear this."

"But why?" the nine-year-old wanted to know.

Joe looked at his daughter sadly. He shook his head as if she should know. As if the answer to that question should have been inbred. "Because we're Yankees fans," he said finally. "That's why."

Joe—Louise's grandfather—was the archetypal Yankee fan. He lived and died by their every pin-striped stroke, their every pin-striped pitch. And he adored the ever pin-striped Lou Gehrig, with whom he shared a love for the game and a common last name. Joe was even at Yankee Stadium on June 2, 1925, the day first baseman Wally Pipp got hit in the noggin by a batting-practice pitch and the Iron Horse got the nod to start the game in his place.

But, by the same token, Margaret had a thing for the Mets.

"You wouldn't like the Mets if you were a boy," Joe would tell her.

"You're not making any sense," she would argue.

But Joe was making perfect sense—at least in his mind. He had wanted a son—oh, how he had pleaded with his wife, how he had made her promise. How he had prayed to the good Lord above. Give me a baseball-loving boy to keep me company at the games.

But even God can get the order wrong. Even God can fuck it all up. And a little after 11:00 A.M. on March 15, 1959, Joe's wife of loving years gave birth to the little girl he never dreamed of, then died on the delivery table as she cradled the just-born in her arms.

"You weren't supposed to die," Joe whispered up at the heavens night after night. But the heavens never answered back. Instead, he'd hear a cry, then realize his daughter needed him.

And though Margaret wasn't the dreamed-of son—she was as female as Cleopatra, with a head of wild black hair, wilder blue eyes, and a smile that made foundations crumble—she did inherit her father's love for the game. Unfortunately for Joe, it was for the wrong goddamn team.

But despite their obvious baseball disagreement, Joe showered his daughter with every ounce of pride he could muster. He loved his little girl, teaching her how to catch a baseball, how to throw, and, most importantly, how to hit. If only he had bothered instructing her in the finer points of birth control.

It was in 1976, just a week or so after her seventeenth birthday, when Margaret announced that she was pregnant.

"Who's the father?" Joe demanded.

"I don't know," she said, knowing full well.

"What do you mean, you don't know?"

She shrugged. "Could be any number of people."

"Didn't you ever hear of birth control?"

"Not from you."

He sighed. Margaret noticed it was the same sort of sigh she had heard at the conclusion of the 1969 World Series, as Joe flipped off the TV and glared at his daughter, then pregnant with reverence for her blessed Mets. He finally spoke up: "You're seventeen years old, for Christ's sake."

"And how old were you the first time you had sex?"

He pondered that question for a moment; then, realizing the answer was "too old," at least by the virginal standard of the day, said, "Age doesn't have anything to do with it."

"Exactly."

"Do you want to get an abortion?"

Margaret shook her head and answered as if she had given the situation a lot of thought. "No," she said matter-of-factly, "I want the kid."

Joe sighed again—the Miracle Mets' rendition redux. Then he smiled, finally, as Margaret knew he eventually would, and said, "I'm just telling you one thing."

"What's that, Dad?"

"It better be a boy."

But that summer, as Margaret lumbered about in her seventh month of pregnancy, Joe took ill. Tests revealed prostate cancer—malignant and spreading. Doctors gave him two to three months at best. "Just give me enough time to see my grandson," was all he asked, but that was more than they could promise or deliver.

Joe lived just long enough to see his beloved Yankees finish their season with a record of ninety-seven wins and sixty-two losses, atop the American League East. He died shortly thereafter, a few hours prior to the team's roster being introduced to a hostile Kansas City crowd at the start of their divisional playoff against the Royals. Coincidentally, his grandchild was born five days later, just as Chris Chambliss hit a solo home run in the bottom of the ninth to break a 6–6 tie and send the Yankees to the World Series—a World Series in which they were swept by the Cincinnati Reds, four games to none.

Watching those four games, the newborn Louise suckling on her left nipple, Margaret couldn't help but think that if the cancer hadn't killed her father, the way the Yankees performed in the 1976 World Series would have most assuredly caused his demise.

Louise Kathleen Gehrig was a precocious child with an appetite for pizza and baseball—she could outhit, outthrow, outrun, outcatch, and outfield any boy on her Little League team, the New Haven Rockets. Margaret had seen to that, teaching her every nuance that Joe had held so near and dear to his heart. And when it came to high school, well, she was just too good for the girls' softball team, and consistently made the starting lineup of Robert Kennedy High's Democrats—the regional champs four Louise Gehrig years in a row.

Spunky, sarcastic, and dangerously flirtatious, she was the spitting image of her mom—the hair, the eyes, that smile— who'd never take *no* for an answer. She'd never have to, and despite the prevailing winds of conservative thought that farted throughout her childhood years, she wasn't about to let any Young Republicans dictate the way she planned her life.

I'm going to be the first female to play in the major leagues." She had been thinking it for years, but on that fateful November 1992 Tuesday evening, when the right-wing flatulence ended with a Democratic kick to the groin, the then sixteen-year-old said it out loud to the only other person she knew would believe her.

"How?" Margaret asked. Not, *why?* Never, *why?*

"I'm not sure yet," was her reply.

"Well, if you need some help figuring it out, let me know."

Louise followed in the footsteps of both her grandfather and mother and attended Yale University upon graduating from high school. But unlike her maternal predecessors, she studied neither law nor business economics. Instead, she opted for a major in modern literature, with a minor in baseball.

She was generally considered a terror on campus— opinionated, stubborn, and dangerously bright. When, during her freshman year, Billy "Spit" MacPherson, coach of the Yale Bulldogs, refused her a tryout, she organized a citywide boycott of the team's home games, employing the help of both the daily *New Haven Register* and the weekly *New Haven Advocate,* as well a half dozen local radio stations, WTNH—the local ABC television affiliate—and numerous local merchants and feminist groups. Yet despite the local media frenzy, it took New York radio personality supreme Imus in the Morning to finally break the coach's and/or Yale's back.

Broadcasting on the all-sports WFAN-AM, Imus interviewed Louise daily.

"So, are you on the team yet?" Imus began one such interview, but before Louise could respond, Imus continued, "Let me just say this about Billy 'Spit' MacPherson. He is a low-rent, gutless worm. He's a coward. A panty-sniffing sissy-boy. 'Spit' MacPherson couldn't coach a Brownie squad."

After a short pause, Louise asked, "Are you through?"

"Well," Imus said, "yes. For now."

"The coach seems to think I don't have the abilities needed to play on his team."

"Let me ask you this. How many games have the Bulldogs won this year?"

"None."

"That's right. None. Zippo. They're oh and sixteen. *Oh and sixteen!*" he screamed. "They suck! And he won't even give you a tryout."

"He won't even take my calls."

"Yeah, well," he said, suddenly lowering his voice, "he won't take our calls either."

One of Imus's cohorts said, "Can you blame him?"

"Who's the president of Yale?" Imus asked.

"George Bush," Louise said.

"Oh, right."

"I don't think he'll take our calls either, boss," another cohort said.

"Wanna bet?" Imus said. "Get him on the phone. We're going to get to the bottom of this."

And after a number of telephone attempts—including a live on-air interview with Bush, during which the ex-one-term president asked, "Didn't I get enough flack from you during the ninety-two election?" To which Imus replied, "Obviously not"—

Louise received the tryout she so desired. Watched by Imus and by all the local media and celebrities he could muster, Louise got three hits and a walk during her five plate appearances, including a ninth-inning home run that won the game for her squad. She was given a uniform and a number, and played at first base for the remainder of the college season—a total of thirty-seven additional games. Her batting average over that stretch was .423, which included seventeen doubles, nine triples, and eight homers. She also had forty-nine stolen bases and a perfect fielding percentage.

"Not bad for a girl," Coach MacPherson said at the press conference following the last game of the season, adding with a shrug, " 'Course those stats ain't bad for a boy either."

By the time Louise graduated Yale, she was the world's most famous amateur athlete, having won every major amateur athletic award short of an Olympic medal. (Women's baseball and/or softball was not an Olympic event, and as for her playing on the men's squad, well, the Olympic committee would not even open the possibility up for discussion.) Her picture had graced the cover of every sports journal and magazine, including *Sports Illustrated,* which asked the prophetic question: "What's next for Louise Gehrig?"

Gary Tomlin, then working as a scout for the newly formed expansion club the Manhattan Meteorites, was looking for a team of great players, the best players Matt Stern's millions could buy—"Think free agency," Stern had ordered—to put on the field during the team's debut season in the year 2000. It was then the summer of 1998, and he had one very specific idea as to what Louise should do next. And it came as no surprise to him that she held similar notions. But first it needed the approval of Matt Stern, the owner of the new baseball franchise.

"I've got a wild idea," Tomlin had explained.

"Shoot," Stern said.

"I wanna sign Louise Gehrig."

Seated behind the massive oak desk of his newly furnished president of the Manhattan Meteorites office suite, the young billionaire smiled. Unlike his contemporaries, Stern got into the baseball business not to make money, but to have fun. He had inherited a little over three billion dollars on his twenty-fifth birthday, and six years later he had barely made a dent in it. In fact, every scheme, every reckless notion, seemed to turn a profit.

Even his first venture, cable superstation NYTV—available free to every American with cable TV—was in the black within two years of its inception. Stern's secret: R-rated movies, uncut and with very limited commercial interruption. No other superstations, not Ted Turner's TNT, not USA, not WOR, not the Sci-Fi Channel, could or would deliver that. At least not for free.

So, with the three billion quickly becoming four, maybe five—he had lost count—Stern figured it was time to stop scheming and time to play. And baseball seemed just the game. And Louise Gehrig was just the type of player he wanted playing on his team. She was talented, and she certainly was controversial. Of course, it didn't hurt matters any that she was also beautiful.

"The commissioner will have a shit fit," he said.

"I can just see his face now."

"All beet red. As if Mr. J. Danforth Quayle were about to explode."

They both laughed at the image.

"It's discrimination if we can prove she's worthy," Stern said.

"But will the courts agree?"

"The Supreme Court, maybe. As long as Norven Dougherty's still running the show." Stern shrugged, then thought for a moment. "Will she go for it?"

"Are you kidding?"

"Then set up a meeting. Louise Gehrig is going to be my star first base"—he stopped himself short, then grinned mischievously—"my star first base*person.*"

Matt Stern's decision to play a female at first base was not appreciated by the majority of other baseball team owners, whose reaction was swift and predictable. They sued. They lost. They appealed. They won. Stern appealed. He won. Louise Gehrig was going to play major league baseball.

Then the other owners made a mistake. Instead of giving up, giving in, hoping for the best, or in the case of Louise's performance, the worst, they appealed one last time, to the highest court in the land.

Chief Justice Norven Dougherty banged the gavel down hard against the aged oak bench.

Clack! it echoed. *Clack! Clack!*

He glanced about the courtroom. On one side, the mighty: thirty-one of the richest, most powerful men and women in the country; their teams of lawyers, headed by Jim Zorian; and their newest commissioner, J. Danforth Quayle—a puppet on thirty-one strings—a giddy, ignorant, pretentious clod if ever there was one. And let's not forget the dog, that yelping little flea-infested mutt that Dougherty wanted to drop-kick through the courthouse's windows.

On the other side, the not-as-mighty, the underdog: Matt Stern, an extremely rich, moderately intelligent, though not blatantly powerful man; his lawyer, Ronald Manelli; and the person who started it all, a young woman referred to incessantly as Ms. Gehrig. And let's not forget truth—the little thing called truth, which Mr. Zorian and his coalition of legal whiz kids would gladly drop-kick anywhere at any time, window or no window.

And in the middle, the league presidents: a home run king and a Yogi, who both claimed impartiality, though Dougherty knew better. He knew they'd both gladly drop-kick the commissioner and most of the owners. Drop-kick them over any center field wall. Going, gone . . . and good-bye! The assholes are outta here. Let's play ball!

Zorian approached the bench. "Justice Dougherty," he said. "Let's . . . be . . . reasonable."

The chief justice cackled out a small laugh. Reasonable? I'll show you *reasonable*. "Mr. Zorian," he began. "The arguments you and your team have presented border on the ludicrous." He spoke slowly, letting his words ring out, ring true. "The old-boy network, men's clubs, men only need apply—these are ancient concepts. And, thankfully, foreign ones—at least before this bench. To deny a completely qualified person a job based on gender is not only illegal in this country, it's irresponsible, reprehensible, and downright callous." Dougherty cleared his throat and took a sip of water from a half-filled glass sitting off to one side of the benchtop. He continued, "To me it would be an open-and-shut case. Open-and shut, *just . . . like . . . that.*" He snapped his fingers three times accenting the words, then smiled at Ms. Gehrig. "No argument there. But," he conceded, the smile fading fast, "my fellow justices have convinced me otherwise."

Zorian's mouth fashioned itself into a disbelieving grin. He went to speak, but stopped himself short, preconsonant—*just . . . in . . . case.*

"There *is*"—he let the small word stretch out on his seven-mile tongue—"the possibility of personal injury to be taken into account." Dougherty coughed, and suddenly looked tired, and very, very old. "Is Ms. Gehrig physically capable?" He shrugged and held out his weathered, veined hands palms up, all the while wishing God would whisper the secret word in his ear.

Louise stared at the chief justice, clenching her jaw in hard reserve. I will not cry, she said over and over in her head. Under no circumstance will I cry. Her mind clouded over, a tropical rainstorm of sudden doubt and confusion. And she too wished for some sort of fiber-optic hot line to the man upstairs. Please God, if you're listening. Or Grandpa, if you're up there. All of us know that this is right. This is real. This isn't a lost cause, it can't be. There's no such thing, remember?

The courtroom was still for a moment, strangely peaceful as Dougherty's wish and Louise's plea crossed lines on their tele-pathic way up to the heavens. Then a rumble began to grow from those reporters in attendance. Whispers and gasps from the mighty thirty-one, a slight canine-ish yelp, and even a de-ceivingly sexual moan.

"Is he?"

"Can it be?"

"No way."

Dougherty banged his gavel.

Clack! Clack!

"Order!" his voice boomed, the color and vitality inexplicably returning full force.

Silence. Dead silence.

He continued, eyeing the young woman, searching her soul one last time to see if he'd come up with the same answer, the same conviction, the same will to win. "Is she strong enough? Is she quick enough? Is she tall enough? Tough enough? Can she blow major league bubbles? Will PMS affect her batting average? All the whys, hows, and whatnots presented so eloquently by Mr. Zorian. So many questions. So many doubts. So many clichés. So many damn *what-ifs*. But in the end there's only one question that has to be answered. Is she"—and he stretched out the word into two or three syllables—"*good* enough?" He shook his head sadly, then suddenly began to nod. "I most assuredly think so," he said. "So, I suggest a compromise of sorts," Dougherty said, a mischievous smile making an appearance on his mouth. "A test, if you will. And since all of my fellow justices seem to agree, it will stand."

Zorian turned and mumbled to one of his associates. "Son of a bitch!"

"The court has ruled that the plaintiff will be given the opportunity to prove her abilities." Another sip. "South Field. Saturday afternoon. The Manhattan Meteorites at home against last year's world champions." He cleared his throat, then stared down Zorian. "That should limit the protests from the peanut gallery." He peered over at Ms. Gehrig. "I expect to see you at first."

She nodded frantically, unable to conceal her excitement—hell, there was no reason to. Standing, speaking loudly, enunciating every syllable, she said, "Thank you, Justice Dougherty. Thank you so very much."

He nodded back, a warm smile, and maybe even, yes, definitely, a twinkle in those old chief justice eyes.

Matt Stern and Ronald Manelli were beaming—smiles were plastered to their mugs. Smiles radiating first disbelief, then astonishment: We did it and Hey, that wasn't too tough.

The league presidents leaned forward with their, "Let us be the first to congratulate you." They shook Stern's and Manelli's hands, and even gave Ms. Gehrig a hug.

As for the mighty thirty-one—they found comfort in the womb of their overstuffed wallets, and shed a collective tear for the supposed integrity of the game.

The mutt, it could only whimper.

As did baseball's commissioner.

Dougherty grinned contentedly at the scene. "Ladies and gentlemen," he said, "court is adjourned." And as he raised the gavel high for one last crack at the top of the bench, Matt Stern whispered to his attorney.

"What now?" he said.

A shrug. "I guess you play ball."

3

Bart Giamatti Is Spinning in His Grave

With interest in baseball declining throughout the nineties, Commissioner J. Danforth Quayle had faced a predicament: how not only to serve in the "best interest of the game" but also to answer to twenty-eight extremely wealthy, overtly powerful leeches. It was sort of like being vice-president, without ever having to publicly spell a word. It was exactly like having to kiss twenty-eight asses simultaneously.

Things had not gone well in recent years. His predecessor was fired when a lockout at the beginning of the 1997 season failed to break the players' union's back, and the union went on to win a suit that raised the minimum annual salary to $183,750. The salary cap the owners so desired never materialized. Same for the end to free agency.

In June of that year came his turn at bat. He accepted the owners' offer immediately, and immediately the ridicule began, commencing on ABC's highly rated late-night entry, "The David Letterman Show." For close to four and a half years America's television viewers had been denied a Top Ten list featuring the ex–vice-president. But on the night Quayle ascended to baseball's highest position, Letterman's comic disdain was back in full force.

The Top Ten Reasons Ex–Vice-president J. Danforth Quayle Will Make One Fine Commissioner of Baseball:

10. Knows all the words to "Take Me Out to the Ball Game."

9. Loves warm beer.

8. The respect and admiration he'll receive from players of Latin American descent for his awe-inspiring regret over never having studied Latin in high school, thus resulting in his inability to speak their native language.

7. Very little spelling.

6. Think of the fun he'll have figuring out realignment.

5. George Steinbrenner will listen to him.

4. Pine tar! Pine tar! Pine tar!

3. Family Values—two words that every major league ball player lives by.

2. He wouldn't be a heartbeat away from anything.

And the number-one reason ex–Vice-President J. Danforth Quayle will make one fine commissioner of baseball: He's got nothing better to do.

⦿   ⦿   ⦿

And that was only the beginning of the abuse.

But J. Danforth was not about to be discouraged. He was not about to be made a fool of. He'd prove himself—and turn out to be the greatest baseball commissioner of all time. Or at least that's how he saw it.

If only he could turn baseball's problems on end, inside out. If only he could take them long, take them downtown—*those problems are outta here!* He thought long and hard. Realignment—the placing of teams that were actually located in the eastern portion of the country in the eastern divisions, and teams from western states in the western divisions—had already failed once, back in the mid-nineties, so that was out of the question.

He toyed with the DH—the designated hitter. Should he bring it over to the National League? Or possibly eliminate it entirely? He shrugged. The infield fly rule suddenly popped into his head. What the hell *was* the infield fly rule anyway? Who knew? He sighed deeply, and moved on.

How about interdivisional play? he thought, having heard many a sports announcer cry out its potential. Or maybe a shortening of the season, with an additional playoff round or two featuring wild card teams from each division—maybe the teams with the best home records? Or, he thought, exciting himself by the prospect, what if the teams with the best records got the home field advantage during the playoffs?

No, what was he thinking? None of those ideas would work. Or at least none could be sold to the owners—at least not in his lifetime. No, J. Danforth needed the concept that would not only turn baseball back into the national pastime, but would also help to further line the pockets of his twenty-eight bosses.

What could it be?

Shorter games?

No, that'd leave less time for commercials.

More afternoon games?

No again, prime-time commercial space is a lot more valuable.

Damn!

Cheaper tickets?

Yeah, right.

Then one morning while sitting on the commode, reading about the cultural elite in Section D of *USA Today*, it came to him—the perfect solution. A nothing-short-of-brilliant solution. The only solution: expansion.

Expansion! Expansion! Expansion!

Yes!

Hallelujah!

Amen!

Baseball would award four new franchises—two American League, two National League—on January 1, 1998, for play to begin with the 2000 season.

The owners were ecstatic, as they'd be sharing part of the two-hundred-million-dollar franchise fee each of the four new baseball entrepreneurs would be coughing up just for the privilege of owning a team, as well as part of the overall broadcasting package, which would now be expanding.

Over a dozen American cities, as well as Mexico City and Winnipeg, vied for the right to bring baseball home to their citizens. But in the end only four prevailed: San Francisco, Memphis, New Orleans, and the borough of Manhattan.

When play commenced in the first spring of the twenty-first century, the major league baseball divisions would be aligned as follows:

American League East
Atlanta Indians
Baltimore Orioles
Boston Red Sox
Detroit Tigers
Memphis Sideburns
Milwaukee Brewers
New Jersey Yankees
Toronto Blue Jays

American League West
California Angels
Chicago White Sox
Kansas City Royals
Minnesota Twins
Oakland A's
San Francisco Bay Buccaneers
Seattle Mariners
Texas Rangers

National League East
Buffalo Expos
Chicago Cubs
Florida Marlins
Manhattan Meteorites
New York Mets
Philadelphia Phillies
Pittsburgh Pirates
St. Louis Cardinals

National League West
Arkansas Astros
Atlanta Braves
Cincinnati Reds
Colorado Rockies
Los Angeles Dodgers
New Orleans Jazz
San Diego Padres
St. Petersburg Giants

In awarding a franchise to Matt Stern, the choice was obvious. He was the most financially sound of all the applicants. Young, ambitious, charming, bright, and, as J. Danforth's college-aged daughter remarked on more than one occasion, cute enough to eat, Stern would make baseball exciting again in a city that had more than enough room for an extra team. Besides, the crosstown rivalry with the Mets would most certainly heat up ticket sales, especially if either team got locked into some kind of pennant race. And with the money Stern was threatening to spend, a strong finish was more than a great possibility for his expansion club.

Stern's instructions to Gary Tomlin were, quite simply put, "Get the best."

"The best is gonna cost you. You could be talking a payroll in the sixty million range."

"I don't give a fuck. Make it a hundred million. Just give me an exciting team, a dream team, a superstar at every position. One that has a shot at winning it all." He smiled a billion-dollar smile. "That's all I'm asking."

"That's all?"

"Well, that and an end to world hunger. But first things first."

"Y'know, expansion teams are expected to lose in their first few years."

"Good. We'll take 'em by surprise. The suckers won't know what hit them."

"It's your money."

With that comment, Stern began to laugh. "Not for long," he had said. "Not for long."

⚾ 4 ⚾

Enquiring Minds Want to Know

All twenty-five players on the Manhattan Meteorites active roster showed up for the post–Supreme Court–sanctioned-game press conference, showered and smelling sweet. The nine starters, as well as P.J. Strykes, manager Lefty Johnston, and Matt Stern, sat at a twelve-seat dais. Microphones were poised before each of the participants, while the remaining players stood behind the seated starters.

The media room at South Field was an elaborately designed expandable ballroom of sorts that gave members of the ever-expanding sports media world a chance for anything from an intimate one-on-one to something of presidential proportions. This conference, with close to 120 members of the fourth estate waiting on every blessed Meteorites word, bordered on the far edge of the latter.

"Ms. Gehrig. Any comment on Justice Dougherty's decision?"

Louise and her teammates had been given news of the verdict as they exited their clubhouse and headed for the press conference. "You're in," Matt Stern had said. High fives and butt pats all around, and in the middle, Louise's gracious smile. "Thanks," she had said. "Any time," Stern had replied.

All eyes in the media room turned toward the first baseperson, who shrugged innocently, then bit down on her lower lip before saying, "The only thing that could possibly be better than this is going to the World Series. Which we'll do in October."

"Aren't you being overly confident?"

"You saw what we just did to last year's champs."

"What do you have to say about this, Lefty?"

Lefty Johnston was grinning from ear to ear. In his opinion, the Meteorites were one of the most talented baseball teams he had ever had the pleasure to watch, let alone manage. And Johnston had managed some of the best—as well as some of the worst. Yet, despite one team that went 29–133, he ranked in third place for the highest winning percentage—.539—among all active managers with at least five years experience in the majors, and he had three World Series rings in his collection of personal memorabilia. At the age of fifty-eight, with eighteen years of playing experience and nineteen years of either managing or coaching, all on the major league level, he had been contemplating hanging up his hat for good, trading it in for a sun visor and a sailboat. He'd sail about the Keys with Martha, his wife of thirty-nine years, by his side. They'd pull into port only long enough to get supplies and to pick up and/or drop off the grandchildren. Yeah, that sounded about right. Then along came Matt Stern and Gary Tomlin, the latter insisting to Stern that Lefty Johnston was the man. But Lefty wasn't so sure, and told the new owner he'd think about it. He really wasn't interested—despite that guaranteed three-year, $5.25 million contract offer—until the name Louise Gehrig began popping up. A girl, for Christ's sake. His interest became doubly piqued, triply piqued. He asked Tomlin to send over some videotapes from her Yale days. Then, together with Martha, they watched Ms. Gehrig hit, field, run the bases—in slow motion, fast motion, backward, frame by frame, every which way the VCR would allow. "I've never seen anyone play like that," he had said at the time, to which his wife replied, "You've never *seen* a player like that." She saw the twinkle in his eyes, and knew before he did what his decision would be. "Don't worry," she had said. "The Keys'll always be there. And the grandchildren, they'll just be a few years older."

"Ladies and gentlemen of the press," Lefty said, still beaming, moving a well-chewed toothpick from one side of his mouth to the other, "I'd say Gehrig knows a great baseball team when she sees one."

"This question is for Bob Dixon. Don't you feel you overreacted out there when you charged the mound?"

Bob laughed just slightly; he could feel the question coming from a mile away. "I heard what Goetz was saying. And I'm not about to let any son of a bitch talk to one of my teammates that way."

"So it had nothing to do with that teammate being female?"

"Look," Bob said, shaking his head slightly, staring through the reporter who asked. "First he hits her, then he's calling her every name in the book. Sure, the circumstances might have had something to do with it. But she's the one who had something to prove, not Rocky Goetz. He's got his Cy Young Award, his World Series ring. He reacted the way he did because she was making him look bad. A *girl* making the unhittable Rocky Goetz look bad. His ego couldn't take it. So, I decided to teach him a little lesson. Was my reaction due to the fact that Gehrig here is female?" He shrugged. "Maybe. Do I regret my actions?" He shook his head. "Not in the least. I'd do again in a heartbeat. In fact, I can't wait until the next time we face the son of a bitch."

"Any comments, Lefty?"

"I've always believed a team's gotta stick together. What Rocky did was uncalled for. He got what he deserved."

"Jamaine, why'd you sit out the brawl?"

Jamaine Young, the team's leadoff hitter, had been the National League's crown prince of the stolen base three years running before a nagging hamstring injury sidelined him for the better part of two seasons and he was released from his long-term contract with the Florida Marlins. Stern, seeking a top-notch leadoff man, signed Young on the spot. It was a pay-for-play contract. A one-year guaranteed salary of $250,000. Pocket change, really, when the game's top players had entered the annual eight-figure salary race. But this contract included a clause: If Young led the league in stolen bases, he'd be paid a $5 million bonus and be given a three-year contract extension worth close to 20 million. At the time it was a gamble Jamaine was more than willing to take. At the time Jamaine had no clue that there'd be a woman on the team.

He stared at the reporter who asked. "I've got a lot of bases to steal, man," he lied. "Got to protect the hamstring. Ain't nothing else to it."

But deep down, Jamaine Young was disgusted. What's a girl doing in the major leagues? It was a question he had asked his wife, his family, and his friends, though he didn't dare say anything to Matt Stern or his teammates, or even to Lefty. They all seemed to love her; Louise Gehrig just couldn't do any wrong. Only some of the wives and girlfriends seemed to understand his feelings. Or were they just jealous? Most probably, when he thought about it. Jealous that they'd lose their man to a teammate. What a crock. And now here he was, once the fastest man in the majors, stuck on what would surely be a laughingstock team, cellar dwellers. But at least he had that 5 million to shoot for. And 5 million bucks could definitely make him forget about Louise Gehrig. Well, maybe.

"Louise, what are you going to do with all the money?"

"I need to get a place in New York." She shrugged. "The rest I'll invest, I guess. I don't know. Money was never the issue. Playing baseball was."

Gary Tomlin had arranged the meeting. Matt Stern traveled to New Haven and met with the celebrated amateur ballplayer. Then, in the comfort of the living room of her State Street loft apartment, he offered the following: "Here's the deal. I want you to play first base for the Manhattan Meteorites. I know there's going to be a battle—the most ferocious on these shores since the Civil War. But we've got a year and a half to work out the particulars. I'll pay all the expenses. We'll hire the best lawyers, the best of everything. I'll give you a five-year contract. If you get to play, I'll pay you $5 million your first year, 6 million per year your second and third years, and 8 million per the last two. And I'll throw in a $2 million signing bonus. If this doesn't work out and you never get to take the field, you keep the signing bonus. Any questions?" "Only one," Louise said. "Where do I sign?"

"Do you have a nickname yet?"

Louise began to answer with a shake of her head, but was cut short by P.J. "Yeah, she's got a nickname all right."

Louise raised an eyebrow toward the team's closer.

P.J. flashed a devilish grin. "We're gonna call her 'Balls.' "

Louise smiled and blushed. Those closest to the first baseperson gave her an encouraging pat on the back or shoulder.

"Why Balls?"

"Cause for someone who ain't got any," P.J. explained, "She's got 'em in abundance."

After the laughter and round of respectful applause died down—laughter and applause during which Louise stood and bowed slightly to her teammates—a reporter asked, "What's next?"

"Today is Saturday, February nineteenth," Lefty said. "Opening day is six weeks away. Speaking on behalf of the team, I think it's time we got our asses down to Florida for a little conditioning."

"The team looked in pretty good condition to us."

"Wait'll you see us in April!"

THE BASEBALL BEAT

by Arnold Loiten

There are few things in life that are pure. There are fewer things left to cherish. Even fewer things to honor. There's Mom, of course. Not all moms, but certainly yours and mine. There's democracy, the belief that all men are created equal. There's our freedom of speech and of religion. There's God. There's family. And there's baseball.

I played baseball as a child. Who growing up in the mid-sixties didn't? I played stickball, and softball, and Little League. I was pretty good, too. I played first base most of the time. And I usually batted somewhere in the heart of the order.

I bring this up because I came from a large family. There were eight of us in all. Mom, Dad, four sisters—one older, three younger—and me. And still, after the hundreds of baseball games in which I participated, I never once remember any of my sisters wishing that she too could be playing right alongside me. I never remember my mom encouraging them. What I do remember is Mom and one or more of my sisters rooting me on from the bleachers. Calling out my name. Chanting, "Go Arnie! Hit it out of the park!"

Of course, things were different back then. There were rules. One such rule—possibly the great Judge Kenesaw Mountain Landis's most brilliant action as commissioner of the game—banned women from signing professional baseball contracts with men's teams. It was formalized on June 21, 1952, and stood as law until just a few hours ago.

Which brings me to today, when things are just as different, though hardly better.

Today, billboards with giant condoms perch on quaint roadsides. Today, armed murderers walk the streets while innocent citizens hide behind locked doors, unable to legally arm themselves, unable to feel safe in their own homes. Today, I would be playing right alongside my sisters. I would be battling them for a spot in the starting lineup. And when I looked into the stands, I'd see my mother rooting them on. Telling them to beat the pants of the other worthless little boys.

Today, a man named Matt Stern has changed the face of the greatest of games. He hasn't just scratched at the surface of baseball's integrity, he's defiled it. And for what motive? Greed, of course. What other motive is there, but lust perhaps? And while I can't at this time speculate on the latter, I can and will on the former. Stern, a man who already has a lot of money, will make a lot more this year. He will line his well-lined pockets with the cash of little girl's dreams, with the credit cards of their hopeful moms. And he will do this while breaking the spirit of so many. So many who loved and lived for and by the game. Fans and players alike. People like you. People like me.

And what of Stern's players? Cy Young Award winners and future Hall of Famers reduced to a circus sideshow. To be laughed at, to become cellar dwellers. Well-paid cellar dwellers, to be sure. Ah, greed again, rearing its evil head. The things some of us will do for money.

Which brings me to Louise Kathleen Gehrig, the young woman who will be playing first base for Stern's expansion Manhattan Meteorites. My feelings for Miss Gehrig have run the gamut over these past months. I started out hating her, hating what she stood for. But my hate and anger mellowed and were transformed into pity, by way of confusion and sadness. I pity her because I know she will fail. I know that she is not strong enough, talented enough, or bright enough to make it in the world of big-league ball. She is a pawn. Well paid, as are all of Stern's chess pieces, but ultimately the first piece to fall. Ultimately a laughingstock, the answer in future editions of Trivial Pursuit to the question, "Who was the only woman to ever play major league baseball?"

Yet her humiliation is of no real concern. Miss Gehrig will get over it. She'll retire from her short stint in the majors a millionaire. What more could she have asked for? What more could she want? Yes, the things some of us will do for money.

The real humiliation is American in nature. For today we have lost the purity. We have suffered the disgrace. And we are all a little less alive because of it.

Rest in peace, great game. I'll remember you fondly.

⦾ 5 ⦾

Moses Speaks

In the hours, days, weeks, months, and eventually, years following the Meteorites-Braves matchup and the subsequent Supreme Court ruling that allowed Louise Kathleen Gehrig the right to play big-league ball, the topic Women in Baseball became the single most discussed and overanalyzed American issue since the assassination of President John Fitzgerald Kennedy. To some, like Arnold Loiten, baseball beat writer for the *Atlanta Journal-Courier,* it was a greater tragedy: "American's darkest moment," "the day baseball died," and other such clichés. Even National Rifle Association spokesmodel Charlton Heston felt a need to get his two cents in, and claimed, "Today I am ashamed of being an American."

He was not alone.

Kevin Thomas Willard sat in the family room of his Atlanta home. He had gazed into the crystal ball and was blinded by its light. He stared ahead, blinking rarely, seemingly hypnotized by the darkened television screen. The remote control belonging to his videocassette recorder rested in the palm of his outstretched right hand. He had just hit rewind and was waiting. Waiting to watch it again.

It was 4:23 A.M. His wife, Geraldine, had given up on trying to coax him to bed almost three hours back. "Please come to bed, Kev," she had said. "I'll let you do, y'know."

No response.

"It's not that big a deal."

"It's a very big deal," he had explained. A very fucking big deal indeed.

"It's just a game."

"Not anymore."

Geraldine gave up, thinking *shucks*, if letting him, y'know, didn't get him to bed, nothing would.

The VCR's counter registered four zeros. Kevin squeezed the remote and pressed play. The TV came to life. The Atlanta Braves' logo filled the screen. Their theme song sweetened the air of the den. Two announcers spoke of the historic importance of the game they were about to watch. They rambled about Louise Gehrig's amateur statistics. They wondered whether she'd be able to prove herself in nine innings, and if she did, what impact would it have on America's game? Then they turned and, like most anyone else who could receive the Turner Broadcasting System–televised game through cable, watched in some sort of stunned disbelief.

It was Kevin's fourth time viewing the game. He had viewed it live earlier in the day. Then he caught the news conference and resulting special reports. Then he watched it again, despite the objections of Geraldine and his four daughters—Debbie, aged sixteen; Kelly, aged fourteen; Lisa, aged eleven; and Cheryl, aged nine—who wanted a little Saturday night primetime action for themselves. At eleven he caught the news, then ESPN's "SportsCenter," then he watched the game again—that time was hard, the hardest thus far. But at least he hadn't cried. No, Geraldine wasn't yet asleep—especially with her talking about doing y'know. He realized back then that the tears would have to wait. And wait they did. Until now, when, in the bottom of the first, with Louise Gehrig stepping to the plate, he could let them loose. A torrential downpour of sobs and sniffles and snot. His wife saying *just a game* echoed in his head and he cried even harder. His oldest daughter telling him it was *a giant step for womankind* echoed as well and that made him angry. But the cataclysmic hatred he felt could not overpower the sadness. The absolute dread that something special was lost forever. That all he cared for in life, all that mattered, was somehow ruined. Spoiled forever by some bitch from New Haven, Connecticut.

Man, that pissed Kevin Thomas Willard off.

⊕ **6** ⊕

What Do You Want
on Your Tombstone?

The initial complaints, protests, warnings, and outright threats came in the form of short notes and/or long letters delivered via the myriad of overnight delivery services: Federal Express, DHL, Express Mail, et alia. Just under four hundred that first business day alone. Most were addressed to Matt Stern, Chief Justice Dougherty, and/or Louise, but no one was exempt. Not Commissioner Quayle, not Jim Zorian, not Bob Dixon, not Lefty Johnston, not even Rocky Goetz—who received a missive deeming him, among other things, a "sissy-boy" who couldn't even "strike out a girl."

Federal Bureau of Investigation special agent Wesley Selden, who had assisted on the case involving baseball great Hank Aaron and the threats he received when he approached and then surpassed Babe Ruth's home run record, found numerous similarities between some of the words hurled at the Gehrig group and those sent off to Aaron twenty-six years earlier. He was put in charge of investigating any potentially dangerous situations, and from the moment the decision was handed down that Louise would have to prove her abilities on the field, he put his special-agent mind on full alert. There'd be trouble—of some sort. He was sure of it. It was one thing in the minds of

rednecks the country over for a black man to break a white man's record, but for a woman to play a man's game. Well, that obviously could never be tolerated. Uh-uh. No way. Not in this lifetime.

While most of the mail got no more hateful than calling Dougherty and/or Stern an "asshole"—a few of those letters even containing Meteorites season tickets returned for an imagined full refund—a few got nasty, your typically misspelled misogynistic ignorance, while others managed to get even nastier than that.

In particular:

One to Stern was filled with the usual assortment of Nazi hy-

perbole combined with some good ol' anti-Semitic, white su-
premacist "Hitler's master plan will prevail" rhetoric.

One to Dougherty was simple enough in its malice. "The
baseball season opens April 3. Too bad you won't be alive to enjoy it. I know everything about you, Judge. Old men make the
best targets." It was signed, "Sniper."

And one to Louise, short (the shortest of any of the letters)
and unsigned, was quite to the point. And for a reason he
couldn't yet decipher, it was the letter which bothered Selden
most. It was a drawing really. Not so much a letter. A crude
drawing of a tombstone whose epitaph read: Louise Gehrig.
R.I.P.

That one gave the FBI agent shivers.

Louise never saw that threat, at least not at first, or any of the
others, for that matter. Neither did Lefty Johnston, Bob Dixon,
or the rest of the Meteorites players. Matt Stern had wisely
hired numerous secretary types to go through all incoming mail
and to sort it into appropriate piles. The FBI pile was, at least
during the weeks immediately following the Dougherty decision, the largest. But Stern believed that would change, and that
the pro-Louise pile—letters that expressed pride, satisfaction,
and great honor, and there were a number of them—would
gain momentum, overtake the competition, and eventually win
the race. And for the time being, he would only mention to his
players that "there have been some threats. . . ." That would be
enough. "Concentrate on the game," he'd say. "The proper authorities will concentrate on the problems. No one is at risk."
And Louise and her teammates would nod and say they understood, all the while wondering what sick comments were being
hurled their way like flaming fastballs from the asshole of hell.

Norven Dougherty, on the other hand, read through every
piece of his mail, and in the case of the threats, wished there
were some sort of return address so he could fire back a re-

sponse. "Fuck you," he'd write over and over and over again. Or maybe, "Come and get me. Asshole." He didn't care. Threats had long ago ceased having any effect on this Supreme Court justice. There had just been too damn many. Too damn many over the years. Too damn many to count.

But there were many, in fact, who felt differently about Louise and her movement. They provided kinder, gentler words, of sorts.

In his "Shooting from the Lip" column in the New York *Newsday*, Mike Lupica wrote: "Hello, Louise Kathleen Gehrig. Welcome to the world of major league baseball. It's a cutthroat world of what-have-you-done-for-me-lately. Unforgiving and demanding and crowded by journalists just like me. At the outside, Louise Kathleen Gehrig, you've got about twenty years here. There's only one rule that I know of, Louise Kathleen Gehrig: 'Goddamnit, never get caught stealing third with nobody out.' "

During his nightly "SportsCenter" commentary, ESPN commentator Chris Berman said, "Today we begin a new chapter in the history of baseball. A woman, Louise *Please-Baby-Please-Baby-Baby-Baby-Please* Gehrig, is the starting first baseperson for the expansion Manhattan Meteorites baseball team. She is five foot seven, looks better in a baseball uniform that any player I've ever seen, and, as was witnessed by the world this past Saturday afternoon, has the sweetest swing this side of the Commerce Comet. Whether or not she can ever match his stats, only time will tell. But as far as this reporter is concerned, I'm rooting for the future. Best of luck, Balls! Knock 'em dead!"

And during his syndicated late-night TV gabfest "Up All Night," Christopher "Mad Dog" Russo rambled on mostly about what a "fox" the Meteorites' first baseperson was. But when pressed by his guest, actor-comedian Chevy Chase, as to whether or not he believed women should be playing major league baseball, Russo said, "This girl made Rocky Goetz look like a chump. *A chump!* So, yeah, I'd have to say she deserves a shot. I mean, Chevy, you saw the way she swung the bat. It's scary."

"And, don't forget," Chase said, a mischievous grin playing on his lips, "she's a fox."

"Whoa," Russo continued. "You got that right. The girl is H-O-T. And she can play. Wonder if she's got a boyfriend."

The *Wall Street Journal* took a different approach to Louise's newfound right to play. They covered the financial end. What did Louise Gehrig mean to the wallets and pocketbooks of those involved?

Starting small, they estimated that at Meteorites road games, attendance would be up at least 15 percent—all those extra fans clamoring to see Louise play, to see history being made—and in some cases equaling and/or exceeding the expected attendance of local rivals. That is, the Meteorites would draw as many fans into the brand spanking new Wrigley Stadium—a domed stadium that seated close to a hundred thousand fans—in Chicago as would the St. Louis Cardinals.

Next came the Mets, who would sell out not only their seven Shea Stadium games against the Meteorites, but catch some of the overflow from the perpetually sold out South Field.

Next up came sneaker manufacturer Reebok, which was the first company to sign Louise to a long-term, extremely lucrative endorsement deal contingent upon the Supreme Court ruling in her favor. For years the company had been attempting to market their woman's athletic shoe line, yet sales paled in comparison to rivals Nike, L.A. Gear, Converse, Avia, and their like. But with a visible and viable spokesperson like Louise promoting the product via television commercials and magazine and newspaper advertisements, Reebok during the coming year would see its market share grow in leaps and bounds.

And lastly, Matt Stern: based on the *Journal's* estimated income projections, the renegade billionaire would actually see a profit during the Meteorites' first year in business—a feat never before realized by an expansion team in the history of professional sports. The journal went on to deem Stern "one of the savviest players in today's billionaire game."

⑪   ⑪   ⑪

And then there was late-night talk show guru David Letterman. A longtime baseball junkie, he lovingly wrung every possible Louise-related joke through his nightly Top Ten wringer.

Louise Gehrig's number-one rejected nickname: Nipples.

The number-one Meteorites' clubhouse pickup line: Is that a bat in your pocket, or are you just happy to see me?

Louise Gehrig's number-one pet peeve: That Dan Quayle jerk.

The number-one product that *will not* be endorsed by Louise Gehrig: Cruex.

7

It Ain't the Four Point Six Ounce–Size, Smooth Mint Gel Crest Toothpaste Pump Dispenser, It's the Motion

Louise was thirteen, fresh out of eighth grade, when she finally got up the nerve to ask her mom, "Who's my dad?"

They were seated in a booth, enjoying their biweekly excursion to Modern Pizza on State Street in New Haven, just a few blocks away, a brisk walk, from their St. Ronan Street home. The large, brick-oven-cooked, mozzarella pie—*well done, but not burnt*—had just arrived, along with Margaret's second beer and a refill of Louise's cola.

Margaret bit into her first slice and shrugged. Thinking, I guess she's old enough to know, she said, "Bobby Wielechowska."

"I beg your pardon."

"Bobby Wielechowska," Margaret said. "He played shortstop for the Mets."

Louise suddenly became excited. "My dad was a Met? How come you never told me?"

"Honey. Have you ever heard of Bobby Wielechowska?"

Louise thought for a moment, the expectant smile vanishing just as suddenly as it had appeared. "No," she said.

"And neither has anyone else."

"Then . . ."

"He was a hot young prospect," Margaret said, looking away with a come-hither smile and a faraway gaze. "And I mean *hot.*" She took a sip of beer and shook her head. "Damn, he was cute. He came up in late August 1975. You might remember reading that the team was doing all right that year."

"Seaver went 22–9, with a 2.38 ERA. He won the Cy Young."

A nod. "In August they still had a chance. But they were weak at short. So, they bring up Bobby from Triple-A. And he just tears it up. In thirty-four games he batted .457, with fourteen home runs. Man, he had a sweet swing." She looked up at her daughter. "I went to one game and smuggled in a banner that read: Bobby, Will You Marry Me?"

"Mom, you're blushing."

"I made the sports report on the evening news. I thought my dad was going to kill me."

"Was he embarrassed by things like that?"

"He was embarrassed because it was the Mets." She laughed. "Hell, if I'd had a crush on a Yankee, he'd have paid for the hotel room."

"Really?"

"Maybe not."

"So, how did this Bobby what's-his-name—"

"Wielechowska."

"Right. How did he become my dad?"

"We fucked."

"I figured out that much. I mean, what led up to this immortal coupling?"

"Are you being sarcastic?"

"Only a little."

Margaret glared, just for a moment, in a stern motherly sort of way, then took another swig and another bite, and continued. "In early February 1976 . . ."

"Early February?"

"February sixth, okay?"

"Okay," Louise said, smiling.

"There was a baseball card show at the Ramada Inn in North Haven. Bobby was signing autographs. His rookie card, y'know. I waited in line, and when it came to my turn, I handed him the card to sign and asked him if he was staying at the hotel. He nodded and said, 'Room 212.' I asked him if eight o'clock sounded good. He said it did. And, well, at eight o'clock I showed up at his room. At eight fifteen I left"—a shrug—"pregnant with you."

"Not too slutty."

"I couldn't help it. It was something about the uniforms. I had a thing for guys in home whites."

"Had."

"Have. Okay? Have." A shrug. "Things were different then."

"I know. Free love and all that."

"Free love was the sixties. Don't confuse your decades."

"Sorry."

They sat in silence for a moment, eating and sipping.

"Didn't you ever hear of rubbers?" Louise asked.

"Your grandfather wasn't much on sexual education."

"Unlike you."

"Exactly." She took a bite of pizza. "Back then sex couldn't kill you. The worst thing that could happen was you got pregnant." Another shrug. "Bobby didn't have any with him. So, I told him to be careful and not to come inside me."

"But he did anyway?"

"You'll find out soon enough that men have very little control over their sexual organs, before, during, or after the actual act."

"Can't wait."

Another few bites.

"What happened to Bobby?"

"This is the good part."

"Why? How bad was he?"

"You've heard of the Mendoza Line?"

A nod.

"Well, for a while there it looked like it was going to be called the Wielechowska Line instead. During the first two months of the next season he batted a dismal .047, with no home runs; and he had a league-leading twenty-one errors."

"Twenty-one errors in two months?"

A nod.

"And you slept with this guy?"

"He was cute."

"Are you sure he's my dad?"

"Absolutely."

"Man." Louise reached over and grabbed her mother's beer. Bringing the bottle to her lips, she took a long swig.

"And what do you think you're doing?"

"After that, I need a drink."

Margaret laughed. "I can't argue with that."

"So, what happened to him?"

"Bobby?"

A nod.

"He was sent back down to the minors, played out the rest of the year, then disappeared."

"Y'mean, he didn't, like, become a sports announcer, or something like that?"

"Louise. He could barely speak in complete sentences. About the only audible thing he said to me was, 'Man, where'd you get those hooters?' That was like the only two-syllable word he knew—hooters."

"So, my baseball abilities weren't inherited from my father."

"Pray they weren't inherited from your father."

"But, then how? I mean, why?"

"Let's just say the spirit of Lou Gehrig is watching out for you."

"What the hell does that mean?"

"Dammed if I know. But it was something your grandfather said all the time."

"But Lou Gehrig was a Yankee."

A shrug. "Nobody's perfect."

Ten years later, Louise was again sharing a Modern Pizza pie with her mom, though they now were both drinking beer, and on this night there was something to celebrate.

A banner was hung by the owner over the take-out window. It read: Congratulations Balls! (It had originally read Congratulations Louise, but a waitress had X-ed out her name and written in the word Balls with a thick black magic marker.)

"It doesn't get any better than this," Louise said.

"Tell me that in October," Margaret said.

"You really think we can do it?"

"You've come this far. And I'm not about to bet against you when you're on a roll."

"I'm gonna miss this place."

"You've always got the off-season. You can eat a lot of pizza in six months."

After a few bites and sips, and even a heartfelt handshake from the mother of a family of four sitting in an adjoining booth, Margaret leaned forward in the booth and whispered, "Tell me about the shower."

Louise was confused at first. Matt Stern was having a separate shower built in the clubhouse specifically for Louise. The National League owners would reluctantly have to follow suit. But at this early date, only a makeshift shower curtain sort of separation could be rigged. "No big deal," Louise and most of her teammates had said at the time. They were teammates. They'd manage.

"Nothing to tell," she told her mom.

"Oh, c'mon. You take a shower with twenty-four men and you tell me there's nothing to tell."

"Mom," Louise said. "There was a curtain separating us."

"And you saw nothing at all."

"Not a thing," Louise said, wishing her mom would change the subject.

Margaret lowered her voice even more. "Please," she begged.

"Please what?" Louise asked.

"Give me some details."

"There are none."

"Louise Kathleen Gehrig."

Louise took a deep breath. She had played this game with her mother before, and knew that Margaret would not give up until she heard what she wanted, even if what she wanted to hear was being made up. "Fine," she said. "What do you want to know?"

"Well, first off, how was it?"

Louise took a slow slip of beer while she searched for the right cliché. *Wet* was the only suitable word that came to mind, but forget it. She knew where her mother would take that. So, unable to come up with anything else appropriate—appropriate meaning no double meanings—she said, "Interesting."

"Interesting? Magazine articles about menstrual cycles are *interesting*. You took a shower with twenty-four of the best-looking men to ever walk out onto a baseball field, for Christ's sake. That's gotta be a whole lot better than interesting."

"Okay," Louise said, "it was hot. Is that what you want to hear?"

A nod. "Hot is good." She smiled. "Wet would be better. But hot will do." She took a sip of beer. "So, how big was Dixon?"

Louise almost choked on her pizza. "I beg your pardon?"

"Bob Dixon. I had such a crush on him when he was a Met. Man, did I have it bad."

"Another Bobby what's-his-name?"

"Wielechowska—that's your father. Show some respect. And no, Dixon can play."

"Until he was traded to the Red Sox."

"You know damn well that the only Boston player worth the buttons on his uniform was Bill Buckner."

"I know, Mom."

Margaret shrugged innocently. "I'm just curious. I want to know how big he is. You know, his . . ."

"I know, Mom."

"Well?"

"I don't know, Mom," she said, suddenly wishing she hadn't played along. She shrugged. "Cucumber size."

"A large cucumber?" Margaret asked. "Or a small one?"

"I don't know."

"Louise."

"Medium size, I guess."

"That's too general."

"What do you want?"

"Precise measurements, down to the last erect millimeter."

Louise thought for a moment, all the while devouring a slice of pizza and downing the rest of her beer. "Okay," she said, ready to get the game over and done with, "A Crest toothpaste pump dispenser."

"Original flavor or smooth mint gel?"

"For Dixon?"

"Uh-huh."

"Definitely the smooth mint gel."

"Four point six ounce or the eight ounce family-size dispenser?"

"Hmmm. I'd have to say the smaller one."

"That's doable. I can live with four point six ounces." She thought for a moment, her eyes getting that faraway glaze, then said, "How about P.J.?"

Louise laughed, a variety of grocery store items flying past in her head. She choose one at random. "A Ball Park frank."

"Before or after plumping?"

"Definitely before," she assumed.

"Ooh, not good. We'll have to cross him off the list."

"What list? Are you planning on seducing all of my teammates?"

"Well, one or two of them, maybe."

"Mom."

"I mean, if you're not going to sleep with them. You're not going to sleep with them, are you?"

"No, I am not."

"Then someone might as well have some fun."

Louise ordered another round of beers, then said, "You're incorrigible."

"And proud of it. But you know I'm kidding."

"Um."

"What about Jesus?"

Louise visited the freezer section, and figured she was going to have some fun with her mom's head. "A roll of Pillsbury Poppin' Fresh chocolate cookie dough."

Margaret gasped. "You're kidding."

Louise shook her head and smiled.

"I'm getting hot flashes," her mother said; then, laughing, she added, "I don't remember reading about *that* in the Bible." The drinks arrived and each took a long swig. "Reggie Borders?"

The checkout line. "A Chap Stick."

"The poor man. No wonder he's so insecure. Darryl White?"

The bread aisle. "A Devil Dog."

"A Devil Dog?"

"Uh-huh."

"But those aren't exactly round."

A confident shrug. "Neither was his dick."

"There's a comment due here about those white stripes of creamy filling. But I'll resist."

"Thank you."

"No problem. Elvis Jones?"

Soap aisle. "A Shout Power Stick laundry stain remover. Lemon scented."

"Two point eight ounce or family size?"

"The regular."

"Hmmm."

"So, you want me to get you some phone numbers?"

"No, I don't want you to get me phone numbers."

"Thought I'd ask."

"I'll be forty-one soon. I can get my own dates."

There was a short pause as each reached for one of the last two remaining slices, and then Margaret said, "Y'know what?"

"What?"

"I do think this is going to be a fun year."

Louise took a swig of beer and nodded.

Two fellow pizza lovers—guys wearing Meteorites baseball caps—walked up to her booth. "Knock 'em dead, Louise," one of the guys said, giving her the thumbs-up.

"Yeah," said his friend, "bring a World Series ring home to New Haven."

Smiling, she said, "I'll do my best."

Pulling a copy of the late edition of the *Daily News* from under his arm, the first fan displayed the back page and asked, "Would you please autograph this for me?"

Louise nodded, the smile continued—My first major league autograph, she thought. Taking a pen and the newspaper, whose back headline screamed Go Balls! over a photo of her sliding into second base, she turned and asked, "What's your name?"

"Steve."

Above her picture but below the headline she wrote: "Steve—Never stop dreaming!—Louise Gehrig."

She handed the tabloid back to Steve, who read the passage and asked, "About you?"

Louise laughed. "About whatever it is you need to keep your spirit alive."

He nodded and repeated his thanks, his friend said, "Nice meeting you," and they were off.

Margaret shot her daughter a get-used-to-it smirk as both began to grin from ear to ear.

"A fun year," Margaret repeated with a slow, steady nod.

"Y'know what?" Louise said.

"What?"

"I think you might be right."

Back home at her State Street loft, Louise began packing. She made neat little piles of what she'd most likely need for a month and a half in the Florida sun.

The Meteorites' spring training facility was a shining new multimillion-dollar complex built over the long-deserted ruins of a housing complex in Homestead. Louise had driven by it in its midconstruction phase during her last trek to the Keys. Being located south of Miami, she knew she'd need little of what had been keeping her toasty through the current and brutal New England winter.

So, with the TV blasting in the background—the same ESPN's "SportsCenter" that had caused Kevin Willard such grief—she picked out shorts and jeans and tank tops and T's. She carefully chose panties and bras and socks, and even threw in a few summery dresses, a couple of blouses, and that black skirt–blue top combination.

Placing the piles into her suitcase and carry-on, alongside a couple of Julie Smith paperback mysteries, the folding combination travel iron–blow dryer, an old travel alarm clock, and that one lucky magnet—a 3-D portrayal of Jude, patron saint of lost causes—Louise turned her attention to the nightly sportscast, one devoted almost entirely to her not-as-lost-as-she-first-believed cause.

Commissioner Quayle's face filled the screen. He was just beginning to read his official statement when Louise sat down on her sofa, glass of juice in hand, and made herself comfortable.

". . . was inevitable. And we must respect the decision of our highest court, just as we must respect and recognize the contributions that Ms. Gehrig will make to the game of baseball. In this day and age, we need to be able to turn to our national pastime for a little relief from the . . .".

Her mind began to wander, away from Quayle, away from the magic of the day, back—thirteen years back—to what she liked to refer to as *my favorite memory.* It was a tenth birthday present to end all.

Margaret had handed her an envelope. "Happy birthday, kid," she had said.

Louise turned the envelope over a few times. Envelopes were things you got from great-aunts and distant relatives. Envelopes weren't something a ten-year-old got from her mom. Moms gave you boxes—bit boxes. Crammed with toys and dolls. Or better yet, a new baseball mitt.

"An envelope?" Louise said finally.

"Just open it."

Bobbing her head to some crazy tune that only ten-year-olds and the Good Humor Man can hear, Louise ripped open the envelope, all the while wondering if Margaret had finally flipped out beyond repair. She half expected a Macy's gift certificate, or worse, one of those U.S. savings bonds. So, when the two multicolored tickets fell into her hand, she really didn't know what to say.

She read the words, to the best of her ten-year-old ability. They were mostly words she knew. Game six. 1986 World Series. Mets vs. the American League Champions. Shea Stadium. October 25, 1986. And as Louise tried to figure out what a Loge Box 376-A was, her mom was saying something about not being able to afford tickets to the first two home games, but that the Series should go at least six games.

"At least," Margaret said. "Definitely." Then, "Well?"

But Louise didn't know what to say. She had been wrung through the emotional baseball gamut, what with the nerve-racking National League Championship Series against the Astros. So, like any confused ten-year-old Met fan, she started to cry. Not because she was happy, but because she was worried. What-ifs clouded her head. Here in her little hands she held

World Series tickets—the greatest birthday present in the entire world. But what if the Astros won the league championship? What if the American League champs finished off the Mets in four or five games? Or vice versa. Damn, Louise thought to herself, this was probably her once-in-a-lifetime chance to ever see a World Series game live, and it might not even happen. She turned and ran screaming to her bedroom, the tickets clutched to her chest, leaving Margaret with a what-the-fuck? expression tacked onto her face as she asked, "Should I have gotten you a new baseball mitt instead?"

But the days and the apprehension passed. The Mets *did* defeat the Astros—in six games. Boston knocked off the California Angels in seven. And though they lost the first two games at Shea, the Mets went on to win two out of three at Fenway Park. Thus on October 25, Louise got the baseball birthday treat of all time.

And now, thirteen years later, as she sat on her sofa with Quayle babble in the background, the goose bumps flared as recollections of that historic tenth inning replayed in her mind. Mookie Wilson and that ball through Bill Buckner's legs, and Ray Knight running home, his arms flailing in the air. Man, that's when it hit her—like a brick load of desire in overdrive. She was only ten, but she knew nothing could ever top that feeling. Nothing would ever make it go away. And nothing could ever replace it.

Not a fucking thing.

Louise needed it. Even then. It was almost an adult feeling of need. One of those if-I-don't-get-it-I'll-die. Desperate and invigorating—all at the same time.

She *had* to play ball. She *had* to get to the show. She *had* to know what Ray Knight was feeling as he rounded the bases and headed home. And there was only one way to find out.

Grabbing hold of the remote control, Louise took aim. "Danny boy, you've got to go," she said. She took a deep breath, followed by a slight clearing of her throat, and zapped to MTV, where the latest video from the Red Hot Chili Peppers filled her apartment with scenes of weird funkiness in glorious black-and-white. She watched for a minute, remembering how her mother always loved the Red Hot Chili Peppers; then, shutting the TV down altogether, she high-tailed it off to bed.

It took Louise the better part of an hour to drift off to sleep. The what-ifs returned full-force. Not Mets what-ifs, but Louise what-ifs. She tossed and turned but couldn't seem to switch her mind to pause. Fast forward—yes—where the picture was a cloudy question mark. Rewind—maybe—where everything was full of promise. But not pause—where confidence ruled. So, settling in for slow motion, as she finally did, she floated off to dreamland.

She dreamed she was in the maternity ward of some big-city hospital. But she wasn't the patient. Margaret was. She had just given birth to an eight-pound, seven-ounce bouncing baby boy.

After the usual cooing and oohing and ahhing, Louise asked her mom, "Who's the father?"

But before Margaret could answer, Bob Dixon came strolling into the hospital room. He carried an armful of flowers. "I am," he said, walking over to Margaret's side.

"But . . .," Louise said.

"No, I am." It was Jesus Maldonado. Like Bob, he carried flowers. He walked over to Margaret's bedside, squeezing Bob more or less out of the way. "How's my little boy?" he asked, patting the just-born's head.

"How's *my* little boy?" It was P.J. Strykes. He carried flowers and a well-stuffed shopping bag that carried the FAO Schwarz logo.

"How *my* little boy?" It was Reggie Borders, coming in just behind P.J., pushing him out of the way.

"Don't you mean *my* little boy?" Lefty Johnston said, following his star pitcher into the room.

"*My* little boy," Elvis Jones said, standing at Lefty's heels.

"Mine," Jamaine Young said, his face appearing suddenly at the room's window.

"Mine," Jeff Carter said, emerging from the tiny maternity room bathroom.

"Mine," Sandy Downs said, crawling out from under Margaret's bed.

"He's mine!" Bob Dixon yelled.

"Mine!" Jesus yelled right back.

"Mine!" P.J. screamed.

"No, mine!"

"Mine!"

"Mine!"

"Mine, mine, mine!"

Louise managed to catch her mother's eye. "What's going on?" she cried out in protest.

But Margaret could only shrug and say, "It's the uniforms," before turning back her loving attention to what had developed into a full-blown baseball brawl right there at the foot of her maternity room bed.

⊕ **8** ⊕

Magnetized

The Meteorites first spring training went well, considering the media attention and hype that had been flung their way. ESPN, CNN, all four networks, *Sports Illustrated*, *Baseball Weekly*, the *Sporting News*, *USA Today*, and all four New York dailies had assigned reporters to around-the-clock coverage of the team. "If Louise Gehrig sneezes," many an editor had ordered, "I want our readers to know about it."

During the last two weeks of February, the team worked over the basics: bunting, hitting the cutoff person, pickoff moves, the suicide squeeze, the double steal, et cetera, et cetera, and so on, ad nauseam.

During one of the many team meetings, Lefty Johnston, with a copy of the official baseball rule book sticking out of his right hip pocket and a toothpick sticking out of the left side of his mouth, asked, "Who can explain the infield fly rule?"

Blank faces and a couple of shrugs.

"Dixon," Johnston barked.

The catcher shook his head. "Sorry."

"P.J."

"Not me, boss," the relief whiz said.

"Elvis."

A shrug.

"Jamaine."

The center fielder rolled his eyes. "Why don't you ask Gehrig?" he said.

"Christ!" was Lefty's reply. "How about it, Gehrig? Do you maybe know what the infield fly rule is?"

"Well," Louise said, clearing her throat. " 'An infield fly is a fair ball, not including a line drive nor an attempted bunt, which can be caught by an infielder with ordinary effort, when first and second, or first, second and third bases are occupied, before two are out. The pitcher, catcher and any outfielder who stations himself in the infield on the play shall be considered infielders for the purpose of this rule.' "

As Louise stopped to take a breath, Jesus Maldonado let out a long low whistle.

She continued, " 'When it seems apparent that a batted ball will be an Infield Fly, the umpire shall immediately declare "Infield Fly" for the benefit of the runners. If the ball is near the baselines, the umpire shall declare "Infield Fly, if Fair."

" 'The ball is alive and runners may advance at the risk of the ball being caught, or retouch and advance after the ball is touched, the same as on any fly ball. If the hit becomes a foul ball, it is treated the same as any foul.' "

"Very good," Johnston said.

"I'm not finished," Louise said, and as her manager pulled the rule book from his pocket and turned to Rule 2.00—Definition of Terms, she added, " 'If a declared Infield Fly is allowed to fall untouched to the ground, and bounces foul before passing first or third base, it is a foul ball. If a declared Infield Fly falls untouched to the ground outside the baseline, and bounces fair before passing first or third base, it is an Infield Fly.' "

Her teammates stared in awe, some at Johnston, whose lips moved along with her sounds, but most at Louise, who bravely continued on.

" 'On the infield fly rule the umpire is to rule whether the ball could ordinarily have been handled by an infielder—not by some arbitrary limitation such as the grass, or the base lines.

The umpire must rule also that a ball is an infield fly, even if handled by an outfielder, if, in the umpire's judgment, the ball could have been as easily handled by an infielder. The infield fly is in no sense to be considered an appeal play. The umpire's judgment must govern, and the decision should be made immediately.

" 'When an infield fly rule is called, runners may advance at their own risk. If on an infield fly rule, the infielder intentionally drops a fair ball, the ball remains in play despite the provisions of Rule 6.05. The infield fly rules takes precedence.' "

There was a moment of silence, broken by Elvis Jones, who hooked a thumb in Louise's direction and with a convincing nod said, "What she said."

Bob shot Jamaine a sarcastic look. "But you knew that, didn't you?"

Jamaine sort of grunted out a play-along laugh.

Lefty smirked, just barely. "Great," he said, putting the rule book away. "Now can anyone explain what Gehrig just said."

Another round of blank faces and shrugs, until two by two, all eyes turned back toward Louise.

At the end of that particular meeting, Bob Dixon approached Louise and said, "Should I ask?"

"As a kid I wanted to know everything there was to know about the game," Louise explained. "So I memorized the rule book—one rule at a time." A shrug. "Thought it could help."

"Little did you know."

"Yeah." She smiled. "At nine I hadn't yet grasped the difference between knowing and understanding."

"I'm thirty-six and I still get that wrong."

Manager Johnston gave his players two days off before the start of the official spring training season and the Meteorites' first scheduled game.

"Just behave yourself," he warned. "And remember, everything you do is being videotaped for the six o'clock news and photographed for use on the back page of the *New York Post.*"

The players smiled and nodded and took off in about a dozen different directions. Jesus Maldonado, with setup pitcher Al King and the team's number-four starter, Roberto Garcia, in tow, sidetracked Louise.

"Hey, Gehrig," Jesus said. "How you spending your days off?"

Louise shrugged. "Gonna catch up on my reading."

"You read too much."

She ignored the comment. "Maybe you should try it sometime."

"Don't think so."

"Why?"

"I'm just not into it."

"No, I mean why did you ask about how I was spending my free time?"

"Oh. 'Cause me, Al, and Robbie are going down to Key West. Wanna come?"

Many thoughts immediately rushed through Louise's mind, none repeatable. "I don't think that'd be a good idea," she said.

"You can always read in Key West," Jesus said. "Sit out on a dock, frosty drink in one hand, a book in the other."

"Thanks," Louise said, "for offering."

"But no thanks, right?"

"Right."

He pulled her off to the side, away from the earshot of King and Garcia, and gave her a cute shrug. "Can't blame a guy for trying."

"You're not just any guy, Jesus."

"Meaning?"

"You're my teammate."

"Oh," he said. "I see. And no nookie-nookie between teammates."

"No nookie-nookie with *this* teammate. What you do with any of the other guys is none of my business."

And it wasn't that the thought of a few off days in the Keys didn't set Louise's little button on panic mode. Just the opposite, in fact. It was just that, at that point in time, Louise couldn't spare the concentration. Men and sunshine and tropical drinks had to take the back burner, at least during this period of major league adjustment. Love would come, but later.

And as for settling down, getting—damn, the word stuck in her throat—*married*—well, it just wasn't to be found on her agenda. At least the old immediate, five-year-plan agenda. To Louise, the only ring she could picture on her finger was of the World Series championship variety.

Do you, Louise Gehrig, take this bat, to have and to hold, from this day forward, for better for worse, in slumps and in streaks, for singles and homers, to love, honor and cherish, till trade do you part?

I do! she could see herself shrieking joyously. *Oh, Lord, do I ever.*

And though she'd be the first to admit that the sight of a tall, hard body could definitely get the juices a-flowin', even sex for sex's sake was out of the question. At least recently. There was too much damn work to do. Batting practice, running, fielding. Louise didn't just want to be the first female to make it to the majors, she wanted to be the best first baseperson in the game. She wanted stats that would make her old grandfather, watching from up in heaven, proud—girl or no girl. And with workouts like that, even at twenty-three, she was too tired to engage in sexual activities. Think about them? Well, that was another matter. But to move on those thoughts. No, thank you. Not right now.

She did, however, have the energy for a few diversions of the noncarnal variety—hobbies of sorts, nothing that would eat into her run-producing abilities. There was reading, of course. And jazz—old jazz—especially Billie Holiday, though Dexter Gordon and his saxophone would do in a pinch.

Then there were magnets—refrigerator magnets—and Louise had quite the collection.

On the sunny February afternoon the Meteorites beat the Atlanta Braves 5–1, the fridge in her State Street loft apartment was covered with 516 magnets of every shape and variety, from the expected: a series of all thirty-two major league baseball team logos—to the imported: a brass Eiffel Tower, a wooden Big Ben—to the corny: various and sundry cartoon characters warning about the chubby-wubby dangers of overeating—to the downright bizarre: an unrolled Stars and Stripes condom frozen in Lucite, a 3-D Jesus (Christ, not Maldonado), and a corner collection she dubbed Duval Street, featuring magnets from most every bar in Key West from the Hog's Breath Saloon to Sloppy Joe's—one for every lover she had ever found in paradise. What was it about Key West? And thank God they didn't have a baseball franchise.

On many an occasion, someone would ask, "Do you have any hobbies? I mean, other than baseball?"

And after the royal reaming during which Louise would most assuredly get across the point that baseball was *not* a hobby, she'd mention her magnets.

"Refrigerator magnets?"

"Refrigerator magnets."

"Oh," would be the most likely response.

Louise had a thing about leaving people speechless. And though it was usually accomplished with her bat, she'd take it from wherever it came, be it her hitting abilities, her refrigerator magnets, or her performance after one too many strawberry margaritas from one of Key West's far too many bars.

⚾   ⚾   ⚾

For four weeks in March, Louise and her teammates rehearsed for their upcoming six-month run—an engagement split between their home field on the Lower East Side of Manhattan and fifteen unfriendly ballparks on the road—hoping, always hoping, for that extended postseason engagement. Man, *dreaming* for that fourteen-game extension. The Meteorites' spring training consisted of a grand total of twenty-five faux games against teams from both leagues, including the Atlanta Braves, the Buffalo Expos, the Los Angeles Dodgers, the Florida Marlins, the New Orleans Jazz, and, of course, the New York Mets.

They played well, they played hard, and with the exception of backup catcher Jo Jo Manzi, a free agent via Toronto, twisting his ankle, they sustained no notable injuries. Jo Jo would be able to rejoin the active roster by mid-April, and besides, Dixon was healthy enough to play every day. In fact, he was having a career spring training—his bat a smoking gun. He averaged .445, with eleven homers, and soon found himself batting cleanup.

The Meteorites spring training record was 13–12, tying them for second overall with the Atlanta Braves in the race of all National League teams. Only the Mets had a better winning percentage, with the crosstown rivals going 17–9.

Louise appeared in all but one game, batted .319, and hit seven doubles, one triple, and three home runs. And much to teammate Jamaine Young's chagrin, she led all major leaguers in two categories by stealing sixteen bases and scoring twenty-nine runs. Her numbers were good—very good, some reporters wrote. Then, quickly, they added, but this *is* spring training. And as everyone—especially those on the sports beat—knows, spring training don't mean shit, jack.

⚾   ⚾   ⚾

With every Louise hit, or at least every stolen base, seemed to come an endorsement deal, or an offer of one. Both Coke and Pepsi were vying for her attention, as were McDonald's and Burger King, and the people representing Calvin Klein underwear, Guess jeans, Campbell's Hungry Man soups, Revlon cosmetics, Chevrolet, Soft & Dri antiperspirant, Tampax brand tampons, and of course, Wheaties. The Mars Corporation even offered to market a candy bar in her name.

Louise informed Guess and Calvin Klein that she was indeed flattered that they'd ask, and thank you, but . . . no. As for Tampax, she just sort of laughed it off with an "I don't think so." McDonald's and Burger King were places she never ate, Chevies were cars she didn't drive, Soft & Dri wasn't her brand of antiperspirant, and Wheaties wasn't her cereal . . . so, no. As for Campbell's, it intrigued her to no end to be the product spokesperson for Hungry Man soups—would they change the name to Hungry Person soups, perhaps?—but soup had never found a place in her gastronomic heart. Again, no. Regarding Revlon, she told them to contact her when they stopped testing their products on animals. And as for the Mars Corporation, a Louise Gehrig candy bar was tempting indeed, but something about millions of teenage boys claiming to have just eaten a Louise Gehrig made her feel, if nothing else, ill at ease.

She did, however, tell both Coke and Pepsi to put their money where their mouths were, while accepting an offer from the Chrysler Corporation to be the spokesperson for their new Jeep Wrangler.

The commercial featured clips of Louise sliding into bases, getting base hit after base hit after base hit, and making diving stabs at line drives, all cut to shots of her driving a Wrangler through the toughest of terrains, up mountainsides, through rivers, over New York City streets. Her one line was simple enough. As she pulled the Wrangler up to the fanciest of restaurants, stepped out, and handed the keys to the valet parking attendant—who quickly pulled it into the parking lot filled with Rolls-Royces and Lamborghinis—Louise, dressed elegantly and to the hilt, turned toward the camera and said, "The new Jeep Wrangler. It's built tough." And with a devastating smile, she added, "Like me."

Overnight with Howie

"We've got Joey from Bensonhurst on the line. You with me, Joey?"

"Sure am, Howie. You might remember me. I called about a month and a half ago. The night before that Supreme Court game."

"Okay."

"I told you how mad I was, and you told me to calm down 'cause baseball needed a change."

"A lot of callers were angry that night."

"I suppose."

"Do you have a question, Joey?"

"Well, yeah. Sorta. I read in the papers and heard on the FAN that the Mediocres have sold out like every game this season."

"People want to see Louise Gehrig play."

"I think that's a travesty. This ain't baseball no more."

"How so?"

"It's a freak show."

"Joey, have you seen her play? Did you see the Atlanta game? Or any of the spring training games."

"Yeah. So."

"So, you're going to call this program and tell me that Louise Gehrig doesn't deserve to play pro ball?"

"It just ain't right, Howie. It just ain't right."

"Why not?"

"She's a girl. Why do ya think?"

"Yeah. One who'll probably make it into the Hall of Fame in twenty or so years."

"Man, now you're making me mad. How can you even say that? The Hall of Fame? It just ain't right."

"What team do you follow, Joey?"

"The Mets, I guess."

"What are you going to do when a woman plays for the Mets?"

"It ain't gonna happen."

"Oh, it'll happen. Mark my words. And it's going to bring life to a game that's barely survived the turn of this new century. Baseball owes its survival to people like Matt Stern and Louise Gehrig."

"This call's going nowhere."

"You can say that again. Here's Dave from Danbury. Are you with me, Dave?"

 PART TWO

Play Ball

There is no greater pleasure in the world than walking up to the plate with men on base and knowing that you are feared.

—Ted Simmons

MANHATTAN METEORITES

2000 Season Schedule

April

Mon. 4/3—Buffalo Expos—7:05 PM
Tue. 4/4—Buffalo Expos—7:05 PM
Wed. 4/5—Buffalo Expos—1:35 PM

Fri. 4/7—AT Philadelphia Phillies—7:35 PM
Sat. 4/8—AT Philadelphia Phillies—7:05 PM
Sun. 4/9—AT Philadelphia Phillies—1:35 PM

Tue. 4/11—AT Pittsburgh Pirates—7:05 PM
Wed. 4/12—AT Pittsburgh Pirates—7:05 PM
Thu. 4/13—AT Pittsburgh Pirates—7:05 PM

Fri. 4/14—AT Chicago Cubs—8:35 PM
Sat. 4/15—AT Chicago Cubs—2:05 PM
Sun. 4/16—AT Chicago Cubs—2:05 PM

Mon. 4/17—Florida Marlins—7:05 PM
Tue. 4/18—Florida Marlins—7:05 PM
Wed. 4/19—Florida Marlins—1:35 PM
Thu. 4/20—Florida Marlins—7:05 PM

Fri. 4/21—Pittsburgh Pirates—8:05 PM
Sat. 4/22—Pittsburgh Pirates—1:35 PM
Sun. 4/23—Pittsburgh Pirates—1:35 PM

Tue. 4/25—AT Los Angeles Dodgers—10:35 PM
Wed. 4/26—AT Los Angeles Dodgers—10:35 PM

Thu. 4/27—AT San Diego Padres—10:35 PM
Fri. 4/28—AT San Diego Padres—10:35 PM

Sat. 4/29—AT Colorado Rockies—3:35 PM
Sun. 4/30—AT Colorado Rockies—9:35 PM

May

Mon. 5/1—AT Arkansas Astros—8:35 PM
Tue. 5/2—AT Arkansas Astros—8:35 PM

Thu. 5/4—Chicago Cubs—7:05 PM
Fri. 5/5—Chicago Cubs—7:05 PM
Sat. 5/6—Chicago Cubs—1:35 PM
Sun. 5/7—Chicago Cubs—3:05 PM

Mon. 5/8—AT Buffalo Expos—7:35 PM
Tue. 5/9—AT Buffalo Expos—7:35 PM
Wed. 5/10—AT Buffalo Expos—1:35 PM
Thu. 5/11—AT Buffalo Expos—7:35 PM

Fri. 5/12—St. Louis Cardinals—7:05 PM
Sat. 5/13—St. Louis Cardinals—1:35 PM
Sun. 5/14—St. Louis Cardinals—1:35 PM

Tue. 5/16—New Orleans Jazz—8:35 PM
Wed. 5/17—New Orleans Jazz—2:35 PM

Thu. 5/18—St. Petersburg Giants—7:05 PM
Fri. 5/19—St. Petersburg Giants—7:05 PM

Sat. 5/20—Cincinnati Reds—7:05 PM
Sun. 5/21—Cincinnati Reds—1:35 PM

Mon. 5/22—Philadelphia Phillies—7:05 PM
Tue. 5/23—Philadelphia Phillies—7:05 PM
Wed. 5/24—Philadelphia Phillies—1:35 PM

Fri. 5/26—AT New York Mets—8:05 PM
Sat. 5/27—AT New York Mets—7:35 PM
Sun. 5/28—AT New York Mets—1:35 PM
Mon. 5/29—AT New York Mets—1:35 PM

Tue. 5/30—AT Florida Marlins—7:35 PM
Wed. 5/31—AT Florida Marlins—7:35 PM

June

Thu. 6/1—AT Florida Marlins—1:35 PM
Fri. 6/2—AT Florida Marlins—7:35 PM

Sat. 6/3—AT St. Petersburg Giants—1:35 PM
Sun. 6/4—AT St. Petersburg Giants—1:35 PM

Mon. 6/5—AT New Orleans Jazz—8:35 PM
Tue. 6/6—AT New Orleans Jazz—8:35 PM

Thu. 6/8—AT Cincinnati Reds—1:35 PM
Fri. 6/9—AT Cincinnati Reds—7:05 PM

Sat. 6/10—AT Atlanta Braves—2:05 PM
Sun. 6/11—AT Atlanta Braves—5:05 PM

Tue. 6/13—St. Louis Cardinals—7:05 PM
Wed. 6/14—St. Louis Cardinals—1:35 PM
Thu. 6/15—St. Louis Cardinals—1:35 PM
Fri. 6/16—St. Louis Cardinals—7:05 PM

Sat. 6/17—Colorado Rockies—2:05 PM
Sun. 6/18—Colorado Rockies—1:35 PM

Mon. 6/19—San Diego Padres—7:05 PM
Tues. 6/20—San Diego Padres—7:05 PM

Thu. 6/22—New Orleans Jazz—2:35 PM
Fri. 6/23—New Orleans Jazz—8:05 PM

Sat. 6/24—Arkansas Astros—1:35 PM
Sun. 6/25—Arkansas Astros—1:35 PM

Tue. 6/27—Los Angeles Dodgers—7:05 PM
Wed. 6/28—Los Angeles Dodgers—7:05 PM

Thu. 6/29—AT Philadelphia Phillies—7:35 PM
Fri. 6/30—AT Philadelphia Phillies—7:35 PM

July

Sat. 7/1—AT Philadelphia Phillies—7:35 PM
Sun. 7/2—AT Philadelphia Phillies—1:05 PM

Mon. 7/3—AT Pittsburgh Pirates—7:05 PM
Tue. 7/4—AT Pittsburgh Pirates—7:05 PM
Wed. 7/5—At Pittsburgh Pirates—1:35 PM
Thu. 7/6—AT Pittsburgh Pirates—7:05 PM

Fri. 7/7—AT Buffalo Expos—7:35 PM
Sat. 7/8—AT Buffalo Expos—1:35 PM
Sun. 7/9—AT Buffalo Expos—1:35 PM

Tue. 7/11—ALL STAR GAME—8:05 PM
South Field, New York City

Fri. 7/14—New York Mets—8:05 PM
Sat. 7/15—New York Mets—1:35 PM
Sun. 7/16—New York Mets—3:05 PM

Mon. 7/17—AT St. Louis Cardinals—8:35 PM
Tue. 7/18—AT St. Louis Cardinals—8:35 PM
Wed. 7/19—AT St. Louis Cardinals—2:35 PM

Thu. 7/20—Arkansas Astros—7:05 PM
Fri. 7/21—Arkansas Astros—7:05 PM

Sat. 7/22—Los Angeles Dodgers—1:35 PM
Sun. 7/23—Los Angeles Dodgers—1:35 PM

Mon. 7/24—San Diego Padres—7:05 PM
Tue. 7/25—San Diego Padres—7:05 PM

Wed. 7/26—Atlanta Braves—8:05 PM
Thu. 7/27—Atlanta Braves—1:35 PM

Fri. 7/28—Chicago Cubs—7:05 PM
Sat. 7/29—Chicago Cubs—1:35 PM
Sun. 7/30—Chicago Cubs—8:05 PM

August

Tue. 8/1—Colorado Rockies—7:05 PM
Wed. 8/2—Colorado Rockies—1:35 PM

Thu. 8/3—St. Petersburg Giants—7:05 PM
Fri. 8/4—St. Petersburg Giants—7:05 PM

Sat. 8/5—Buffalo Expos—1:35 PM
Sun. 8/6—Buffalo Expos—1:35 PM

Mon. 8/7—AT Florida Marlins—7:35 PM
Tue. 8/8—AT Florida Marlins—7:35 PM
Wed. 8/9—AT Florida Marlins—1:35 PM

Thu. 8/10—AT Cincinnati Reds—7:35 PM
Fri. 8/11—AT Cincinnati Reds—7:35 PM

Sat. 8/12—AT St. Louis Cardinals—8:35 PM
Sun. 8/13—At St. Louis Cardinals—2:35 PM
Mon. 8/14—AT St. Louis Cardinals—8:35 PM
Tue. 8/15—AT St. Louis Cardinals—8:35 PM

Wed. 8/16—Atlanta Braves—1:35 PM

Thu. 8/17—Atlanta Braves—7:35 PM

Fri. 8/18—Florida Marlins—7:05 PM
Sat. 8/19—Florida Marlins—1:35 PM
Sun. 8/20—Florida Marlins—1:35 PM

Mon. 8/21—Cincinnati Reds—7:05 PM
Tue. 8/22—Cincinnati Reds—7:05 PM

Thu. 8/24—AT Colorado Rockies—3:35 PM
Fri. 8/25—AT Colorado Rockies—9:35 PM

Sat. 8/26—AT St. Petersburg Giants—7:35 PM
Sun. 8/27—At St. Petersburg Giants—1:35 PM

Mon. 8/28—AT Arkansas Astros—8:35 PM
Tue. 8/29—AT Arkansas Astros—8:35 PM

Thu. 8/31—Philadelphia Phillies—1:35 PM

September

Fri. 9/1—Philadelphia Phillies—7:05 PM
Sat. 9/2—Philadelphia Phillies—1:35 PM
Sun. 9/3—Philadelphia Phillies—3:05 PM

Mon. 9/4—Buffalo Expos—7:05 PM
Tue. 9/5—Buffalo Expos—7:05 PM

Thu. 9/7—AT Chicago Cubs—2:35 PM
Fri. 9/8—AT Chicago Cubs—8:35 PM
Sat. 9/9—AT Chicago Cubs—2:35 PM
Sun. 9/10—AT Chicago Cubs—2:35 PM

Tue. 9/12—AT Atlanta Braves—7:35 PM
Wed. 9/13—At Atlanta Braves—7:35 PM

Thu. 9/14—AT New Orleans Jazz—8:35 PM
Fri. 9/15—AT New Orleans Jazz—8:35 PM

Sat. 9/16—AT San Diego Padres—10:35 PM
Sun. 9/17—AT San Diego Padres—4:05 PM

Mon. 9/18—AT Los Angeles Dodgers—10:35 PM
Tue. 9/19—AT Los Angeles Dodgers—10:35 PM

Thu. 9/21—New York Mets—7:05 PM
Fri. 9/22—New York Mets—8:05 PM

Sat. 9/23—New York Mets—1:35 PM
Sun. 9/24—New York Mets—1:35 PM

Mon. 9/25—Pittsburgh Pirates—7:05 PM
Tue. 9/26—Pittsburgh Pirates—7:05 PM
Wed. 9/27—Pittsburgh Pirates—1:35 PM
Thu. 9/28—Pittsburgh Pirates—7:05 PM

Fri. 9/29—AT New York Mets—7:35 PM
Sat. 9/30—AT New York Mets—7:35 PM

October

Sun. 10/1—AT New York Mets—1:35 PM

2000 PROMOTION DATES

Opening Day	Monday, April 3
Warner Brothers Music Sample Day	Wednesday, April 5
Soho All-Natural Soda Calendar Night	Tuesday, April 18
Earth Day	Saturday, April 22
Manhattan Meteorites Cap Night	Thursday, May 4
Topps Baseball Card Day	Saturday, May 6
New York Times Sports Bottle Day	Sunday, May 14
Citibank Beach Towel Day	Sunday, May 21
WFAN Fanny Pack Night	Friday, June 16
Manhattan Meteorites T-Shirt Day	Sunday, June 18
Snapple Sun Visor Day	Saturday, June 24
Baseball Weekly Free Issue Night	Friday, July 14
Manhattan Meteorite Tube Sock Day	Sunday, July 16
PETA Vegetarian Night	Thursday, July 27
Donruss New York Baseball Hero Card Day	Saturday, July 29
American Airlines Kids Fly For Free Day	Saturday, August 5
Ocean Spray Sports Bag Day	Sunday, August 6
Rolling Rock Sweat Band Night	Thursday, August 17
Sony Home Electronics Giveaway Day	Sunday, August 20
Trojan Condom Safe Sex Night	Friday, September 1

NYTV SuperStation Pin Day	Sunday, September 3
Half-Priced Ticket Night	Monday, September 4
Calvin Klein Perfume/Cologne Sampler Night	Friday, September 22
Fan Appreciation Day	Sunday, September 24
Manhattan Meteorites Sweatshirt Night	Thursday, September 28

9

Ready

Manhattan's South Field—situated in the area located just north of the entrance ramp to the Williamsburg Bridge, south of East Houston Street, east of Pitt Street, but west of the FDR Drive—was a virtual replica of the old Wrigley Field, which was torn down in 1997 to make room for the new Wrigley Stadium. It featured the same capacity (38,710), the same dugout, the same bullpen, even the same vines—vines which Matt Stern purchased from the Cub owners, at the outrageous price of an even hundred thousand dollars, and had transplanted to the edge of his center field wall. Stern figured that if he was going to build a ballpark it was going to be modeled after the best. And though many thought the best was easily Baltimore's Camden Yards, or possibly Toronto's Sky Dome, to the young owner the best was Wrigley—hands down—bricks, grass, bleachers, and all.

On Saturday, April 1, in the year 2000, Louise Kathleen Gehrig, along with her manager, teammates, and coaches, arrived at South Field. She was assigned locker number 12. Dixon's was to the right of hers, Jamaine Young's to the left. After loading in and hanging up her gear—4's of every size and variety were sewn or etched or Sharpied onto everything—she made her way from the clubhouse, down the walk that led to the six steps that led up to the dugout, out onto the field, and over to first base. Her base. Her home. Her Valhalla, Holy Land, and honeymoon bed all rolled neatly into a tight little rubber-covered white square.

She looked about the field and inhaled deeply. The cool April air—not New York air, but South Field air, baseball air, Amazon rain forest air, all-good-things-must-last-forever air—filled her lungs. The smell of the freshly manicured grass made her just a little high. A little woozy, a little funky in the head—like when watching a Key West sunset. Like when reading Tom Robbins. Like when listening to Billie Holiday croon "Body and Soul." Like when standing before Lou Gehrig's Cooperstown display—that bat, that glove, that uniform, that number 4. Like being in love? Maybe, she thought.

Louise sat down on the base and dug her hands into the dirt where the baselines would soon be drawn. She sunk her fingers greedily in. This is mine.

"Hey, Gehrig."

She didn't have to turn—the voice, a perpetually gruff bark, was easily recognizable.

"Hey, Lefty," she called back.

"Mind if I join you?"

She patted the ground to her left. "Plenty of room."

The Meteorites manager strolled from the dugout and took a seat next to his first baseperson. "How's it shaking?" he asked.

"It's shaking," she said, a slight nod, a slighter smile.

"You ready?"

"I've been ready for a long time."

"I know that. But are you *ready*?"

Louise thought for a moment—those Game Six highlight reel details: Run Ray! Go Ray! You can make it! Yes! flashing before her eyes. Was she ready? Was she ready? Was she *ready*? Oh, fucking yes—in every language, every symbol. YesYesYesYes Yes!—then taking one of those long, lingeringly deep breaths, she answered, "Yeah."

"Good."

Lefty pulled a 750-count package of Forster flat toothpicks from his jacket pocket, popped the pointy end of one into his mouth, and offered the package to Louise.

"No thanks," she said.

Lefty put the small blue-and-white box away.

"What about you," Louise asked. "Do you think I'm ready?"

He chewed on the Forster for a minute, then said, "I think you've been ready for a long time."

"No, but am I *ready?*"

He laughed, and nodded, bobbing his head to some crazy tune that only baseball managers, ten-year-olds, and the Good Humor Man can hear. His head filled with memories of his distinguished past—those glory days with the Orioles, his triple crown in 1970, the not such glory days with the Giants, playing against Aaron and Rose and Mantle and Clemente. And now Louise. A new dawn of glory was approaching—that swing. "Yeah," he said, finally, "you're *ready.*" He sucked on the toothpick for a moment, then spun it around and jabbed it into the opposite corner of his mouth. "Is there anything you need to know?" he asked, with the hesitancy of a dad about to explain the facts of life to his nine-year-old.

"Yeah," Louise said. "There's one thing that's been bugging me."

"What's that?"

"Why me?"

"Y'mean, is it luck, talent, brains, ambition, natural ability"— he snorted a half laugh—"balls?"

"I guess."

He turned to face her. "I'd say just the right combination of all of the above." He shook his head and looked away. "And goddamn, Balls, if you ain't got the sweetest swing I've ever seen."

Louise thanked Lefty for the compliment, then turned to face him. "Are you blushing?" she blurted out, leaning close, examining the miracle—baseball managers just *did not* blush.

Lefty stood up quickly, and just as quickly made excuses, disappearing back toward the dugout. Louise watched after him, she too now blushing—blushing like the time just after her first kiss. Sure, she had socked the guy. Coldcocked him right in the face, breaking his nose, but afterward, after the apologies and the blood, she had blushed. Because, hell, she was only eleven—he was twelve—and she had never been kissed before.

Such moments warrant a little innocence. But being told by your manager that your swing was sweet—well, Louise wasn't sure. Maybe it was the same thing. She just wasn't sure.

Louise's instructions to her mother were simple enough: "Find me a place I'll be comfortable in. Preferably downtown." But when she arrived at the penthouse apartment taking up the entire twenty-third floor of the West Village postmodern high-rise on Charles Street, just a block from the Hudson River, when she glanced at the sunken living room with its gleaming hardwood floors, the recreation room with its seventy-five-inch direct-view television monitor and the state-of-the-art sound system, and the wraparound balcony giving her an unobstructed view of, seemingly, the entire tristate region, she just looked at her smiling mom and said, "Are you nuts?"

"You don't like it?"

Louise continued the inspection: The bathroom had an environmental shower large enough to comfortably accommodate the entire Meteorites starting lineup at the same time, and the Jacuzzi tub seated four.

"It's comfortable," Margaret insisted. "And it is downtown."

"What is this costing me?"

"Not that much, considering. We're in a depressed market remember? It was actually quite a bargain."

"How much of a bargain?"

"A million five."

"One million, five hundred thousand dollars?"

"Uh-huh. And the previous owners covered the closing costs."

"How nice of them."

"You don't like it?"

"It's not that, Mom. It's just a little, y'know, too much."

"Too much money?"

"We're talking about one and a half million dollars."

"Which, as if I have to remind you, is a drop in the bucket. Between salary and endorsements, and I'm not even taking into account what you might get from Coke or Pepsi, you could probably buy a half dozen of these this year alone."

Louise sighed. "I guess."

Margaret pointed toward the living room windows. "Look at that view. Do you have any idea what kind of party you can throw on the Fourth of July?"

"Mom, I'll be in Pittsburgh on the Fourth of July."

Margaret bit at her bottom lip. "Oh. That sucks. Well, think of the party I can throw."

"Umm."

Louise continued to examine. In the kitchen she discovered the double-size Sub-Zero fridge with steel doors—steel doors virtually covered in her magnets. And for the first time since entering her new home, she smiled.

"There's room for more," Margaret said. "I had to take that into account when looking for a place."

Louise ran her fingers over the collection. A few made her smile. The David Letterman magnet even got her to laugh. It always did, this raised-eyebrow mug shot from the cover of *Esquire* magazine. And one, in particular, made her own eyebrows do a little drunken tango. It was shaped like a sideways eight, an infinity symbol with perfectly rounded circles. One was filled with the Meteorites logo—the bright yellow M outlined in black, in a circled background of black pinstripes on white. The other was filled with the number 4, raised and likewise bright yellow outlined in black, over the selfsame background. And over the 4 was the name Gehrig, in bold black letters.

"Thought you'd like that one," Margaret said.

"Yeah," Louise said, the word squeaking out of her throat. Because though she had spent a good part of her young life dreaming of playing major league ball, she had never once given thought to having her own refrigerator magnet. That thought had never crossed her mind. Not for a moment. But seeing it there in all its yellow and black and white glory, surrounded by Fido Dido to one side and Ted's Creamy Root Beer to the other, by Hemingway's face for Sloppy Joe's to the top and that little man holding the sign that read Intense Excitement to the bottom—it made her laugh. It gave her goosebumps. But most of all, it made her want to play baseball all the more. Because now she knew that next year there'd be another official Louise Gehrig refrigerator magnet. And another the year after that.

"What do you think of the apartment now?" Margaret asked, breaking her daughter's code of silence.

The answer was far away, in a voice Margaret recognized from whenever Louise got in her baseball mind-set. "I love it," she said.

That was all the approval Margaret needed to hear.

Agent Wesley Selden was especially busy the weekend preceding the Meteorites premiere opening day. Letters had been pouring into the South Field main office at the rate of about a thousand a day. He had a lot of words, a lot of hate to sift through. Sure, words of praise, admiration, and even love could occasionally be found, but praise, admiration, and love never made it to Selden's eyes. Only hate.

Tombstone, as the "Louise Gehrig. R.I.P." author was dubbed by those in the FBI office, was the most vigilant of any of the antifans. Seven letters a week, with two always arriving on Monday to make up for the lack of mail delivery on Sunday. And though the drawing of the tombstone never changed over the six-week period prior to opening day, the message occasionally varied, if only slightly. Once a week, on one of the two Monday-delivered letters, Louise's name would be X'ed out with six small, identically sized X's, and over it would be scrawled the word "baseball."

The postmark on the number ten–size white envelope was always New York, New York 10002—the South Field zip code. But Tombstone's identity was a mystery. Selden didn't have a clue. But something about Tombstone, some forty letters later, still gave the agent the willies. And with thirty-eight thousand plus fans due at the opening day celebration, the possibility that one of those fans would be a psychopath was something Selden would bet the rent money on.

Now all he had to do was spot him.

The first pitch on Monday, April 3, was set for 7:05 P.M., and at a little after 3:00 P.M., Margaret accompanied her daughter to a small South Field get-together, a party for players, coaches, and what friends, family members, and significant others were deemed worthy to attend.

"Oh, my God," Margaret said moments after entering the clubhouse. "There's Bob Dixon."

"He's our catcher, Mom," Louise said in her no-big-deal voice. "Remember, the four point six ounce-size, smooth mint gel Crest toothpaste pump dispenser?"

"How could I forget," Margaret said dreamily.

Louise smiled and turned toward Bob. "Hey, Bob!" she yelled. "C'mon over here. I want you to meet my mom."

Bob, who had brought no friends, family members, or significant others to the opening day celebration, walked over and extended his hand. "Nice to meet you," he said.

"Likewise," Margaret said, shaking the catcher's hand.

"Mom's had a crush on you for years," Louise said.

"Really?" Bob said. "Have you sought counseling?"

Margaret nodded. "I'm afraid it's incurable."

"Well, if you two will excuse me," Louise said; and, shooting a mischievous smile Margaret's way, she walked over to Reggie Borders, the day's starting pitcher. "Hey, Reggie. Nervous?"

He nodded in an oddly silent manner. "I'm always worried I won't live up to my potential." He looked at her. His eyes were wide and wild—frightened like a deer's caught in headlights. "I'm worried I won't pitch a perfect game."

"But isn't it enough to just do your best?"

"That is my best. I pitched four of 'em in high school, three in college, and another three in the minors. But I've never pitched one in the majors. Five years and I've never pitched a perfect game."

Louise felt suddenly uncomfortable, as if she were somehow responsible for his misery. "But you're a great pitcher," she said. "How many one-hitters do you have?"

"Seventeen. But a one-hitter isn't a no-hitter. And a no-hitter is what I want every time out. A no-hit, no-walk, perfect game."

"Aren't you being a little hard on yourself?"

He turned and stared through her. "If I'm not hard, who will be?"

"Lefty," Louise shrugged. "Isn't that his job?"

Reggie smiled. "He's a good man. But he's a softy. He doesn't understand how every hit, every base on balls kills me just a little. Like cigarettes, every hit takes a day off my life." He smiled and slapped his own knee. "I'm gonna get me something to eat. Hungry?"

"Ahh . . . no, thanks."

Reggie nodded and walked over toward the buffet table. Louise felt a sudden chill run down her spine. She saw P.J. Strykes eying her from his locker point of view, and headed off in his direction.

"A bundle of laughs," he said, with a nod toward Reggie, who was munching down a ham-and-cheese grinder.

"Is he always so cheery?"

"You'll learn never to talk to him before a start."

"But he's a great pitcher."

"I know that. You know that."

"Everyone does, except Reggie Borders?"

"Something like that."

They both turned and glanced over at Margaret and Bob, who seemed to be hitting it off, laughing, making what Louise would easily classify as serious eye contact.

"Where's your significant other?" Louise asked the relief pitcher.

"Don't have one at the moment. Baseball schedules require a lot of patience on the part of the"—he searched for a word—"other." He flashed a smile. "And if you could make one sweeping generalization about the, ahh . . ."

"Others."

"I've dated, is that patience was not one of their virtues." He nodded at Sandy Downs as the left fielder and his wife walked past. "How 'bout you?"

"No time," Louise said. "And no patience."

"Aha! Speaking of patience, how are you and our beloved center fielder getting on?"

"What are you talking about? Jamaine worships me."

"Goddamn incentive clauses."

"You should talk."

"Yeah, well. It's different with pitchers."

"Umm. Every time I steal a base I can feel the spikes."

"Wait'll they count."

"Between him and the wives, I'm not exactly feeling loved," Louise said.

"Screw the wives," P.J. said. "They're just jealous because you have a life."

"Do I detect hostility?"

"Not really. Mall hair makes me irritable."

Louise laughed. "Well, maybe you'll get to take out some of that frustration on the mound."

"Today? No. Today, I'm just collecting splinters. The chances that I'll get to pitch with Reggie starting are slim to none. So, I just sit out in the bullpen and root you guys"—he smiled broadly—"and gals on."

"Only one gal."

"For now."

"I don't know. You think there'll be others?"

"That depends on you."

"Thanks for putting the future of women in baseball on my shoulders."

"I didn't put it there, Balls. You did."

At 4:30, the clubhouse was cleared of visitors. Margaret walked past her daughter and squeezed her hand. "Thank you so much," she said.

"Any time," Louise said.

"Knock 'em dead."

"I will."

"See you after the game."

With everyone gone, the players changed into their uniforms and settled down to hear whatever words of inspiration and wisdom Lefty would offer up as a sacrifice to the Great God of Skippers on this, their opening day.

"Before you step out to stretch or warm up or take BP," he began, "there are a few things I'd like to say. It's nothing new. I don't know any words that can make you win. No one does. And I don't care that the Mike Ditkas and the Pat Rileys of the world might believe otherwise. Winning comes from inside. From the gut, from the soul. Any good ballplayer knows that. And you are all good ballplayers. But winning today is almost an aside. When you take the field, you'll become part of history. Today everything changes. The world you know and love, the world you marveled at as children, will be different"—he looked over at his starting first baseperson—"once *you* take the field." He paused for a moment, and swallowed hard. "I had all but given up on baseball. No. Change that. I *had* given up on base-ball. I had had enough. It just didn't interest me anymore. Then you came along. And I thought that maybe baseball had a future. And I saw you swing a bat, and I *knew* it had a future, and that I wanted to be a part of that future." He turned away, clasping his hands together and bringing them up to rest against his chin. He whispered, "And here we are." He turned back and looked into the faces; then, clapping his hands to-gether with all the authority he could possibly muster, Lefty smiled and said, "Now let's go out there and kick some Buffalo butt."

Outside the grounds of South Field, a group of anti-Gehrig pro-testors had set up camp behind the outfield bleachers. A few hundred strong, they carried signs and placards, they shouted, they chanted. "Gehrig go home! Gehrig go home! Gehrig go home!"

A few hundred feet from where they stood, a group of pro-Gehrig supporters protested the fact that the anti-Louise group was protesting at all. They too carried signs and placards. They booed and hissed at the anti-Gehrig group. They shouted, they chanted. "Go, Gehrig, go! Go, Gehrig, go! Go, Gehrig, go!"

When heard together, as it usually was, their battling protest sounded more like: "Go Gehrig Gehrig go go home!"

Agent Selden patrolled the area, taking in the absurdity of it all. Silly, he thought to himself reading a sign that read A Woman at First Base Is Like a Fish on a Bicycle. Just plain silly.

Plainclothesmen had been stationed throughout the stadium, in every rest room, and at every entrance. They were all in radio contact with one another and Selden. And with a little over thirty minutes to go before the first pitch, five men had been arrested. Four for being drunk and disorderly. The fifth when a handgun was found in his binocular case.

Selden was immediately on the scene. "Do you always bring handguns to ball games?" he screamed at the culprit.

The man was lying facedown on the ground. He was handcuffed. One FBI agent had a semiautomatic pistol of some sort pointed at his head. "I grabbed the wrong case!" the man yelled, insisting, "I thought those were my field glasses."

Selden turned to the arresting agent. "Who is he?"

The agent flipped open the man's wallet, which contained every sort of identification imaginable, including a platinum American Express card, a Diners Club card, an Optima card, two gold Visa cards, a gold MasterCard, and a Discover card.

"Should I book him for having too much credit?" the agent asked.

Selden cracked a slight smile. "Just get him out of here," he said, not about to waste his time with a wacko under arrest. There were wackos running free—wackos with binocular cases containing who the fuck knows what?

Shit! he thought, just as a voice in his headset told him there was a problem at Gate E.

At 6:55—with New York's weather god granting baseball a clear and mild evening with temperatures hovering around sixty—the announcer chosen to be one half of NYTV SuperStation's Meteorites play-by-play team, Kurt Rybak, walked onto the field and took his place behind a microphone set up just behind home

plate. "Ladies and gentlemen," he said. "Welcome to South Field. Welcome to history. Welcome to the new world order."

The 38,710 in attendance applauded respectably, a few even hooted and hollered, and then they all became absurdly quiet as Rybak introduced the players and coaches who made up the Buffalo Expos.

But as soon as the last Expo ran to the field, the crowd came alive. They cheered, they screamed, and millions of something-special-is-about-to-happen goose bumps ran rampant in the South Field stands.

"And now," Rybak's voice boomed, "introducing your Manhattan Meteorites. Number forty-seven. Manager Lefty Johnston."

Lefty ran out of the dugout, shook hands with the Expos' manager, then took his position a few feet up the first-base line from home plate.

"Number eleven. Center fielder, Jamaine Young."

Both Lefty and Jamaine received a respectable, if not enthusiastic, round of applause by any standards. No one could have possibly been prepared for what happened next as the 38,710 strong rose to their collective feet and roared.

"Number four!" Rybak yelled above the noise. "First baseperson, Louise Gehrig!"

Louise stepped from the dugout and ran toward Lefty.

"Welcome to the big leagues, Gehrig," he said.

She shook his hand, gave Jamaine a forced high five, then took her place a foot or so up the first-base line. The goose bumps were working overtime. Stop it, she whispered in her head. Stop that right now.

As Rybak introduced number nine, shortstop, Jesus Maldonado, Louise turned to Jamaine and commented on the noise. "I don't know if they love me or hate me."

"Gehrig, it's pretty simple actually. Get a hit, make a good play, they love you. Strike out, make an error, we'll all wanna string you up."

"And if I steal a base?"

"I'll steal two." He flashed her a shit-eating grin. "This ain't spring training no more."

Rybak continued:

"Number eighteen. Catcher, Bob Dixon.

"Number two. Right fielder, Jeff Carter.

"Number twenty-seven. Left fielder, Sandy Downs.

"Number nineteen. Second baseman, Elvis Jones.

"Number thirty-one. Third baseman, Darryl White.

"And warming up in the Meteorites bullpen, number sixteen. Starter, Reggie Borders."

Rybak then introduced the other pitchers, backup players, relievers, coaches, and trainers, and added, "And now, to sing our national anthem, Warner Brothers recording artist Michael Stipe."

And the onetime lead singer from R.E.M. stepped up to the mike and delivered a soft, soothing rendition of "The Star Spangled Banner," while every man, woman, and child at South Field took off their hats, if indeed he or she were wearing one, covered their hearts and sang along. Many cried. Many smiled. And all the goose bumps that had erupted when Louise was first introduced suddenly returned and soon found themselves marching up and down the first baseperson's arms and legs and back and neck and toes. Louise Gehrig was awash in tingles and tremors as Stipe sang, "Oh say, does that star spangled banner yet wave . . ."

⚾   ⚾   ⚾

"Throwing out the ceremonial first pitch," Rybak said, "National League president and home run king, Hank Aaron."

All eyes and cameras at South Field turned toward the front row of seats just to the home plate side of the Meteorites dugout. Aaron stood and waved to the many who clapped at the mere mention of his name. Instead of having Aaron toss the first pitch to the home team's catcher, as was the custom, Matt Stern felt that Louise would be the most worthy recipient of Hammering Hank's magic. So, taking a stand twenty-five or thirty feet from Aaron, she waited as cameras clicked, flashes flashed, and the clamor from the thirty-eight thousand plus seemed to reach another sort of frenzied crescendo.

Aaron nodded her way—a big, confident grin—and threw the ball. A little overhanded lob. Louise caught the pitch easily and ran over to Aaron. While she was handing him back the

souvenir ball and posing for the baseball photo-op of the de-
cade, the baseball legend grabbed the future legend's hand
and, squeezing it firmly, whispered, "Don't let the sons of
bitches get to you and you'll be all right."

She nodded and squeezed his hand back. "Thank you," she
said, not sure what else to say in the presence of such a man.

Wesley Selden just wanted the game over and done with, but it
was still a few minutes away from starting. Over two dozen arrests thus far, all drunken and disorderlies, except for the one
incident of mistaken binoculars. Still, there was such a commotion, such a crowd—it was an explosive situation to say the least.
Or as a fellow Fibbie said, "It don't get more explosive than
this."

"What's that?" Selden asked, distant, keeping his eye on the
group of anti-Gehrig protestors.

"It's so loud," the agent explained.

"No. No," Selden said, glaring at the agent. "What did you
just say? Exactly."

"I said, it don't get more explosive than this."

"Shit!" Selden said, as suddenly a warning light clicked on in
his head. "Son of a bitch." And he was off, before the agent
could even ask him what the hell he was getting at.

"Play ball!"

The top of the first inning was a breeze for number sixteen.
Reggie was in complete control. And after he struck out the
side on eleven pitches, the crowd at South Field gave the
pitcher a standing ovation as he walked back to the dugout.
Louise and the other seven on the field could only slap Reggie
on the back or butt with lines like "Great job" or "Good going."
He was making their job easy, he was making the Expos look
like the helpless bunch of minor leaguers they actually were.

In the bottom of the first inning, Jamaine Young hit the first
pitch over the head of the Expo shortstop for a single.

Then it was time—time for history and twenty-one-gun sa-
lutes. Time for electricity and courage. Time for Elvis sightings
and a Ben & Jerry's chocolate chip cookie dough ice-cream
shake. It was time for Louise to step out of the on-deck circle
and into the batter's box.

The Expo pitcher set, wound, and delivered. Jamaine took
off and had a clean steal of second, while Louise watched as the
ball smacked into the catcher's mitt.

"Strike one."

She likewise held off the next pitch, arguably just off the
plate. But the ump gave it to the pitcher. She swung at the third
pitch, fouling it into the left field stands. The first Balls souvenir. She caught a part of the next pitch, but not enough to warrant a hit. The ball looped into short center field and was easily
put away by the Expo second baseman.

Walking back to the dugout, angry with herself, Louise failed
to notice that at least half of those in attendance at South Field
were nonetheless standing and clapping.

"Don't worry about it," Lefty said as she passed, a quick pat
to her behind. Lefty would never get used to *that*, but with everyone else doing it, and him patting everyone else, he didn't
want his star first baseperson to feel left out. "Uh-huh. Yeah,
right," his wife would later comment. "Anything you say, dear."

But of all the thoughts that ran through Louise Gehrig's
mind as she took a seat on the bench, the most prevalent was
not that she had blown her first big league opportunity, not that
she had looked bad to the fans and the press, but that she had
not done her job. She had not moved the runner over to
third—as was the goal in this situation. And that pissed Louise
off. Royally.

⑩   ⑩   ⑩

It took Wesley Selden and his team of FBI agents until the third
inning to check and double-check the contents of every trash
container in and around South Field. Selden half expected to
find another binocular case of sorts—one containing something
ultimately more lethal than a handgun—a bomb, maybe, a det-
onator rigged to a few pounds of plastic explosives.

"What would we have done if we had found anything?" one agent asked as they made their way around the field box seats.

"Evacuate," Selden answered.

"Yeah, sure."

Selden nodded and looked about at the thousands. It would have been a deadly situation, to say the least. One the special agent was glad he didn't have to deal with. At least on this beautiful opening day.

"Welcome back," Kurt Rybak said to the NYTV SuperStation audience. "It's the top of the ninth and the score is still tied, zip-zip. Reggie Borders has been nothing short of stupendous, wouldn't you say, Junella?"

And Junella Wingi, Rybak's play-by-play sidekick, agreed. "He has to be. The Meteorites have obviously left their bats in Florida."

"True enough. Not a very auspicious start for Louise Gehrig's career."

"The night's still young, Kurt. Give her a chance."

As lackluster as the Meteorites' offense was, such was the brilliance of Reggie Borders's opening day performance. Going into the top of what should have been the last inning of play, the Expos had no hits, no walks. Three more outs and he'd have his perfect game. But it wouldn't count, not unless his teammates could score in the bottom of the ninth—it wouldn't count unless they won. And he, better than anyone else, knew that he was tiring, and could not keep up the strikeouts forever.

After getting the leadoff hitter to fly out to left field, an easy catch for Sandy Downs, Reggie got into trouble with the Expos' next batter. Foul ball after foul ball after foul ball, and a few pitches out of the strike zone later, the count was full and the batter seemed to have the definite edge. If Reggie walked him, there would go the perfect game, though the no-hitter would still be intact. If Reggie shot one down the middle, the batter could possibly take it deep, and there'd go everything.

But Reggie was not about to give in. He let loose with a change-up which the batter fouled off into the upper deck. Another change-up, another foul. A curve—the batter just got a piece of it, tipping it off into his own dugout. Another change-up, another foul. A curve, a foul. Reggie had had enough. He let go with a fastball, low and away.

Clack.

The batter connected, blasting a bouncing line drive toward the gap between first and second. Louise saw the bullet coming her way. She took one step to her right, then another, then lunged for the ball. It clapped into her glove. She rolled over, made it to her knees, then reached into her glove and underhanded the ball to Reggie, who was covering at first. On replays it was obvious that the ball made it into Reggie's glove a frame—or one-thirtieth of a second—before the runner's foot touched first base. And luckily for the Meteorites, luckily for Reggie Borders, the first base ump had excellent eyesight.

"Out!"

Reggie let out a long stream of air. He looked over at Louise, who smiled back. And, man, for the first time in his professional career, Reggie Borders wanted to give a teammate a kiss smack on the lips. Louise just wanted him to get his perfect game, and the team to win.

Reggie struck out the next Expo batter and walked silently off the field. He had pitched a perfect nine innings, facing the minimum of twenty-seven batters. It was up to his teammates to do the rest.

Going into the bottom of the ninth, the Meteorites had racked up a total of seven hits and five walks—a total of twelve players left on base. A dozen players unable to score. After flying out in the first, Louise struck out to end the third, hit a line drive directly at the third baseman to end the fifth, then popped out again in the seventh.

Now she was in the on-deck circle, waiting, hoping, for Jamaine Young to get on base, and for another chance to bring him home.

To save their ass, The Expo brought in the one man on their team who could actually throw hard strikes, left-handed closer John Holliday. With three pitches, he had Jamaine swinging to the wind and heading back to the dugout. "Fuck!" the Meteorite center fielder muttered along the way, just that one word over and over and over again.

It was Louise's turn. She shot one look back at her teammates, Reggie in particular—he stared straight ahead, looking at no one or anything—then stepped into the batter's box.

Holliday was a pitcher Louise could hit. The Expos' catcher knew that, as did Holliday. So he laid off the fastball and nibbled at the corners.

"Ball one!" the umpire yelled.

The still-capacity crowd went wild.

"Ball two!"

More cheers.

Louise swung at the next pitch, fouling it off into the stands.

"Strike."

Holliday let go again, low and away.

"Ball three."

Louder—chants of "Louise" echoing through the night.

She held off, but Holliday's next pitch was right down the middle.

"Strike two."

And the count was full.

Rising to their feet, the thirty-eight thousand plus clapped and stomped. Their theme song was "We Will Rock You," sung loud and off-key. But the sheer volume and enthusiasm made up for any musical wrongdoings.

Holliday set, wound up, and let fly.

Louise closed her eyes and drew a deep breath as the ball shot past and clapped into the catcher's glove.

"Ball four."

And she could breathe—slow, long breaths as she trotted over to first.

In the dugout, every player was standing on edge, half on the field, half off. Every player except Reggie Borders, who sat still, barely breathing, just existing, waiting for the moment of victory or defeat. Waiting, too nervous to sweat.

Holliday glared at Jesus Maldonado for a long moment, then wheeling around, he attempted to pick Louise off. But she dove back just in time, then stood, and brushing herself off, knew for certain that second was hers.

The ball had not even left Holliday's hand by the time Louise was on her way full force into second base. The steal was so clean, so indisputable, that the Expos' catcher never even threw the ball over. It was uncontested, and the volume in South Field shot up another couple dozen decibel points to sonic boom level.

Shaken by what was a rare stolen base when he was on the mound, Holliday turned and glared at Louise. Who smiled back, then winked. She mouthed the words, "Third base belongs to me, babe," setting the hairs on the back of Holliday's neck standing on end—part panic, part rage.

Holliday turned and let loose a fastball that was clocked at 101 miles per hour. But when he spun back toward second to face his real adversary, Louise was nowhere to be seen. Instead, the crowd was chanting, "Go! Go! Go!" his catcher was standing and shaking his head, Jesus Maldonado was doubled over laughing, and everyone in the Expos' dugout was pointing over at third, where Louise stood, brushing the dirt off her uniform, smiling the most beautiful smile he had ever seen.

But Louise wasn't interested in Holliday's confounded glare. She couldn't care less about the hysterics of thirty-eight thousand plus screaming out her name. No, at that point, moments from the end of her first professional game, she cared about only one other human being. And he was seated in their dugout. But instead of seeming lost and utterly helpless, Reggie Borders actually had a Mona Lisa grin peeking out one of the corners of his mouth. His eyes were glued to Louise—their breathing in sync, their heartbeats pulsing as one.

For the principals, all sounds suddenly ceased except for the ones that mattered.

Louise digging in, getting her footing, ready to make it home at whatever opportunity.

Jesus, hands sticking to his pine tar–covered bat handle, digging in. Always digging in.

The catcher, slapping a fist into his mitt, slapping the signs against his thigh.

Holliday, breathing, nodding, glancing back quickly over his shoulder at third, fingering the ball, digging in.

Louise studied his every movement—she read his breathing—the slight up-and-down heaving of his chest—and after he glanced back at her for the third time, she took off.

As soon as it registered on Holliday that Louise was attempting to steal home, he let loose with a sloppy fastball, high and outside. The catcher had to jump up to make the catch. Jesus immediately backed off from the plate and dropped to his knees, motioning to Louise to slide in low and outside. She followed her teammate's advice. And just as the catcher's mitt came down toward the plate, Louise's outstretched hand brushed the corner. The ump dropped to one knee and dramatically spread his arms out wide. Jesus threw his arms around Louise, and the entire Meteorites' dugout minus one emptied onto the field. The players, Jamaine included, carried away in the emotion of the moment, descended upon their first baseperson and lifted her to their shoulders. Louise tried to take in as much of what was happening as possible, considering her for-she's-a-jolly-good-fellow situation. She saw Holliday and the rest of his teammates being sucked up by the vacuum known as the visitors' dugout. She saw her mother in the stands, cheering, screaming, hugging the people who were seated to the sides and behind her. And she saw Reggie Borders, standing at the lip of the dugout, watching, smiling, tears streaming down his face.

| Buffalo | 000 | 000 | 000 | 0 | 0 | 0 |
| Manhattan | 000 | 000 | 001 | 1 | 7 | 0 |

As the thousands poured out of South Field onto the Lower East Side streets, Special Agent Wesley Selden felt a sudden wave of calm. The big game had come and gone without incident. He laughed just slightly to himself; only 161 more to go. He was walking west on East Houston Street, from Gate E, around the center field bleachers, back toward Gate A, walking and enjoying the warm April night, when something flapping in the light breeze caught his attention. It hung from the pole of a streetlamp. He moved over for a closer examination, and a sudden chill ran up and down his every limb. Then a sudden rage. It was a flier—an eight-and-one-half-by-eleven-inch sheet of white twenty-pound bond paper. And on the flier, a tomb-stone. A very familiar tombstone, with the all-too-familiar epi-taph, "Louise Gehrig. R.I.P."

Selden reached up and ripped the sheet down. He folded it carefully and looked a few hundred feet down the street toward the next street lamp pole.

"Fuck," he muttered out loud.

Sure enough, the rectangular sheet glowed slightly in the bright lights from the South Field parking lot. He ran toward it, ripping it in half as he ripped it off. Glaring down the block, an-other pole, another flier.

"Son of a bitch!" he yelled loud enough for anyone in his im-mediate vicinity to hear.

He stopped for a moment and looked around him. Six or seven poles lined his field of vision, and every one was pock-marked with a white rectangle, some with two or three. He turned toward the parking lot and looked at the thousands of cars. Windshield after windshield after windshield, there was a flier, maybe two, held graciously in place by the windshield wipers.

Selden radioed a few of his subordinates and told them to scour the area. "Retrieve every fucking one of these things," he ordered.

The rage subsided, replaced by frustration, and maybe a touch of humiliation. He walked back toward the almost empty stadium and wondered what game number two would bring. Then he wondered about game number one. Had the Meteor-ites won? And what part had Louise played? Hell, he had been so busy preserving and protecting, and weeding out the loons, that he never once looked at the scoreboard. And to think, he thought, I love baseball. He laughed. I've gotta find another line of work. Now that was a common thought, and after twenty-seven years with the bureau, a familiar one. An old drinking buddy of a notion that always made Wesley Selden feel warm and comfortable inside.

ⓝ   ⓝ   ⓝ

Click.

The TV went dead. Kevin Thomas Willard lowered the remote control and sighed. He sat in the dark, dreary silence of
his living room for a few moments before standing and wad-
dling off to bed. He was tired, very tired. And very, very sad.

"Are you okay?" his wife, Geraldine, asked.

He nodded just barely a couple of times, then sat on the
edge of the bed, lay back, and slipped under the covers.

Geraldine put aside the current issue of *Redbook* magazine,
reached over, and gently touched her husband's shoulder.

He pulled away, shrinking to the very edge of the bed.
Geraldine knew that sign all too well. It had been commonplace
for the past month and a half. And it all had to do with that
Gehrig, the baseball girl. She found herself hating the Meteorites' first baseperson, not because of anything to do with baseball, but because of the effect Louise Gehrig had had on her
husband, on her marriage. She just wanted Kevin back. Back to
his old sloppy, farting, cursing self. His corny jokes and blind bi-
ases. His wham-bang, thank-you-ma'am quickies. His beer
belches and sport binges. Now there was no other sport—not
even his blessed Atlanta Braves could make him smile. No, it
seemed as if Kevin had forgotten how to smile. He could only
shiver and shake and cry. He was the man she loved, the man
whose children she had borne, and he seemed extinct. For this,
Geraldine Willard despised Louise Gehrig. She hated her to the
very essence of her soul.

⚾   ⚾   ⚾

It was approaching 3:00 A.M. when the cab carrying Louise and
her mom pulled up in front of the Charles Street high-rise.
Exiting first, Margaret noticed that the variety store across the
street was open around the clock. As Louise paid the driver,
Margaret took off in its direction.

"Where are you going?" Louise asked.

"I want to see if the early editions arrived yet."

"Mom, it's late."

"It's early."

Louise entered the lobby of her building. The doorman, a

tall Jamaican American with the heaviest of accents, greeted her. "Hello, there, Miss Gehrig."

"Hey, Ziggy," she said.

"You played good tonight. I know. I saw it on TV."

"Thank you."

Margaret entered the lobby. She immediately held the back page of the *Daily News* up, face high, for her daughter to see. Over a photo of her riding on the shoulders of her teammates ran a banner headline which read: Gehrig the Great. Lowering the paper, Margaret beamed, "They love you."

Louise shook her head, and the two women headed toward the elevators.

"Good night, Miss Gehrig," Ziggy said.

"Night."

In the elevator, Louise grabbed the newspaper from her mom and perused the back page. "Assholes!" she said.

"What's that?"

"Reggie Borders pitches a perfect game and he doesn't even get a mention until the third paragraph."

"Reggie doesn't sell newspapers."

"That's bullshit."

"It's business. Reggie is a great pitcher, but otherwise he's a bore. You ever see a quote attributed to Reggie Borders?" Margaret took Louise's silence as an answer. "Didn't think so."

"It was a perfect game," Louise said; then she added in a whisper, "His dream."

"And playing the pro ball was your dream," Margaret said. "And yours was the more improbable."

"Umm."

Exiting the elevator and entering her apartment, Louise threw the newspaper onto the coffee table and flopped herself down on the living room sofa in the same jumbled movement.

"Other than being annoyed with the editors of the *Daily News*," Margaret asked, taking a seat beside Louise, "how are you feeling?"

"Tired. Totally. As if I lived and died a thousand lifetimes during that ninth inning."

Opening up the newspaper and spreading it out on the coffee table, Margaret flipped through the back pages as if looking for something in particular. She suddenly cracked a smile and gazed over at her ballplaying daughter. "Guess what?"

"What?"

"The Meteorites are in sole possession of first place."

Louise sat up and tried to focus on the standings. Sure enough, the Mets, Cubs, and Phillies had all lost their opening day games to teams in the Western Division, while the Marlins, Cardinals, and Pirates wouldn't be commencing their seasons until later that day.

"Well, what do you know?"

"Think you can hold on?" Margaret asked.

Louise smiled. "Would *you* go and bet against us when we're on a roll?"

✪ 10 ✪

Through Wind, Rain, Sleet, or Snow

After the opening day telephone pole and car windshield fiasco—every newspaper in the country ran a front-page copy of the R.I.P. tombstone flier—Wesley Selden doubled the number of agents assigned to the case. He set up a makeshift office in the bowels of South Field and prepared himself for a long haul.

The letters continued to pour in but at a lesser volume. And though they were fewer in number, they were meaner in spirit, full of ugly, hateful sentiments that at times made Selden despise the entire human race. "What are we," he asked his associates, "if capable of this?"

Tombstone continued sending his missives. Seven a week, as usual, with two arriving in Monday's mail. And though there was no letter the day after opening day—"Finally!" Selden exclaimed—two arrived that Wednesday, making him shiver with disgust. But there was a difference—not in the tombstone and epitaph, which remained the same, but in the postmark. That was new, and to Selden, confusing. A New York City postmark he could understand. This was, after all, the city's new ball club—tempers would be expected to flare. But Atlanta, Georgia? Why would anyone down in Atlanta care if the Manhattan Meteorites had a woman at first base? Didn't the city have enough of its own sports-related problems to worry about? What with a perpetually last-place football team? What with a perpetually last-place basketball team? What with the state still reeling from the 1996 summer Olympic Games debacle? Maybe it was because baseball was the only area in which the peach state excelled, Selden reasoned. Or maybe it was because baseball didn't adhere to borders and boundaries. It was a national language. And to some fanatics in Georgia, the people up north were fucking it up.

⑪   ⑪   ⑪

Because of the sudden and immediate media attention given to these threats against Louise, Matt Stern, not about to risk losing his wisest investment, decided it was time she be completely apprised of the situation.

A meeting between Louise and Selden was set up in the latter's office the morning before the third game of the season—a Wednesday afternoon outing against the Expos. Like every meeting he had ever attended since taking the FBI pledge of honor upon graduation from the bureau's academy, Selden taped his conversation with Louise.

He played the tape numerous times since, and was always confounded by her calm, as he had been that day, seated across the desk from the first basewoman. Staring into her lovely blue eyes—she really does have beautiful blue eyes, he remembered thinking at the time—admiring her courage, her talent, her ambition, her guts.

Louise: And how many of these fliers have you received?

Selden: Forty-two, as of opening day. Not counting the ones stapled to telephone poles around the stadium, and placed on car windshields in the parking lot.

Louise: Forty-two?

Selden: One a day, every day, since the Supreme Court–sanctioned game against the Braves.

Louise: You'd think people would have better things to do with their time.

Selden: So, you can understand why we're concerned.

Louise: It's your job to be concerned. It's my job to play ball.

Selden: Doesn't this frighten you?

Louise: Should it? What's the chance that this man—

Selden: We've yet to determine Tombstone's sex.

Louise: Tombstone?

Selden: Our nickname.

Louise: Cute.

Selden: It's not intended to be cute, just short and practical.

Louise: Of course.

Selden: But you were saying.

Louise: Right. What are the chances that this person will really do anything? Aren't I, in all honesty, in greater peril when I cross the street, or drive to the ballpark?

Selden: In this city, yes. But you're right. In most cases, suspects like Tombstone never do anything other than send harassing letters. Eventually that gets boring and they're off to some other obsession.

Louise: So, most likely I'll be okay.

Selden: I'm here to make sure you'll be okay. We just want to keep you apprised of the situation. Especially after the . . .

Louise: The letter made the papers.

Selden: Exactly.

Louise: So, I'm apprised.

Selden: Yes, you are.

Louise: Is there anything I can do to help?

Selden: Cooperate, and keep your eyes open.

Louise: You never know when the guy sitting next to you is a certifiable loon?

Selden: That's a good rule to live by.

Louise: I do have one question.

Selden: Shoot.

Louise: Why Tombstone? I mean, hasn't there been a lot of other hate mail?

Selden: Tons.

Louise: So, what was it about these letters in particular?

Selden: Ms. Gehrig.

Louise: Please. Call me Louise.

Selden: Fine. Louise. After twenty-seven years in this line of work, you develop a kind of sixth sense. Either that, or you get killed on the job. And there's something about those letters that put me on edge. I don't know what it is exactly, but they give me this queasy feeling in the pit of my stomach. That's all I can really tell you. It's a hunch, not a fact.

Louise: After twenty-seven years, that's good enough for me.

Selden: Thank you for coming in.

Louise: No problem. If you need anything, you know where to find me.

Selden: At first base.

Louise: Right. It was nice meeting you.

Selden: The pleasure's all mine, believe me.

Clichés, Lineups, & Paperbacks

It was Memorial Day weekend by the time the Manhattan Meteorites had their first meeting with their crossborough rivals, the New York Mets. Louise's team was four games over the .500 mark with twenty-six wins and twenty-two losses. They were tied for second place with the Florida Marlins, a game and a half back from the first-place Mets. The four-game road series with the Mets, followed by another four-game road series with the Marlins, would give professional and amateur baseball analysts the planet over some idea as to what the team was really made of. Would Matt Stern's cookie hold up or ultimately crumble away like dream teams of so many seasons past?

On the national level, Meteorites announcers Rybak and Wingi were responsible for baseball's newest, and ultimately the season's hottest, cliché—a take on the old Tinker to Evers to Chance—when, during the third game of that opening series against Buffalo (Warner Brothers Music Sampler Day), with an Expo on first, the next batter hit a ball directly at shortstop Jesus Maldonado, who tossed it to Elvis Jones at second, who in turn rifled it to Louise at first. "The first double play of the year," Rybak said at the time, adding, "Maldonado to Jones to Gehrig."

"If you don't mind me saying so," Wingi interrupted, "Jesus to Elvis to Louise sounds a hell of a lot snappier."

"Jesus to Elvis to Louise," Rybak repeated with a slight laugh.. "I like it."

And so did every baseball fan in America. The phrase caught on quickly, and just as quickly banners began to appear at every Meteorites game, home or away.

Then there was the merchandising—as if Matt Stern wasn't making enough money. There were Jesus to Elvis to Louise T-shirts and Jesus to Elvis to Louise bumper stickers. There were caps and buttons and coffee mugs. There were banners and a full-color poster. There was a song—a top-ten hit by the super-star rap group Salt 'N' Pepa—and the accompanying MTV video. There were cigarette lighters, ceramic banks, and of course, a Jesus to Elvis to Louise refrigerator magnet.

On the lineup level, Lefty had made a few appropriate changes to the bottom half of the order. The top half—well, they played like a manager's dream.

Going into the Memorial Day weekend Mets series, the Meteorites' starting lineup looked like this:

> 1—Young—#11
> 2—Gehrig—#4
> 3—Maldonado—#9
> 4—Dixon—#18
> 5—White—#31
> 6—Carter—#2
> 7—Downs—#27
> 8—Jones—#19
> 9—pitcher

On the commercial endorsement level, it was a Friday morning, the beginning of the Memorial Day weekend, when Louise received the script for her intended Coke commercial—the Atlanta, Georgia–based soda giant had won in the Coke-Pepsi bidding war with a three-year, $36 million contract offer. The script called for Louise to be lounging poolside, surrounded by hunks in pin-striped swim trunks. The script maintained that she'd be wearing a Meteorite yellow-and-black bikini, her baseball cap, and sunglasses, and that between sips from a bottle of Coke, she'd be flirting with the hunks. Her one big line: "A girl's gotta know how to relax."

It took Louise less than thirty seconds to make telephone contact with the company's advertising representative.

"What is this shit?" she demanded.

"Louise?"

"Yeah, this is Louise."

"Is there a problem?"

"You bet your ass there's a problem."

"With the script?"

"Uh-huh. You've got me lying around in a bikini like some beer commercial bimbo."

"Yeah," the representative said, stretching out the word into three or four syllables.

"Would you have Shaquille O'Neal lying around a pool in his jockstrap? I don't think so. You'd show him on the basketball court. In uniform."

"So, what are you saying?"

"I'm an athlete, God damn it."

"But you're not Shaq."

"And I'm not Niki Taylor either."

"People like seeing women in bikinis. Sex sells, remember?"

"It doesn't sell me."

"We thought it'd be, ah . . ."

"It's not me."

"Louise. Think of it as a different take on your image. Baseballs and bikinis. Cute, huh?"

"Fucking adorable."

"Would you prefer to be wearing a one-piece?"

"I'd prefer to be wearing my uniform. You didn't hire me for my boobs, remember?"

"Yes, well. Sure."

"Change it."

"I don't know if that's possible. It's been approved. . . ."

"I don't give a rat's ass if it was approved by God. Change it, or I'll be hawking Pepsi faster than you can say, 'New Coke.' "

"Ah . . . Pepsi? You wouldn't do that."

"Oh no? Watch me."

Louise slammed the receiver down hard, and counted slowly to ten. By the time she reached seven, the phone began to ring. It was the Coke representative calling to apologize for the mix-up. Somehow the wrong ad copy had been sent. A mistake. "Please accept our apologies."

And later that day, Louise received the "correct" commercial script. One which had her working up a good sweat on the ball field—the hitting, stealing, catching routine—then cooling off with an ice cold Coke.

"Ahh . . . !"

⑪　　⑪　　⑪

And on the personal level, going into the Mets series, the star first baseperson was, well, if nothing else, bruised. Life on the road was tougher than she could have ever imagined. Three days in Philly, a travel day, three days in Pittsburgh, no travel day, three days in Chicago. And by the time she got to L.A., San Diego, Denver, and Arkansas, she was reduced to seeing nothing but airplanes, hotel rooms, ballparks, and the insides of paperbacks. She read a lot in her first two months of pro ball—more than even she'd like to admit—and, heaven forbid, even succeeded in turning a few of her teammates on to the written word.

It began during a never-ending rain delay in Pittsburgh. Louise pulled herself into a corner of the visiting players' lounge, pulled out an old paperback edition of *Even Cowgirls Get the Blues,* and dug in. She hadn't made it through a paragraph before Jesus Maldonado took a seat next to her and said, "So, Gehrig, you're reading westerns now?"

She turned to book around as if to remind herself of its title, then smiled. "Not exactly," she said.

"You read a lot."

"Maybe you should try it sometime."

"Nah. I read all those books in high school. They weren't for me."

"See, that's the problem," Louise said, placing a bookmark in and closing the novel. "In school they don't teach you how to enjoy reading. They assign you these books that you're *supposed* to read. But the thing is, for most people, these quote-unquote classics are a little too heavy. If the teachers took time to find out what each student cared about, then assigned an appropriate book"—she shrugged—"well, then reading wouldn't seem like such a chore."

"So, um . . . what you're saying is?"

"What I'm saying is that you don't like reading because you've never read anything that you'd like."

Jesus just sort of looked at her for a moment, then mumbled, "Huh?" Then he listened carefully as she tried to explain.

Two days later, just prior to a Friday evening game at Wrigley Stadium, Louise approached the shortstop and handed him a bag stamped with the familiar Waldenbooks logo.

"A little present for you," she said.

He eyed the package cautiously, and just as cautiously opened it, pulled the paperback edition of *Delta of Venus* from the wrapping, and turned it over gingerly a few times in his hands. "Thanks," he said. "I guess."

"Give it a chance."

"Ann-aise," he said, attempting to pronounce the author's first name.

"An-a-ese," Louise corrected him. "Anaïs Nin." She reached out and touched Jesus' hands. He looked up and into her eyes. "Trust me, Jesus. Once you start this book, you won't want to put it down."

Jesus gulped hard. Such pretty eyes, he thought, nodding in agreement, or at least understanding; and he placed the book in his gym bag, where it remained, forgotten, until after the game—a game the Meteorites lost 18–3. A laugher, their first. Then later that night, alone and bummed about the error and

two strikeouts that helped lead his team to the embarrassing defeat, he remembered Louise, and thinking of his first
baseperson, he remembered her present. What the hell, Jesus
figured, TV sucked, so he might as well give it a shot. He
reached into his gym bag and plucked out the paperback.
Then, making himself comfortable, mimicking the way he had
seen Louise sit and read so very many times, he opened to page
one, a short story titled "The Hungarian Adventurer," eyed the
first few words, then forged ahead.

The next day during batting practice, Louise asked Jesus if
he had yet to begin the book. She expected polite excuses, or
maybe an abrupt subject change.

"Begin it?" Jesus said, his eyes suddenly flushed with excitement. "I couldn't put it down." He shook his head. "Man, you
didn't tell me it was like that."

"Like what?"

"You know." He lowered his voice. "All kinky and shit."

"I told you you'd like it."

"That scene with the pocketknife. It made my heart race."
He nodded excitedly. "This Anais chick, she sure knows how to
write. Wait'll I show this book to P.J. He's gonna flip."

⑪   ⑪   ⑪

P.J. *was* next—a volunteer of sorts.

"Hey, Balls. What's all this about Jesus reading?" he asked
Louise during the bottom of the second inning of the first
game of their four-game home stand against the Marlins. "Next
thing you know he's gonna apply for a library card. What
gives?"

"He found something he likes to read."

"So I've heard." They both turned their attention back to the
game for a glimpse of Jeff Carter striking out.

"Damn," Louise muttered.

"He'll break out of it," P.J. said.

She nodded.

"Have any suggestions for me?"

She turned to face P.J. "Suggestions?"

"As in, have you read any good books lately?"

Louise couldn't help but laugh. "Well, yes. As a matter of fact, I have." She looked away, then turned back quickly. The team's closer stared at her expectantly. "You're serious?"

"Totally."

"Okay. What sort of books do you usually like?"

"Usually? Balls. Look. I haven't picked up a book since my junior year in high school. And that was *The Scarlet Letter,* which I read only because I was under the impression that if it was about an adulteress, there had to be some pretty hot sex scenes."

"Were you disappointed?"

"Like I said, haven't picked up a book since."

She nodded. "What are you looking for?"

"Answers. Reasons. The secrets of the universe. And I want to laugh."

"Hmmm."

"Any titles come to mind?"

Louise nodded confidently. "A few."

⚾   ⚾   ⚾

By the next road trip—eight games in four cities in eight days— Bob Dixon had joined Louise's little reading club. His immediate preference: legal thrillers à la John Grisham, Scott Turow, Steve Martini, Paul Levine, et alia.

And heading into the Mets Memorial Day weekend, Lefty Johnston (mysteries), Reggie Borders (cyberpunk and sci-fi), and number-two starter David Gaston (high-tech political thrillers) were likewise aboard.

Louise was doing damn well in the English lit department. She was doing well hitting, great stealing bases. The endorsement contracts kept coming in. Her magnet collection was growing by veritable leaps and bounds. If only she weren't so damn lonely. If only her mother and her catcher weren't suddenly head over heels in love.

⚾ 12 ⚾

Private Conversations

The love story known as Margaret Marie Gehrig and Robert Leonard Dixon began shortly after the Meteorites' first nine-game road trip. After the first fascinating opening day chat accented with so many cautious smiles and that serious eye contact, Bob's head was left swirling from his first baseperson's mom. It was all he could do to concentrate, and yet he was having a career year—a few years after he should have called it a career. It seemed all he had to do was step into the batter's box and swing away. Going, going, gone. *Good-bye!* And he'd shake the vision of Margaret's smile out of his head just for a minute to watch the ball careen off the scoreboard or fly over the left field bleachers, and he'd begin the old catcher's version of the home run trot. To Bob, there were four speeds for running the base paths after you belted one out of the park: fast, slow, hot dog, and old catcher. His was the slowest by far, but not on purpose.

Back in New York after that Philly-Pittsburgh-Chicago swing, Bob finally got up the nerve to approach Louise and ask her opinion. "Got a minute?" he began.

"Sure, Bob. What's up?"

"I've, ah, been meaning to ask you about, well, your, ah, mother."

"What about her?" Louise asked.

"Well," Bob continued, "I was sort of wondering . . ."

"Spit it out, Bob."

He took a deep breath. Asking a friend if it was okay to date her mom was harder than he thought. Even at the age of thirty-six.

"She seeing anyone?"

"No," Louise said cautiously. "Why?"

Her tone threw the catcher for a loop. He suddenly felt like a teenager asking for permission to grow up. "Would you mind very much if I gave her a call?"

She stared in lieu of a response.

"Y'know. To ask her out."

It took a moment or two, but Louise finally managed to shrug out an answer. And even though her mind was running in overdrive (Of course I'd mind. You think I want to overhear locker-room talk about my own mom?), she knew Bob was different, or at least she hoped he was different. He seemed different anyway. "Why would I mind?" she said, finally.

"Well, it is your mother."

"Yes. But she's an adult," Louise said, thinking, Some of the time.

"Great," Bob said. "Thanks."

"No problem."

And that night, Louise called Margaret at her home in New Haven. On the first attempt the line was busy. On the second—busy. The third—busy. It took Louise eight tries before hitting pay dirt.

"Hi, Mom," she said.

"Louise. You'll never guess who just called."

"Bob Dixon."

"Well, yes. How did you . . .?"

"Are you going out with him?"

"Well, I did have a wonderful time talking with him that—"

"When?"

"Louise Kathleen Gehrig, are you going to let me finish a—"

"I'm sorry."

Margaret cleared her throat. "We're going to dinner on Saturday night, after the Pirates game."

"Oh."

"Now all you have to say is, "Oh."

"That's it. Oh. Short and to the point, Mom. *Oh* just kind of says it all."

  ⑪   ⑪   ⑪

By the Memorial Day weekend series with the Mets, Margaret and Bob were in deep. Everyone knew it—the press was having a field day: Dixon Gehrig Affair, Not Louise, Her Mom!—and the participants couldn't care less. They were happy. They were carefree. "Take our picture! Why should we care? We're in love!"

Louise wondered how it felt. Over the past ten years she had allowed herself to fall into lust on a few too many occasions—a few too many to remember. But love. It sounded nice, but what the hell was it? (Where the hell was it?) (Why the hell was it?) Right now she'd have settled for a good clean fuck. No, make that a good clean Key West fuck, complete with daiquiris. It had been many a month—a year and a half to be precise—and after being constantly surrounded by two dozen gorgeous men, after being constantly reminded by all those love scenes in all those books, her privates were furious with her for the lack of attention.

We don't have time, she'd try to explain.

What about masturbation? the privates demanded.

But Louise didn't have an answer. Usually, by the time she made it to bed, she was just too damn tired.

Sorry, she'd say.

But to little avail. Vaginas, like their male counterparts, had a mind of their own. And, time or no time, excuses or none, this first baseperson's most private of parts was going on strike.

Fine, Louise said, not about to argue with her pussy. If it wanted to wage a war of silence—so be it.

  ⑪   ⑪   ⑪

The four games with the Mets proved little in regard to which of these two teams might eventually be crowned the division champs come Sunday, October 1. While the games were exciting, gut-wrenching, standing-room-only local-rival matchups, they showed both teams to be rather evenly matched. The Meteorites won the first by a score of 5–3, the Mets captured the next two—3–2 in eleven innings and 7–4—and the Meteorites managed to win the last on a brilliant pitching performance by Reggie Borders, 6–0. Both teams had power and speed. Both had pitching, defense, and a solid starting lineup. Either could take the National League East, and only the prevailing winds of luck and season-ending injuries could know for sure how each team would stand in a little over four months.

Writing in his *Newsday* column, Mike Lupica summed up the series best: "For thirty-five years New York's baseball fans have yearned for a local rivalry to equal those from the days when the Dodgers, the Giants, and the Yankees all called New York City home. They dreamed of a subway series between the Yanks and the new kids in town, the Mets. Volumes were written on the likelihood—who would possibly prevail? When, why, and how? It was a citywide obsession that led nowhere. The closest the two teams probably came was in '85, when both finished second in their respective divisions, just a few games out of first, and again the next year, when the Yanks repeated second place and the Mets, of course, went on to win it all. But in the years that followed, talk of a subway series vanished. Hell, fans of either team would have been happy with more of those second-place finishes—second place was surely better than the basement. Then, last year, the inevitable. Mr. Steinbrenner moved the Bronx Bombers to New Jersey and the usually hapless Mets were alone, abandoned in the big city.

"But all of that was forgotten this past weekend—L.A. could have their Dodgers, the Giants were history, and even Steinbrenner was granted a reprieve. The Mets had a rival—a real crossborough rival named the Manhattan Meteorites. A crossborough divisional rival with a woman at first base. And New Yorkers had a subway series—not a World Series. But a four-game series of nail-biting baseball that probably had the late A. Bartlett Giamatti smiling up from beyond the grave. Both teams played long. Both teams played hard. They sweated. They bled. They stole bases and they hit home runs. And in the end they each won two.

"They'll meet again come mid-July. This time on the Meteorites' home turf and for three games—one or the other will have to come out ahead. One or the other will prevail. And I don't know about you, but my odds are even and I can't wait. Because as far as New York, as far as professional sports, as far as life in general—it just doesn't get any better than this."

Kevin Thomas Willard watched the four-game series on the thirteen-inch black-and-white TV set in his room in one of Atlanta's many transient hotels, all the while thanking the good God above for the advent of cable TV. He had left his wife and four daughters a month earlier, in the end of April, after a series of blowouts that left him on the verge of suicide. As usual, he videotaped the games—having purchased a used Goldstar-brand VCR for twenty dollars from a pawnshop located off the hotel's lobby—then watched them over and over ad nauseam. He watched and studied Louise's every move, her every nuance. When she blinked. When she laughed. When she seemed distracted and would stare off into baseball space. When she turned. What angles she faced. Her usual seat in the dugout.

He had it all down—every detail, every trait—etched onto the lining of his brain with a nail of distress.

◐ 13 ◑

Slumpin'

"And here come the Meteorites," Kurt Rybak announced. "Down to their last three outs in this dreadful two-game series against the Atlanta Braves. Baseball just doesn't get any uglier than this."

"And it's a shame," Junella Wingi said, "because fans of the game were really looking forward to this showdown between Louise Gehrig and Rocky Goetz."

"Gehrig versus Goetz—the rematch. It's all the sports pages have been screaming about. Well, that and the fact that Dixon and Louise's mom are an item."

"I think you're confusing the sports page with the gossip columns."

"There's a difference?"

"Most of the time, no."

"And their relationship is a lot more interesting to read about than that Tombstone nut."

"I'll have to agree with you there. Those fliers give me the creeps."

"How do you think they make Louise feel?"

"I know I couldn't handle it."

"She's a tough woman."

"Absolutely, which brings us back to the subject at hand."

"Gehrig versus Goetz."

"And if you consider Louise the clear-cut winner of the first matchup back in February."

"When the game didn't count."

"It counted for Louise."

"True enough."

"Then, Rocky would have to walk away with the belt this time around."

"Absolutely. And with the score eleven zip here in the top of the ninth at Atlanta's Fulton County Stadium," Rybak explained, "Meteorites reserve outfielder Dean Matz steps up to the plate."

"He'll be batting for relief pitcher Pete Coleman, who gave up that grand slam in the eight."

"He couldn't get anyone out."

"Just up from Triple-A and his ERA is infinity."

"Welcome to the show, Pete."

"Matz is batting .291 with three homers on the year."

"A home run would definitely be wasted here."

"Not much short of an all-out rally would help at this point."

"Rocky sets, he delivers, and, oh, boy, Matz makes it easy."

"Pop fly to short. One out."

"These Meteorites' bats have really cooled since the Mets series."

"And how," Wingi said. "And with one hundred games left in the season, the team finds itself five games out of first behind the Mets."

"But as we all know, a lot can happen in a hundred games. Standings can change."

"Standings can change in ten."

"True enough."

"Speaking of standings, over in Chicago they've just started the eighth inning, and the Reds are down seven zip to the Cubbies."

"That loss'll put the Braves eight games up on the second-place Reds, twelve and a half games up on the Rockies."

"With thirty-nine wins versus twenty-four losses, they're certainly playing like world champs."

"To be fifteen games over the .500 mark on June eleventh. Incredible."

"Young steps up to the plate."

"In case you weren't watching, he was ejected in yesterday's game for arguing a called third strike."

"It's frustrating. His error in the fifth inning of yesterday's game gave Atlanta the go-ahead run."

"Looks like Sacker is calling for Rocky's curve. The pitcher sets. Delivers."

"Jamaine swings right through it."

"Rocky's savoring this one."

"Can't you get fined for smiling like that?" Wingi asked.

"Could be," Rybak said. "Could be."

"Another curve. Whoa! Strike two."

"Jamaine needs to learn that patience is a virtue."

"Especially in these sorts of situations."

"Sacker's calling for another curve."

"That'll be three in a row."

"There's the windup."

"Strike three."

"Jamaine looks mad."

"If I were Lefty Johnston, I'd send him to the showers right now. He needs to cool off."

"And the crowd in Fulton County Stadium rises to its feet and begins the familiar chant."

"Gehrig. Gehrig. Gehrig."

"But unlike the fans in South Field, these people aren't cheering her on," Rybak said, adding, "no, sir."

"I'm surprised Lefty's sending her out."

"She's playing in the majors now. She's got to get used to it."

"Balls is suffering through the first slump of her young career," Wingi explained. "With only three hits in her last thirty-two times at bat, her average has dropped below .270."

"But she still leads all of baseball in stolen bases."

"By one, over Jamaine Young."

"I wonder with the incentive clause in his contract, if that leads to any clubhouse tensions."

Wingi laughed. "I'm sure there are other more obvious tensions in that clubhouse."

"Yes, well," Rybak said, clearing his throat.

Another laugh. "Louise steps into the batter's box."

"There's that smile plastered to Rocky's face again."

"I'm sure there's something in the rule book about gloating. It's one of those borderline calls."

"Like balks?"

"Something like that."

"Pete Sacker is calling for a curve, low and away, but Rocky is shaking him off."

"He wants to go after her with his fastball."

"Sacker gives in—a heater right down the middle."

"Rocky's feeling confident. And with the way he's pitched today, I can't say that I blame him.""

"True enough."

"Balls digs in, then steps out, and the ump calls time. Rocky's smile is suddenly replaced by what appears to be a string of obscenities."

"Pitchers hate that."

"Now Louise is the one who's smiling."

"She steps back in. Y'know, if she gets an out, it'll be the first time in her professional career that she's made the last out in a game."

"It's gotta happen sooner or later."

"Rocky sets, winds up, and delivers. Just outside. Ball one."

"Even during a slump, Louise Gehrig can shake any pitcher's confidence," Wingi said.

"Sacker again calls for an outside curve. Rocky shakes him off. It's gonna be another heater."

"Even though he's not about to lose the game, I think Rocky Goetz is playing with fire. If Louise gets a hit in this spot, she suddenly looks like the hero, despite Rocky's fine pitching performance."

"He's got it out for her," Rybak agreed. "No question about that. But right now, he's on a tear. I'll give him the edge."

"Rocky sets, winds up, and . . ."

"Mother of God. That pitch must have busted the radar gun. Strike one."

"Louise seems startled.

"Sacker once again calls for an outside curve, but Rocky isn't

having any part of it. He gets the call he wants, sets, winds up
. . . and Louise connects. A fly to right field. Deep but playable.
Brown has it for out number three. The game and this series
are thankfully over."

"That's five losses in a row for the Meteorites."

"The team has definitely lost some of its momentum. They
look tired."

"I couldn't agree with you more, Kurt. And I think I can
speak for every player on the team when I say, the All-Star break
can't get here fast enough."

◍ 14 ◍

The Family That Jeers Together ...

Security for the two games in Atlanta was the tightest it had been for any since opening day. Wesley Selden had seen to that. He and a group of five handpicked agents converged on the stadium the morning of the first game and gave it a most thorough going-over. Another handpicked agent guarded Louise around the clock, escorting her to and from the stadium, standing guard outside her hotel room at night.

"Is this really necessary?" Louise had asked Selden.

"I think so," was his reply.

The Tombstone letters had continued unabated, with the Atlanta postmark remaining constant. So the local authorities had been warned: *There might be trouble!*

And though countless locals were arrested for drunk and disorderly conduct, and though the Tombstone letters arrived up in New York at the South Field mail room almost like clockwork, no Tombstone fliers were plastered around and about the stadium grounds. None were pinned under car windshield wipers. Not one. In fact, the entire two days went off without any real bothersome incidents. Even Selden's blood pressure low-ered itself to something approaching what would be considered normal on any average human being of the agent's age, height, and weight.

It was almost too easy.

Kevin Thomas Willard and his wife, Geraldine, attended both of the games—though one was seated nowhere near the other, and neither had the slightest inkling that his or her estranged spouse was present.

For both of the games, Kevin sat alone in the far reaches of the upper deck. He had purchased both tickets at the Fulton County Stadium box office for a grand total of seventeen dollars.

Geraldine sat with her four daughters, Debbie, Kelly, Lisa, and Cheryl, in a field-level box normally occupied by bigwigs—advertising representatives, perhaps?—from the Coca-Cola Cor-poration. Or at least that's what the plaque on the railing near the seats led her to believe. She had purchased the tickets from a man in the Fulton County Stadium parking lot for an exorbi-tant price. She didn't care about the cost. She wanted to get up close and personal with the young woman who had taken her husband away.

Kevin sat silently through the first game—a Saturday after-noon outing. No smiles. No cheers. In fact, during the seventh-inning stretch, a five-year-old sitting directly behind Kevin asked his father, "Is that man dead?"

"I don't think so," was the father's reply.

"Then what's his problem?" the five-year-old persisted.

"Maybe he's just sad."

During Sunday's early evening matchup, Kevin actually man-aged a sigh, and once nodded his head with what might have reasonably passed as enthusiasm when Rocky Goetz struck out a side that included Louise.

But sighs and nods seemed to be all Kevin Willard had left in him. It was as if all life were gone—evaporated, run out. He was flat, indifferent. Dead, just as that kid had thought. He just didn't have it in him anymore.

As for Geraldine and her daughters—daughters whose loyalty to their mom overrode any pride they might have secretly felt for Louise's accomplishments—they screamed and cheered through both games whenever the Braves gave even the slightest effort. And when the Meteorites got up to bat, they *booed* their hearts out. Especially for Louise Gehrig. They'd chant— "Gehrig go home! Gehrig go home! Gehrig go home!—and yell obscenity-laced clichés that women had no place on the ball field, that women belonged in the kitchen or the bedroom. Even the men seated around them—large drunken macho sport types—were baffled, embarrassed, and even a little offended by their deafening display.

"Fuck off!" Geraldine would yell when anyone told her to please keep it down or think of her children.

She was not about to be denied her God-given right to protest the fact that a woman was playing first base on a major league baseball team and that, because of that fact, God damn it, her life had come apart at the non-leather stitched seams.

Overnight with Howie

"And here's our buddy, Joey from Bensonhurst. You with me, Joey?"

"Sure am, Howie."

"Let me guess. You're calling with a big, fat I told you so!"

"The biggest."

"And why is that?"

"'Cause she's choking."

"Every ballplayer has bad days. Ever hear of a slump?"

"But this is a permanent one."

"And you're willing to bet the rent money on it?"

"Howie, I'm so sure that come, say, late July, Louise Gehrig is gonna be picking a lot of splinters out of that cute little butt of hers, that I'd bet my life on it."

"And I'm sure you'd find takers for that bet."

"So they wouldn't have to listen to my calls anymore."

"Actually, Joey, we all find your calls rather entertaining."

"Thanks."

"So, what's your prediction for the All-Star Game?"

"Gehrig strikes out. She's gone by the second inning."

"Doesn't it bother you that she's received more votes than any player in the history of All-Star voting?"

"Even I voted for her."

"You what?"

"Gotta see her fail, Howie. Gotta see her fail. It's what us baseball fanatics are living for."

"It's what you're living for maybe."

"No, really. You mark my words. Robinson—"

"Cole Robinson, the American League starting pitcher."

"Right. It'll be strike one. Strike two. Strike three. You're out. Good-bye Louise Gehrig. See ya later. Time to sit down."

"We'll just have to wait and see."

"Whoosh."

"Whoosh?"

"Whoosh. The sound of Robinson's fastball."

"I see. Well, I hate to cut this short, but we've got to take a break."

"Okay. Talk to you after the All-Star Game."

"I'm sure you will."

"You can bet on it."

"I'd bet on that before betting against Louise Gehrig."

◉ PART THREE ◉

The All-Star Break

The pitcher has got only a ball. I've got a bat. So the percentage in weapons is in my favor and I let the fellow with the ball do the fretting.

—Hank Aaron

2000 MIDSEASON STANDINGS

AMERICAN LEAGUE

East	W	L	Pct.	GB
Milwaukee	50	35	.588	—
Boston	51	36	.586	—
New Jersey	51	37	.580	.5
Toronto	47	39	.547	3.5
Detroit	44	44	.500	7.5
Atlanta	43	44	.494	8
Baltimore	40	48	.454	11.5
Memphis	27	60	.310	24

West	W	L	Pct.	GB
Texas	53	34	.609	—
Chicago	49	38	.563	4
Minnesota	45	40	.529	7
Seattle	46	42	.523	7.5
Oakland	44	43	.506	9
California	43	43	.500	9.5
Kansas City	42	45	.483	26
San Francisco	20	67	.230	33

NATIONAL LEAGUE

East	W	L	Pct.	GB
New York	51	36	.586	—
Manhattan	49	39	.557	2.5
Florida	43	44	.494	8
Buffalo	42	45	.483	9
Chicago	41	46	.471	10
St. Louis	40	48	.454	11.5
Pittsburgh	39	48	.448	12
Philadelphia	37	49	.430	13.5

West	W	L	Pct.	GB
Atlanta	56	32	.636	—
Cincinnati	49	38	.563	6.5
Colorado	45	43	.511	11
Arkansas	44	44	.500	12
St. Petersburg	43	44	.494	12.5
San Diego	41	45	.477	14
New Orleans	39	47	.453	16.5
Los Angeles	38	49	.437	18

15

Purgatory

For Louise Kathleen Gehrig, the All-Star break—a much-needed five-day break in which she, Bob Dixon, and Reggie Borders, the chosen three starters, would only be needed for a solid two innings or so of play while their fellow teammates could rest and relax completely—began on Sunday at 4:28 P.M. as she and her teammates exited Buffalo's Memorial Stadium after their 13–2 rout of the Expos. It was the Meteorites' third win in a row, a sweep of Buffalo on the road.

At this, the so-called halfway point, the Meteorites were two and a half games out of first place, with forty-nine wins and thirty-nine losses, thanks largely to an extremely hot streak after their debacle in Atlanta.

The Mets held the lead, as they had since April 7, and the Marlins had, for the most part, fallen out of the race and were now a distant third, playing one game under .500 ball.

And while most analysts gave the older, wiser, more experienced Mets the edge, their pesky crossborough rivals just would not go away.

As for stats: catcher Bob Dixon ruled all of baseball in the home run department with a total of thirty-four. He was batting .324 with eighty-seven ribbies.

After seventeen starts, Reggie Borders was 13–3, with one no-decision. His ERA was 1.37, and his strikeout total was 175. He had thus far pitched eight complete games, and had the no-hitter, as well as three one-hitters, to his credit.

Number-two starter David Gaston was 9–5 with a respectable 2.93 ERA, while Sean McKnight, the Meteorites' number-three starter was 8–4, with an earned run average just over 3.00.

P.J. Strykes had nineteen saves, as well as four wins. His ERA was 1.89. He'd be the first to tell anyone that he'd have at least 50 percent more saves if "Reggie Borders didn't throw so god-damn many complete games."

And while Louise and Jamaine Young held the one-two spots, respectively, for stolen bases, Balls had a considerable lead: her seventy-one steals to his sixty-two. A fact which did not sit well with the center fielder, whose head was no longer so filled with visions of 5 million dollar bills dancing the rumba en route to his checking account. A fact which pissed the center fielder off to no end. It sucked being wrong, and as much as he hated to admit it, he might have been just that in his initial appraisal of Louise. She was an okay player—he'd never in a million years admit it out loud to anyone—but she still had no right playing in the majors. *That* just wasn't right.

Louise had started every game and was currently batting .299, with twenty-three doubles, seven triples, and ten homers. She had fifty-one RBI's to her credit and had now scored seventy-eight runs. A two-week slump notwithstanding, she was having one hell of a rookie year.

Boarding the jet that would take them home, Louise took her usual seat in the next to last row. She was tired, honestly more tired than she could ever remember being. But sleep wasn't a possibility, at least not a realistic one. She knew the feeling though it didn't have a name. "Wired" would most likely do. But not really. So, settling in sort of sideways and lifting her sore legs onto the vacant seat beside her, she pulled out the paper-back of the moment and tried to focus. But with the words swirling on the printed page and her head beginning to pound, she decided a beer—with God's blessing ice cold—would be more in order.

At the front of the jet, where the alcohol always seemed to be kept, Louise retrieved a canned Rolling Rock and three aspirin tablets from a stewardess, then headed back to her seat. On the walk back up the aisle, she passed the men who had become her closest friends over the past four months, brothers of sorts. A few were asleep. One or two watched the on-board movie. But most read: P.J. was thumbing through Jack Kerouac's *On the Road,* Reggie was halfway finished with Philip K. Dick's *The Man in the High Castle,* manager Lefty had discovered the pleasures of Jim Thompson, Bob Dixon was finally getting around to *The Firm,* Darryl White had borrowed Jesus' copy of *Delta of Venus,* Jeff Carter was reading *The Jungle* by Upton Sinclair, Jo Jo Manzi was plowing through the latest from Harry Crews, David Gaston was on a severe Michael Crichton kick, and Jesus had just started D. Keith Mano's *Topless.*

"Baseball's Book Club"—what the team was dubbed by Mike Lupica in one of his Sunday columns—"may very well be Louise's greatest miracle," he wrote.

The label made Louise smile. She felt like a satisfied high school teacher—that wasn't so painful, now was it?

Sitting down, taking the first long sip, she put the book away and dug her Walkman out of her carry-on. She popped an old jazz tape into the player and put on the headphones. Another sip.

"Ahh . . ."

Thank God for Billie Holiday.

Louise wanted almost to sing along. "Lady sings the blues. She's got them bad. She feels so sad . . ."

Another sip. A little massage for the bridge of her nose. That's it. The headache—that dull behind-the-eyes pain that had been with her, on and off, mostly on, since just before the beginning of her slump—eased away. She had managed to work through the slump. Patience, that seemed to be the key. Patience and practice—hours of BP with Gary Tomlin. And suddenly she was hot again.

Now, she'd use these five days to work through the pain. All of it. The dull ache in her head, soreness in her muscles, and the itch between her legs.

Question: How can a woman surrounded by so many gorgeous men be so goddamn lonely and horny?

Answer: when she's their teammate.

Louise closed her eyes, sighed, and forced a smile.

Sing it, Billie, she thought. Sing it.

⬤   ⬤   ⬤

That Sunday evening, Bob Dixon and Margaret Gehrig had dinner in a little restaurant on Bleecker Street in the Village. It was Louise's favorite Manhattan restaurant, the NoHo Star, and they asked her to come along.

"Really, Mom," Louise argued. "I'm tired. You guys go and have a good time."

"Please," her mother pleaded. "I never get to see you anymore."

Louise sighed. She was tired—too tired to argue, too tired to think, too tired and what the hell. "Okay," she said finally.

And after the three were served their first round of drinks, Margaret turned to her daughter and said, "Louise, there's something we'd like to share with you."

Louise looked expectantly from her mom's face over to Bob's and back to her mom's. Her heart sank, her stomach flip-flopped. She knew what was coming next.

"Bob has asked me to marry him," Margaret continued, tears suddenly coming from her eyes. "And I've said yes."

Louise would have most likely said oh, if it weren't for the tears. Her mom's tears. It had been a long time since she had seen her mother cry—had she ever seen her mother cry? Hell, it had been a long time since she'd seen her this happy. She reached over and hugged her dearly.

"When did this all come about?"

"Bob called me last night from Buffalo."

Louise turned to the catcher. "You proposed over the phone?"

"I couldn't wait any longer," he said with an innocent shrug.

How sweet, Louise thought. "Then you deserve a hug too."

And after that hug, looking back and forth at both members of the happy couple, she couldn't help but wonder what the back page headlines would be. Dixon to Marry Balls' Mom, or maybe, Will Balls Call Dixon "Dad"?, or even Will Dixon Adopt Balls? Her mind swirled at the possibilities.

"So, when will this all happen?" Louise asked.

"We figure late October, early November."

"After the Series," Bob explained.

"The one we'll hopefully be playing in?" Louise asked.

"The one you will be playing in," Margaret said.

Louise nodded, but for the first time since taking the field in early April, she didn't feel confident that her team would go all the way. First there were the Mets. If only—and what a big *if only* that was—the Meteorites could somehow manage to take over and keep hold of first place. Then what? There'd be the Braves, that's what, trying for another World Series ring. And the Western Division champs had home-field advantage this year. Shit! She shook it off and downed the beer. Man, she thought, something's wrong, something's missing. If only—another if-only, life was chock full of too fucking many *if-only's*—she knew for sure what.

⚾   ⚾   ⚾

Louise spent what seemed like a good portion of Monday morning lounging in the Jacuzzi tub that could easily seat four—she'd have been more than satisfied with a cozy twosome, thank you very much. The day's All-Star festivities didn't begin until 7:00 P.M., and those really didn't require that much concentration, at least as far as Louise was concerned. The events included the home run derby, in which she would not participate, and the celebratory dinner and dance that followed. No playing, at least not for Louise Gehrig—just a lot of smiling, nodding, signing autographs, and rubbing elbows with many of the heroes of the sport she now called home.

She probably would have passed on playing in the game altogether if not for the convenient fact that it was taking place at South Field.

When asked to chose the location for the first All-Star Game of the new century, Commissioner Quayle decided the honor should go to one of the four new baseball parks: San Francisco's Garcia Stadium, Memphis's Elvis Presley Memorial Stadium, New Orleans' Delta Dome, or Manhattan's South Field.

Placing the four names in a hat, he blindly reached in and pulled out the slip marked South Field. And though it was the smallest of the four, the New York City location would nonetheless give the All-Star Game a much-needed boost—being in the Big Apple would make it one of the media events of the summer, third in importance only to the Democratic and Republican national conventions.

Well, second in importance.

Louise mingled in the National League dugout during the home run derby. This year, five players from each league competed in the prestigious event. Each was allowed to step into the batter's box and swing away until he or she missed three times. Though little was proved by the competition, various sponsors usually donated thousands per homer to a charity of the hitter's choice.

Since he was leading his league, and all of baseball for that matter, in homers, Bob Dixon was the last man to go to the plate. The American League hitters were winning at least this competition, having hit five balls out of the park versus the National League's three. Bob would quickly even the score.

Louise watched proudly as "Dad," as she jokingly called him in the clubhouse, hit the first two balls into the South Field bleachers.

"Way to go!" she yelled from the dugout. And getting his attention, getting him to turn to face her, she added, but only mouthed, the word "Dad."

He missed the next two balls, swinging sloppily through them. And when he turned to glare into the dugout, Louise needed to turn away and cover her mouth otherwise her laughter would have been heard loud and clear on the other side of the East River.

Bob took a deep breath, adjusted both his stance and his grip on the bat, and turned to face the pitcher. Then, suddenly figuring what the hell, he broke batting concentration and pointed the index finger of his right hand out toward the left field wall.

Not understanding exactly, the pitcher turned and half expected to see some sort of commotion. But when he noticed nothing peculiar, he turned back and shrugged. But Bob's finger remained impassive. The left field wall! that index finger screamed.

Grooving to the allusion, a number of National Leaguers, Louise included, cheered the Meteorite catcher on, not so much for his abilities, but for his nerve at publicly satirizing Babe Ruth's legendary called home run.

Not getting it in the least, the pitcher set, wound up, and delivered.

Crack!

⑪   ⑪   ⑪

With the theatrics behind them, the players and their families assembled in the top-floor banquet room of the Marriott Marquee Hotel, a gleaming edifice of glass and concrete towering over the ever lovely Time Square, for an evening of food, drink, dance, and maybe even a little baseball talk thrown in between bites and gulps and two-steps.

Louise, a couple of beers to the wind, was standing and speaking with Bob, Margaret, and Jonathan Diggers, an old Red Sox teammate of Bob's and the American League's starting shortstop for All-Star Game, when the latter asked, "Balls, how come you didn't take part in the home run derby?"

She smiled graciously. "I'm not a home run hitter."

"She's too goddamn modest," Margaret said. "She led all of college baseball in home runs two years in a row."

"And she's got ten on the year in the majors," Jonathan said.

"I have a dozen teammates who'd give back half their salary for ten dingers at the All-Star break."

"That's only 'cause they know next year's salary would be doubled in return," Bob said.

"Thank God for arbitration," Jonathan said.

"I doubt that he had anything to do with it."

"I'm not a power hitter," Louise explained. "I only get homers when pitchers make mistakes. And seven pitchers made ten perfect fastball goofs."

"Why only seven pitchers?"

"She's got four homers off Eddie Bonaventura," Bob explained.

"Old Eddie. That's too funny," Jonathan said. "He's with the Cards now, right?"

"Uh-huh," Bob muttered.

"What's his deal?"

"I guess I rattle his bones," Louise explained with a smile.

"I can understand that. The voice came from a fifth party. Louise, Bob, Margaret, and Jonathan turned. "I'm not interrupting, am I?" that voice asked.

"You," Jonathan said sarcastically, "interrupt." He smiled and held out a hand. "You bastard." Then turning to face the others, he said, "Balls, Margaret, I'd like you to meet the darling of the American League, Cole Robinson."

Cole stuck out a hand in Margaret's direction. "Margaret," he said; then, repeating the action with Louise: "Ms. Gehrig. I've heard so much about you. It's a pleasure to finally get to meet you."

"The pleasure's all mine," Louise said, eyes up, eyes down, eyes right, eyes left—taking in the tailored black Armani sports jacket, the worn white linen shirt buttoned all the way to the top, the Levi's 501s and the boots—Doc Martins, black and greasy. He was tall, six two, maybe six three, and sort of lanky. His hands were bony, the fingers long, as if they could swallow a Rawlings cushioned cork center hardball whole. Definitely, she thought, the pleasure's definitely all mine.

"So, how's life in"—and Bob made as if the words stuck in his mouth like peanut butter—"New Jersey?"

Cole laughed. "All my life I dream of playing for the Yankees, and when I finally get into pinstripes, they're the New Jersey Yankees. New Jersey! Can you believe it? It's just not right."

"Come on over to the Meteorites," Louise suggested with a smile. "At least you'll be playing in New York."

There's only one reason I'd want to play for the Meteorites, Cole thought, and that's because I'd get to see more of you. But the words that came out of his mouth sounded more like this: "With Reggie Borders on your team, I'd be relegated to the position of number-two starter. I'm happy being number one."

"Good ol' Cole," Bob said. "Humble as always."

"When you're good you might as well admit it," Margaret said.

"Exactly," Cole agreed with a warm smile. "And I'm great, damn it."

"Getting a little hot in here for me," Jonathan said, tugging at his collar. "I see Ozzie Smith over there. I got to grill him about this Eddie Bonaventura thing."

"What are you gonna ask?" Louise said.

"How come he doesn't tell Eddie to just walk you?"

"Last time I faced him, they tried to walk me intentionally. By mistake he throws one right down the middle, and *whack*, outta the park."

"You're kidding?" Jonathan said.

"Ask Bob," Louise said.

Jonathan looked at the Meteorites' catcher, who just nodded and smiled—shit-eating grins didn't come more pronounced.

"Too much," Jonathan said with a slight shake of the head and an accompanying laugh before heading over to bust the ass of the Cardinals' manager.

Turning away for a moment from Cole's piercing gray eyes, Louise caught a glimpse of her mother's right hand, held confidently by Bob's left, and smiled.

"I've heard rumors about that smile," Cole said, quietly, so that only Louise could hear.

"And I've heard rumors about your pickoff move," Louise countered.

"Pickup?" Cole asked.

"No," Louise said, enunciating carefully. "Pickoff."

He cleared his throat. "I don't allow many stolen bases."

"We'll see," she said.

Just then the band providing entertainment for the evening finished its obliteration of Van Halen's "Jump." A few in attendance applauded as the vocalist said, "We'd like to slow it down now." Then, turning to face his bandmates, he said, "Hit it, guys." The drummer counted to four and they began a passable rendition of Rod Stewart's "Tonight's the Night."

"Great tune," Bob said.

"Then let's dance."

And before Louise could stop her mom and tell her, Please don't leave me alone with Cole Robinson because I'm libel to jump his bones right here, right now, before she could beg, Stop, don't go, before she could issue a warning sign—Danger, Danger, Warning Will Robinson—red light STOP!—Bob and Margaret were pressed cheek to cheek, lost in each other's arms as the vocalist's voice creaked in effigy to Rod the Mod.

"So," Cole said, thinking, Here I am, suddenly alone with the most beautiful woman in baseball. He searched for words—any words—then, modifying the thought, asked, "Enjoying your first year?"

Louise nodded, So much was running through her mind, things like why can't this guy be on our team, then her own last-minute corrections like, no, then I'd never be able to concentrate. "I guess," she said. "I'm a little tired."

"It's a lot harder than most people think."

"Can't argue with that."

"Good," he said. "I hate being argued with." He motioned over toward the bar. "Care to join me in a drink?"

"Ahh, yeah. Sure," she said. "Why not?"

They walked over and sat down at one end of the room's antique wooden bar. Louise ordered a Rolling Rock. Cole said he'd have the same.

"I hear you're a real book nut," he said.

"You seem to hear a lot about me."

"A lot's said, and I pay attention."

"Fair enough. And yeah, I like to read. You?"

"Got an M.A. in English."

"So, what are you doing here?"

"Teacher salaries haven't hit that elusive seven-figure mark

yet." He shrugged. "Figured I had ten, twelve good years. I'd
play 'em out, then move on. I don't live for baseball. It's a
game, the greatest game in the world. And I have fun with it.
But I refuse to turn every pitch into a life-or-death situation."

"I know pitchers like that."

"The best example's on your team. Just think what Borders
could do if he'd only relax."

"Then again, maybe the stress is part of his game plan."

The drinks arrived. Cole lifted his and toasted. "To books,"
he said.

Louise clinked her bottle against his. "And baseball," she
said.

"Here, here."

Keith Hernandez, the Atlanta Braves' manager and skipper for
the National League's All-Star team, had a starting lineup that
looked like this:

        1—Joey Lawrence/Braves—#46—SS
        2—Louise Gehrig/Meteorites—#4—1B
        3—Quinton Clark/Mets—#19—RF
        4—Bob Dixon/Meteorites—#18—C
        5—Theordore Humphrey/Reds—#37—CF
        6—Ron Attwood/Dodgers—#25—LF
        7—Rick Rodgers/Marlins—#9—2B
        8—Michael Brown/Cubs—#58—3B
        9—Reggie Borders/Meteorites—#16—P

And though the ex-Met ex-Card ex–other team's Gold Glove–
winning first baseman despised the fact that Gehrig and Dixon
were voted onto the team he had to manage—voted in over the
Braves' first baseman, Lenny Varga, and catcher, Pete Sacker—
Hernandez nonetheless would do his damnedest to win, even if
it meant starting Reggie Borders over Rocky Goetz. It had nothing to do with Borders being the better pitcher—a fact which
Hernandez would never admit. It had to do with the fact that

Dixon was catching, and he and Borders connected. Or so Hernandez argued in his head.

After Michael Bolton's rather flat rendition of the national anthem and the ceremonial first pitch from President Bill Clinton, the teams took to the field.

Seeing that the game was being played in a National League park, the American Leaguers were up first. It took Reggie Borders all of thirteen pitches to strike out the side. And though Hernandez would be one of the last to ever admit it, even he was impressed with that fastball.

With the commercial break over, Joey Lawrence stepped into the batter's box to face Cole Robinson. Louise was in the on-deck circle, swinging a fungo bat over her head, reliving in her mind the end of the previous evening.

⚾   ⚾   ⚾

The beers had continued to flow and the talk had moved from modern literature to favorite films to "what about music?" to a diatribe about those who supported Republican presidential candidate Rush Limbaugh and his running mate, Patrick Buchanan.

"Maybe they're ill," Cole suggested.

"Cancer of the prudent judgment?" Louise suggested.

"Something like that," he said. "I mean, there's got to be an explanation."

"Their duty is to save the moral fiber of this great land while there's still something to save."

"The Rush/Pat moral fiber, you mean. Women in the kitchen—and not on the ball field, blacks in the back of the bus, and homosexuals in jail," Cole said; then, puffing out his cheeks, he mimicked Limbaugh, adding, "Where they belong."

"Like us, like you . . . like *now*," Louise said, also puffing out her cheeks. "I take it you're voting for Al Gore."

"Hell, if the GOP gets in, I'm packing my bags."

"To go where?"

"Some Caribbean island. I'll buy a little place on the beach and spend the rest of my life lying in the sun, drinking daiquiris, reading everything I can get my hands on." He laughed just slightly.

"What?"

"Maybe I'll even try to churn out my version of the great American novel."

She took a sip of beer. "Sounds nice."

"Yeah," he agreed. "What about you, Louise? Ever dream of running away?"

A nod. "Only to Key West.

"Ahh. But the trouble is, Rush would be Key West's president, too."

She laughed slightly. "You obviously haven't been to Key West."

"Never had the pleasure. But I'm game. We could book a flight now. We'll leave the morning after the World Series is over."

She mimicked an announcer. "Cole Robinson. You and your teammates have just won the World Series. What are you going to do now?"

"And I'd yell, 'I'm going to Key West.' " He smiled. "How's that sound?"

"Like you're dreaming."

The smile faded. "What do you mean?"

"We'll sweep you in four games. It won't even be close."

But before Cole could respond, before he could even gather his wits up off the floor, Bob and Margaret sauntered off the dance floor and approached, while the bartender called "Drink up," and the lights in the banquet room were turned up on high.

"We're heading home," Margaret said.

"Can I share a cab?" Louise asked.

"Don't see why not."

Louise turned to Cole, held out her hand, and said, "It was really nice talking to you."

"Yeah," Cole said, shaking her hand. "See you tomorrow, I guess." Helplessly, he looked over at Margaret, who smiled warmly, then at Bob, who just sort of shrugged.

"Bye," Louise said.

And she, along with Bob and her mother, were off, leaving

Cole standing at the bar, wondering and hoping—wondering if he had done something, if he had perhaps said something, maybe the wrong thing, and hoping that the dueling feelings in his heart and groin would one day go away.

⦿　　⦿　　⦿

Atlanta Braves shortstop Joey Lawrence had worked the count to three balls and one strike when Cole let loose with a slow curve that connected with the handle of his bat. The ball careened into shallow center field and was easily put away.

One out.

The sold-out South Field crowd rose to its feet as Louise strolled over to the batter's box. She nodded a good evening to the umpire, caught the eye of Toronto Blue Jay catcher Rick Coviello, then turned to face Cole. He looked good enough to munch on standing there on the mound, she thought. A Cy Young Award winner in his rookie year for the Oakland A's— with twenty-four wins versus four losses, and an ERA of 1.54—who, when his three-year contract was up, accepted George Steinbrenner's offer of a pat 10 million a year for five years, plus bonuses, Cole Robinson *was* an impressive figure on the mound. And though at that moment he was thinking similar thoughts, something more or less about Louise's impressive figure, butterflies nonetheless flew loop-the-loops in his stomach as he stared her down.

The crowd exploded into cheers of "Balls! Balls! Balls!—met by nothing, not a single cheer for Cole.

Louise took her position and smiled at the pitcher.

That smile, Cole thought, that goddamn smile.

Rick sent Cole the appropriate signs—a fastball, right down the middle. Cole nodded, then set. Suddenly a smile appeared at the corners of his mouth. You won't be smiling for long, Louise thought. And then Cole winked. *What the fuck!* Louise thought, suddenly flustered. But before she could step out of the batter's box and ask the ump for a time-out, Cole wound up and delivered. Louise could only watch the ball sail by.

"Strike one."

Okay, Louise thought. If you want to play it that way. Sure, the velocity of the pitch had startled her—the boy could throw—but it *was* just the first pitch. And Louise Gehrig *always* took the first pitch.

Cole procured another fastball sign. Moving into position, he wound up and let it fly.

"Strike two."

Shit, Louise thought, staring at Rick's glove, that was low. She shot a look back at the ump, then turned to glance at Cole. The son of a bitch was beaming. He knew that was a lucky call—lucky for him.

Okay, fine!

Louise stepped out of the batter's box, asked for and received time. She needed to catch her breath. She needed to think. She could hit Cole, she knew it. She could hit anyone. She believed that. She had to. And so far, she hadn't exactly been proven wrong. But something was very wrong. Her concentration was off, all funked up. She wasn't in the baseball mind-set. Instead, the feelings that were crisscrossing through her five-foot, six-and-three-quarter-inch frame had everything to do with certain extracurricular activities that had been missing from her program. Damn it, she thought, what I'm feeling has nothing to do with baseball.

Out on the mound, Cole really wasn't faring much better. Sure, the count was in his favor. But big fucking deal! He was out there on the mound, like a love-struck teen with two and a half quarts of blood rushing into his jock, another two and a half quarts rushing to his heart, and he couldn't help himself, Just the sight of her made him weak in the knees.

Stepping back into the batter's box, Louise raised the bat onto her shoulder, then turned and smiled at Cole. He took a deep breath, wiped the sweat that had been accumulating on his brow, then tried to focus on Rick for the called pitch. Nodding at the single finger, Cole set, wound up, and delivered. But the pitch was low and inside—Louise jumped back, the crowd groaned mightily, and the ump yelled, "Ball one!"

Taking a deep breath, Louise stepped back in, then turned and glared at Cole. There were no smiles to be found—on either the pitcher or the batter.

Louise adjusted her stance as usual, just a little, digging in her left foot. Rick once again gave the sign for a fastball and inhaled as Cole began his windup.

"Ball two."

This time, Rick had to reach to catch the high outside fastball. On the mound, Cole spun around and rubbed at his temples. "Shit," he muttered loud enough for the shortstop to hear.

Rick, figuring a visit to the mound would be worth his while, stood and trotted over.

"You okay, man?" the catcher asked.

Cole exhaled loudly. "Just dandy," he said.

"Hey," Rick said. "Let's just walk her and get it over with."

"No way," Cole said. "Can't do that. I can't give in to her. Not out here."

"It's your call."

Rick ran back to the plate, took his position, and gave Cole the sign. A slider. The pitcher smiled. Okay, Cole thought, a slider it is. Louise adjusted, Cole set, wound, and delivered, and the ump shrieked, "Ball three!"

The crowd applauded, Rick shook his head, Cole muttered something profane, and even Louise had to admit that she was on the lucky side of that call.

With the count full, Cole knew it was best to revert back to his best pitch. So when Rick called for another slider, the pitcher shook him off. A curve? No. The heater, inside? Cole nodded and set.

Louise began her swing the moment the ball rocketed out of his hand.

Crack!

Cole watched the ball career into short right field—a clean line drive single. He watched Louise run to first. He watched her tag the base, then turn and stare his way. He watched as her teammates cheered her on, cheered along with the thousands in attendance. He too wanted to cheer. He too wanted to chant, "Gehrig! Gehrig! Gehrig!" But he could only shake his head and appear peeved—that was the least he could do for his fellow American Leaguers. Yet, deep down he was happy. Deep down he felt chills. Deep down he was kissing her passionately. Deep down they were ripping each other's uniforms to shreds. Deep down they were climaxing again and again and again. Deep down Cole Robinson was in love.

⬭   ⬭   ⬭

Quinton Clark of the New York Mets was up next, but Cole's mind was not so much on getting him out as it was on not letting Louise steal second. He leaned over, rested his pitching wrist on its respective knee, and glared at Rick. He nodded at the sign for a curve, stood, set, then whipped around and rifled the ball to first base.

Louise, who had been leaning—ready to jump, one foot on the grass—dove back in, her hand slapping the base a millisecond before the first baseman's mitt smacked up against her outstretched arm. It was close—as close as calls can possibly get without being a dead heat—but the first base ump spread his arms out wide.

She called time, stood, dusted herself off, tagged up, then turned and scrutinized the pitcher, sending spiked valentines of love through those pretty blue eyes.

Cole grinned contently, then turned once again to face Quinton Clark, who, before even stepping into the batter's box, had prepared himself for countless pickoff attempts. Bob Dixon, who now stood in the on-deck circle, had warned Quinton, "If Louise gets on base, expect to spend eternity in the box. It'll be like purgatory," Bob said, offering up a shrug and an "I think he's got a crush on her" to Quinton's question of, "How come?"

Rick gave Cole the sign—the same sign. The pitcher nodded, set, and again swung around and unleashed a rocket to first.

Louise was back easily this time. The throw was off line and was almost missed altogether by the first baseman. She smiled smugly. "C'mon Cole," she thought, half mouthing the words, "Let's see what you've got."

Cole stuck his tongue hard into his right cheek, gripped the ball, and smacked it into his glove a few times before taking his place back on the mound. He threw a conciliatory glance at home plate, then spun around to glare at Louise. She had one foot on grass, one on dirt, taunting Cole. Or was he taunting her? Either way. Taking a huge, deep breath, Cole stared somewhere in Rick's direction, spotted the sign—the same sign, then set and . . .

Whoosh!

It was the sound the ball made—a flat-lined lightning bolt from Cole's right hand to the glove propped inches from the fair ball side of first base. Louise was too far gone, too far out, when she heard it. And she knew. Son of a bitch! she thought as her attempt to get back to the base fell short.

"You're out!" the umpire bellowed.

"I know," Louise muttered, standing, hustling back toward the safety of her dugout. And on that top step she brushed off her uniform, all the while never taking her eyes off the mound. It was an overheated gaze that burned an *L.G.* brand into the back of Cole Robinson's neck. He could feel it. And though he smiled, and though he beamed, and though he doffed his cap to the cheering of his teammates, deep down he felt as if he had just suffered the most premature of ejaculations, and he wasn't sure if he'd get a chance to come again.

Only Louise knew differently. Those around her—the fellow National Leaguers in the Meteorites' dugout—figured she was mad, as she rightly should be. Hell, the woman had never been picked off before. And that always burns. Especially the first time. Especially when you're fast. Especially when you can steal a good base. And Louise *was* fast. Louise could *definitely* steal a good base. But though her skin was flushed red, though her breathing was hard, though she shook with what appeared to be rage, Louise "Balls" Gehrig was not mad. No, anger had never even crossed her mind. Not in the least. Sex? Yes. Absolutely. You better fucking believe it! She was hot. She was horny. Hotter and hornier than she could ever remember being—well, hotter and hornier than any time since she had put on a major league uniform. The only thing Louise wanted at that moment was to fuck Cole Robinson. Fuck him blind, fuck him stupid, fuck him inside out. And God damn it if she didn't hate him for making her feel that way.

⑪   ⑪   ⑪

Louise got a chance at All-Star redemption when she came to bat in the bottom of the third. With the score two-zip in favor of the National Leaguers, and Cole gone from the mound, replaced by the new "Iron Horse," forty-three-year-old Dave Stewart, now sporting a Memphis Sideburns uniform and having another one of his myriad "career years," Louise stepped to the plate and, on the second pitch, launched a rocket to the extreme reaches of right field. A stand-up triple and two RBI's for the rookie. She'd take it.

Keith Hernandez pulled Louise out of the game at the end of the fourth inning, with the score 5–0. "Good work, Balls," he said, slapping her behind for emphasis.

She nodded her thanks and took a seat beside her stepfather-to-be. "How long you think he'll keep Reggie in?" she asked.

Bob shrugged. He didn't have a clue. Except that he was thinking what Louise was thinking, which was the exact same thought that was currently running through the collective mind of every player, every fan, every journalist: No one had ever pitched a no-hitter in the All-Star Game.

But by the end of the next inning, Rocky's moaning had finally gotten through to Keith. "When do I get to pitch?" he had asked at least a dozen times since the conclusion of the second inning. But with a perfect game going—through five, Reggie had faced the minimum fifteen American Leaguers—Keith was reluctant to pull him.

But pull him he did. "Now," he said, then softly, so no one would hear, "or never," He eyed Rocky, and joylessly added, "Go get 'em."

Reggie Borders, thinking it was his fault he was pulled from the game, took a seat next to his fellow Meteorites and proceeded to watch as American Leaguer after American Leaguer lit up Rocky Goetz like a white trash Christmas tree.

The ace of the Atlanta pitching staff gave up six runs in two-thirds of an inning, and would have been charged with losing the game had not the National Leaguers managed to win during their last at bat.

| American | 000 006 000 | 6 | 9 | 1 |
| National | 022 010 002 | 7 | 12 | 0 |

Geraldine Willard watched the All-Star Game from the relative comfort of her Atlanta home, her four daughters by her side. It was an All-Star party of sorts. Geraldine had invited everyone she knew, with but one exception. She invited Debbie and Kelly's boyfriends. She invited the couple next door. She invited the woman who styled her hair. Hell, she even invited that cute assistant manager at the local bank branch who helped her secure a loan against the house when her husband up and disappeared.

And during the party Geraldine and her guests drank and ate and enjoyed the game, yelling, screaming, cheering every player on. Every player but one.

The party's theme was conceived by her eleven-year-old daughter, Lisa. It was a dual theme, simple, and very much to the point: To hell with Kevin and To hell with Louise Gehrig too!

⚾   ⚾   ⚾

FBI special agent Wesley Selden spent most of the game roaming the grounds of South Field, keeping an eye peeled for Tombstone flicrs. He found none. And neither did any of the other agents assigned to the case. All was clear. All was cool. All was peachy keen, hunky-dory. All was Ziggy Stardust and the Spiders from Mars. It was a beautiful midsummer Manhattan night. Warm, with a three-quarters moon lighting the sky. A perfect night for baseball, one of the announcers must have said, one of the writers must have written. Even the fans who attended the game were surprisingly well behaved. The game began, they cheered or booed in all the right places. The game ended, they went home. "It don't get more peaceful than this," one of the other agents commented to Selden as the last of the fans made their way onto the Manhattan streets.

"Yeah," Selden said with a half grunt as thoughts of baseball's halfway point morphed into everyday weatherman terminology, phrases like, the calm before the storm, or more precisely, the eye of the storm. "A little too peaceful for me."

At the postgame reception it took Louise no time to find Cole Robinson. He was standing by the bar, holding two fresh Rolling Rocks. One poised in her direction.

"Thought you might like a beer," he said, clearing his throat imperceptibly.

"Thank you," she said.

They sipped and looked about, nodding and smiling at teammates and friends—anything not to catch each other's glance.

"So, ahh . . .," Cole said.

"Yeah," Louise agreed.

"Uh-huh," he countered.

"Umm."

"Absolutely,"

She just nodded.

What more was there really to say?

"Look, I know this might sound strange," Louise said after a second beer. "Or maybe forward, or maybe, I don't know. Maybe it's not strange at all. Maybe you're used to it."

"What?"

"Would you like to go out tomorrow night?"

Cole opened his mouth, but no words came out. He reached for his throat, as if to see if something were missing, then finally nodded.

"You would?"

"Uh-huh," he said then, forcing a cough, "Ah, yeah. I'd love to. But."

"There's a but?"

He nodded. "Unfortunately."

She waited for an explanation.

"The team leaves tomorrow for Seattle. We're playing an afternoon game on Thursday."

"Shit," she mumbled, half under her breath.

"I could check into catching a later flight," Cole said, thinking, attempting.

Louise shook her head and looked away. She suddenly felt uncomfortable, wishing she'd never asked. "Don't do that," she said, figuring once she got her hands on Cole she wasn't about to lose him to a red-eye.

He nodded, then nervously asked, "Can I get a rain check?"

Louise smiled, just slightly, then looked into his face.

"I mean," he continued, shuffling his feet—a little dance of desire, hypnotized by her smile—"can we maybe try again at some future date?" Now he returned the smile. "Eventually our schedules have got to mesh. We both play for New York teams, right?"

Louise began to nod at this point—slowly, slightly, never lessening that smile.

"Well, New Jersey in my case," Cole continued. "But close enough."

"Absolutely."

"Absolutely close enough?"

"No," Louise said. "Absolutely you can have a rain check."

"Thank you."

"My pleasure."

$$\text{\small ⊕} \qquad \text{\small ⊕} \qquad \text{\small ⊕}$$

Kevin Thomas Willard did not watch the All-Star Game. He sat before his TV, the *Guide* in one hand, a Budweiser in the other, but he just could never bring himself to turn the damn thing on. It hurt too much—that pain in his heart, that pain in his head. The everything, the near and dear. The memories and dreams, every crack of the bat—what could be and if-only's. He was breathing hard. Sitting alone in the dark, taking a sip, tossing the *Guide* to the floor, he wished it were over. He wished he could die. He wished Louise Gehrig would die. He half sang, half whispered the words, "God, why have thou forsaken me?" to the tune of "If I Were a Rich Man," then began to cry.

It just hurt too goddamn much.

THE BASEBALL BEAT
by Arnold Loiten

The very first All-Star Game was played on July 6, 1933, in Chicago's old Comiskey Park, though, of course, at the time, no one considered the ballpark all that old.

It was a day game, played on a hot and exceedingly humid midsummer afternoon. A game which reached baseball fans across the country through the miracle of radio.

Some forty thousand very lucky fans did get to see the game live. Did get to see the American League win by a score of 4–2, due mainly to a two-run homer by none other than Babe Ruth during the third inning. The losing pitcher was St. Louis's Wild Bill Hallahan. The winning pitcher, New York's Lefty Gomez.

There are, of course, no video tapes of that game. There aren't even any tapes of the radio broadcast. And most likely only a few photographs exist, though I could lay my hands on none to accompany this column. And that's a shame. Because it was a historic game, not just because it was the first All-Star Game, but because its participants were true All-Stars, in every sense of the word.

Besides Ruth, Jimmy Foxx was there. Chuck Klein played. And Mel Ott. There was Pie Traynor, and another Lefty, also a pitcher, whose last name was Grove. There was Mickey Cochrane, and Joe Sewell playing the last year of a Hall of Fame career. There was Charlie Gehringer, the Mechanical Man from Detroit, and Frankie Frisch, who hit the game's other home run. And, of course, there was Lou Gehrig, who would go on to play in five other All-Star Games before his career was cut short by the deadly illness which now bears his name.

Today things are different or at least they seem that way. The All-Star participants are voted in by the fans—well-meaning sorts, don't get me wrong—who unfortunately turn the proceedings into a popularity contest.

Being an All-Star no longer means that you are the best at your position. It means only that you are a fan favorite. Maybe you make the best sneaker commercials. Or give the best interviews. Or your rap CD sold millions of copies. Or you were picked by *People* magazine as one of the fifty most beautiful people in the world. Or, maybe, just maybe, you're a woman. That could probably get you on the All-Star team.

I can think of one Gehrig who got there that way. The original, well, he had to rely on his talent, his power, his run-producing potential. The copy just had to born the right sex. I wonder what the original would think. Would Lou feel proud? Or would he wonder just the heck was going on?

You certainly know my feelings on the matter.

◎ 16 ◎

Pizza 'n' Roses

A little after 3:00 P.M. the following day, Cole Robinson sat in a
the main cabin of the New Jersey Yankees' personal jet. He,
along with his teammates, coaches, their manager, and the New
Jersey beat reporters, was awaiting clearance that would allow
the 707 to leave its assigned gate and head over to the runway,
where it could wait a bit longer for more clearance to fly, baby,
fly. He had tried reading—he couldn't concentrate. He attempted to take a nap—he wasn't sleepy. He figured he'd start
up a conversation with one of teammates, but all they wanted to
talk about was the All-Star Game—all they wanted to talk about
was Louise Gehrig, and the awe-inspiring way he had picked her
off first base. But Louise Gehrig was the last thing Cole needed
reminding off. She already pervaded his every thought—
walking, sleeping—since their meeting at the Marriott All-Star
get-together, more so since the beers, and on into extra innings
since the game itself. His mind had a hard-on and his heart a
boner. His crotch, well, that was dented beyond repair.

He sighed, then glanced at his watch.

Three fourteen.

It was now or never.

He stood up and began walking to the front of the plane.

"Where the hell you going?" Yankee manager Dave Winfield asked before Cole could safely duck out the doorway.

"I, ah," he said, half in the plane, half out, "well . . . you see."

"Yeah," Winfield barked. "What?"

Cole exhaled deeply. "I forgot something," he said, then added, "I'll catch up with you in Seattle." Halfway up the runway, he could still hear his manager screaming—about what, he didn't really understand. Cole wasn't scheduled to start until Saturday—what difference did it really make if he was there on time for Thursday afternoon's game? Okay, he finally admitted as he stood in front of an American Airlines booking agent, in the middle of a pennant race it made a difference. But not a great one, and besides, he'd make it. A bit the worse for wear, but he'd be there, cheering on his teammates from his place on the bench. Yeah, that was more important than seeing Louise.

Right.

Sure.

Fuck!

"May I help you?" the American Airlines agent asked.

"Yeah. I need to book a red-eye to Seattle."

The agent pushed a few buttons on her computer keyboard, then informed Cole, "There's a flight to Seattle, with a stopover in Chicago. It leaves at 6:12 P.M."

"That's not late enough," Cole said.

"How late would you like to leave, sir?"

"Midnight. One A.M. Later if possible."

The agent smiled cordially. Then, looking into the desperate face of the customer standing before her, she realized he wasn't joking. "I'm sorry," she said. "We have another flight through Dallas–Fort Worth that leaves at 8:02. But nothing at midnight."

"What about any of the other airlines?" Cole asked.

"I'm checking," she said, eyeing her computer screen. "Delta has a flight that leaves at 7:14 with stops in Memphis and Salt Lake City." She looked up at Cole, sadly shaking her head. "I'm afraid our 8:02 is the latest."

"How 'bout in the morning?" the Yankee asked. "What's the earliest?"

"We have a 7:09 flight that'll get you to Seattle at 12:53 P.M."

Cole thought for a moment. He could make a clean break

from first class—his luggage, which was currently waiting along with his teammates, coaches, their manager, and the New Jersey beat reporters for clearance to take off, would already be at the ballpark. Five minutes to sprint from the gate to the taxi stand. Twenty minutes, give or take a few, to get to the park. Hell, he'd make it in plenty of time for the 1:35 first pitch. "I'll take it," he said, handing the agent his Platinum American Express card. "First class."

⋒   ⋒   ⋒

It was a little before 5:00 P.M. when Margaret asked, "Are you gonna sit at home alone all night and sulk?" She utilized the most aggravated tone she could muster.

"I'm not sulking," Louise said, sulking.

"No," Margaret agreed, "you're being pathetic."

"Thanks."

"Don't thank me. You should have gone home with him the other night."

"I wasn't ready."

"But you're ready now?"

"I don't know. I just want to see him."

"Well you're not seeing him tonight." Margaret glanced at her watch and sighed. "For Christ's sake, he's halfway to Seattle by now."

"But I don't feel like going out," Louise said for what seemed like the hundredth time that night.

"It'll do you good."

"I feel like staying home."

"Staying home won't do you any good. You'll just sit and mope and eat your heart out over something you can't control. Listen to your mother."

"I don't know."

"C'mon," Margaret said. "There must be someplace you're in the mood for."

Louise's brain hemmed and hawed. Cole Robinson's arms didn't seem like anyplace her mother could take her.

Then Margaret employed a secret weapon, a temptation that had always—from the time Louise could shovel food into her own mouth—worked on her little girl. "How long has it been since you've had good pizza? I mean, really good pizza?"

Louise, unable to control that smile reflex, smiled, and let out a little half laugh, half breath. It had never occurred to her—a visit to a long lost friend. "A long time," she said with a little shake of her head.

"How's Modern sound?"

"It sounds great," Louise said. "But isn't it crazy to drive two hours one way to get a pizza?"

"Bob'll drive," Margaret said shrugging her motherly shoulders. "That's what men are for."

"Oh," Louise said. "So, that's what they're for."

"You didn't know?"

"I was never really sure."

"Well, now you know."

"Yeah," Louise said. "Now I know."

And suddenly with the thoughts of her own personal small mozzarella pie—well done, but not burnt—playing on the taste buds of her mind, she felt, well, better. At least a little. Pizza— original New Haven brick-oven pizza—was the one and only thing that might have a shot of pushing Cole Robinson, at least temporarily, out of her mind.

⚾   ⚾   ⚾

It was a little after 6:00 P.M. when Cole Robinson, carrying an armful of red roses, stepped into the lobby of the Charles Street high-rise Louise called home. Ziggy smiled as the pitcher approached.

"You Cole Robinson, man?" he asked.

"Ah, yeah. I guess," Cole replied.

"That's some pickoff move you got."

"Thank you."

"I expect you'll be wanting to leave those for Ms. Gehrig?"

"Well, if it's not too much trouble," Cole said, "I'd like to give them to her myself."

"'Fraid that's not possible, man."

"Not possible," Cole repeated.

"She left for the evening with that crazy mother of hers, and the catcher man, Mr. Dixon."

"Left?"

"Yeah, man. Just a few minutes ago. Went for what she called the best pizza in the galaxy."

"Pizza?"

"Yeah, pizza."

Cole swallowed hard. "Did she happen to say what time she'd be back?"

"Late," Ziggy said. "I think." He motioned toward the flowers. "You apologizing for the pickoff?"

"What's that?" Cole asked, his mind running in every direction but clear.

"The flowers. They for the pickoff?"

"Oh. No. Not really."

"I see," Ziggy said, flashing a smile the size of Jamaica. "The big time New Jersey Yankee pitcher has got a hankering for Ms. Gehrig. Is that it?"

Cole began to blush. He wasn't sure what to say, what to admit. He hated the notion that what he said to this doorman might be all over the New York tabloids come sunup. "No," he said, attempting to think fast. "They're just flowers."

"Three dozen red roses."

"Four."

"What's that?"

"Four dozen red roses."

"That's not *just* flowers."

Cole stammered, searching for the right word, then finally settled on, "Is there someplace I could leave them?"

"Leave them with me, man. I'll make sure Ms. Gehrig gets 'em."

"Okay," Cole said, nodding and hoisted the flowers over the security desk and into Ziggy's arms. "You sure she'll get them?"

"I promise," Ziggy said. "I'll hand them to her myself."

Cole nodded.

"Would you like to leave a note, maybe? So she knows who they're from?"

"Um," Cole said, thinking. He sure seemed to be doing a lot of that lately. "No. I'll give her a call."

"Okay."

"Bye," Cole said, turning and heading for the exit.

"Good-bye, Mr. Robinson," Ziggy said. "It was nice meeting you."

Cole looked back over his shoulder before heading back out onto the West Village street. "Yeah," he said absentmindedly. "Nice meeting you, too."

Louise's homecoming to Modern Pizza was just the distraction she needed.

"I can't believe we drove two hours for pizza," Bob said as the infamous threesome placed their orders.

"You drove, honey," Margaret corrected; then, motioning toward Louise and herself, she added "We gossiped about Cole Robinson."

"Uh-uh, *honey*," Bob said sarcastically. "You listened. *I* gossiped about Cole Robinson."

And that much was true. During the two-odd-hour ride up Interstate 95 to State Street in New Haven, Margaret and Louise asked the questions, and Bob supplied the answers—as best he could. They were, after all, only leaguemates, not teammates.

"What about girlfriends?" Margaret asked, somewhere between Greenwich and Stamford.

"Only one that I know of," Bob said. "What's her name? That model? Jennifer Hansen."

"Cole dated Jennifer Hansen?" Louise asked.

"They lived together for about two years," Bob said. "You never heard about that?"

"Never paid much attention to Page Six," Louise said, shaking her head, wondering what the hell Cole would want with someone like her after he had had someone like Jennifer Hansen—*Vogue* cover girl Jennifer Hansen, *Cosmopolitan* cover girl Jennifer Hansen, *Playboy* cover girl Jennifer Hansen—Jennifer Hansen was as overexposed and popular as a supermodel could be.

"She's the real reason he split from the A's," Bob said.

"Come again," Louise said, suddenly trying to shake images

of Jennifer Hansen's goddamn toothpaste-perfect smile from her head.

"During his last year in Oakland, Cole caught her in bed with Peter Glavine."

"The catcher?" Margaret asked.

"*His* catcher," Bob said. "Remember when Glavine caught his hand in the car door? It was like late July, early August, 1998."

"Ballplayers are always catching their hands in car doors," Margaret said.

"It's what the PR people say when the injury's on the embarrassing side," Bob explained.

"What can be more embarrassing than slamming your hand in a car door?"

"Oh, being caught with your star pitcher's live-in model girlfriend and having that star pitcher kick the living crap out of you."

"Is that what happened?" Louise asked.

Bob nodded. "Cole broke Glavine's hand and his nose. An official season-ending car-door slam." He shook his head. "Cole should have claimed a car door got him as well, for all the good he was to the A's those last two months. Lost eight straight games. His ERA went through the roof. And when his contract was up, returning to the A's wasn't even a consideration. Steinbrenner offered up the bucks. Cole didn't hesitate a second."

The threesome was quiet for a moment, and then Louise asked, "What happened to Jennifer?" She shuddered at the realization of how foul the name really tasted.

"Threw her out on her ass," Bob said with a slight smile. "She was living with the lead singer of the Red Hot Chili Peppers within the week."

"How come I never read about this?" Margaret asked.

"No one ever wrote about it," Bob explained. "Believe it or not, we protect our own every once in a while."

At about the West Haven exit of I-95, Margaret asked her daughter why she was so quiet.

"Just wondering," Louise said, "if he's still got a thing for her."

Margaret turned to face Bob. Only he in the car might hold the answer to *that* question.

"Louise. Last year Cole Robinson went 25–5 for the Yankees, with an ERA of 1.39. You couldn't buy a hit off the guy. Trust me on that one. Remember, the Red Sox only won the division by one game. You know who was in second place—our old friends from the Bronx."

"New Jersey," Margaret corrected.

Bob laughed. "Yeah. Our blood rivals from Jersey."

"So, you think he's over her?'

"I'd bet on it. I've never seen a more focused pitcher." He laughed slightly before adding the kicker. "And when he wasn't pitching, he'd be sitting off in the shade somewhere, reading.

That made Louise smile. A smile that lasted through the beers, through her small mozzarella pie—well done, but not burnt—and even through the two-hour ride home. A ride home fueled by thoughts of Cole Robinson.

It was during the pizza that Bob dropped the most fascinating of bombs. Discussing a certain major leaguer who'd been suffering through a season-long slump, Louise made the comment that he was flirting with the "Wiclechowska line."

"Bobby Wielechowska?" Bob asked.

"Yeah," Louise said, exchanging a little curious eye-talk with her mom. Why? Do you know him?"

"We've shared a few beers."

"Oh, really," Margaret said.

"Yeah. He played for the Mets for about an hour."

"I know."

"Mom used to have a crush on him."

"It was Bob's turn to say, "Oh, really." He smiled. "Him, too?"

"I was young."

"If only he did as well with the bat as he did with the ladies," Bob said.

Silence.

"He, ah, y'know? He always had a reputation as a real ladies' man."

"Yeah," Margaret said, clearing her throat. "So . . . ?"

"What's he doing now?" Louise asked.

"Umping in the minors," Bob explained. "I thought for sure he'd make it to the big leagues this year." He pulled another slice from the pizza pie and took a bite. "Probably next year."

⚾ ⚾ ⚾

"Roses?" Louise said, stepping into the lobby of the Charles Street building.

Ziggy held them out to her as she approached. "Yes, ma'am," he said with a beaming, no problem Jamaican grin. "From a certain Mr. Cole Robinson, pitcher for the New Jersey Yankees."

Louise took hold of the forty-eight roses, gripped them, thorns and all, to her chest, and headed toward the elevator. "Thanks," she mumbled as she waited for the elevator door to slide open.

She looked around, half hoping her mother would pop out of the lobby woodwork, half not. Margaret was off to spend the night at Bob's. "You'll be okay?" she had asked.

"I'll be fine," Louise insisted, never for a moment thinking that Cole would have skipped his flight and arrived at her door, roses in hand. Hell, she had never even given that a thought. If it had so much as peeked into her mind, she'd have sat at home, pizza or no pizza, and waited for—*oh, my God*, dare she think it—her knight in pinstripes (Grandfather would be so proud) to arrive.

Upstairs, after placing the roses in three different vases (she didn't have one large enough to hold that many flowers) Louise glanced at her answering machine. The message counter registered 3.

Taking a deep, deep, so very deep breath, she jacked up the volume and pressed play.

Beep.

"Louise. It's Matt Stern. You're probably not going to believe this, but the office just received a call from David Letterman's producer. It seems they've had a cancellation for tomorrow night and are wondering if you would appear as a guest on the show. I told them I'd get in touch with you immediately and get right back to them. So, give me a call as soon as you get this message. Okay?"

Beep.

"Congratulations! You've just won an exciting all-expenses-paid, four-day, three-night vacation to beautiful Paradise Island in the Bahamas. To claim your prize, call 1-900-555-1957, Monday through Friday, eight A.M. to seven P.M., Eastern Standard Time. The call will cost you $4.95 a minute. The length of the average call is five minutes. Your claim number is: 101792-KCB. Please have that number ready when you call."

Beep.

"Louise, It's Cole. Cole Robinson. At the last minute I was able to catch a later flight. Well, actually, I just sort of jumped planes before takeoff. I was hoping maybe we could get together. But I guess I missed you. I'll try calling again tomorrow, from Seattle. Bye. Oh, yeah. Hope you like the roses."

Beep. Beep. Beep.

Or at least that's what she might have heard.

But Louise was not about to sit around and listen to messages from anyone other than Cole Robinson. As soon as Matt Stern's voice became identifiable, she hit fast forward, then hit it again before the computerized voice telling her about her exciting trip to Paradise Island in the Bahamas could even get halfway through the word *congratulations*. But on the third message, she let the machine play. And after Cole said his line about her liking the roses, after those three beeps, she hit rewind, then play, and listened to message number three all over again. Then, pulling a few of the roses from the closest rose-filled vase, she pressed the soft petals to her face and inhaled deeply, repeating the replay process with her answering machine, half to memorize the sound of his voice, half to once again experience the strange but wonderful tingles.

It was a little after ten the next morning when Louise, asleep in a bed of Cole Robinson–red rose petals, awoke to the persistent ringing of her telephone. Thinking, hoping, dreaming it might be Cole, Louise lunged for the phone.

"Hello," she said in her best attempt at a wide-awake voice.

"Louise," said the voice on the other end of the line. "Matt Stern. How come you never called me back last night? I thought you loved David Letterman."

"Ah," she said. "Matt. Um." She ran her tongue on the pizza and beer-coated insides of her mouth. "What? What are you talking about?"

" 'The David Letterman Show.' "

"What about it?"

"They want an answer."

"An answer to what?"

"Didn't you get my message?"

"Message?"

"On your answering machine."

It took Louise a moment to remember her rapid fast-forwarding. "Oh, my machine," she lied. "It's, ah, I've been having problems with it. It's not working."

"You should say that on the tape. I'd have kept trying to call."

"Sorry."

"S'okay," Matt said. "So, what about it? Do you want to appear on the Letterman show tonight?"

Reality-check time. "David Letterman? Tonight?"

"I've got to let them know right away."

"Yeah," Louise said. "I guess. Sure."

"Good. I'll have the producer call you with the details."

"Okay."

"By the way," Matt said. "Tuesday doesn't count."

"What's that?" Louise asked.

"The pickoff. The All-Star Game doesn't count. You still have yet to be picked off. Your streak is alive."

"Streak," Louise said, thinking about Stern's words—*Tuesday doesn't count*. Yes, it did. Tuesday most certainly did count. "Yeah." And she forced a smile Matt could not see.

"Well, let me go and call the Letterman people."

"Okay."

"Have fun tonight."

"Right. Thanks."

"Bye."

"Bye."

Cole made it to Seattle's Kingdome just as the owner-manager of a local Jiffy Lube completed his rendition of the national anthem.

"Nice of you to show up," Winfield barked.

Cole nodded hellos to everyone on the bench, then took a seat. It'd be at least three hours before he could get to a telephone. Three hours which turned into four hours, which turned into four hours, thirty-two minutes—a 272-minute game during which the Jersey Bombers' butts were collectively kicked by the Mariners.

New Jersey	021 000 020	5	7	3
Seattle	104 900 30	17	21	0

As soon as the game was over, Cole lunged for the clubhouse, and in lunging for the clubhouse, lunged for the telephone. He had no need to pull out any slips of paper with Louise's number crudely scribbled down. He knew it by heart. He had had four hours and thirty-two minutes to memorize it forward, backward, and inside out.

On the fourth ring, the answering machine picked up. "Hi," the tape said in Louise's unmistakable tone. "I'm not here. But you're an adult. You *know* what to do at the beep."

Cole nodded to himself, and smiled. "Hi," he said. "It's just me again. Cole. Cole Robinson. Hoping to catch you at home. I'll, ah, I'll try again later. Bye."

He hung up and joined his teammates at the postgame press conference, where skipper Winfield said something or other about it being "only one game," and that the team had played hard, and that they'd come back strong tomorrow. "We've got to take it one game at a time," Winfield concluded. "That's all we can do."

Cole nodded quietly in the background. Then he just as quietly headed to his hotel room, ordered up a room service dinner, ate, read a couple of chapters from Carl Hiaasen's latest, then fell quickly into a deep, Louise dream–filled sleep.

He awoke many hours later, when a teammate called his room with the announcement, "Hey, turn on 'The Dave Letterman Show.' That Louise Gehrig chick is gonna be on."

17

Commercial Breaks

At one minute before 11:00 P.M. Eastern Standard Time some bigwigged head honcho boss-type at the American Broadcasting Companies' headquarters in New York had had enough, had seen enough, had heard enough. He pulled the plug on the Republican National Convention about an hour into Rush Limbaugh's acceptance speech, cued up the local news, and informed the affiliates that come eleven thirty, "The David Letterman Show" would be on the air. It was the decision of a lifetime, one that gave Letterman his highest overnight Nielsen ratings ever. American viewers, who had likewise grown tired from four days of imbecilic prattle, turned to Letterman in droves—even his critics, even fans of Jay Leno and Arsenio Hall, even fans of Christopher "Mad Dog" Russo, even fans of Charlie Rose.

And that evening, after an opening monologue made up entirely of quips about the Republican National Convention and after Rush Limbaugh's Top Ten Favorite Classic Rock Tunes, with number one being Queen's "Tie Your Mother Down," Letterman came back from the commercial break—a commercial break during which bandleader Paul Shaffer and the Late Night Jazz Ensemble performed a funked-up rendition of "Take Me Out to the Ball Game"—sat back, smiled, and flipped back a handful of light blue index cards, then made the following introduction: "My next guest leads all of major league baseball in stolen bases. And yet that hardly tops the list of her extraordinary accomplishments. She's the first baseperson for the Manhattan Meteorites. And you may know her as Balls. Ladies and gentlemen, please give a warm welcome to Louise Gehrig."

Louise walked onto the Letterman set, much to the hoots and hollers of the many males in the audience—males used to seeing her dressed in a uniform and cap, not in a sexy black dress with a hemline well above her baseball knees, nor with her long black locks flowing freely onto her superbly sculpted shoulders—and greeted the talk show host, then took a seat by his side.

"Welcome to the program," Letterman said.

"Thank you. It's a pleasure to be here," Louise said, "even on such short notice."

"Yes, well. Rush had to cancel at the last minute. You know how these things are."

"Sure," Louise said. "He's out there making the world safe for people just like him."

"Ooh," Letterman said. "That's a scary thought. That there *are* people just like him."

"Someone has to be buying his books," Louise concluded.

"Indeed," Letterman said, a huge goofy grin playing on his mouth. "So, is major league ball every thing it's cracked up to be?"

"It's a living," she said, a beautiful smile playing on her mouth. "Not all of us can be talk show hosts."

"That's debatable," Letterman said.

"I really can't imagine doing anything else."

"You're not the, say, secretary type?" Letterman sat back in his chair and lowered his voice down into the pompous range; then, clearing his throat, he said, "Honey. Type that up for me right away. And, ah, while you're at it get me a coffee."

Louise smirked. "Yeah. Right. Type this."

"Whoa," Letterman whooped, along with about half the studio audience.

"I was never the submissive type," Louise said.

The talk show host laughed. "That's too bad," he said, in a crummy Groucho Marx shtick.

"For you," Louise joked, "exceptions could be made."

Letterman blushed the first baseperson's way, obviously smitten. "We'll talk after the show," he joked back, in the most suggestive voice he could possibly muster.

"Maybe I can help you with your swing."

"Yeah," Letterman said, suddenly standing, staring out at the studio audience. "It's been fun. Thank you all for coming. See you tomorrow night." Then reclaiming his seat, fanning himself with the light blue index cards, and wiping nonexistent beads of sweat from his forehead, he turned back to his guest. "Now, we'll have no more of that, Ms. Gehrig."

"Yes, sir," Louise said with a blush and a smile.

Letterman straightened his suit jacket, adjusted his tie, and read his next question off one of the light blue index cards. "So, ah, who's the fiercest pitcher you've faced?"

"Cole Robinson," Louise said, so quickly that it seemed as if she were expecting the question.

"Really?"

"Uh-huh."

"But you got a hit off Cole just the other night."

"I can get a hit off just about anybody," Louise said, much to the studio audience's delight. "He picked me off."

"How about Rocky Goetz?"

"He's good," Louise said with an almost innocent shrug, "but not unhittable."

"Is anyone?" Letterman asked.

"I don't know. I sure would have liked to face Doc Gooden in '85, or maybe Nolan Ryan. Or Roger Clemens, or maybe Randy Johnson, when he was on. Those are the people I watched growing up. As for the pitchers of today, I think Reggie Borders is one of the best. I've taken BP off him, and asked him to let loose. Forget it. It's like facing an automatic weapon. I couldn't even see the ball. He struck me out with three pitches."

"Wow," Letterman said, once again tapping the edge of those

light blue index cards against the top of his desk. "But can he pick you off first?"

"I don't think so," Louise said. "But what makes him such a great pitcher is that that's nothing he'd ever have to worry about. He'd never let me get there in the first place."

"Right," Letterman said. "We've got to take a break, but when we return, Louise Gehrig will give us her official World Series picks."

◍   ◍   ◍

And after the commercial break—during which Paul and the band performed a synth-pop cover of "Joltin' Joe DiMaggio"—Letterman, as promised, asked Louise her predictions as to which team would win each of the four divisions.

"The American League West?" Letterman said.

"I really shouldn't be answering this," Louise said.

"It's just between you and me," Letterman promised. "I won't tell a soul."

"Umm," Louise said, smirking. "Okay. American League West. The Rangers seem to be walking away with the division, but don't rule the White Sox out yet."

"I would never do that," Letterman said. "Okay, what about the AL East?"

"That's the toughest to call. You got the Red Sox, the Yankees, and the Brewers. Any one of those three teams could take the division. Even the Blue Jays have a chance."

"But, and not to insinuate that you are, if you were a betting man," Letterman said, pausing for a moment to slightly slap the side of his head, almost as if he were trying to lodge his brain back into place, "woman, a betting woman, whom would you put the rent money on?"

"But I'm not a betting woman," Louise said, adding, "Never even bought a lottery ticket."

"Never?"

"Never."

"Y'know," Letterman said. "All you need is a dollar and a dream."

"So I've heard," she said.

"But c'mon, you've got to have a favorite between those teams."

"Not really. I don't usually follow the American League."

"Okay. Personally," Letterman said, "I think the Brewers are gonna do it this year."

"Why's that?"

"Oh, I don't know. I guess I just hate the Red Sox, and I can't take the Yankees seriously since they've moved to New Jersey." A smattering of boos and hisses from the studio audience caused Letterman to laugh once, loudly. He turned to face them, and laughing, said, "Oh, sure. Since when are you all on New Jersey's side?"

"That's as good a reason as any to hate the Yankees," Louise said finally.

"Hey. What do I know? The Yankees will probably win it all."

"Not if I have any say in it," Louise said, much to the audience's delight.

"Okay. So, we've got the American League covered. What about the National League?"

"Well, it doesn't take a baseball genius to predict that Atlanta's gonna win the West."

"Even I could predict that. Hey," he said, beginning to laugh goofily, "speaking of the Braves. Do you remember Bob Horner? Played for them in the early eighties. Man oh man, was he fat."

"First base, right?"

"And third."

"Big home run hitter."

"Big, period."

"What about him?"

"Oh, nothing," Letterman said. "I just like picturing him straddling first base." He laughed, again wiped at his brow, then cut himself short with a sucking-in of air and a stretched out "yeah." And after the briefest of pauses, he resumed. "So, now what about your division? Is it gonna be you or the Mets?"

"What about the Marlins?" Louise asked diplomatically. "Or the Pirates, or the Cubs?"

"Ahh," Letterman said, waving them off. "Everyone knows it's gonna be one of the New York Teams. I want to know which one. C'mon. Give me some inside dope. What's your strategy? What's Lefty got up his sleeve? How are you going to win the division?"

Louise shrugged almost innocently, then offered, "By winning more games than the Mets."

"Good answer," Letterman said. "And is that a possibility?"

"I certainly hope so," Louise said. "We'll certainly try."

"Good," Letterman said. "It should be an exciting pennant race." Then, stretching out his hand, he said, "It's been a pleasure meeting you. I wish you all the luck in the world. And I hope to be seeing you come October in the World Series."

Louise nodded and smiled, then shook the talk show host's hand. And as Letterman said something about being right back, Paul and the band began a rocking interpretation of Terry Cashman's "Willie, Mickey and the Duke (Talkin' Baseball)."

Cole Robinson turned off the television in his hotel room. He looked at his watch, still set to East Coast time. It read 2:58 A.M. Late, he thought. But was it too late? Not willing to risk another encounter with her telephone answering machine, he picked up the receiver, punched the 8, which was the number that was supposed to be punched if a guest of the hotel wanted to make a long-distance call and have it charged to his hotel bill, then dialed Louise's home number.

"Hello," she said, a bit drowsy, picking up on the third ring.

"Louise," he said. "It's Cole."

"Cole," she repeated, trying to decide if this was reality or if it was a dream.

"Yeah. I'm sorry if I woke you. I just saw you on the Letterman show and I wanted to call."

They both mentioned the flowers immediately, their voices overlapping. Louise said, "The flowers were beautiful" at the exact same millisecond in time as Cole asked, "Did you like the flowers?'

Then they both laughed.

It was the first of many times they'd be thinking or saying or doing the exact same thing at the exact same millisecond in time. Such was seemingly a prerequisite for great romance—and to have a great romance was something that flittered about in both of their minds.

Overnight with Howie

"And here's Joey from Bensonhurst. Go ahead, Joey. Tell us, 'I told you so.' "

"I told you so. I told you so. I told you so!"

"Well it wasn't exactly a strikeout for Mr. Robinson."

"Howie. It was even better. Ol' Cole did something no pitcher in the National League could manage to do. He picked her off. It was a beautiful sight to behold."

"I'm sure you just have been roaring."

"Roaring. Man, I genuflected in prayer. I put up a shrine to the mighty Cole. I would kiss his feet. I, I, I would . . ."

"I think we get the picture."

"Now Ms. Louise Gehrig and her team of know-nothings are gonna sink faster than a pair of cement shoes in the East River."

"You sound pretty sure of yourself."

"Hey. They're two and a half games back. After this weekend's series with the mighty Metropolitans, they'll be five and a half back. Bye-bye Mediocres. So long Louise Gehrig."

"We'll see."

"Another unbeliever."

"Oh, so there are actually others who agree with you?"

"More than you'd think, Howie. More than you'd think."

"How many?"

"A lot."

"No, really. How many. I want numbers. I want reality, not some Bensonhurst fantasy."

"A few."

"What's that? Two, three."

"Something like that."

"So, in all of New York, you've only been able to find two or three people who agree with you that Louise Gehrig has no right playing pro ball?"

"Well . . ."

"That's not a very good percentage, Joey. Counting you, and giving you the benefit of the doubt, that's four out of about 12 million. I got a better chance of winning Lotto than I do meeting up with someone who agrees with you."

"Just watch, Howie. I'll be proven right."

"In your dreams, Joey. In your dreams. Right now we've got to take a commercial break, but when we return, we'll hopefully be talking to Cole Robinson, the Yanks' starting pitcher tomorrow evening against the Mariners. We've been having a little problem getting through. Seems his phone has been busy. But we'll try again, and then maybe we'll get to ask him what he thinks about Louise Gehrig."

⊕ **PART FOUR** ⊕

The Second Half

I'd rather hit than have sex.

—Reggie Jackson

⑪ 18 ⑪

Through Wind, Rain, Sleet, or Snow Revisited

Baseball's second half began on a much quieter note for Special Agent Wesley Selden. Sure, there was the ever-persistent Tombstone—the daily mailings had never varied: the Atlanta, Georgia, postmark, the size and make of the envelope, the brand of twenty-pound white bond upon which the copies were made. But the most amazing aspect to Selden was not Tombstone's perseverance, but the fact that the U.S. mail service was so damn reliable. Hell, the agent thought, didn't *his* cards and letters always arrive a day, maybe more, late? Didn't the payments *he* sent out on time always make it to their destination a day or two after their due date? He was sure of it. Yet these threats never missed a day. Fucking U.S. Postal Service, he had laughed to himself almost daily.

The rest of the loonies—the bigots, the Republicans, the members of the Klan—well, they seemed to be on hiatus. On an extended All-Star break. Let 'em stay there, Selden thought. Tombstone was more than enough.

After three and a half months, the Federal Bureau of Investigation—an investigatory unit that could crack the bombing of the World Trade Center in less than a week—had no clues, no leads, no nuthin' that would lead them to whomever this Tombstone was. They had talked to every employee at every branch of the Atlanta post office. *Nothing!* They had checked every store where the easily identifiable envelopes and paper were sold. *Nothing!* They had checked art supply shops and art schools. *Nothing!* They had checked ten years' worth of rap sheets for virtually every resident of Fulton County, short of parking tickets and arrests for jaywalking. *Nothing!* They had interviewed Arnold Loiten. *Nothing!* Hell, they had even talked with Limbaugh and Buchanan. *Nothing!* Selden and his agents had turned over every Atlanta, Georgia, stone—tomb, pebble, or otherwise—twice. *AND NOTHING!*

So, on the Friday after the All-Star break, a Friday during which the Meteorites would be hosting the crossborough Mets, it came as no surprise to Wesley Selden when, at precisely 9:17 A.M., the bag of daily mail for South Field was opened to reveal orders for tickets, fan mail—oh, how Louise now got oodles of that—utility bills, credit card applications, a *Victoria's Secret* catalog, something from Ed McMahon, and that number ten–size white envelope.

"Just one for you," the young woman in charge of going through the mail said to Selden as she handed him Tombstone's daily exercise in exasperation.

"Thanks," the agent said.

The young woman cracked the gum she was chewing. "My pleasure," she said.

⊕   ⊕   ⊕

The three-game series against the New York Mets flew by in a quite literal crack of the bat for Louise and her teammates. It was a dream series, so to speak, one in which every aspect, every nuance of the game, clicked into place, at least for the home team.

Bob Dixon added four homers to his total, while Louise added that many in stolen bases, getting some eight hits in fourteen times at bat. But theirs weren't the only hot bats. Seemingly every Meteorite player was touched by magic—that rainbow dust of Babe Ruth ash that a few times every season covers a team or two and makes their every move into a soon-to-be textbook example of baseball genius. Nothing could go wrong, and even mistakes scored runs.

As for the Mets, well, everything did go wrong—even an obvious home run was called a foul ball by the umpiring team. It was a nightmare, a three-game nightmare they'd just as soon forget.

The Meteorites won the first game, 9–1, amassing a total of eighteen hits. They won the second game, 12–4, putting up a fifteen under "hits" in the box score. And they were leading in the third game by seven runs to the Mets' none.

Reggie Borders was on the mound with one out in the top of the ninth when he gave up a bloop single to one of the Mets' utility outfielders. It was only the second hit off Reggie that sunny Sunday afternoon—Manhattan Meteorite Tube Sock Day. But still it bothered him, depressed him, annoyed the fucking shit out of him. He faced down the next batter and quickly worked the count to two strikes. The next two pitches were fouled off. Then Reggie hit pay dirt.

"A bouncer right into the glove of Jesus Maldonado," Kurt Rybak announced.

"An easy double-play ball," Junella Wingi said. Jesus to Elvis to Louise."

"The Meteorites have swept the Mets and now find themselves in sole possession of first place."

"Wow! I've got goose bumps all over."

"How do you think they feel down on the field?"

"I think they feel fantastic!"

"True enough."

Down on the sweet-smelling grass of South Field, the Manhattan Meteorites players hugged and jumped and butt-patted one another into oblivion, to a soundtrack of cheers from the 38,710 fans in attendance. The fans had once again witnessed a miracle—never before in the history of professional sports had a first-year expansion team led its division beyond the halfway point. Never had a first-year expansion team lead its division three games into the season.

"I don't fucking believe it," Jesus Maldonado yelled as they arrived in their clubhouse.

Bob Dixon just sat and shook his head in disbelief. "First place," he said. "Christ!"

Louise just smiled—the experience was numbing, out-of-body, fucking weird.

"Hey, Gehrig," Jesus said. "We fucking did it, man. We fucking did it." He threw his arms around the first baseperson and hugged her so hard that he lifted her a few inches off the floor.

Lefty looked around at his players, and thought, This feels good. Really good. Now if we can just hold on.

Cole Robinson and his pin-striped teammates weren't having equal luck against the Seattle Mariners. They won only one game out of four, and that by a score of 1–0 on a nothing less than inspired pitching performance by Cole. And after their weekend series the team suddenly found itself three games out of first, in third place behind the Red Sox and the Brewers, and only a game up on the fourth-place Blue Jays.

It was frustrating, but not nearly as frustrating as the fact that the Yankees were heading home for a quickie three-game series against the Indians while the Meteorites were heading out on the road for a quickie three-game series in St. Louis.

That was real frustration.

On the night that the team found itself in sole possession of first place, Margaret and Bob decided that their wedding would take place on Saturday, November 11, and that, if it was okay with Louise—and Margaret was quite sure it would be—they'd get married in the presence of but a handful of friends, family members, and teammates, in the living room of her Charles

Street apartment, with the New York skyline standing in as a witness in the background.

It was then that Bob suggested they ask his old Mets teammate, closer John Franco, to marry them.

"He's a justice of the peace," Bob explained.

"Think he'd do it?" Margaret asked.

"Are you kidding. He'd kill me if I didn't ask."

"Then it sounds good to me."

"Are you sure? I mean, if you prefer to check into the church thing."

"Bob. When was the last time you went to church?"

"Um. When I got baptized," he said. "I think."

"Right. And I didn't even have Louise baptized. I tried, but the priest, this old friend of my father's, told me the godparents weren't suitable. I asked why, and he explained that they weren't Catholic. I explained they weren't any religion. And he said that was even worse."

"So, what'd you end up doing?"

"I told him to go fuck himself. That I didn't want or need to belong to a club that didn't want me as a member."

"So, a big church wedding isn't your lifelong dream?"

"It's never even crossed my mind."

"C'mon. Never?"

"Honest."

"So, I should call John?"

"Getting married by John Franco would be an honor."

Bob smiled.

"What are you thinking?"

"Ah, just that I'm glad I asked."

"What? About John Franco?"

"No. You to marry me."

⚾ 19 ⚾

Streakin'

Pending marriages and sexual tension aside, the Manhattan Meteorites were on a serious midseason roll. After sweeping the Mets at home and then the Cardinals out in St. Louis, they returned home for a seventeen-game home stand and quickly won their next six games: two against the Astros, two against the Dodgers, and two against the Padres. Counting their three straight wins over Buffalo immediately preceding the All-Star break, the team had aced fifteen in a row, and with their arch enemies—if a first-year expansion team can actually *have* an arch enemy—the Atlanta Braves coming into South Field for a midweek two-game series, they were 61–39, twenty-two games over .500. The hottest team in baseball was about to take on, well, the hottest team in baseball. And with that much heat, sparks would most assuredly fly.

⚾   ⚾   ⚾

"True enough."

"Y'know, I heard that before the game," Junella Wingi announced to her and Kurt Rybak's NYTV audience, "tickets to yesterday afternoon's and tonight's games were being scalped outside the stadium for as much as five hundred dollars each."

"It's madness," Rybak said. "New York City has gone completely nuts for this team."

"But you have to admit. Anyone who came to South Field yesterday got their money's worth—no matter what they spent on tickets."

"True enough. Reggie Borders was dazzling."

"Dazzling isn't good enough. There isn't a word in any language to describe last night's performance. I mean, when was the last time a pitcher threw two no-no's in the same year?"

"I know Nolan Ryan did it in '73," Rybak said. "Let me pull up the old *Baseball Encyclopedia* on the computer screen. Here we go. Yeah. Ryan in '73 for the Angels. Jim Maloney had two no-hitters for the Reds in '65. Virgil Trucks had two in '52 for the Tigers. A year earlier, Allie Reynolds did it for the Yankees. And Johnny Vander Meer for the Reds in 1938."

"So, Reggie is only the sixth pitcher in history to have two no-hitters in the same year."

"And he's in some pretty interesting company. I've never heard of half those guys.

"How many Hall of Famers?"

"Only Nolan."

"Old Nolan is in a league by himself," Wingi said. "Hey, while we're waiting for the game to start, I wanted to ask you what you thought about tonight's national anthem?"

"It was fabulous," Rybak said. "I just never thought I'd live to see the day when the New York City Gay Men's Choir could perform at a sporting event and actually be accepted."

"Accepted? They received a five-minute standing ovation."

"True enough. And then there's the food."

"It's PETA Vegetarian Night here at South Field. No hot dogs, no burgers."

"Veggie burgers."

"Have you tasted one?"

"Actually, with a little hot sauce, it was very good."

"The crowd seems to be eating them up."

"And speaking of the crowd. That sound in the background

can only mean one thing. The Meteorites are taking the field. It's time to get this show on the road."

"Strike three."

"Rocky Goetz is on tonight."

"Tell me that after Louise has a shot at him," Wingi said. "Or Dixon."

"There's the familiar chant of *Gehrig*. Geh-rig! Geh-rig!"

"Louise saunters over to the batter's box. She's tipping her hat to the crowd. Is that a million-dollar smile or what?"

"It's a five-million-dollar smile," Rybak said. "It's priceless."

"Braves catcher Pete Sacker calls for a curve, low and away. But Rocky is shaking him off. Sacker repeats the sign. Rocky again shakes his head. And it's time for a little conference at the mound."

"It's a little early in the game for conferences on the mound, don't you think?"

"Not when Balls is at the plate."

"Bats don't get any hotter. Unless they're in the hands of Bob Dixon."

"Louise is batting .647 over the past fifteen games. Her season average is up to .331. And her steal total is just five short of a C-note. A career year and she's only a rookie."

"Do I smell Hall of Fame?"

"If she can keep it up. Absolutely."

"She'll be the only other player besides Nolan Ryan to make it in with 100 percent of the vote."

"I hate to disagree," Wingi said. "But you know there'll be some bozo who doesn't vote her in because of the gender factor. Y'know, the Arnold Loitens of the world."

"And that's a shame."

"The meeting's over."

"Looks like it got a little hot out there."

"There's a definite rivalry between Rocky and Louise. "It's almost as if he had something to prove."

"He's a man, isn't he?"

"Uh-huh."

"What? No comment?"

"I don't want to disgrace my gender."

"Never."

Rybak cleared his throat. "Moving on. Sacker gives Rocky the call for the fastball."

"Obviously what the pitcher wanted."

"Uh-huh. Rocky sets. He winds up, and, whoa!"

"Strike one."

"I think that pitch gave the radar man whiplash."

"Louise just watched it."

"She rarely swings at the first pitch."

"Make that absolutely, positively never."

"True enough."

"Louise digs in a little. Sacker gives Rocky the universal sign for the fastball."

"Yeah. But check out which finger he's using."

"Pete Sacker's not a happy camper."

"Maybe he can see into the future."

"Rocky sets, winds up, and . . ."

"She hits a rocket."

"Wow!"

"That ball is going . . . going."

"That ball has left the building."

"A home run for Louise Gehrig."

"Her twelfth of the season."

"Did she smoke that? Or what?"

"Check out Rocky. He's just glaring at her as she rounds the bases."

"We've seen every one of Louise's dingers but I'd have to say she's enjoying this one the most."

"Even more than the ones off Eddie Bonaventura."

"And she just got her fifth homer off ol' Eddie last week."

"The crowd is going absolutely nuts."

"They love her."

"What's not to love?"

"Jesus holds at second."

"That ball was just inches short of being a home run."

"Rocky is definitely rattled."

"Louise can do that to pitchers."

"And so can the next batter," Wingi said.

"Forty-five home runs on the year with sixty-one games to go, counting today's."

"Think he can do it?"

"I don't know, but it's sure gonna be fun watching him try."

"Dixon steps in. Sacker sends the sign."

"He's calling for the junk ball, but Rocky's shaking him off."

"Don't tell me he's gonna throw the fastball. That used to be Dixon's Achilles' heel. But not this season."

"Sacker gives him the sign for the slider, but Rocky shakes him off again. The catcher stands, takes a few steps toward the mound, then shakes his head and turns around."

"He shook himself off."

"Sure enough, he's giving Rocky the sign for the fastball. And here comes the pitch."

"And there goes number forty-six!"

"And RBIs number 111 and 112."

"Not bad for a thirty-six-year-old."

"Not bad for anyone."

"And look at that. Braves skipper Keith Hernandez is walking to the mound. It looks like this is going to be it for Rocky Goetz."

"Rocky is livid."

"I don't think he's ever been pulled this early in a game."

"Hernandez wants to stop the bleeding."

"This is going to murder Rocky's ERA."

"Maybe next time he'll listen to his catcher."

"I doubt it."

"And the game is in the books."

"It couldn't end fast enough for the Braves."

"True enough."

"Final line score. The Braves: one run, five hits, two errors, with seven men left stranded. The Meteorites: seventeen runs, twenty-one hits, no errors, with five players left on base."

"And we'll be right back with the happy recap."

Atlanta	000	100	000		1	5	2
Manhattan	306	401	12		17	21	0

That night, Cole Robinson called Louise from his hotel room in Memphis. "I just saw the highlight reel," he said. "It was all Meteorites."

"We had a good night."

"Yeah. I'd say so." He laughed slightly. "Think we could borrow some of your magic. How about if you and your stepdad-to-be come over and play in pinstripes for a while."

"Don't you think someone might notice?"

"Only because we'd be winning games."

"C'mon," Louise said. "You're not doing that badly."

"We're still in the race, I guess."

"Four and a half games is not a lot at this point in the season."

"I guess."

"I guess you'd prefer to be seven games up?"

"That'd be fine for starters."

"Oh, yeah," Louise said, smiling. "What else would you like?"

Cole sighed. He knew she was smiling, could feel its warmth, picture its colors, radiating over the fiber-optic lines. Ahh . . . technology! "To finally get to turn in that rain check. I guess."

"You guess?"

"No, I know. Yeah. That's what I want more than just about anything."

"The feelings are mutual."

"I hope so."

"They are," Louise said, wishing she too could see Cole in the flesh. For two weeks she had dieted on late-night calls and news highlights, and desperately wanted more. But just as fate can be unkind to lovers, so can major league baseball schedules.

And no two schedules were more opposite than those of the Yankees and the Meteorites. When one team was at home, the other was on the road. It was as simple as that. The Mets filled in the blanks—they played half their home games competing for baseball fans with the Yankees, the other half against the Meteorites. It all sort of worked out—except for Louise and Cole.

And though they most likely could have found a way to be together—to cash in Cole's rain check—they both realized sadly that such an effort would only draw attention—vast amounts of press: screaming headlines and sound bites from Rush Limbaugh—to their situation. And a media blitz was the last thing they needed, the last thing they wanted, even if it would somehow symbolize that they had finally succeeded in obtaining what they needed and wanted most.

⚾ **20** ⚾

Everybody Was Kung Fu Fighting

The Meteorites' winning streak continued one game beyond the Atlanta series, then ended at eighteen when the Cubs won their fourteen-inning Saturday afternoon matchup, 8–7. But, as more than one baseball analyst was quick to point out, with a record of 64–40, the Manhattan team could play .500 ball for the remaining two months of the season and still win the division. The Mets were eight games back and barely holding on. The Marlins had slipped to fourth place with a record of 49–51, while the Cubs had moved into third place with a three games over .500 record of 53–50.

Over in the NL West, the Braves might as well have been popping their Dom Pérignon corks. Despite the two losses to the Meteorites, they had the best record in all of baseball, 70–33. They were *the* team, the bad boys of baseball—in the tradition of the '86 Mets or the '89 A's—rude, crude, and nasty. The Braves could come back from almost any deficit—they knew how to win. And they were absolutely intent on repeating as world champs, Louise Gehrig or no Louise Gehrig.

The first two weeks of August were kind to both divisional leaders. The Meteorites won eleven out of fifteen, after taking the rubber game in the Chicago Cubs series that had ended their winning streak. The Braves were 10–5, with an eight-game winning streak on their side, as they ventured back to the mean streets of Manhattan for their midmonth two-game series in South Field. Rocky Goetz was scheduled to pitch the second game, and he couldn't wait. He was itching to once again face off against the Meteorites' first baseperson. He was as eager as all hell.

The Meteorites won the first of the two games against Atlanta, a Wednesday afternoon meeting, on a ninth-inning dinger from Bob Dixon—his fifty-second—by the score of 4–3.

That evening Louise went to dinner and the movies with her mom, and afterward they grabbed a few ice cold Rolling Rocks at The Cowgirl Hall of Fame & Bar-B-Q on Hudson Street, just around the corner and down the block from where Louise lived.

When Louise arrived back at her Charles Street apartment, the message counter of her telephone answering machine registered 1. She glanced at her watch. It was approaching 1:00 A.M., but Cole and his teammates were in Anaheim playing a night game against the Angels, one that wouldn't be over until at least 2:00 A.M. East Coast time. She shrugged—maybe there was a rain delay—then punched the play button.

Beep.

"Louise. It's Matt Stern. I assume you've heard the news about Justice Dougherty. The press has been calling nonstop for a statement. Give me a call as soon as you get in, and we'll come up with something appropriate. Bye."

Beep. Beep. Beep.

"A heart attack," Matt Stern explained.

"When?"

"Last night apparently. I guess he never showed up for a dinner engagement at his daughter's, and she got worried."

"But he seemed so full of life."

"That he did. I had asked him to throw out the first ball at our last home game of the season."

"Was he going to do it?"

"Are you kidding? Said he wouldn't miss it for the world. He called it 'the first game of the rest of Louise Gehrig's baseball life.' "

"Yeah," Louise said, all the other words choking up somewhere in her throat.

"But, hey . . . Dougherty lived a long time—especially considering the enemies he made. I'm sure he had no regrets."

"That's something, at least."

"It's more than most of us can say."

Louise hung up and headed off to bed, wondering about regrets, cosmic, personal, and otherwise. Then she thought about enemies. Tombstone. What had Louise done to justify his/her/its hatred? Other than to be born female.

"Not a blessed thing," she said aloud, drifting off into dreamland.

⚾   ⚾   ⚾

The next afternoon, Louise called Mike Francesca during his drive-time shift on the FAN and relayed her sorrow to the tristate listening audience: "I am deeply saddened by the death of Justice Dougherty," she told him. "If it hadn't been for him, I don't believe I'd be playing professional baseball. But granting me permission to play was the least of his accomplishments. The man was at the forefront of the civil rights movements. He supported women's rights, abortion rights, and always the right to free speech. He was a great man. An honest man. A man who followed his heart. And he will be greatly missed."

"If you could say something to Dougherty," Francesca asked, "what would it be?"

"I had a dream last night, that he and my grandfather, Joe Gehrig, became friends, and they were watching all the games together from these great field box seats up in heaven. They were sitting between Lou Gehrig and Babe Ruth. Jackie Robinson, Casey Stengel, Shoeless Joe Jackson, and Ty Cobb were sitting in the row behind them."

"That's a pretty wild dream."

"Yeah. And if that's somehow the case, I'd ask him to say hello to my grandfather for me. To tell him that I'm doing okay, and that I love him."

⑪　　　⑪　　　⑪

The next evening, Lefty Johnson asked Louise if she'd prefer to sit out the game. "No," she said, explaining, "I haven't missed a game yet. I'm not about to start now."

Reggie Borders was pitching, his twenty-fifth start of the season. And with his current record of 18–5, with that one no-decision, and an ERA of 1.67, the Cy Young looked quite in the proverbial bag.

For the Braves, Rocky Goetz was on the mound, making his twenty-fourth official start—one game had been lost to a rain delay and later rescheduled. He was 15–6, with two no-decisions and an ERA of 2.89—abnormally inflated due mainly to his last outing against the Meteorites. But still, the Cy Young would most assuredly be his, if the voters could only pretend Reggie never existed.

There was a definite buzz in the air of South Field as the Manhattan team took the field for the start of the game. The night was hot, in the very high eighties, and the sun was lingering in the sky, not sure if it should set, or maybe too damn lazy to. Or maybe the old sun knew what was coming, tipped off by Norven on his way to the cosmos.

The game started predictably enough with Reggie striking out the Braves leadoff man, Joey Lawrence. But then Atlanta center fielder Charlie Kravitz choked up on his bat and blooped a single into shallow right. It was his first hit ever against Reggie Borders. Lenny Varga, the Braves' first baseman, was next. He worked the count full before graciously grounding a perfect double-play ball Jesus Maldonado's way—Jesus to Elvis to Louise—and Reggie was out of the inning, and out of what little trouble there might have been.

⑪　　　⑪　　　⑪

It was Rocky's turn. Jamaine Young wasn't really a problem. Hell, Jamaine usually couldn't rent a hit off Rocky Goetz—not even if he agreed to pay for mileage. And sure enough, he popped up to the foul side of first base and was quickly retired by Lenny Varga.

Next came Number Four. Rocky had played out the scenario a hundred times in his head, and every time it was better—just *that much* better than the time before it. Man, revenge can be sweet.

Pete Sacker figured the first pitch call didn't matter much— Louise Gehrig never swung at the first pitch—but still, he wanted Rocky to understand that there wasn't a chance in hell that he was going to let him toss a fastball her way. It wasn't happening, not this time. Pete knew his team had enough problems winning a game from the Meteorites, and he wasn't about to lose one to stupidity, ego, or both.

Louise stepped into the batter's box.

Damn, Pete thought, the cheering gets louder for her every turn at bat. He watched as she nodded toward the umpire, and even sort of smiled his way. Pete smiled back, thinking, She's a good-looking woman. Then turning his attention to Rocky, he gave the pitcher the sign for a curve, low and away.

Rocky nodded.

What the fuck! Pete wondered, he's actually listening to me. Pete repeated the sign, just in case Rocky had misunderstood. The pitcher just nodded again, then smiled.

"Okay," Pete said under his breath.

Rocky set, wound up, and let fly.

The ball hit Louise high on the back of her right thigh—just below the derriere, where the muscle was hard. But it stung, stung like a motherfucker, she thought, dropping her bat, taking a few steps toward first, then a few toward the mound.

"C'mon, bitch!" Rocky yelled, a rabid foaming grin distorting his mouth. "Or are you too much of a pussy?"

"I'll show you who's a pussy!" Louise screamed. Then she lunged, she flew, and she landed feet first into Rocky's protective cup—a protective cup that cracked and gave way and hardly protected under the force of Louse's Bruce Lee–like kick.

Standing and brushing her uniform free of the pitching mound dirt, Louise looked down at the pitcher lying crumpled into a tight fetal position, his hands pressed hard against his throbbing groin. "Asshole," she muttered, turning on her cleats and heading toward the Meteorites dugout.

Passing the home plate umpire, who was giving her the thumbs-out sign indicating that she'd been tossed from the game, Louise said, "Yeah. Yeah. I know." Then motioning back toward the mound, she added, "I think he's out too."

The umpire nodded back just slightly, and even seemed to smile.

The crowd in South Field cheered and screamed and chanted her name.

She stepped down into the dugout, then back out for a moment—a curtain call of sorts. She waved to the crowd and screamed back, "That one's for you, Justice Dougherty!" As she walked past her startled teammates, who stood just short of the top step and gawked, Louise told Lefty, "I'll be in the shower."

"Okay," he said. Then glancing across the infield, he caught the gaze of Braves skipper Keith Hernandez, who shrugged and held out his hands, palms up—What can you do? Exactly, Lefty thought, watching as a few of the Atlanta players helped Rocky Goetz off the field.

What the fuck can you do?

⚾   ⚾   ⚾

BALLS KICKS ROCKY'S!

That *New York Post* front-page headline was Louise's favorite. It screamed out from newsstands everywhere the next morning—it screamed out over a photo of her landing a Bruce Lee–like kick at Goetz's nuts. She liked the image and headline so much, she had a copy framed. Once it was ready she would hang it in the living room of her Charles Street apartment: a war trophy of sorts.

A lot was written and even more was said about Louise's conduct toward Rocky Goetz. And while most thought it was an appropriate reaction—he was, after all, throwing at her—a select handful, including columnist Arnold Loiten, felt she should be at least fined, and maybe suspended.

During an interview by WFAN personality Ed Coleman, teammate Jamaine Young was among the many who offered his support.

"As much as I want to hate her," Jamaine said, "she goes and does something like this, and even I've got to sit back and cheer her on."

"I take it you're not Rocky's biggest fan?" Coleman said.

"He's got a little too much ego for my taste."

"If you don't mind me saying, that's coming from a ballplayer who's often been accused of thinking a little too much of his own abilities."

"Ed, I'm the first to admit it. I can be a real hot dog at times. But Rocky, he goes beyond that. He goes beyond being a jerk. He's an asshole, in the grandest sense of the word."

Coleman laughed, wishing that his listeners could have heard Jamaine's last sentence as uttered, and without the annoying, but FCC-regulated, *beep*.

$$\text{(ID)} \quad \text{(ID)} \quad \text{(ID)}$$

The public was likewise in Louise's corner. Even die-hard jockheads—the sort who usually bitched and moaned about a girl playing a man's game—phoned in the myriad radio sports talk shows to express their definitive opinions:

"She's got guts."

"She's got balls."

"Gotta give her credit."

"She stood up for herself. I respect that."

"Never thought I'd be saying this, but I'm a Louise Gehrig fan. She's the best thing to ever happen to the game."

"I love her."

"She certainly doesn't play like a girl."

"I just traded for her in my rotisserie league."

"I stopped following baseball about ten years ago, and she's brought me back."

"Louise Gehrig, will you marry me?"

Geraldine Willard was one of the few who felt Louise needed to be punished for what she did to the mighty Brave. Fined, or suspended, or slapped around—something. She couldn't be permitted to just get away with it. Could she? Certainly not, Geraldine figured. *Absolutely* not.

It had been months since Geraldine had seen her Kevin—since she lost him to the Meteorites' first baseperson. And though she at first enjoyed the newfound freedom, that cute assistant manager from the bank, the couple of one-night stands with hot young hunks from Atlanta's hippest nightspots, and this writer she had just started seeing, Geraldine was beginning to miss her husband. She hated to admit it, but she still loved the lunkhead. And she'd gladly do anything—definitely *this,* and even some of *that*—if only he'd return. But she hadn't heard from him—not a word. And now the girls were beginning to whine—they all wanted their father back.

Geraldine sighed as images of where Kevin could possibly be played hide-and-seek in her head. Was he with her? Had he met her? Had he, well, done *this,* done *that,* or even *the other* to her? Damn it all, she thought, suddenly beginning to cry, appropriate punishments—a few embarrassing, a few debilitating, and a few far more deadly—filling the spaces left by the vacated tears. Damn that Louise Gehrig. This was all her fault. All her fault. Damn her!

On the Monday morning following "The Night the Cup Cracked," as it was dubbed by Mike Lupica, Louise was vacuuming her living room when her buzzer sounded. It was Ziggy telling her that a parcel had been left by the mailman. A parcel that was too large to fit into her mailbox.

A few moments later, that parcel was resting on her kitchen table. She stared at it. No return address. Just the To: portion of the priority mail label had been filled out. Over the stamp was a goddamn Atlanta, Georgia, postmark.

Louise thought for a moment about calling Agent Selden, but then, figuring she was just being silly, just being childish, she pulled a knife from her utensil drawer and sliced away at the packaging tape.

The box opened without a kaboom. It opened to reveal another box within, cradled lovingly by hundreds of little white styrofoam puffs. A Louise Gehrig action figure box. It was colorful, in Meteorite yellow and black, with Louise's smile plastered across the front. The doll inside was Barbie sized, dressed appropriately in Meteorite home whites. Accessories included a bat, a ball, and a glove.

"Hmmm," was what Louise uttered as she opened the top of the box and attempted to pull out the doll. A gasp was what was heard next in her kitchen, as only the tiny cap-covered head came out, severed as it was, by what was apparently a serrated-edge knife, from the rest of the doll.

Louise fought off the first wave of nausea as she placed the head down on the table and upended the box. The doll's arms and legs, hands, feet, and torso fell out. Not broken away, but also severed into countless pieces.

Holding the doll's body in her hands, she noticed the tears in its uniform. The number 4 had been ripped clear off, and the shirt was sliced open at the breasts.

"Jesus Christ!" she said when she examined the pants. They too were cut, sliced wide open at the crotch. But instead of revealing what should have been the doll's generic genitalia, details had been painted on: lifelike pinks and browns, and even a tuft of hair.

The masterpiece was even signed. In the tiniest of scripts, across the doll's right buttock, it read, "Tombstone."

⚊ 21 ⚊

About That Rain Check ...

Friday, September 1, 2000, was Trojan Condom Safe Sex Night at South Field. Every person over the age of fourteen attending the Meteorites' meeting with the Philadelphia Phillies would receive a free three-pack of Trojan lubricated latex condoms, each white pin-striped and emblazoned with the black-and-yellow Manhattan Meteorites logo.

"We better win this one," Lefty said to players before they took the field.

"What makes this game any different?" Bob Dixon asked.

"The condoms."

"Excuse me."

"If we start losing, you'll see condom balloons everywhere. It'll take hours to clean up the field."

"Think so?"

"Bob, all you need is one drunken idiot to start it off. Then to anyone who's had a beer or two, it'll seem like the greatest idea since the *Hindenburg.*"

Elvis Jones, who was listening in on the conversation, asked, "The what, skipper?"

Lefty turned to face his second baseman. "The *Hindenburg,*" he repeated. And when that got no reaction, "The zeppelin. A really big balloon."

"A really, really, really big balloon," Bob explained.

Elvis almost shrugged, but not exactly.

"Don't worry about it, Elvis," Lefty said. "Just go out there and kick some cheese steak butt."

Luckily for the grounds crew, the Meteorites did win, beating the Phillies by the score of 6–4.

| Philadelphia | 001 000 030 | 4 | 9 | 0 |
| Manhattan | 200 011 02 | 6 | 11 | 0 |

Later in their clubhouse, after the press conference, after the shower, after everyone was dressed and just about ready to go home, Louise grabbed for her gym bag. She could barely lift it.

"What the hell's in here?" she asked.

A few teammates shrugged innocently, but it was P.J. who cracked up first. Between laughs he asked, "Forget to eat your Wheaties, Gehrig?"

"I don't eat Wheaties, P.J.," Louise said. "Remember, I just got that Special K endorsement deal." Then, against her better judgment, she unzipped the canvas bag, and found it filled, found it jam-packed to the seams, with Meteorite condoms.

"It was Strykes's idea," Jesus said. "Honest."

"And a good one," Louise said with a keen smile, rezipping the bag, heaving its shoulder strap onto her shoulders, and heading toward the clubhouse exit.

"Hey," P.J. said, his laughter suddenly on pause. "Where you going?"

"Home," Louise said.

"You're taking the rubbers?"

"Yeah," she said, walking up to the closer, breathing-distance close. "Unlike you, P.J., I've got use for them."

Every teammate except P.J. burst out laughing. He was too busy blushing a dozen shades of red.

"Gentlemen," she said, tugging on the shoulder strap and raising her eyebrows Groucho Marx high, "if you'll excuse me"—she cleared her throat—"I've got some work to do." And Louise was off and out of the clubhouse, thinking all the while, I wish."

After the action figure incident, Wesley Selden was keenly aware of Louise's every move. He held back that Monday afternoon, and refrained from scolding her for opening what could have so easily been a mail bomb. Then he strongly suggested a bodyguard. Louise said she'd think about it. He insisted that she never again open a strange package without calling him first. To that she agreed.

Selden didn't really care whether or not she'd agree to the surveillance he had placed on her building. Around the clock, an agent would be within lunging distance. Drinking coffee at the shop across the street. Eating a slice of pizza next door. Reading a newspaper in a car up the block. There. Aware. Keeping an eye out. Louise didn't have to know.

On the road. Well, that was another story. But the bureau had its ways, it had its secret ins and outs, and Selden was a master at manipulating them. Hell, he had helped bring down Colombia's most notorious drug lord, keeping an eye on a ballplayer should be a piece of cake.

Their win against the Phillies was the exception for the Meteorites and not the rule, at least at that point in the season. The end of August had been hard on Louise and her teammates. During the fifteen-game stretch that took them through to the Labor Day weekend, the National League East leaders won only four games, and suffered through their longest losing streak of the season—six games: two each against the Rockies, the Giants, and the Astros, on the road—which, on Sunday, September 3, after a loss to those last-place Phillies, left them with a record of 81–56 and only four games up on the suddenly surging Mets.

Even Bob Dixon's bat had cooled—only two homers in the last two weeks of August, giving him a fifty-four on the year. He still needed six to tie Ruth, seven to tie Maris, and eight for a record of his own, and he had but twenty-seven games left in which to belt them out of the park.

The Braves, on the other hand, were on a steamroll to the land of the statistician's dream. At the same point in the season—with a month, the pennant chase month, to go—they were fifty games over the .500 mark, with some ninety-two wins versus forty-two losses, and playing some downright brilliant baseball. They were the only team with a magic number in reach—and that magic number was *four.* Any combination of Braves wins and second-place Cincinnati losses would mean a clinch of the pennant for Rocky Goetz and his teammates.

Over in the other league, the race between the Red Sox and the Yankees had suddenly taken on monumental proportions. The teams were locked in a dead heat race for first place—if public opinion polls were taken on such matters, the results would have them each possessing the exact same win-loss record, plus or minus, of course, three games. One day the Boston team would be in the lead, two days later the New Jersey Bombers would have taken their place. As for Milwaukee's club, the Brew Crew had fallen completely out of the race and were suddenly battling the Orioles for fifth place. The Blue Jays were stuck in third and fading fast because of injuries and some of the most stubborn slumps in recent baseball history.

To the AL West, the Nolan Ryan–managed Texas Rangers seemed the most likely division winners. They were nine games up on the second-place White Sox, and holding strong. Only a complete collapse of their top-notch pitching staff could possibly stop them from winning the West. And that, as most baseball analysts were quick to point out, was a very long shot indeed.

The Yankees were on the road over the Labor Day weekend for a two-game weekend series against Seattle followed by another two-game series against the San Francisco Bay Buccaneers. Like the Meteorites, they were playing a rare night game on the Monday holiday.

That morning, munching down a light breakfast in his City by the Bay hotel room, Cole Robinson, lustfully aching from head to toe to the tip of every appendage, glanced over what agony September held for both the Meteorites and his Yanks.

From San Francisco, Cole and his teammates would travel to Atlanta for a four-gamer against the Indians, while Louise and company would face off against the Cubs at home.

Each team had Monday the eleventh off, then the Yanks returned home for eight games, three with the Red Sox, two with the Tigers, and three with the Sideburns, while the Meteorites took to the road for four consecutive two-gamers, against the Braves, the Jazz, the Padres, and the Dodgers, respectively.

Then the Meteorites returned to South Field for four against the Mets and four against the Pirates, while the Yanks took to the road for two each against the Royals, Twins, White Sox, and Rangers. They were up in Boston for the final three games of the season, while the Meteorites traveled across town for their final three at Shea Stadium.

"Jesus Christ!" he muttered to himself, tossing the schedule aside. Another month. And then came the playoffs. Fuck!

He finished off his breakfast and was just about to hop into yet another cold shower when the phone in his hotel room began to ring. At first Cole continued toward his ice voyage, but after the seventh ring, figuring it might be important, he headed back into the room, reached over, and pulled the receiver from its bed.

"Hello," he said unenthusiastically.

"At least try to sound as if you're happy to hear from me," Louise said on the other end of the line.

"Louise," Cole said. "I didn't think it'd be you. I figured it was Winfield calling to scream about something or other. Y'know?"

"Yeah," Louise said. She knew all too well about road trips and constantly ringing hotel room telephones, though screaming managers were not part of her regular schedule.

"So, what's up?" Cole asked.

"I was wondering what you're doing next Monday," she asked.

He grabbed the schedule from the table. "Flying home, I guess."

"And where you flying home from?"

"Atlanta. Why?"

"We're flying into Atlanta on Monday."

Cole grunted a short, cheerless laugh. "That figures."

"No," Louise said. "You're not getting it. We have an afternoon game at home against the Cubs on Sunday and we don't play the Braves until Tuesday night. You have an afternoon meeting against the Indians on Sunday afternoon and you—"

"Don't play Boston until Tuesday night," Cole said, his mind suddenly clicking into gear. "So, if you catch the first plane out of New York on Sunday afternoon . . ."

"And you catch the last possible flight back home on Tuesday . . ."

"We'll actually . . ."

". . . be able . . ."

". . . to spend . . ."

". . . some time . . ."

". . . together."

⊕   ⊕   ⊕

That Labor Day night, Louise had the first five-hit game of her short career—three singles, a triple, and her fourteenth home run of the season. Couple that with four stolen bases, and the Meteorites' first baseperson couldn't help but snap the team's collective slump. Her energy, her vitality, her precision, were contagious: Jesus Maldonado hit for the cycle, Bob Dixon added two dingers to his inspiring total, and Jeff Carter hit two out of the park as well. And making his twenty-seventh start, Reggie Borders pitched a three-hit complete game shutout.

Buffalo	000	000	000	0	3	2
Manhattan	321	121	41	15	23	0

⚾   ⚾   ⚾

On the left side of the continent, Cole Robinson was doing
Reggie one better. A two-hitter against the Buccaneers—one of
the most brilliantly pitched games of his career. He teased, he
taunted, he pitched boner after boner his opponent's way, but
all the San Francisco Bay Buccaneers could come up with was a
series of quick, but premature, ejaculations—like teenagers in
heat, they fell to their more sophisticated rivals.

New Jersey	005	000	001	6	9	0
San Francisco	000	000	000	0	2	0

⚾   ⚾   ⚾

The rest of the week was a blur—a high-speed train ride of hits,
outs, and one or two hideous errors, a high-speed train ride
leading toward that desired head-on in-tunnel collision.

Both the Meteorites and the Yankees swept their short series
against Buffalo and San Francisco, respectively. Then Louise
and her mates took on the raging Cubs while Cole and the
Yanks traveled to Atlanta to face the recently displaced Indians.

But while the Cubs were no match for the hormones that had
put the Manhattan team back on track, the Indians proved themselves serious about a possible spoiler role—if they couldn't take
the pennant, and they never had a chance, then why should anyone else? Winning the first three easily against the unexpectedly
hapless New Jersey Bombers, the Indians bragged about a
sweep—it would be their first four-game sweep of *any* team this
season, their first four-game winning streak, and for it to happen
against the first-place Yankees would definitely be a feather in
their cap.

But on that Sunday afternoon, September 10, in the year
2000, the Indians would be facing Cole Robinson—not the average old Cy Young Award–winning Cole Robinson, but the Cole
Robinson who, in a few eternal hours, would be holding court
with Louise Gehrig. And while the old Cole Robinson could oc-

casionally be beatable, could occasionally give up the odd run, this new, improved model was a motherfucking terminator of a pitcher to end all.

Cole hadn't planned on pitching the greatest game of his career. He only wanted to pitch the fastest—not velocity-wise, but time-wise. He wanted to be in his rent-a-car and out of the stadium within two hours of the first pitch.

Walking out of the dugout with his catcher, Cole barked the following instruction: "All fastballs."

"What was that?" the catcher asked.

"Fastballs. Nothing but fastballs."

"But what if—"

"No signs are needed."

"What is this, a no-huddle defense?"

"Call it whatever you want."

Once on the mound, Cole threw one quick warm-up pitch, and nodded to the umpire that he was indeed ready to begin. The first Indian stepped to the plate. Cole set, wound up, and delivered.

"Strike one!" the ump yelled.

Shaking his head slightly, the catcher tossed the ball back to Cole, who immediately set, wound up, and let fly.

"Strike two!" the ump yelled.

With a small smile playing at the corners of his mouth, the catcher flung the ball back to Cole, who set, wound up, and again delivered.

The batter muttered something like, "That's too fucking fast," but was drowned out by the umpire calling, "Strike three, you're out!"

The Yankees catcher smiled broadly and tossed the ball back to Cole. He wasn't really sure what the pitching ace was up to, but if could throw a fastball like that, then, hell, let him.

Six pitches later the inning was over.

Back in the Yankees' dugout, Yankee skipper Dave Winfield asked Cole, "You okay, kid?"

"Fine. Why?"

"You seemed to be in a hurry out there. I kept wondering where the fire was."

"No fire, Coach," Cole said, knowing better. "Just feeling on."

"Okay," Winfield said. "Just figured I'd ask."

During the top of the ninth inning, the Yankees' catcher took a seat at the far end of the dugout next to Cole Robinson. "Nervous?" the catcher asked.

Cole turned and sort of looked his way. He wondered, Could anyone possibly know? Then he nervously asked, "About what?"

"The no-hitter."

"No-hitter?" Cole repeated, adding a question mark to the phrase.

"Only three more outs to go," the catcher said.

Cole laughed. "Oh, yeah. Right."

"Well are you?"

"Nervous?" The pitcher took a very deep breath. "Yeah, a little," he said.

The catcher nodded, then turned his attention out to the field. The bases were loaded and his teammates had the opportunity to add to their one-run lead. But one pitch and a double play later, it was time to retake the field. "Just fastballs, right?" he asked, standing.

"Just fastballs," Cole said, darting past on his way to the mound.

"Thought so."

Nine pitches later, Cole Robinson had the first no-no of his career in the history books. And though the Indians' pitchers had limited his Yankee teammates to only one run, one run was enough.

New Jersey	000	001	000	1	7	0
Atlanta	000	000	000	0	0	0

Complete game time: one hour, forty-eight minutes.

Immediately following the last pitch of the ninth inning, Cole turned and headed toward the dugout. The Yankees catcher considered running over to give him a bear hug and congratulate him, as was the no-hitter custom, but after a split second of mental deliberation, thought better of it.

The first person to speak to Cole was a reporter, his video shooter in tow. He shoved a microphone in front of the pitcher's face and, as was the Walt Disney Corporation custom—reporters everywhere knew they could earn a cool ten grand if they delivered a plug for Disneyland or Walt Disney World from a major pro player immediately following some historic sporting moment, such as the winning of any championship, the hitting of a hole in one, the breaking of some supposedly unbreakable record, or the pitching of a no-hitter—said, "Cole Robinson, you've just pitched your first no-hitter. What are you gonna do now?"

Cole glared at the reporter and, enunciating a little too perfectly, said, "It's none of your fucking business," before pushing him out of his way. Then, a few rushed giant steps later, the pitcher ran into Winfield at the top of the visiting dugout steps. He yelled over the roar of the appreciative Atlanta crowd, "I'm leaving now. I'll catch up with the team in Boston on Tuesday."

But before the Yankee skipper could order Cole to stay for the postgame press conference, before his mind could even think up an order of any sort, Cole was gone, down the dugout steps, through the visitors' clubhouse, out to the parking lot, and into the front seat of his Avis rent-a-car. Cole was not about to sit around and argue—he had just pitched a perfect game for Christ's sake. And now, finally, he'd get to celebrate. Fuck the postgame press conference. Fuck the press. Fuck Walt Disney. Cole had a date with Louise Gehrig and he needed to prepare. He needed everything to be right, he wanted everything to be perfect. He needed, he wanted . . . *argh* . . . if only he could breathe.

Louise was hardly having such luck. On the hot streak of her young career, she couldn't buy a strikeout, she couldn't rent a lazy pop fly right into the glove of the Cubs' center fielder, she couldn't even borrow an easy out. And man, if that wasn't driving her crazy.

Sunday afternoon's game against the Chicago team was the Meteorites' sixth win in a row and their second rout in three days. And by the bottom of the fifth inning, the game was already pushing three hours. Watching teammate after teammate after teammate get on base, Louise, usually the calming force in the dugout, was a pacing, sweating, cursing, nervous wreck, while other bench warming Meteorites, once gung ho sorts who'd yell and spit tobacco, chose to sit back, relax, catch up on their reading. Louise wanted to scream to her teammates, "How can you read at a time like this?" But she knew they'd never understand.

The nonstarting pitchers in particular were each immersed in what P.J. Strykes called the Bloodsuckers Union, a collection of seemingly every worthwhile vampire book ever written from Bram Stoker to Nancy A. Collins to Anne Rice. When Louise had asked P.J. about the vampire obsession, with a frightening straight face he told her that after reading *Interview with the Vampire* he wanted more than anything to be a vampire. "Louis or Lestat?" Louise has asked, not at all surprised when the team's star closer chose the latter. And though she for a moment considered informing P.J. that the vampire he so admired was most likely bisexual, if not altogether gay, she thought better of it for two reasons: 1) If she didn't tell him, he'd probably never know, and 2) Maybe he already understood more than she could possibly ever explain.

⚉ ⚉ ⚉

When the last Cub out was finally recorded at 6:11 P.M.—four hours, thirty-six minutes after the 1:35 first pitch—Louise and the gang had amassed a total of sixteen runs on twenty-three hits to the Cubs' two runs on four hits. And though two runs against the usually unhittable Reggie Borders might have made many a team proud, the Cubs had looked so bad for thirty-six consecutive innings that they just hung their heads and disappeared into South Field's visiting clubhouse.

Chicago	000	100	010	2	4	4
Manhattan	602	300	50	16	23	1

One second—not more, possibly less—after Elvis Jones caught a pop-up for the final out, Louise ran to her locker, threw on an old pair of jeans and a well-worn black silk shirt, traded in her cleats for a pair of Doc Marten's, and let down her hair. Then, grabbing her gym bag, she said good-bye to Bob Dixon, and was off. Only Dixon, out of all the Meteorites, and the Yankees for that matter, knew of this Atlanta rendezvous. Louise had asked him to explain to Lefty and anyone else who might ask that she needed to leave early, and would meet up with the team at Fulton County Stadium.

And though Bob half expected Lefty to put up some sort of fuss—the postgame press conference and whatnot—the Meteorites' skipper simply shrugged and said, "Okay."

"Okay?" Bob asked. "It's not a problem?"

The manager shrugged. "The way Louise has been producing, she wants to cut out early once in a while and catch up with us later, you think I'm gonna argue? Hell, she can even have Tuesday's game off, if she wants. The kid deserves a rest."

Bob thought to himself for a moment, then, figuring what the hell, asked, "Can I have Tuesday's game off?"

"No," Lefty said.

"But I've been producing."

"You've been having a phenomenal season," Lefty said. "But you need as many at bats as you can get. If I remember correctly, you're after this record. Or do I have to remind you?"

"Ah, no. You don't have to remind me."

"As I calculate it, you're still a few dingers short."

"A half dozen."

"With nineteen games left."

"Got'cha."

"Good. Now hit the showers."

Louise made the 6:55 P.M. American Airlines flight out of La
Guardia Airport with seconds to spare. She settled into her first-
class seat in an otherwise empty first-class cabin. She had three
hours and some nine minutes in which to work herself into an
even more delirious frenzy. Relax, she thought to herself. Relax.
Relax. Re-*fucking*-lax! She exhaled deeply a few times, then
turned to her personal video screen, switching it on just in time
to catch the afternoon's sports roundup. The big news was
Cole's no-hitter, with his sixteen strikeouts edited together into
a string of jump-cut delirium. Then there was another win for
the Meteorites, and a loss for the Braves—their third in a row.
And though their magic number was down to one, the sportscaster more or less announced that their next opponents—
Louise and company—were not about to willingly give the
Braves that pennant-winning pleasure. The sportscaster went on
to add that Braves manager Keith Hernandez was considering
keeping pitching ace Rocky Goetz out of the upcoming two-
game series against the Manhattan team. "I can't risk losing
Rocky," Hernandez said.

That made Louise laugh, and even took her mind away from
Cole. A steward interrupted the vision of her cleats connecting
with Rocky's groin with the question of, "Can I get you a
drink?"

"Yeah," Louise said, suddenly and inexplicably relaxed, relaxed and very happy. "What do you have?"

At the postgame press conference, Special Agent Selden pan-
icked when Louise Gehrig was a no-show.

"Where's Louise?" he asked Lefty.

The manager shrugged. "Wanted to leave early. Told Dixon
she'd catch up with us in Atlanta."

Selden kept the string of obscenities that were bouncing
around in his head to himself. After the press had had its turn,
he cornered, then questioned the catcher.

"What's up with Louise's little disappearing act?"

"I beg your pardon."

"Where'd she go?" Selden asked.

A shrug. "Just told me she needed some time to herself," Bob lied. "Why?"

"Why the fuck do you think?" Selden said, punching the closest locker. "We've got some fruit loop running around who'd like to see her dead."

Louise's instructions echoed in Bob's head. "Don't tell anyone where I'm going, or who I'll be with. Especially Selden." He feigned ignorance. "I'm telling you what she told me," he said. "I'm sure she'll be all right."

Selden didn't say anything else. He just backed off and radioed for his supporting players to meet him in his makeshift office. It was one thing to watch her from a block away. But he knew he couldn't save her life if he didn't even know where she was.

Louise always hated Atlanta's William B. Hartsfield International Airport—of all the airports in all the cities into which she and her teammates regularly flew, none was more confusing or less rewarding. Seats were uncomfortable, the concession food sucked, and even the news racks had a bad selection of magazines. But as she raced from the Boeing 707, her carry-on slung over her shoulder, she had no complaints. In fact, she had never been happier to see an airport before, and would have probably even loved the food, marveled at the wide and varied selection of reading material, and fallen fast asleep in one of the plush waiting area chairs, if she hadn't been in such a hurry to get the hell out of there.

"The Hyatt," she said, slipping into the backseat of an awaiting taxi cab. The anxiety was back—coupled with fear and a little nausea. But as the cab took to the Atlanta streets—Peachnuts onto Peachfuzz and finally onto Peachtree—and that gleaming tower with the familiar Hyatt logo appeared on the horizon, the feelings in the pit of her stomach melted into a blessed rush, and the Manhattan Meteorites' star first baseperson couldn't help but smile. She was in Atlanta with some forty plus hours to kill. And so was Cole Robinson. And all those weeks—almost nine weeks—of aural stimulation via whispers and niceties and highlight reels—would finally come to a head. Damn, she thought to herself with a funky little smile as she slipped the driver thirty bucks and told him to keep the change, this had better be worth the wait.

22

Reciprocation

Louise walked briskly through the highly polished lobby of the Hyatt Regency, straight toward the elevator banks. Pressing the call button, she looked around at the collection of chrome and ferns that seemed to prevail in all big-city hotels. The elevator went *ding*, its door opening. She entered the empty car alone, pressed the button for the twenty-second floor, and was off.

Trying to ignore a Muzak version of Gang of Four's "I Love a Man in a Uniform," Louise thought about the easy anonymity—walking unnoticed, un-may-I-please-have-your-autographed—with which she had crossed the hotel lobby. It was amazing how much difference a baseball cap, or lack thereof, could make.

On the twenty-second floor, the elevator once again went *ding* before opening its door. She exited the car and read the highly polished brass plaque which gave directions: Suites 2201–2205 to the right; Suite 2206–2210 to the left. She turned right and headed down the hall, passing the first four doorways—2201, 2202, 2203, and 2204—single doorways each, before reaching the massive double door marked 2205. That was the room Cole promised he'd be waiting in. She had checked the handwritten note to herself in the cab just before it pulled up to the hotel entrance, then again in the elevator. And now she checked it one last time. Yup—2205, that's what he'd said. So, taking a very, very deep breath, Louise put the crumpled note back into her pocket and knocked.

Once.

Twice.

"Hello," Cole said, opening the door before Louise could get in that crucial third knock.

"Hi," Louise said.

It was an *Annie Hall* sort of moment: Louise standing in the hallway, her knocking arm still pitched and ready to hammer lightly on one of suit 2205's double doors—well, la di da, la, la.

Cole stood in the open doorway, a gracious smile plastered to his face. Neither was breathing—not really. And neither could think of anything to say. They just stood and stared—like bad wax figures sans uniforms from a hellish nonexistent Madame Tussaud offshoot museum in Cooperstown, New York. Even their minds were on pause. Only their hearts seemed to be working properly, and putting in a hell of a lot of overtime at that. Pumping, rerouting all that blood to destinations south.

Louise spoke first. "Can I come in?" she asked.

"Ah, yeah," Cole said, moving aside. "Of course."

Louise entered suite 2205, brushing past Cole Robinson—the magnetic pull of her silk shirt against his cotton button-down, her 501s against his. She looked about the massive room. "Very nice," she said.

"Thanks. I did my homework. Every guidebook said this place had the grandest rooms in all of Atlanta."

"Yeah," she said, taking in the gleaming parquet floors and miles of orientals, the tame Van Gogh and Picasso copies, the oversize sofa and love seat, the entertainment center—Billie Holiday was playing softly, something from the Verve box set— the small breakfast table, the desk, the balcony peeking through the sheer curtain–covered double sliding glass doors, and the other doors, all wood, leading to, well, other parts of the suite. She nodded. "Grand is definitely the word for it."

"There are two bedrooms," Cole said. "I've taken the one through there." He pointed at one of the doors, the only open one. "I left the bigger one for you," he added, sincerely, pointing at yet another door—a double door, which was closed.

Louise nodded. A flophouse with a fold-up bunk bed would have sufficed. But this was nice. Definitely doable.

"Can I get you a drink or anything?" Cole asked, suddenly sounding more like an airline steward than a baseball player.

"A shower," Louise said, very aware of the splashes of Chanel Number Five covering layers of perspiration. "I could really use a shower."

Cole smiled. "Check this out," he said, leading the way into the bedroom reserved for Louise.

"Jesus!" she half muttered upon entering the room. It was as large as the parlor, with a monster-size bed—bigger than king-size by at least a yard in both directions—perched up on a raised platform, another entertainment center, a dressing area, a walk-in closet, and more bureaus than Louise could ever begin to fill.

"Over here," Cole said, standing before yet another door.

Louise walked over and peeked in. It was a master bathroom virtually identical to the one in her Charles Street apartment. "I don't believe this," Louise said.

"What?" Cole asked. "Is something wrong?"

"No," she said. "Not at all." She inspected the Jacuzzi tub for four, the environmental shower; hell, even the faucets were an exact match. "It's like this bathroom and my bathroom at home came from the same set of blueprints."

"Really?"

"Yeah," she said.

"You have a bathroom like this at home?"

"Doesn't everybody?" she asked with a sexy smile.

He smiled back. "That is a serious shower."

"And how would you know?"

"I had some time to kill, so I washed up."

"I thought this was my room."

"I didn't think you'd mind."

She harrumphed loudly. "Well, okay, I guess. This once. But don't let it happen again."

"I won't. I promise."

That silence again.

A few shrugs.

"Well," Cole finally said. "I'll let you take yours."

"Okay."

More shrugs.

Cole moved toward the doorway.

Louise turned on the water. Hot.

"Cole," she said.

"Yeah."

"Y'know, we could always take a shower together."

He gulped hard and nodded twice. "We could?"

"Would definitely break the ice."

"No ice," he agreed.

More silence.

Louise shrugged and kicked off the Docs, then began unbuttoning the silk shirt—first the cuffs, then the front, beginning at the top.

Cole watched, mesmerized and lost in a libidinous daze.

"Are you going to join me?" Louise asked. "Or just watch?"

Cole inhaled and thought, Either would be just fine, then reversed himself, admitting that the former would be a hell of a lot more enjoyable than the latter—at least at this early stage. He kicked off his shoes and went to work buttoning down the cotton button-down.

"That's more like it," Louise said.

Cole stepped forward into her arms. They kissed, their tongues dancing about in each other's mouths as they helped each other out of the remaining articles of clothing, then clumsily into the steaming shower. The sensation of the cold ceramic tiles against Louise's back versus the hot spray of the shower on her arms and side, and all that coupled with the heat emanating from Cole—his mouth, his hands, his cock as they explored her every curved inch—was way too much for the first baseperson to take. Louise came quick, and she came sudden. Once, twice, hell, she lost count—it was an endless string of little oh's, and that was just BP.

"Would you like something to eat?" It was Cole playing the part of steward again.

"Yeah," Louise said, thinking it was time to refuel. "Dinner'd be nice." Looking over the room service menu, she decided on a large spinach salad, a fresh baguette, and some crème brûlée for desert. To drink they agreed on a bottle of Beaujolais. While Cole ordered up the meal, Louise replayed the previous hour or so in her head. First there was the shower—she'd rate that an A+. It had been a long time for her, but an even longer time for Cole, who hadn't, well, since Jennifer. And judging from his quick finish, Louise didn't doubt that for a minute. Though he didn't last much longer during the second inning, she had to admit that the huge bed was a much better playing field, and damn, the man had God-given ability with his mouth. Uh-huh. Another A+—no arguing that. She could still feel the repercussions—an army of tingles marching outward from her privates. *Hut-two-three-four, we want Cole to lick some more.* She giggled to herself—oh, they call this puppy love—then sighed.

"What's so funny?" Cole asked.

"Nothing," she said. "Just feeling silly."

He lay back down next to her on the bed.

"How long until we eat?"

"Twenty to thirty minutes."

Louise smiled. "Twenty to thirty minutes, huh?" she said, thinking, Damn, that's more than enough time.

"That's what the man said."

"In that case . . . ," she said, then nothing more, as she rolled over on top of him and took a hungry nibble at his tongue, all the while proud of herself for saving that gym bag filled with Meteorites condoms, all the while ecstatic that they were finally being put to some good use.

After dinner Cole disappeared into the bathroom for a moment and very self-consciously brushed his teeth, flossed, then gargled. Louise thought about doing the same for a moment (the Hyatt's house salad dressing definitely had more than a sprinkling of garlic), but then thought otherwise. She had a different agenda to follow, one in which bad breath mattered little.

She looked about the room for a clock of some sort, and spotting one ticking away on the marble mantel of an oversize fireplace, she saw that it was almost two o'clock, Monday morning. Ninety-nine point seven percent of Atlanta's population was most probably fast asleep, or at least en route. So, wearing just an oversized T-shirt—a Yankee shirt, one of Cole's—Louise stepped out onto the suite's balcony—its very private balcony. It was warm and clear. The stars were out in droves and the moon was full. A handful of lights twinkled on and off in the slapdash skyline.

Through with dental hygiene, Cole returned. Noticing his lover's balcony jaunt through the sheer curtains, he watched for a moment, the sharp mint bite of the mouthwash still stinging his lips. Louise was leaning forward, staring at everything, staring at nothing, her elbows resting on the balcony's railing. She swung her hip slightly from side to side to the beat of a Billie Holiday tune piped out from the main room. In the bent forward position, the T-shirt covered only the top portion of her behind. The sight made Cole shake, and feel, well, light-headed. It reminded him of the first time he saw a Van Gogh. He wanted so badly to reach out and touch the swirls of paint, to feel what the artist experienced, what the artist thought, what Van Gogh saw. In one afternoon at some forgotten museum, he had returned to stand before the painting at least a half dozen times. Each time the feeling was greater, more complex, and absolutely exhilarating. And though Cole knew he could never experience what God was thinking when he created Louise Kathleen Gehrig, Cole marveled at the notion that he could touch her swirls.

Taking one last long lingering look at Louise, he blinked down hard for a moment—like an instant camera his mind forever freezing that image. Cole needed to take that image with him through life so he could die a happy man. Cole needed to take Louise with him through life—that fact seemed so obvious. So painfully obvious. At least at the moment.

He took a deep breath and stepped out onto the balcony. "What do you see?" he asked, suddenly standing very close behind her.

Louise turned to face him. She smiled a dreamy faraway smile and dropped slowly to her knees.

"Hey," Cole said.

She loosened the belt of his terry cloth robe and let it fall open. It took only to the count of four in her head for Cole to spring to life. She nibbled at him slightly, and scratched the underside of his balls with her fingernails.

He gasped. "But what if . . . ?"

"Ssshhh," she said, never taking her eyes off the intended target. "And concentrate on the stars. I want this to last."

Louise and Cole never once left their hotel suite that Monday. When the maid knocked on the door and informed them that she needed to clean up the room, they told her to go away, that they'd just mess it up again anyway. They ordered room service breakfast, room service lunch, room service dinner, and room service snacks. They sipped wine out of each other's belly buttons—luckily they both had innies—and made love inside and out, backward and forward, upside down and raw. Once, during an extended session of dual oral stimulation, they turned on the local news for laughs, just to catch a glimpse of the day's baseball highlights and maybe a quickie interview with one of their teammates or managers. But only Rocky Goetz was on, talking about being pulled as the starting pitcher in the Braves' next outing against the Meteorites. "It's not fair," he complained. "I think Keith is making a big mistake."

On Tuesday morning—a *late* morning which followed another one of those *early* morning balcony jaunts, one during which Cole handily returned the previous morning's favor—Louise was the first to wake. She was cuddled up against Cole's chest. It was warm and already very familiar—as if she couldn't imagine ever not waking up in his arms. She inhaled deeply—she wanted to take his scent with her, up to the plate that night, and hit a homer for the God of scents. She groaned just slightly, involuntarily, and lifted her left leg up higher against his. Damn, was she sore. But damn, if she didn't want to do it again. Cole made a delicate snoring sound—just one little exhale. Louise smiled, and found it, well, cute. Nuzzling her face to his chest, she stuck out her tongue and playfully licked at random. Cole growled. Louise licked again, then moved her face over an inch or two and sucked at his nipple. He opened an eye. She peeked up, her mouth still very attached to his nipple. His one open eye rolled down in its socket and made contact with her prying baby blues.

"Morning," she said, removing the nipple from her mouth for just enough time to get out the two syllables, then retreating back for another helping.

"Morning," he said, simultaneously opening the other eye and forming a huge grin. "How long have you been doing that?"

She pulled back for a moment, gazed at the nipple, then said, "Not long enough," before digging right back in.

Cole closed his eyes. The first-thing-in-the-morning sensation of Louise was a trip. He knew that waking up alone in his New Jersey home on Wednesday morning would be one of the most depressing experiences in his life, but he couldn't think about that now, now as her hands began to move downtown. No time to think about that, he thought, succumbing.

Louise stroked gently with her hand. The most predictable aspect of the most predictable species, she thought, marveling somewhat at the intensity of this wake-me-up hard-on. Louise's mouth was ready for more than a nipple, and it was time to take the plunge south of the border.

Oh, my, every part of Cole's body gasped. "What do you want me to concentrate on now?" he asked, in between rushed breaths.

"Nothing," Louise said, stopping for a moment. "I just want you to come."

And come he did, groaning loud enough to wake a sleeping infant in suite 2204, an infant whose illegal alien nanny was performing much the same act upon the infant's millionaire father, while the infant's also wealthy mother, supposedly out at a power breakfast, was actually in a sleazy rent-by-the-hour motel, repeating Louise's moves, almost exactly, on a high-powered but ultraconservative Republican party bigwig, a bigwig whose much younger second wife was also executing similar French foreign policy on their Spanish-speaking but scandalously sculptured gardener, while the bigwig's teenage son from marriage number one was doing likewise with his dad's longtime hunting buddy, a fellow conservative most active in the GOP. That was where this one chain of head ended.

⊕   ⊕   ⊕

Another would begin in a few hours. Geraldine Willard was sure of that. Today's visit would be her third to the Hyatt Regency's top-floor Windows on the World Restaurant, her third such "afternoon luncheon appointment" with Arnold Loiten, the baseball beat columnist for the daily *Atlanta Journal-Courier* newspaper. Geraldine wasn't overwhelmed by Arnold's company. And she found him mediocre, if not altogether oafish, in bed. But he liked to spend money—to wine and dine. And that Geraldine enjoyed. And he detested Louise Gehrig. To that Geraldine could relate. And he had guaranteed admission to the *Journal-Courier's* reserved box in Fulton County Stadium. Those were worthwhile perks for a little sexual attention. An even swap considering her current status. So, she spirtzed on some perfume—Eau du Cher, direct from the Home Shopping Club—and clipped on her sexiest, most dangliest earrings, and soon she was ready. Her taste buds could hardly wait.

⊕   ⊕   ⊕

Cole's flight to Newark International Airport left the William B. Hartsfield International Airport at 2:12 P.M. It was due into New Jersey at 5:29. He figured if he left the Hyatt by 1:30—if he really, actually was walking out the door by 1:30—he'd make his flight.

Cole and Louise entered the twenty-second-floor hallway at 1:24 P.M. and walked to the elevator banks. He pressed the call button at 1:26, and within thirty seconds a car stopped on their floor and they got in. The car was packed, the after-lunchers from Windows on the World all grooving to a Muzak version of Aerosmith's "Love in an Elevator," but Cole and Louise squeezed in. They made small talk, whispered into each other's ears. Four tourists got off on the seventeenth floor, giving the remaining occupants a little breathing and shifting room. Louise and Cole moved back into one corner. Their whispering evolved into a kiss, as only whispering sometimes can. It was a deep, passionate kiss that made one gentleman on the elevator clear his throat. It was a deep, passionate kiss that made everyone else long for a kiss just like it. Even Geraldine Willard reached down and squeezed Arnold Loiten's hand. She knew that in less than fifteen minutes they'd be locked in some sort of sexual embrace. She smiled at the attractive couple and watched them as their lips finally parted. Then something clicked. Something was wrong. Geraldine gulped hard. That face, she thought. I know that face. Baseball cap or no baseball cap, with or without makeup, hair up or down, in uniform or in jeans and a T-shirt, in cleats or in those hideous black boots, Geraldine Willard would recognize that face in a *Where's Waldo* book.

The elevator car reached the Hyatt lobby and everyone got off. Everyone except Geraldine, who stood in shock.

"Are you coming?" Arnold asked.

She nodded as if she needed a drink of water, or maybe a breath of fresh air.

"Are you okay?" Arnold asked as they stepped from the car.

She shook her head and lifted a feeble finger, pointing it at the quickly fading backs of Louise and Cole. "That couple in the elevator."

"What about them?" Arnold asked with a grossly mischievous smile.

"That was Louise Gehrig."

"No way," Arnold said, his blood pressure shooting up countless points. "Louise Gehrig making out in a hotel elevator?"

Geraldine nodded furiously. "And that's not all."

"What?" Arnold said, taking Geraldine's arm and leading her swiftly in the direction of the taxi stand, where he could see the elevator couple standing.

"The guy she was with," Geraldine said.

"What about him," Arnold asked, focusing on Louise.

"That's Cole Robinson."

Arnold let go of Geraldine's arm and lunged toward the taxi stand. They were kissing—the possible baseball superstar couple. The door to an awaiting cab was open. The man stepped in. "Turn your face, God damn it," Arnold muttered, picking up his speed. There. Motherfucking *there*! The cheekbones. The perfect nose. Holy shit! The chin. Cole Robinson. It *was* Cole Robinson!

Arnold made it through the huge sliding glass doors and stopped short just outside the hotel's entrance. Louise stood watching the cab drive off, then turned from waving good-bye. She walked to the entrance but needed to get by Arnold to get back inside.

"Excuse me," she said, her mind melancholy and elsewhere.

"Sorry," Arnold said, standing aside to let her pass.

Louise, bobbing her head to some crazy tune that only lovers, ten-year-olds, baseball managers, and the Good Humor Man can hear, strolled by and entered the hotel.

Geraldine exited at that exact same moment, just in time to see Arnold sliding into the backseat of an awaiting taxi.

"Where are you going?" she yelled.

"To the office," he yelled, adding, "Baby, you just handed me the sports scoop of the year." He slammed the door shut before she could even comment, and the taxi took off.

Geraldine stood passively for a moment—no longer horny, her taste buds no longer tingling from the Windows on the World food. She was seething. And she wanted to cry. For the second time that year, Geraldine had lost a man to Louise Gehrig. And that trend was going to stop, she thought, the tears beginning to flow. God damn it! It was going to stop immediately.

THE BASEBALL BEAT

by Arnold Loiten

I've spent the last twenty-four or so hours wondering if I should continue writing this column. I kept asking myself, Is there really anything left to say about the great game of baseball? Hasn't it all been covered, ad nauseam, time and time again? Hasn't it all been said before?

Really, now. How much more can be said about the integrity, or lack thereof, of the game? About escalating salaries? About expansion spreading what little talent there is way too thin? About the owners' greed? About the commissioner's lack of power? About stats and slugging percentage? About the greatest of games? About the October Classic? About Ruth, Mantle, and Ted Williams?

How much more can any of us bear to read on the subject of Louise Gehrig?

Two days ago my answer, especially to that last question, would have been, NOT ANOTHER BLASTED WORD. But then a ride in an elevator changed all that.

It was an elevator ride shared with the young woman I've criticized all season. She didn't know I was there. Not that she'd have recognized me on the spot—I tend to blend into the scenery pretty well. But the Lord Jesus Christ could have been standing alongside her, and she wouldn't have noticed him either.

See, Miss Gehrig was otherwise engaged. She was making out, like a teenager in heat in the backseat of his dad's Chevy. Necking, heavy petting, out in public, for all the world to see.

Now granted, we've all been in love, and, if we're honest with ourselves, we've also all been in lust. But usually we have the common decency, the common courtesy to our fellow human beings, to act on those impulses behind closed doors. Not out in broad daylight, on an elevator filled with businessmen, tourists, restaurant patrons, and newspaper columnists.

But, as we have recently discovered, ballplayers do tend to think of themselves as special, above the law and below the moral code of decency to which most Americans hold themselves. Which probably goes a long way in explaining why Miss Gehrig's partner in this stomach-turning crime also saw nothing wrong with the public display of her obvious gropability. For her partner, her lover, if I may jump to the quite obvious conclusion, was also a ballplayer. A fellow major leaguer. Though not a fellow National Leaguer.

Which brings me to why ballplayers should never be considered role models—role models should be parents, or teachers, or someone who can help mold moral fiber. And why they nonetheless are. Let's face it, they're heroes to our kids. They're heroes to you and me. They live out our dreams on the diamond, on the court, on the ice.

So when one behaves badly, we publicly disparage him or her. Sure. We shake a finger in their face and say, "Shame. Shame on you for what you've done." Sometimes a fine or a short suspension accompanies the finger shaking. Most time not. And really, what does a thousand-dollar fine mean to someone earning one, two, three, or more million a year? Nothing! So, the athlete goes on his or her merry way, back to the diamond, or court, or ice. And our kids think, "Hey, what he or she did couldn't have been that bad. Maybe I'll try that too." Admit it, we as adults oftentimes think exactly the same thing.

But that's life in the majors. That's life in professional sports. That's life in the baseball beat reporter's world. And though part of me thinks it's time to just toss in the towel and call it quits, I know I have at least one civic duty left to perform:

Shame on you, Louise Gehrig. Shame on you, Cole Robinson. Shame on you both for what you've done.

Overnight with Howie

"And now, dear listeners, the call we've been waiting for. Here's Joey from Bensonhurst to put the news of the past few hours in perspective as only he can. You with us, Joey?"

"I'm here, Howie."

"What's wrong, Joey? You don't sound like the happiest of campers."

"I'm just so disgusted by everything."

"I take it you mean the as-yet unconfirmed revelations out of Atlanta that Louise Gehrig is involved with Cole Robinson?"

"It makes me sick."

"Can I ask why?"

"It's, it's unnatural. That's why."

"Louise is a very attractive young woman. Cole is a good-looking guy. Both are single, apparently healthy. From my point of view, there's nothing more natural in the world."

"Howie. Ballplayers aren't supposed to sleep with each other."

"Joey. I can understand someone like you having a bird over two macho male major leaguers getting it on. But, c'mon. This is a man and a woman. They aren't even in the same league."

"It turns my stomach. I'll never be able to watch Robinson pitch again."

"You're alone on that one. Beside being admired for his athletic abilities, the man's now a hero to millions of Louise Gehrig fans for his off-the-field activities. We've gotten dozens of calls from listeners who say they'd give anything to be in his shoes. And personally, I can't say I blame them."

"Howie, please. How can you say that?"

"Louise is one very attractive woman. Very attractive."

"Am I the only one who sees what she's trying to do?"

"And what's that? What is Louise Gehrig trying to do, other than play baseball?"

"She's undermining the game."

"Starting with Cole Robinson, I assume."

"Exactly."

"I take it you've heard that Cole threw a no-no the other day. It doesn't sound to me like his career is in jeopardy."

"That's no big deal. It shouldn't even count if he's sleeping with Gehrig."

"You're too much, Joey. I suppose you think the commissioner should pass some sort of antisex rule."

"He should do something. And fast."

"Joey, the Loiten column is just a few hours old. It hasn't even been confirmed."

"But this is an emergency. Quayle has got to act now. Before this goes any further."

"Like to the October Classic. Can you imagine the headlines if the Yankees and the Meteorites make it to the World Series?"

"No one'll watch."

"Are you crazy? The execs over at NBC couldn't dream up a better scenario. Their ad revenues would go through the roof."

"Well, at least we know that's not going to happen."

"I wouldn't bet against it."

"Oh, c'mon. Even if the Yanks can somehow hold on and take the East, can they really make it past the Texas Rangers?"

"Maybe. Maybe. Stranger things have happened."

"And if, now I said if remember, the Manhattan Mediocres actually win the East, do they stand a chance against the world champion Atlanta Braves? I say no."

"And again, I say, stranger things have happened."

"No way."

"You seem to forget that Louise and her teammates have taken six out of eight from the Braves during the regular season— including a blowout last night, and another win tonight, both at Fulton County Stadium. The Braves certainly haven't been playing like world champs. They've been stuck on that magic number of one for a few too many games, if you ask me."

"Tonight's win was a squeaker."

"A win is a win is a win."

"That's deep, Howie."

"It's late, Joey."

"Especially for the Mediocres."

"And on that note, we'll take a commercial break."

 PART FIVE

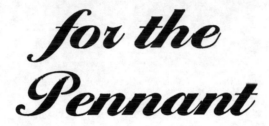

There are only two places in this league. First place
and no place.

—Tom Seaver

◉ 23 ◉

Sleeping with the Enemy

On an overcast Thursday afternoon, September 14, in the year 2000, as a heat wave seemed to have the entire country pressing its air conditioners into overdrive, the Atlanta Braves clinched the NL West with a solid at-home trouncing of the Philadelphia Phillies. They were the first team to guarantee themselves a life in the postseason, but few, outside of Atlanta, were interested. The real front-page sports story involved the off-field activities of Louise Gehrig and Cole Robinson. Were they? Did they? And was it good for you too?

Arnold Loiten's Wednesday evening column alleging the affair was quoted and misquoted, interpreted and evaluated repeatedly throughout the day, the night, and the days and nights that followed.

Sports analysts everywhere shifted their attention from pennant fever to this love connection of sorts. Photos, fan reaction, et cetera, et cetera, and so forth . . . ad nauseam.

While one news tabloid featured snapshots of the lovers melded together inside a heart pierced with crisscrossing baseball bats, another ran photos from the All-Star Game under the blaring headline: PICKED OFF & PICKED UP

⬤   ⬤   ⬤

From the Meteorites' camp came a series of no comments, likewise from the Yankees'. But both teams' respective billionaire owners had called their respective participants aside.

"Is it true?" Matt Stern asked Louise early that Thursday afternoon in the otherwise vacant New Orleans Jazz Park visitors clubhouse, at about the same time that, up in his flashy New Jersey office, George Steinbrenner asked Cole Robinson, "What's going on here?"

Louise nodded and said, "Yes. It's true." While Cole shrugged and said, "I'm in love with her."

Stern nodded. "Are you in love with him?" he asked.

"Yes," Louise said.

While Steinbrenner shook his head. "Love's a pretty strong word, Cole."

"The feeling is pretty strong, Mr. Steinbrenner."

Then both owners asked a virtually identical what-if question regarding the World Series.

"Why don't we cross that bridge when we get to it," Louise said.

Cole's version was, "Shouldn't we be more concerned with the Red Sox right now?"

Both owners nodded and listened and gave their ownerly advice.

Stern ended the discussion by saying, "I'm happy for you, Louise. I really am. From everything I've heard, Cole seems like a great guy. And you make one very attractive couple. But I have to admit I'm jealous."

"Why's that?" Louise asked.

" 'Cause like every man in America, I too am in love with Lousie Gehrig."

Louise smiled and gave Matt a hug.

Steinbrenner, on the other hand, ended his meeting by saying, "I won't stand for anything getting in the way of the Yankees winning the World Series. I hope you understand that."

"I do," Cole said.

"You must always remember that baseball is your life, Cole. And that it must always come first."

"I've won a lot of games for you this year," Cole reminded the owner.

"I know you have. But I don't want it to stop here."

"It won't."

"Very well, then," Steinbrenner said.

And the meeting was over.

No smiles.

And definitely no hugs.

Stern then called Steinbrenner to suggest they release identical statements regarding the affair.

"Good idea," the Yankees' boss said.

"I've already put something together. Let me fax over a copy."

Stern did. Steinbrenner suggested a few alterations. Stern vetoed one of the changes. Steinbrenner understood the reason, but suggested another variation on the wording. A few more changes were made, then a few more. And an official statement was simultaneously released on both the Meteorites' and Yankees' letterhead:

> We would like to put a hasty end to the salacious rumors, and announce that Manhattan Meteorites first baseperson Louise Gehrig and New Jersey Yankees pitcher Cole Robinson are involved on a personal basis. Both the Yankees and Meteorites management strongly believe that this relationship will have no bearing on the professionalism of either player or team. We respect both Ms. Gehrig's and Mr. Robinson's right to privacy, and strongly urge fans and members of the press to do likewise.

Just prior to the Meteorites' Thursday night meeting with the New Orleans Jazz, Jesus Maldonado, P.J. Strykes, and most of the starting players decided it was time for a team meeting.

"Want me in or out?" Lefty Johnson asked.

"Out," Jesus said. "If you don't mind."

"Not at all," Lefty said, picking up his current paperback and heading out to catch come Louisiana rays.

"Louise," the meeting began. It was Jesus doing the talking. "How could you?"

"How could I what?" Louise asked.

"He's an American Leaguer," P.J. said. "It's just, well . . ."

"It's not natural," Jesus said.

"I can't believe I'm hearing this," Lousie said.

"What about us? How do you think we feel?" Elvis Jones asked. "You're our teammate and you're out sleeping with the enemy. Literally."

"Maybe if I was having an affair with Rocky Goetz, I could understand this. But Cole Robinson. What can any of you possibly have against Cole?"

"I've played against him many times," Bob Dixon said, speaking up. "He's a great guy."

"But so are we," Elvis said.

"Yeah. What's wrong with us?" Reggie Borders asked.

"Is that what this is about?" Louise asked, looking from face to face. "That I chose Cole over one of you?"

"Well . . . ," Jesus said.

"Yeah," P.J. said. "That's it exactly." He spread his arms out wide. "Twenty-three guys." He motioned to Bob. "No offense, man, but you've already got her mother."

"None taken," Bob said.

"Twenty-three guys," P.J. continued, "who are all head over heals about you."

"But—" Louise began.

"Let me finish," P.J. said. "This isn't easy to say, and if I stop, I might chicken out. We love you, Louise. We've all talked about it. Every one of us dreams of being your knight in shining armor. And to see you go off with someone from the American League, it's like, well . . ."

"We're the Jets," Jesus explained, "and you're going over to the Sharks."

The odd concept of a baseball player explaining something in *West Side Story* terms escaped Louise for the moment. "I'm touched," she said. "I really am. But you've got to understand that I didn't choose Cole over any of you. I love you all, each and every one of you." She smiled at P.J. "Even you, Strykes."

P.J. would have said something cocky, something sarcastic, and might have, if it weren't for the fear that he'd suddenly break down, a mound of sobbing, blubbering muscle, right there in front of all his teammates. Instead, he forced a smile and nodded meaningfully a few times.

"But you guys were never a possibility. I could never sleep with one of my teammates." Looking around, she caught Jesus' eye for just a moment before he looked away and down. "And most of you already have girlfriends"—she looked over at Sandy Downs—"or wives."

"What if Cole gets traded here?" Darryl White asked.

"Good question," Jesus said. "Yeah, what if that happens?"

"C'mon," Bob said. "You guys are stretching."

"Cole isn't about to become a Meteorite."

"What if I were to get traded?" P.J. asked. "Then would you consider dating me?"

"P.J. You guys are like big brothers to me. Understand?"

A few nods.

"I'm in love with Cole. Truly. Madly. Deeply in love. Please be happy for me."

She looked from face to face to face. A few teammates nodded, Jesus stared at the floor, and P.J., well, their gazes connected for one long moment, and Louise was sure she saw tears.

"Want us to beat the shit out of Arnold Loiten?" Jesus asked.

"Can't you get in trouble for that?"

"There are ways," Jeff Carter said with a menacing smirk.

"Hmm. That's an idea," Louise said. "But let me think about it. Right now we've got other more important butts to kick."

"Like whose?"

"New Orleans, that's whose."

But there was no enthusiasm whatsoever. And though the team's magic number now stood at twelve, they'd move no closer to clinching the division on that hot and very humid New Orleans night.

Manhattan	001 000 100	2	4	1
New Orleans	002 010 02	5	6	0

After the game, they spoke.

"I'm the most envied man in baseball," he said.

"And for good reason," she said. In her hands she held the gift Cole had given her during a break in their Atlanta love play, a diamond-encrusted baseball refrigerator magnet. He had had it custom designed for her at Tiffany's.

"I just can't belive the fuss."

"I can," she said, turning the diamond baseball this way and that so that it could catch the stray rays of apartment light and morph them into rainbows. "It doesn't surprise me in the least."

"But how the hell did they find out."

"We were spotted making out in the elevator."

"I hate when that happens.'"

"Not me. In fact, how 'bout flying out here right now and we'll work on getting caught making out in every elevator in New Orleans."

"That might take a while."

"I've got the time. Hey, we can even invite Arnold Loiten over to watch."

"I'd like to get my hands around his neck."

"Now, now, be kind. He was just doing his job."

"People get paid for being assholes."

"They're called reporters."

"Umm."

"So, how about that little elevator rendezvous?"

"Can I get a rain check maybe, for sometime in November?"

"You and your rain checks."

"I turned in the last one."

"That you did."

"Well?"

"I'll be busy in November."

"Doing what?"

"Drinking daiquiris and soaking up the sun."

"I can drink daiquiris, too, y'know."

"So?"

"So, nothing. Just though you'd like to know."

"I'll file the information."

"You do that."

"I could sure use one now."

"A daiquiri?"

"Or a joint."

"Louise. Is that any way for an all-star to speak? A role model for millions of little girls?"

"Some role model," Louise said, exhaling loudly. "So, what's next?"

"Well, we clinch the AL East, then beat the Rangers in four. You clinch your division, then squeak by the Braves in seven."

"How come you sweep and we squeak?"

"We're the Yankees."

"The team from *New Jersey.*"

"But we're still the Yankees."

"Okay, so we're in the World Series, then what?"

"One of us wins, the other loses."

"Pretty cut-and-dry."

"Yeah."

"Will your baseball ego survive losing the World Series to a girl and her expansion teammates?"

"Never."

"Didn't think so."

"So, you'll let us win."

"Not a chance."

"It was worth a shot."

⑩   ⑩   ⑩

J. Danforth Quayle had expected dilemmas when he took the job as baseball's commissioner. He relished the notion that he'd be able to face down the problems that plagued America's national pastime. There would most likely be strikes and lockouts, an occasional suspension and fine, and, maybe, just maybe, he'd even get to reconsider the Pete Rose situation. But never, *never* in his wildest dreams did he expect to see the day when baseball players would begin dating one another, and he'd have a select group of five team owners call for an impromptu meeting, then show up in his office asking what he and the league presidents planned to do about it.

"Well," he said, "what would you like me to do about it?" That, he figured, was as good a start as any.

The ever-present mutt growled just slightly, and its owner told it to shush.

"Make a ruling," the oldest of all team owners said.

"Such as?"

"No nookie," the female owner suggested.

"You want to rule that nookie between major leaguers will not be tolerated."

"Something," another owner said.

"Anything," said another.

Quayle exchanged glances with National League president Hank Aaron and American League president Yogi Berra.

Aaron cleared his throat. "Gentlemen," he said, eyeing the one female owner, "may I state emphatically that to disallow this union between Ms. Gehrig and Mr. Robinson would be a most direct violation of their civil rights. And believe me, I know a thing or two about civil rights."

And though a few of the owners wondered what civil rights had to do with baseball, they kept quiet.

"We'd be sued from here to kingdom come," Aaron said. "And back."

"But would we win?" one owner asked, facing not Aaron, but Quayle.

"No, sir," Aaron said. "We'd lose, and we'd be made fools of. But then, it wouldn't be the first time baseball's powers that be made asses of themselves."

One of the owners stood suddenly and turned to his associates. "I think we have the answer to our question."

"But . . ."

"No," he said. "We've taken enough of these gentlemen's time." Then turning to face Quayle, Aaron, and Berra, he added, "I take it you'll keep what was discussed here today to yourselves?"

"And away from the press?" Quayle said. "No problem."

"But what about the other owners?" Aaron asked.

"They were all offered the opportunity to be here," the lone female owner explained. "Each and every one of them."

"Including Matt Stern?" Aaron asked.

"Including Matt Atern."

"But only you five chose to attend," Aaron said.

"That's right. We're the only ones who viewed it as a problem."

Aaron grinned. The meeting was over.

After the five multimillionaires went on their merry multimillionaire way, Aaron, Berra, and Quayle held a meeting of their own.

"But *what if* the Yankees and the Meteorites meet in the World Series?" Quayle asked.

"Both teams take the field and try their damnedest to win," Aaron explained; then, lowering his voice to almost a whisper, he said, "It's not like this has never happened before."

"Excuse me?"

Aaron and Berra exchanged nervous glances.

"Baseball players have been sleeping with one another for as long as there's been a game," Berra explained.

"It's just never been publicized."

"That's impossible," Quayle said. "Louise Gehrig is the first woman to ever play the game."

Aaron and Berra stared at the commissioner, but, after a long pause, when he still didn't get it, Berra looked at his National League equal and said, "You explain it . . . please."

"Over the years there have been a number of gay baseball players."

"Gay," Quayle asked, "as in homosexual?"

Aaron and Berra nodded.

The commissioner blanched. He turned first to face Aaron, and then to face Berra. "No," he said simply. Just no.

" 'Fraid so, Dan," Berra said. "Just, no one ever talked about it. It never came up."

"But," Quayle said, "who?"

"That really isn't important."

"Like hell it isn't. These players are role models. I won't have—"

Aaron held up a huge hand to silence the ex–vice-president. "Enough," he said.

"But—"

"It's none of your business. It's no one's business. What people, what baseball players, do in the privacy of their bedrooms is no one's business but their own."

Quayle turned to Berra, hoping he could bring some sense to this immorality play. But Yogi only shrugged. "You know what they say, Dan."

"What, Yogi?" Quayle said, suddenly feeling tired, suddenly feeling old beyond his years. "What do they say?"

"You can being a horse to water," Berra began, "but you can't tell him where to stick his . . ." He motioned downward with an open-palmed hand, then shrugged again—a *what can you do?*

Quayle sat and stared. His mouth was open, and he was perspiring heavily. And he felt, not ill, but, well, rather dead. He stayed that way for some time, long after Aaron and Berra exited his office, long after even his secretary went home. It was a distant cousin of a feeling—this death—uncomfortable but strangely familiar. It took a few minutes of mind scanning to place it. Then it hit. Then it all made sense. Tuesday, November 3, 1992—that night he and Uncle George admitted defeat. It still made vomit well up in his throat and tears well up in his eyes. That's how he felt now, half admitting to himself that maybe this commissioner's position wasn't such a grand idea after all, half wondering which of his childhood's baseball heroes took it up the butt.

Talk show hosts of every ilk—radio to television—had, as one might imagine, a veritable field day with the Louise-Cole affair. From Imus in the Morning to Howard Stern, from Phil Donahue to Sally Jessy Raphael, from Jay Leno to Conan O'Brien, the news became the butt of jokes and speculation, one-liners and skits.

On "The David Letterman Show," host Dave came back from a commercial break—one during which Paul and the band performed a jazz rendition of the old disco hit "Love to Love You, Baby"—and said, "Getting right to it. It's time for tonight's Top Ten list as compiled at the home office in Vatican City. As you might have heard, today it was confirmed that Manhattan Meteorite superstar first baseperson Louise Gehrig is indeed involved with Yankee pitching great Cole Robinson. Tonight's list, The Top Ten Baseball Legends Louise and Cole Might Name a Child After, if indeed they should ever get married and have children."

"So, it's a jumping-the-gun sort of Top Ten List?" Paul asked.

"Exactly," Letterman said, laughing. "And why the hell not?" He tapped the light blue index cards a few times against the top of his desk, giving his mouth ample occasion to stretch itself into the goofiest of grins, then read the list.

"Number ten, Mookie Wilson. Number nine, Coot Veal." He turned toward his bandleader. "Y'know. I think I had that for dinner the other night. Coot Veal."

"A very popular dish," Paul said.

"Yeah," Letterman said, continuing. "Number eight, Firpo Marberry. Number seven, Orval Overall. Number six, Pie Traynor. Number five, Putsy Caballero. No Putsy, you can't borrow the car tonight. Absolutely not. In fact, go to your room, Putsy. Right now." Letterman laughed. "Where was I? Oh, yeah. Number four, Clyde Kluttz. Number three, Joey Buttafucco. Oops, sorry 'bout that. That was from our parallel universe Top Ten list, The Top Ten Characters from Cheesy Real-Life Made-for-TV Movies that Louise and Cole Might Name a Kid After."

"I've always wondered about those parallel universe lists," Paul said.

"And now you know," Letterman said, his eyes going wide in mock horror. "Number two, Mordecai 'Three Finger' Brown. And the number one Baseball Legend Louise and Cole Might Name a Child After, the San Diego Chicken."

Meanwhile, on Christopher Russo's late-night TV gabfest, "Up All Night," The "Mad Dog" shook his head in disbelief, stating repeatedly that Cole Robinson had to be the luckiest guy in the world. "I'm jealous!" he shrieked in his harsh, overbearing sort of way. "I want Louise. I want her, you understand," he moaned. "I want her." And he said he'd love to get the Yankee pitching ace drunk so that maybe he'd get on a bragging rights high horse and spill his guts about some of Louise's most private, most intimate secrets.

It was a thought shared by millions of American men.

Kevin Thomas Willard was one of those men—he was as fascinated by the affair as the next guy. It put Louise Gehrig in a very different light. It put her on a different planet. And suddenly, for the first time, Kevin viewed Louise sexually. He wondered what she looked like naked, fantasized even. How she was groomed, what her most private of parts looked like under some intense OB-GYN sort of scrutiny. He imagined what it would be like to have sex with her. What sort of sounds she made. Or maybe, watching Cole and Louise fuck. Did she come? Or, how often? He spent hours in his room, forward-scanning through rented X-rated videotapes, searching for an actress who even remotely resembled Louise, and when he found one (there were actually two who could pass his litmus test: Holly Goodhead, who made about a half dozen features in the late eighties, and Tori Lynn, who made dozens of extravagantly produced porno epics in the early nineties), he'd watch their scenes over and over again, squinting just so to get that perfect Louise Gehrig effect. Ms. Goodhead, in particular, starred in a few movies featuring *that*, and *that*, in turn, reminded him of Geraldine. He found himself wondering about her, missing her even. But soon those thoughts would be replaced by a longing to once again view one of the Louise lookalike scenes. This is better than baseball, he thought on more than one occasion. This is good.

Nothing was good, at least as far as Geraldine Willard was concerned. At least not at that point in time. She had sworn off men. Totally. The Arnold Loiten incident in front of the Hyatt Regency had been the straw that broke her camel's back. "Enough," she said aloud, over and over and over to herself. "Enough," she mumbled to her daughters. "Enough is enough."

"Mom," her youngest daughter, Cheryl, suggested, "Why don't you just go out with guys who hate sports?"

"Because, honey, guys who hate sports are girly-men," Geraldine explained.

Daughter Kelly agreed. "The only guys worth going out with at school are on the football team."

Cheryl nodded, but she really didn't understand. Her third-grade boyfriend hated sports. He liked to read, and to watch movies, and to kiss. He certainly didn't kiss like a girly-man. But then at the ripe age of nine, Cheryl didn't really know what a girly-man kissed like. Her boyfriend, also nine, was the only guy she'd ever kissed. Maybe it was time to experiment. Then again, she liked him a lot, so maybe not. She shrugged and excused herself from the conclusion of the conversation. Her mother could get boring real quick. And this Louise Gehrig stuff was old news. Real old. And besides, she didn't want to get caught in a lie. Her mom knew nothing about the boyfriend, and Cheryl wanted it to stay that way.

The discussion lasted long into the night, with Geraldine working herself into a rage. To put it simply, she was through losing men to Louise Gehrig. And besides men, she'd given up baseball as well. "Baseball and men—get out of my life!" she screamed later that night from her large and lonely bed. I admit defeat, she thought, crying herself to sleep. I am defeated. The men of the world are yours, Louise Gehrig. All yours. Take them, have them, enjoy them while you still can.

For Special Agent Wesley Selden, who was still pissed off at Louise for her little disappearing act only a few days earlier, the Louise Gehrig–Cole Robinson affair only revived the hate—

hundreds of letters poured into South Field *and* Yankee Stadium. But these were different. Instead of hating Louise for her sex, these new zealots hated her for her sexuality. Morality was the key to these letters. Morality and the Kingdom of God. Family values and the Lord Jesus Christ. According to these "Christians," Louise was preaching sin, fornication, and even sodomy to the defenseless little children of America. Selden read letter after letter after letter, and in doing so renewed his own personal vow of hatred for everything born-again, everything religious. These Bible-thumping fundamentalist fruit loops are going to be the death of me yet, he thought, tossing aside another handful of envelopes. "Get a life!" he screamed at the sack of mail. "Get a fucking life!"

Selden dismissed the moralistic ravings as mostly harmless, despite the nagging memory of the string of abortion doctor murders that ravaged the South in the mid-1990s. The FBI agent hoped Louise's sin wasn't viewed in the same light by these kooks. She was, after all, only fucking. Though, then again, to sexless slugs, fucking could be the greatest vice of them all.

What worried Selden, what sent icy shivers down his arms and legs and spine, what scared him more than the mutilated doll, unnerved him more than Louise vanishing, was a new twist in the Tombstone letters. Thursday's, and now Friday's, immediately following the Louise-Cole announcement, featured a surprisingly improved drawing of the tombstone, wider now, a headstone for two, with a background of clouds and grass and flowers. It was signed even, in an almost feminine script. And the wording was different:

⑪ 24 ⑪

Meant to Be Broken

When Louise returned to her Charles Street apartment on Wednesday, September 20, a package was waiting along with the usual collection of bills, magazines, and Victoria's Secret catalogs. It looked much like the last package, with the same tape, the same lack of return address, and the same goddamn Atlanta, Georgia, postmark.

This time Louise phoned Selden right away.

The special agent arrived within the hour, accompanied by members of the bureau's bomb squad, who carried a large device which Selden explained as a portable X-ray machine. It would determine, he told Louise, if the package contained a bomb.

After much activity, setting up, moving about, turning on, shutting off, readjusting, then turning on again, all accompanied by what Louise thought sounded very much like a cheesy sci-fi soundtrack, the bomb squad experts concluded that the package contained nothing even closely resembling an explosive device. Then they left, but not before one of them secured a Louise Gehrig autograph for his little girl.

Alone, Selden turned to Louise and asked, "Do you want to open it? Or should I?"

"Knock yourself out," Louise said, handing him a kitchen knife.

He sliced away at the tape, pushed back the flaps, lifted off some crumpled sheets of newspaper—the *Atlanta Journal-Courier*—and said, "Cute."

"Cute," Louise repeated.

He turned the box so that she could see inside. But what Louise saw was, in her opinion, anything but cute. The box contained a large pink rubber dildo. One that perfectly resembled the appendage it was designed to replicate—veins, head, and all. And on that pink rubber dildo head was another masterpiece: a caricature of Cole Robinson's smiling face. There was no doubt as to whom the artist was. The name was as clear as day, written in that identical feminine script down the length of the pink rubber dildo shaft—Tombstone.

"I'm assigning you a bodyguard," Selden said. "Until we catch this idiot."

Louise nodded.

"You don't have a problem with that?"

"No," she said. "I have a bigger problem with dying."

The next evening, Louise and her teammates returned to South Field for their final home stand of the regular season—eight games, four each against the Mets and the Pirates. Their won-lost record was a very admirable 92–59 and their magic number was closer, down to single digits and finally in view. It was eight.

Bob Dixon's race to break Roger Maris's single-season home run record of sixty-one continued. His dinger total matched the team's number of losses. Number fifty-seven came on the Saturday, September 16, meeting with the Padres. And a celebration quickly followed the game, a celebration for his four hundred fifty-third career home run, a dinger which helped him bump and replace his boyhood hero Carl Yastrzemski as number eighteen on the all-time home run hitter list, a dinger which he proudly dedicated to his fiancée. The somewhat anticlimatic numbers fifty-eight and fifty-nine came during the September 19 game against the Dodgers out in L.A. One more and Bob would tie Ruth's old record of sixty, two and he would tie Maris, three and Hall of Fame get ready—not that there was now any doubt as to his admittance.

Louise also suddenly found herself in contention to break a record of her own. With 127 stolen bases thus far on the year, and eleven games to go, the rookie first baseperson was only four steals shy of breaking Rickey Henderson's single-season record of 130. Hell, Louise had pilfered four bases in a single game three times already that season, so she figured it was a record she could take. And how would she celebrate? Well, she gave some serious consideration to lifting that record-breaking stolen base high over her head and proclaiming, "I am the greatest," but figured few would get the joke. Instead, she'd probably wave to the crowd, smile proudly, then gladly donate the base to the Baseball Hall of Fame.

When asked to comment on Louise's base-stealing abilities and the possibility that his record might fall, Henderson, now a first base coach for the Arkansas Astros, commented, "She's fast. But she's a girl. So I'll still hold the record. No question about that. I'll still be the greatest of all time."

⬤　　⬤　　⬤

Though Louise and company maintained their hold on first place, their crossborough rivals just would not go away. The Mets held strong through the last month and were only three games back at 89–62. And with seven of the last eleven games against the Meteorites, the four at South Field and the last three of the season at Shea, many baseball analysts were predicting that the still wet-behind-the-ears Meteorites would choke, while the more experienced Mets would forge ahead, only of course to be swept by the Braves in four.

⬤　　⬤　　⬤

Over in the other league, the Texas Rangers had clinched the American League West easily, while the AL East was still up for grabs—a two-team dead-heat race, still, between New Jersey and Boston. Here the analysts were just about evenly split. Though, they argued, the Red Sox had the most recent playoff experience (Boston had prevailed the previous season by only one game over the Yanks), with the loss of heavy hitters like Bob Dixon, they just didn't have the power it would take to win it all. And no matter who won the East, they all predicted, the Red Sox or the Yanks, neither would have a snowball's chance in hell against the charging Rangers. It would be an Atlanta-Texas World Series—that was the general consensus—going the full seven games, with either team capable of pulling it off.

The Meteorites won the first two of their home games against the Mets. Closer P.J. Strykes was awarded his ninth win of the season (versus just one loss and in addition to thirty-three saves) on Thursday night, when he entered a 1–1 tie in the top of the ninth, quickly retired the side, then sat back and watched as Sandy Downs hit the first pitch in the bottom of the inning right out of the park. Gone, good-bye, and, I'll take it.

On Friday night, it was Reggie's turn—another complete game, a five-hit shutout—his twenty-second victory of the season, with the Meteorites winning 6–0.

And while Louise stole no bases during the Thursday night game, she added three to her grand total on Friday, tying Henderson's record. Bob Dixon, however, wasn't as lucky; after two games, and now with only nine to go, he was no closer to his goal. The time was running out, as it had for many in pursuit of the most coveted of batting titles, and the pressure—media pressure, fan pressure, Dixon pressure—was becoming unbearable.

The Saturday afternoon affair was one of those battles of epic baseball proportions: a David versus Goliath matchup where only ERAs suffered.

"Relax," Louise told Bob before taking their turns at bat in the bottom of the first. He struck out looking.

"Calm down," she said in the third. He hit a broken bat blooper to shallow center field and was just as easily out.

"I'm not saying anything this time," she said in the bottom of the sixth, with the score tied at 2–2. He lined one right into the third baseman's glove.

Louise refused to even look Bob's way as they prepared to bat for one final time in the bottom of the ninth, down by one run.

"If anything can bring home a victory it's the combination of Gehrig, Maldonado, and Dixon," Junella Wingi said from the broadcasting booth.

"True enough," Kurt Rybak agreed. "And Dixon is definitely due for a hit."

"He's due for something. He's looked awful at the plate today. Simply awful."

"He's definitely feeling the pressure. You know, no one's even cracked the top ten since 1961. That year Maris took the crown away from Ruth with sixty-one dingers, while his teammate Mickey Mantle got fifty-four."

"The Expos' Darryl Strawberry came closest, with fifty-three homers in '95, George Foster with fifty-two in '77, and Cecil Fielder had fifty-one in 1990 while playing for the Tigers. But otherwise, no one's even been close."

"Add to that the press covering your every move."

"Louise has helped out in that respect, taking a lot of the media heat off of Dixon."

"True enough. But the pressure's still there. It's in his head. He can't escape from it. Not really."

"But can he do it?"

"I don't know. But with fifty-nine, he's tied for third place with Ruth on the single-season home run leader's list. That's not bad company."

"Louise steps up to the plate and the crowd is going nuts."

"Can you blame them?"

"Not at all. She's had one hell of a year."

"Pip Hatfield, the Mets' relief ace, sets, winds up, and . . . ball one."

"She's such a patient hitter."

"Hatfield sets."

"It's fastball all the way."

"Dangerous territory."

"It hit the handle of Louise's bat. Should be an easy out. Feliz flips down his sunglasses. And he . . ."

"He drops the ball! He drops the ball!"

"Can you believe that? Jose Feliz, a three-time Gold Glove winner at short, drops the ball."

"He's pissed."

"He'll be charged with an error on that one. Yeah. It's official—E6."

"It hit the heel of his glove and just bounced out."

"Oh, man, you don't see that every day."

"So, with Louise Gehrig on base, Jesus Maldonado in the batter's box, Bob Dixon on deck, and no outs, I'd say the Meteorites' chances of a last-inning comeback are looking good."

"As the American League president has been known to say, it ain't over till it's over."

"True enough."

"Though I doubt that Louise is going to get that one steal she needs to put her ahead of Rickey. Johnny Mars, the Mets' catcher, has thrown her out three times in five attempts."

"Not many catchers can make that claim. Though I can think of a few who would love to."

"Pete Sacker, maybe?"

"Among others."

"Louise takes only the slightest of leads. Hatfield glares at her, then turns to face down Maldonado. He sets, and delivers."

"Maldonado hits a weak fly to shallow right. An easy out."

"He could really use some of Louise's patience."

"Ain't that the truth."

Junella laughed. "Ain't that the truth? That's a new one."

"Only a variation on the old 'true enough' theme. I figured it was time for a little variety in my life."

"I'm sure our listeners will be glad to hear that," Wingi said. "Dixon steps in. And the cheers are deafening."

"Fifty-nine home runs is worth cheering for. You know the Bambino hit fifty-four or more homers on four separate occasions? Fifty-four in 1920 and 1928, fifty-nine in '21, and, of course, sixty in '27."

"An amazing career. Seven hundred and fourteen dingers in all."

"Dixon still has a way to go on that record."

"Judging from this season, he's got the time. He's looking pretty good for an old man."

"True enough."

Wingi laughed. "Well, speaking strictly as a baseball fan, I hope he shatters the Maris record. I'm selfish. I want to be able to tell my grandchildren I was there when Dixon hit his sixty-second."

"You gotta be rooting for him. And even if he doesn't make it, though I tend to agree with you and think he will, I know I've sure enjoyed the ride watching him try."

"No question. This has been the most exciting baseball season in years, thanks to Louise, Bob, and their teammates."

"Let's not forget Matt Stern."

"Absolutely. The man responsible."

"Louise takes a short lead. The crowd is chanting—Dixon, Dixon, Dixon. Hatfield gets his sign from Feliz. They're going with the curve."

"Doesn't much matter, the way Dixon's been producing—curve, fastball, slider, junk ball—he can hit 'em all." Wingi paused long enough for Rybak to say, "True enough," but when none was forthcoming, she continued. "Hatfield sets, he winds up, and . . ."

"There's goes Louise."

"And there goes the ball! Bob Dixon has hit a screaming line drive that may just do it! Duane Lambert backpedals to the warning track, looks up, and . . . good-bye! That ball has left the building!"

"Number sixty. And though it prevented Louise from being credited with a stolen base . . ."

"I think Louise'll forgive her father-in-law to be."

"It gives the team a much-needed win and puts Bob Dixon only one home run away from tying one of the greatest records in the history of professional sports."

"Listen to the crowd."

"Look at the smile on Dixon's face."

"The pressure valve has been opened for one blissful moment."

"Louise is giving him a hug at home plate."

"The rest of the Meteorites are running from the dugout and surrounding Louise and Dixon. And I don't know about you, Kurt, but I've got a bad case of the goose bumps."

"You've got goose bumps, Bob Dixon has sixty home runs, and the Meteorites have taken three in a row from the second-place Mets and now have a magic number of two."

"It doesn't get any better than this."

"Truer words have never been spoken, Junella," Rybak said. "We'll be right back with the jolly recap."

25

The Appreciative Fan

I can do it. I can do it. I can do it. I can do it.

This was Bob Dixon's mantra as he and the rest of the Meteorites jogged to their dugout after the scoreless top of the first inning on sunny and beautiful Fan Appreciation Day at South Field. He nodded at Louise.

"Nervous?" he asked.

She exhaled loudly. "No. You?"

He shook his head and his eyes went wide. "Scared shit-less."

After working the count full, Meteorites' leadoff man Jamaine Young watched as the next pitch flew about three feet over his head, well out of reach of the Mets' catcher, Johnny Mars. Mars shook his head in disgust as Jamaine ran up the line to take his place on the bag. There was no longer a race between him and Louise for the stolen base crown. He had given up. He had thrown the towel in. Louise had won hands down, fair and mostly square. And though he would never admit that she was faster, he'd agree in a heartbeat that she had the rattle quota on her side. Something about Louise on base threw the defense for a loop.

Of course, the fact that Matt Stern had privately amended his contract didn't hurt. "Get a hundred steals, the bonus and contract extension are yours," Stern told him. "You don't have to do that," Young had said. "I know I don't have to," Stern replied. "I want to."

After that, well, hell, Young could sit back and appraise Louise's abilities for what they were, a God-given talent of sorts. Deep down he could no longer muster the disgust he had originally felt. What's a girl doing in the major leagues? Well, this girl can play, or so he bragged to his wife, his family, and his friends—though he still didn't dare say anything to Matt Stern or his teammates. Or even Lefty. He didn't need to hear an "I told you so." As for all those wives and girlfriends who were initially so jealous of Louise, the Cole Robinson affair nipped that in the bud. Whew! And Thank God! all around. It really wasn't such a big deal after all, Young said to his wife at about the same time that a dozen or so wives and girlfriends said roughly the same thing to their Meteorite husbands or boyfriends. "Sure, dear," was the typical response. "Whatever you say."

Now, with eight games to go, Young needed only three steals to make it to his hundredth of the year. And he'd make it, he was sure of that. So sure he could taste that five million bucks— and they tasted fan-fucking-tastic!

Louise stepped up to the plate. On the first pitch, Young took off. Mars's throw to the covering shortstop was high, and Jamaine had his ninety-eighth by a mile. No contest at all.

"Yes," he said, pumping his fist into the air. "Yes! Yes! Yes!"

Three pitches later, Louise was standing on first—walked on four pitches—and it was suddenly time for Mars and the Mets skipper, Tommy Lasorda, to take a quick trip to the mound to, if nothing else, calm down the pitcher.

Louise scanned South Field—from Jesus standing just outside the batter's box, swinging the bat over his head, to Bob standing in the on-deck circle, stretching with a fungo bat, to the stands packed with the throngs of fans, her mother among them, ardently cheering the team on.

The umpire began the slow walk out to the mound to tell

Lasorda to hurry it up. The Mets' manager nodded, then bounced back to the dugout. Mars reclaimed his position behind the plate, Jesus stepped in, and it was once again time to play ball.

From the on-deck circle, Bob sweated out every pitch. How many more before he stepped into the box and attempted the, well, almost impossible? Would Jesus get a hit, or would it be one of those endless at bats where he fouled off pitch after pitch after pitch? Would he ground into a double play? Or worse, one of those rare triple plays—all he needed was to hit one right into the glove of the second baseman and whammo, Bob would have to wait until the next inning. No, please, no. That, he couldn't take.

He caught Louise's gaze, and smiled at her. She smiled back, that sexy little grin that drove his teammates wild. Jesus fouled off a pitch. Bob sighed and scanned the stands. Margaret was seated a few rows behind the home team dugout. She blew a kiss his way. He beamed and chuckled.

Jesus fouled off another. Bob looked to the electronic scoreboard. The count was three balls and two strikes. Everyone on the team used the scoreboard to keep track when Jesus was at bat.

Bob swung the fungo over his head in wide sweeping circles a few times, then stretched his legs out almost as far as they could reach. Louise wasn't taking any chances with Mars—she had a short lead, especially compared to Jamaine's. Another pitch, another foul.

"Christ!" Bob muttered anxiously. He looked into the stands again, hoping for another kiss, or at least one of Margaret's smiles. That's when the glint caught his eye. A fan dressed in a Yankees T-shirt and a goddamn Braves cap—*the nerve!*—was sitting in the second row, just behind first base. Bob couldn't tell if it was a man or a woman—he or she was thin, but not too tall—but he knew for goddamn sure what was in his or her hand. If it looked like a gun, gleamed like a gun, was handled like a gun—then for his intent and purpose, it *was* a gun.

Bob dropped the fungo and dashed toward Louise. Tombstone, the drawings, the severed doll, and that goddamn dildo all played flash cards with his memory. His heart raced as each step took him closer to saving her life. The gun was raised high, yet to be aimed. Fans along the first base line stood and cheered—not yet understanding what was about to happen. The noise, Bob thought, so much noise—was it the fans or the vessels exploding *I can do it's* in his head?

The home plate umpire extended his arms toward Lefty Johnston: What's going on? The manager shrugged, thinking, Dixon's finally cracked. Not knowing what else to do, the Mets' pitcher turned and stepped off the mound. Johnny Mars stood and removed his catcher's mask. First base coach Gary Tomlin placed his hands squarely on his hips and watched Dixon approached—"What the hell you doing, Bob?" he yelled. Jesus Maldonado dropped the bat and took a few steps toward his freaked-out teammate. He too wondered what was going on—no make that, what the *fuck* was going on. Meteorite after Meteorite stood, or stepped forward, then raced up the dugout steps.

A few more steps, Bob thought, shooting a glance at the stands. Tombstone! I'll kill you, you fucker, if you hurt her. I'll kill you! The gun! Where's the fucking gun? Everyone was watching—Louise, standing in open-mouthed shock, shaking her head, holding her hands palms out as if telling Bob to stop, suddenly very frightened.

I can do it! I can do it! I can do it! Where's the motherfucking gun?!
Then the glint, he saw it—aimed. Perfectly aimed. Bob visualized the trigger being squeezed, the 9-mm slug heading toward Louise's head in some sort of cinemafantastique slow motion. He pounced on her, pushing her to the ground, hearing not the sharp pop of the gunshot but only Louise's shrill scream as the first and only bullet was fired.

26

Guns Don't Shoot Ballplayers, Fans Do

First base was a deep burning red. Purple almost. A shrine of violence. A heavy metal chainsaw kitten attack of blood and sand and bone and shreds of Meteorites home whites fraternized on the once-white bag—some wretched party of bygone hell.

Jesus Maldonado took a few additional steps forward, then stopped cold—dead in his tracks. The pain, man. He could feel the pain. His head swirled and he swallowed back some bile; then, taking a few deep breaths, he pressed on. His teammates needed him.

Johnny Mars fell to his knees in the dirt, then looked to the stands from where the shot had rung out. Fans were mostly screaming and running away, or diving for cover. A couple of business types in suits were wrestling with someone in a Yankees T-shirt and a Braves cap. There was the gun—held high, aimed high, in the air. Another man, this one dressed in a Paul Westerberg T-shirt, stepped in. He raised a fist, then slammed it down into the Yankee fan's face. The Braves cap went flying off, revealing a head of curly gray hair, as the shooter's head snapped back and his knees caved in.

Lefty hustled to the base. "Oh, Christ!" he muttered over and over and over again. "Oh, Christ!" He turned to the stands.

The two men in the suits, along with the Paul Westerberg fan, were holding the shooter down and pummeling him with their fists, screaming at him, three thick necks bulging with veins and color. The gun had been knocked from his hand, knocked from the stands. It lay in the dirt, in front of the rolled-up rain-delay tarp. Lefty turned back to face first base, but the backs of his players circled around the carnage blocked it from his view. Gary Tomlin turned away from the mess and caught Lefty's worried gaze. He shook his head and looked down at the dirt. Lefty suddenly felt very ill, as if he wanted to cry. But tears would have to wait. He could cry later—right now he needed to help.

Special Agent Wesley Selden was standing just inside South Field's Gate E when he received the call that a shot had been fired in the vicinity of first base.

"Fuck!" he screamed, hightailing it into the stadium.

But by the time he made it to Field Box 37, row A, B, C—somewhere in that area—a dozen of New York's finest were handcuffing the shooter and reading him Miranda. One of the men pointed to the field, where one of his fellow officers stood guard next to a gleaming silver 9-mm semiautomatic pistol.

"How the fuck did he get that in here?" Selden asked.

The cop shrugged.

Selden looked back out at the field, past the gun and its guard, over to first base. It was still surrounded—now by players and coaches from both teams, as well as by those ever present members of the press, the videotape rolling, the flashes persistent. I don't want to know, he thought, pictures of Louise flashing off in his mind. I don't want to fucking know.

He turned back to face the shooter—to glare at the son of a bitch.

"Any ID?" he asked the closest cop.

"None."

"Take the fucker into the clubhouse. I want first crack at him."

"But."

"Just do it!"
"Yes, sir."

⊕   ⊕   ⊕

Margaret remained at her seat. She was sitting upright—straight backed—tears streaming down her face. She had seen Bob run, and had wondered why. And then she heard the shot. Over and over again it seemed to echo in her head. She had been caught in the middle of the panic. Over there. Just a few boxes from where she sat. Tombstone. It had to be. Why hadn't she seen him? Why hadn't she done something? Sobs were racking her frame. She wanted to go out onto the field—to rush onto the field. But she was frozen in place. She was stuck in time. The shot, the sound, the explosion of red. She covered her face with her hands and rocked back and forth. "No, no, no," she said. "Please, no. Please, God, no."

The hand on her shoulder startled her. She looked up. It was P.J. Strykes.

"Ms. Gehrig," he said.

She looked into his pain, and screamed, "Oh, no! Please."

"Come with me, please."

Margaret stood, then fell forward and buried her face against P.J.'s chest. He held her tightly and whispered that things would be all right.

⊕   ⊕   ⊕

Margaret and P.J. stepped toward the circle of baseball players surrounding the first base bag. They all turned and stood, and as P.J. and Margaret joined their ranks, a few stepped aside so she could pass. Then they all looked down or away.

Selden was speaking to Lefty, who brushed aside some tears when he spotted Margaret. He looked pale, sickly—she felt worse. She nodded once in his direction, then watched as the medics and physicians from both teams gently lifted Bob onto the stretcher.

"Bob?" Margaret said, suddenly searching the crowd of dazed, frightened athletes. Her eyes were wide. She felt alone, frightened and cold, like when her father died. Then she heard her daughter's voice.

"Mom," Louise said. She was shaking, her uniform covered in blood, but she was standing. "Mom. Are you all right?" she asked, rushing into her mother's arm.

Margaret nodded. "I thought you were," she said. "I thought you . . ."

"I know," Louise said.

"But . . ." Margaret pulled away from her daughter. "Bob?" she said, turning in half circles. The now purple-colored bag caught her eye. So much blood. So much. "Bob," she said again. They were lifting the stretcher. Bob's eyes were clenched shut, and his mouth too, as if he were trying to bite back the pain. Then one of the doctors moved and Margaret saw his leg—his knee—or what was left of it. She took a heaving step forward, then one back. Then she covered her mouth, took three or four deep breaths, and fainted dead away.

When Wesley Selden entered the Meteorites' clubhouse, he asked the other agents and officers to leave. "I want a few minutes alone with him," Selden said.

"This is against regulations," one of the New York City cops reminded him.

"This is the FBI, asshole," Selden snapped. "We don't have the same regulations."

Once they were alone, Selden grabbed the shooter by the throat and slammed him up against the nearest locker—locker number 13. He held the man there, an inch or two off the floor, and glared into his eyes. The shooter was old, in his late fifties or early sixties, skinny, with lots of gray hair. His Yankees T-shirt was ripped and stained with blood, his blood. His face was swollen, his nose broken.

"Tombstone?" Selden snarled.

"What's that?" the old man said.

"I called you Tombstone."

"I heard what you called me. I just can't figure out why."

"Y'know," Selden said, every word accented with spit, "I can't figure that out either."

"I'll tell you why. Cause I hate that motherfucker," the old man said. "That's why."

"What the fuck did Louise Gehrig ever do to you?" Selden emphasized each word with a pulse of added pressure to the man's Adam's apple.

"Louise Gehrig?" the man said through a combination of coughs and spit. "What the hell you talking about?"

Selden loosened his grip. The man slumped back sightly, slipped and banged a hand against locker number 12, then regained his footing.

"Louise Gehrig. Why were you shooting at her?"

The man began to laugh. He shook his head and tried to straighten out his torn T-shirt. "I wasn't shooting at no Louise Gehrig," he said. "Why the hell would I wanna do that? She ain't never done nothing to me."

Selden could feel himself going over the edge, about to explode, to morph into an enraged and fucked-up Dudley Doright. He was most definitely capable of violence—well-targeted, well-deserved violence—and the shooter was pushing all the right buttons. The shooter had entered the double-jeopardy round and was betting his life. "Then who the hell were you shooting at?" Selden yelled.

"That goddamn Dixon," the man said. "I've been a Yankee fan my whole life. I was here, y'know, when Maris hit number sixty-one."

"Big fucking deal," Selden said. "Ten million people had seats to that game."

The man was quiet. "You wanna hear what I have to say, or not?" he asked.

"Enlighten me."

"I've had enough. I ain't seen a good baseball game in Yankee Stadium going on twenty years. And then that George Stein*bummer* goes and moves them to Jersey. What the hell am I supposed to do?" The shooter turned away for a moment, then stared back. "It'll be a cold goddamn day in hell when I sit back and let some no good ex–Boston Red Sox break ol'

Roger's record. That home run, man, that's the one memory I can hold on to. I can't let no one take that away. No one."

Selden turned away and headed for the nearest exit, shaking his head in disgust as he walked. He punched the door to locker number 1 so hard that it would probably need to be replaced. But big fucking deal, he thought. He needed to hit something and the locker probably wouldn't sue back.

"I stopped him!" the shooter yelled after the special agent. "But good. All he can get now is maybe an asterisk next to his name." The shooter cackled out a laugh as six New York City police officers reentered the clubhouse and slapped on the cuffs. "I got him good," he laughed as he was led away. "I got him good."

Selden stepped out from the dugout and took a look around South Field. As a kid he used to dream of walking on real major league grass. But now it was part of a job—a job he was beginning to resent.

Hundreds of fans still milled about, worried looks plastered to their faces. Or curious. Or frightened, perhaps. Many were crying. A few were holding each other. And a few others, well, they just sort of looked dead—just sitting there—dead.

A voice could be heard over the public-address system. It said, "This afternoon's game has been postponed. Please listen to WFAN-AM radio for rescheduling information. We ask that you please vacate the stadium immediately."

Selden passed a group of umpires. He heard them discuss the possibility that the game might be needed to determine the National League division champ.

"Their magic number is two," one ump said.

"But stranger things have happened," said another.

"If we need it, we make it up as a doubleheader this weekend at Shea," the first one said.

"But that would give the Mets the home field advantage."

"Then we make it up here on Monday."

They all nodded.

"Agreed?"

"Agreed."

"Yeah."

"Sounds good to me."

⅏   ⅏   ⅏

Selden walked over to where a group of Meteorites were standing on the field. "Have any of you seen Louise?"

"She went to the hospital with her Mom and Lefty," Reggie Borders explained.

"Thanks."

Elvis Jones spoke up. "You're the FBI guy?"

Selden nodded.

"So, what the deal?" he asked.

"Yeah, why'd someone wanna shoot Louise?" Jamaine Young asked.

"Was that the Tombstone guy?" P.J. asked.

Selden looked away for a moment, and he spotted an Atlanta Braves baseball cap lying on the ground over and in front of where the shooter had sat.

"That wasn't Tombstone," the special agent said. "And he wasn't aiming at Louise."

And suddenly he had the eyes and ears of some of the greatest players in the sport hanging on his every word.

⅏   ⅏   ⅏

Manhattan's Saint Noah of the Divine Roman Catholic Hospital had one of the finest trauma units in all of North America. It was in its third-floor waiting room that Louise, Margaret, and Lefty, then Matt Stern and Special Agent Selden, as well as the ever-present gaggle of reporters and the seemingly unnecessary cops, waited, while in operating room number 9 surgeons did their damnedest to save the future Hall of Famer's leg.

Margaret sat huddled in a corner with her daughter. She had been given a sedative by one of the attending team physicians, as had Louise. Both were ghost white and silent, Margaret's trail of tears having subsided for the moment.

Selden explained the known details first to Lefty and Matt.

"Son of a bitch," the manager muttered. "I don't understand," the owner said. Then, sitting down beside Louise, the agent gently took her hand.

"Hi," she said.

He nodded hello.

"Mom," Louise said. "This is Agent Selden. He's with the FBI."

Margaret looked into his face. "How could you let this happen?" she asked, rather void of emotion.

He swallowed hard. "I've done everything in my power to prevent this sort of thing from happening. But we were looking for people who had a bone to pick with Louise. We never expected anyone would want to shoot Bob Dixon."

"He wasn't aiming at me?" Louise asked.

Selden shook his head and attempted to explain. He stopped short when Margaret began sobbing.

"Are you okay?" he asked softly.

"Just tell me what happened, God damn it!" she shrieked, then softening, "Please, tell me what happened."

It would be almost seven hours before Dr. Joseph Bruckheimer walked from the OR and into the waiting room. He swept past Selden and the cops, past Lefty and the reporters, past all of the other Meteorites who had arrived bearing gifts and tears, right up to Louise and her mom.

They stood.

"Ms. Gehrig," he said, staring hard into Margaret's face.

"Yes."

"I've got some good news."

Margaret took a long-overdue breath.

"We'll be able to save the leg."

Tears once again came to her eyes. "Will he be able to play again?"

The doctor shook his head. "I'm afraid not. The kneecap was destroyed."

"Will he walk?"

Bruckheimer nodded. "Tomorrow we put in a plastic replacement. Then, with a lot of therapy, some patience, a little luck, and some love, he'll be able to walk again."

Ⓜ   Ⓜ   Ⓜ

It was after midnight. Bob was "resting comfortably" on a morphine high in a private room on the hospital's eighth floor. Margaret was in Bob's room, asleep, via the Dalmane highway, on a roll-away bed. Two guards—one a New York City cop, the other one of Selden's agents—stood by just outside the room. "In case," Selden had explained. "In case what?" Margaret had asked. Selden shrugged. "Just in case."

Louise was in the waiting room down the hall. She sat glassy-eyed on an old sofa, a now warm can of Diet Coke held limply in her hand. An old color TV was playing. She stared at it, through it. The news was on. The South Field incident played over and over and over again—and if ever the phrase *ad nauseam* applied, it did here. There were interviews with the shooter—a Bronx native named Andy Shaw who gleamed at the camera, gave a crackling laugh, and shouted, "I stopped him! I stopped that damn Red Sox cold. Your record's safe, Roger. It's safe as long as I'm around." And there were the sports commentators—the expert analysts—who theorized that the Meteorites could not possibly recover from such a shock to their system—at least not in time for the playoffs.

A warm familiar voice came from the doorway. "Didn't your mother ever tell you that TV rots your mind?"

Louise looked up. "Cole?"

He smiled and took one step forward. That was all the time it took for Louise to jump from the sofa and into his arms. He held her with all of his strength, held her and stroked her hair. "It'll be okay," he whispered.

"He tried to save me," she said, pulling away, looking up into his eyes. "He thought I was the target. And now he'll never play again."

"But you weren't the target. This isn't your fault."

"I can't help but think . . . ," she said.

"It'll be okay," he promised. "I promise."

⑪   ⑪   ⑪

The next morning, Margaret found Cole and Louise in the waiting room. He was sitting upright on the sofa, she was curled up, asleep, her head resting on his lap. His Yankee warm-jacket covered her legs and lower body. He stroked the back of her neck gently.

"Cole," Margaret said. "What are you doing here?"

"I had to come."

"But won't you get in trouble?"

"My next start isn't until Friday in Boston. The team can handle the Twins without my rooting them on." He shrugged. "Winfield understands."

"But does Steinbrenner?"

Cole shrugged. "He doesn't have any choice."

Margaret walked over to the coffee machine and poured herself a cup. Then, sitting on one of the adjoining chairs, she took a sip and motioned toward her daughter. "How is she?"

"Okay. I guess. She feels as if this is all her fault."

"I know."

⑪   ⑪   ⑪

Louise woke up feeling ill—the sheer violence, the bloody images playing over and over and over in her mind. She sat up from her resting spot on Cole's lap and bolted from the room. Turning the corner, she ran down the hall, a hand slapped tight against her mouth. The bathroom for the disabled was closest, and it was empty. She opened the door and lunged inside. Then crouched over the toilet, she retched up the gray-haired Roger Maris fan and his goddamn gun. She vomited up his dry cackle, his bullet, and Roger Maris's fucking record. She threw up every one of Maris's hits and homers and even his goddamn errors as well. And with them went Tombstone, and the ever-efficient U.S. Postal Service. With them went the doll, the dildo. With them went Arnold Loiten and all the anger and hatred in the world. With them went all the pain.

She regurgitated them up and flushed them all down—a nice neat package from Louise Gehrig to the citizens of hell.

If only the wound in Bob's leg could disappear as quickly.

Dr. Bruckheimer entered the waiting room. Louise was standing. Cole's warm-up jacket was draped over her shoulders. She looked out the window at nothing in particular. Cole was half asleep, still seated upright on the sofa, his head nodding forward every now and then. Margaret was in the chair, her eyes glazed over, focused on the Yankees logo on the back of Cole's jacket. It was identical to the one on the shooter's shirt. It was identical to the memory of her dad.

The doctor cleared his throat. Six tired eyes turned his way. "He's awake," he said.

"And . . . ?"

"I think he'd like some company."

Margaret, Louise, and Cole filed into Bob's private room. Margaret went immediately to the side of the bed, while Louise stayed at the foot, Cole just behind her. Bob looked first at Margaret—no expression on his face. He looked at Cole— again, no expression. Then he looked at Louise. He thought about how he'd feel if she were lying in the bed, and he was standing by her side. And though this was pain—oh, man, oh, mother-fuck, did this hurt—seeing Louise in his place would hurt more. Of that, Bob was certain.

He turned back toward Margaret and broke the silence. "You still wanna marry a guy who has to limp down the aisle?"

She nodded and sniffled back tears. "Yeah. I do."

Louise stared down at the spot on the bed where the sheet covered Bob's right leg. She wondered what it would feel like to be in his place. To know that she could never again play the game that had given her life, made her life, that was her life.

Bob caught her staring. "It's okay," he said.

Louise looked up and into his eyes.

"I had to save you."

Louise turned and caught her mother's nervous glance. Margaret nodded a little: You tell him. Louise shook her head in small rapid back and forth shakes: No, you! Then they both looked down at Bob and shrugged.

"What?" he asked.

Louise and Margaret raised their eyes and exchanged glances again, then both turned to face Cole. "You explain," Louise whispered.

Bob stared up into the face of the Yankee pitcher. "Explain what?" Bob asked.

"Well," Cole said. "You see, Bob . . ." He cleared his throat, then looked helplessly at Louise.

"Go on," she urged.

"It's like this. . . ."

Bob stared dumbfoundedly. He looked as if someone had just told him the most unbelievable excuse of all time—a record-breaking *my dog ate it, my grandmother died, my car won't start, the rubber broke—all rolled into one*—and he had no choice but to buy it.

"Did anyone bother explaining to this kook that the greatest Yankee of all time was an ex–Red Sox?" Bob asked finally.

"Babe Ruth doesn't matter," Cole explained. "The guy's a Roger Maris nut. Seems he was in Yankee Stadium when Maris hit number sixty-one."

Bob began to laugh. It was all too ridiculous. "That was thirty-nine years ago," he said. "I wasn't even born."

Cole shrugged. "Guess he wanted to preserve the greatest moment in his life."

Bob shook his head. "Then why didn't he just shoot himself?"

Kevin Thomas Willard watched and read everything about the Bob Dixon incident. He couldn't comprehend how anyone who professed a love for the game could shoot down a man who was on the verge of breaking one of the greatest of all professional records. That wasn't a love for baseball, it was a love for the past. Records were meant to be broken. But in close to four decades no one had really ever threatened. And here was Dixon—a good player, sure. A great player, even. A solid producer who usually averaged thirty homers a year. Once he hit forty-three. Twice, forty. But sixty—no one would have ever suspected the ex-Philly, ex-Met, ex–Red Sox had it in him. And damn, if that wasn't what made the game so damn special. That unpredictability. That an average—okay, slightly above average— talent could rise above, could scale the Mount Everest of legends erected by Babe Ruth and Willie Mays and Joe DiMaggio and Hank Aaron and the original Gehrig. That a player, in these days of inflated egos and salaries, in these days of below-average ability, below-average zeal, could become a legend to rival. A legend for today. A living legend. Dixon was amazing. The Meteorites were a miracle team. And Louise, well, Kevin truly and honestly loved her. This was baseball—he finally understood. This was baseball in all its glory. In all its stark, sheer beauty. And for some screwball with a gun to step forward and stop Dixon in his tracks made Kevin angry. For some nutcase called Tombstone to reduce Louise's life to security guards and mail-bomb squads made him seethe. It made him want to kill. It made him want to cry. It made him realize that life was too short to be holed up in a small, dirty room in a transient hotel. It even made him miss Geraldine.

Like her husband, Geraldine Willard was glued to the tube. She had watched every speck of Dixon info. She could picture the shooter. She could hear his laugh. She reran the catcher's sprint toward the bitch over and over and over again. His lunge. The gunshot—barely audible. The explosion of red. The grimace on Dixon's face. The bitch's screams. She memorized the action from every angle—and inch lower and the bullet would have really counted. It would have taken out a large chunk from Louise's thigh. A few inches to the right and it would have lodged in her spine. What a wonderful thought, at least to Geraldine. She felt excited, alive again. And aware. The Dixon shooting made her realize that life was too short to not take action. And it illustrated how easy it was—obviously very easy—to sneak a weapon into a major-league ballpark.

27

Success & Bullets

The arithmetic was simple: with seven, eight if necessary, games left to play, Louise and her teammates needed a combination of Meteorites wins and/or Mets losses that equaled two—*the magic number two*. If, and it was one of those mega-magical-religious if's that baseball fans live and die by, the Meteorites could somehow manage to lose all eight games, *and* if their crossborough rivals could somehow manage to win all eight, the Mets would win the NL East pennant. If the Meteorites won only one of the last eight, *or* if the Mets lost only one of the next eight, there'd be a tie—and one of those infamous one-game playoffs. And as Red Sox fans knew, one-game playoffs could be brutal.

If the Meteorites lost all of their remaining games, and the Mets lost only two, Louise and company would still reign supreme. If the Meteorites won one, *and* the Mets lost one, again, the Manhattan team would be king of the hill. If the Meteorites won two of their remaining games, they won the pennant, *no matter what* the Mets did. It was pretty simple actually—innocent, as far as concepts go.

But violence can destroy innocence. And violence has never been on speaking terms with simple. Violence subscribes to the chaos theory of sporting publications, *Sports Unpredictable.*

With both Louise and Bob out of the lineup for Monday evening's home meeting with the Pirates, and with the frightening perception of doom invading every other Meteorite mind, it came as no surprise to Lefty, Jesus, Elvis, and company that the Pittsburgh team could shut them out. It was the Meteorites most lackluster performance of the season—a 7–0 loss—and if ever the cliché *their hearts weren't in it* rang true, it did on this chilly, rainy late September night.

The Mets, playing the first game in a four-game series in Buffalo, were also unnerved. Catcher Johnny Mars was sitting out the game, as was the team's first baseman. But that lack of offense didn't prevent them from squeaking by the hapless Expos by the score of 3–2.

The Meteorites' magic number remained at two—with six, seven if necessary, games to go.

Margaret watched the game on TV with Bob from his hospital room. That afternoon, Dr. Bruckheimer had replaced Bob's kneecap with a plastic replacement that would soon give Bob the ability to walk "with a limp," to sit, and maybe even to kneel. "But not for a long while."

The painkillers were helping. Bob could barely feel the wound, the throbbing, the sharp, jabbing pang. Barely. But the pain in his head, that soreness in his heart—there were no painkillers for those. The pharmaceutical companies just didn't make something to help you get over the fact that the dream was over.

Louise spent the night in her apartment with Cole. "You need some sleep," her mother had insisted, walking them to the elevators. "Bob will survive."

She nodded and heeded her mom's advice. And in the quiet

privacy of her Charles Street home, she pulled Cole close and asked him to help her take her mind off the pain. They made slow, delicate love, and afterward she fell asleep in his arms.

Locked in his secure embrace, Louise dreamed of her grandfather—a man she knew only from photo albums and her mom's recollection. She felt his large patient hands squeezing hers. She saw his tired old knowing gaze—a Norven Dougherty gaze, or was that old Norven she heard laughing in the other room?—never veering from her curious stare. And she heard his voice, telling her, urging her, in soft fragile tones, "You can't quit now."

And though she knew her grandfather was right, Louise, waking from her dream, couldn't help but ask herself: Was baseball worth dying for?

On Tuesday night, the Meteorites fared slightly better, losing by only one run to the Pirates. Meanwhile in Buffalo, the Mets were getting a good old-fashioned ass-whoopin', losing 7–0 going into the ninth inning, when they miraculously—in a strictly 1969 manner of speaking—tied it up, then went on to win in extra innings.

Louise, Cole, and Margaret watched the Meteorites' game with Bob in his private hospital suite. Considering the situation, Bob was in good spirits—on his way to accepting. He'd have a long life ahead of him. A life with Margaret. And, if he was ever so inclined, he could always return to baseball as a manager or maybe even as a GM.

Besides, the books had helped. Instead of sending flowers, or other soon-to-wither-and-die novelties, the Meteorites players had showered their fallen catcher with a lifetime of reading. Paperbacks were piled high in seemingly every corner of the hospital room—every one inscribed with a dirty little comical ditty or some words of inspiration. A dozen current hardcover bestsellers sat patiently on the nearest night table, and those too were imprinted with a signature of friendship and longing. And over in a Federal Express delivery box sat three extremely rare, noninscribed first editions courtesy of the team's pitching staff.

"See that," Cole said. "You get shot and you get a goddamn library."

"Only in America," Bob said with a sarcastic laugh.

"True enough," Margaret said in her best play-by-play voice. "True enough."

For some three hours the foursome rooted and laughed and drank wine from a couple of bottles the Yankee pitcher had smuggled past the hospital's security staff. And when the gave was over, Cole and Louise made a speedy exit. He needed to catch a red-eye to Chicago, and she needed some sleep.

Louise hadn't been feeling well—the trauma and all—and had once again spent her first few good morning moments bent over a toilet. It would pass, she knew. But she couldn't risk illness now. Not when her team needed her. She had to get over the brink. Bob needed her to survive. "One baseball death in the family was enough," he said, explaining, "I need to play the game vicariously through you."

Louise suited up for the Wednesday afternoon game against the Pirates. She stretched, warmed up, and took BP. But when it was time to play, when 1:35 rolled around on baseball's clock, she knew she wasn't ready. Not just yet. She still felt nauseous and even dizzy. It didn't take Lefty more than a squinty look to recognize something was wrong.

"Why don't you sit this one out, Louise?"

She didn't argue. She didn't even give arguing a thought. She just took a seat on the bench and watched as her team—a strangely unfamiliar team—took the field.

Up in Buffalo, the Mets were likewise playing an afternoon game. And once again, they were losing. By the end of the sixth inning, the score was 10–2 in favor of the Expos.

By the end of the sixth inning in South Field, the score was 0–0. And it seemed as if the players and fans were more interested in watching the scoreboard than in watching the game on the field. Every Buffalo run was greeted by cheers. And as the game's end neared, chants of "Go Expos!" made the rounds.

In the top of the ninth inning, with left-handed relief pitcher Larry Sheer on the mound, a utility outfielder for the Pirates knocked one out of the park, making the score 1–0. It was all the Pirates would need. And the Meteorites would be handed their third loss in a row—meticulously garnished on a silver platter.

But though the game was over, no players and no fans left the stadium. Instead they all turned their eyes toward the giant Diamond Vision screen over the center field wall, upon which was now playing the end of the Mets-Expos matchup. Taking the field in the top of the ninth, losing 14–5, the Mets were not about to lie down and die. They battled back, getting a hit and two walks, then another hit—which scored two runs—and another walk, which loaded the bases with only one out. They now needed seven runs to tie, and a home run would give them four. The Meteorites began to sweat. If the Mets could come back and win this game, the momentum would most definitely be on their side. And suddenly a few of the Manhattan players began feeling like Chicago Cubs circa 1969. Baseballs stuck in their throat. Cough, cough. Choke, choke.

Then, just as suddenly, the next Mets hitter grounded softly to second for an easy double play. The Mets lost. The Meteorites and some thirty-eight thousand fans in South Field breathed a collective sigh of relief. Even the Pirates seem to cheer—there was never any love lost between the Mets and the Pirates. There was never any love lost between the Mets and any team. And now the best they could do was hope for that one-game playoff. The Meteorites had at least backed themselves into a tie for the NL East Division crown.

Once win was all they needed.

After the game, Louise sat with a few of her teammates in their clubhouse. Bottles of champagne were on ice—waiting, just waiting. The bottles would have to wait just a little while longer.

"How's Bob?" everyone asked.

"Better than you'd expect," Louise said.

"Your mom okay?" P.J. asked.

"Yeah. She's calmed down."

"What about you?" Jesus asked.

She shrugged. "I'm scared, y'know? Can't explain it. I just don't feel, well, I just don't feel right. That could have been me. That could have been any of us. How do I know some Rickey Henderson nut isn't gonna come hunting me down because I might break his record?"

"You *will* break his record," Jamaine Young said, "I'd bet the ranch on it." He smiled warmly. "Besides, no one likes Rickey Henderson."

A few players laughed.

Even Louise smiled. "I guess," she said.

"Stern's installing metal detectors," Lefty said. "That should keep the guns outta the park."

"I just don't get it," Louise said.

"It's hard to understand," P.J. said. "But we can't let this stop us. We've been playing like shit out there. We can't afford to lose both you and Bob. We need you out there."

Yeahs all around.

Louise nodded. I'll be back tomorrow. I promise."

"We've got to win this thing," Jesus said. "For Bob and for ourselves. We've played like fucking champs all year. This is the best team I've ever been on."

A number of his teammates mumbled their agreement.

"Let's what we set out to do six months ago," he continued. "Let's prove all those assholes wrong. An expansion team *can* win it all. We know we can do it."

"So, what's stopping us?" P.J. asked.

"Fear of failure," Reggie Borders said.

Louise shook her head. "It's fear of success," she said.

"And bullets," Elvis Jones said. "We're afraid of success and bullets."

"But not necessarily in that order."

⑪ **28** ⑪

Let's Go to the Videotape

On Thursday evening, the Manhattan Meteorites took to the green grass of South Field for their final home game of the regular season. Reggie Borders was starting. He was the first out of the dugout and onto the field. Jo Jo Manzi was catching, and he was right on his tail. Next out was Sandy Downs, heading toward left field, followed by Jamaine Young and Jeff Carter to their respective homes in center and right. Darryl White ran out and over to third base. Then came the might defensive three: Jesus Maldonado, Elvis Jones, and Louise Gehrig.

"Your Manhattan Meteorites," an announcer said over the stadium's PA system. And 38,710 fans were on their feet—cheering, some crying, all chanting: "Win! Win! Win!"

⑪   ⑪   ⑪

"Welcome back," Junella Wingi said. "If you're just joining us, Reggie Borders struck out the side one, two, three in the top of the first, and now it's the Meteorites' turn at bat."

"The team could really use a win tonight," Kurt Rybak said. "Not only because it'd mean clinching it here at home, but for their morale."

"I think having Louise back in the lineup definitely helps."

"True enough."

"I thought you were trying to cut down on those."

"Old habits are heard to break."

"True enough," Wingi joked.

"Jamaine Young steps to the plate."

"He's really had a great year. Especially considering those nagging hamstring problems of seasons past."

"He'd be leading the majors in steals if it weren't for Louise."

"Stan Anderson, the Pirates' catcher, gives the sign. A change-up."

"Woo. Way outside. Ball one."

"We should tell our viewers that the Meteorites have a special video presentation immediately following tonight's game. A video highlights tape from their first season."

"And there are certainly a lot of highlights from this season."

"Anderson calls for the change-up again."

"That one was only a foot or two outside the strike zone."

"Ball two."

"Besides highlights, we've gotten word that there'll be a message from Bob Dixon live via satellite from his hospital bed."

"Time to break out the hankies."

"Most likely."

"Anderson calls for a fastball. Handelsman, the Pirate pitcher, nods, sets, winds up, and . . ."

"Ball three."

"He can't seem to find the plate."

"With a record of nine wins versus fifteen losses, he's got to be a little concerned about where he'll be pitching next year."

"Or whether he'll be pitching at all. Handelsman's hardly a rookie."

"True enough."

"Anderson calls for another fastball."

"Speaking of Bob Dixon. I spoke with Lefty Johnston earlier. He said that he and a bunch of the players visited him in the hospital this morning and that he was in surprisingly good spirits."

"I guess he'll be able to walk again. That's amazing, especially if you've seen the slow-motion replay of the gunshot. That leg exploded."

"Ball four. Jamaine Young goes to first."

"His hundredth steal should be pretty much in the bag right here."

"With Anderson behind the plate, you better believe it."

"It's so good to hear that chant."

"Louise! Louise! Louise!"

"I know I've missed it."

"She seems a little nervous."

"Getting shot at can do that to a person."

"Getting shot at. Getting threatened. She's got a bodyguard following her around the clock."

"And yet she won't give up."

"Louise waves to the crowd."

"Anderson calls for a change-up. Handelsman nods, sets, and . . ."

"There goes Young. What a tremendous jump! And Anderson's throw is way off line."

"Ball one to Louise, stolen base number one hundred for Jamaine Young."

"More highlights for that videotape."

"Louise steps out of the box while the crowd gives Young a standing O. She seems to be taking a few deep breaths."

"Trying to relax."

"She steps back in. Anderson calls for a curve. The pitcher nods, sets, and . . ."

"A fly to the warning track in extreme right field. If it stays fair, it's an easy double. . . ."

"Fair ball! It's a fair ball! And right fielder Johnny Loftus fumbles the ball."

"He just kicked it away."

"Jamaine Young scores. And Louise is on her way to third."

"A stand-up triple."

"Welcome back, Louise Gehrig."

"And the Meteorites take the lead, one-nothing."

"Listen to that roar."

"It's gotta feel good."

"There's that smile."

"I don't want to sound sexist, but there isn't a prettier smile in all of baseball."

"I'll allow that."

"Thanks."

"Any time."

⚉   ⚉   ⚉

The Meteorites won the game by the score of 4–0 and guaranteed themselves a postseason berth. And after the final out in the top of the ninth, the team hugged and patted and screamed and yelled. They celebrated and bowed to the applause like true champions.

Then, turning their attention to the Diamond Vision screen, they watched, along with the 38,710 in attendance, as their fallen teammate spoke.

"Hello," Bob said. He was seated up in the hospital bed. A little color had returned to his face. It was his first public appearance since the shooting. He wore his Meteorites hat, along with the hospital's home whites. "First off, to all my teammates: congratulations. I'm proud to consider myself a part of this team. To our fans, thank you for the support, and for the hundreds of letters that have been pouring into the hospital's mail room since Sunday. Really, I'll never be able to answer them all, but I'll try. I've got a lot of time now." He exhaled deeply. "But it's okay. Life goes on. Baseball goes on." He paused for a moment, fighting the impending tears. "Louise, Jesus, Jamaine, Jeff, Reggie, P.J., Lefty, all of you, there's only one thing I ask. I'm greedy. I want another World Series ring. Understand?" Everyone on the team nodded in unison. "This is the one that means something. This is the one that's history." The tears finally won, as Bob concluded, "Now, go down there and kick Atlanta's ass."

The crowded cheered, many wiping away tears of their own. Bob waved good-bye, and his image was replaced by the first image of the highlight reel: Louise facing Rocky Goetz's fastball on that chilly Saturday afternoon in February, when she proved, beyond any major league doubt, that she could play baseball. The background music: Frank Sinatra singing "New York, New York."

Louise stared up at the video image. Is that really me? she wondered. That girl's young. She's innocent. I hardly feel either. Tonight's was a good game, going three for four and adding one steal to her total—a history-making steal that secured her position in the record books as the player with the most stolen bases in a single season ever. And she was feeling better—no morning jaunt to the toilet. Well, no retching away. She felt as if she might, but she hadn't. So, that was something anyway.

Up on the Diamond Vision screen, one shot faded into the next: opening day, Dixon's first homer of the season, Louise's first steal, the final out of Reggie's opening day perfect game, another Dixon dinger, a double play—*Jesus to Elvis to Louise*, a Jamaine Young steal, a Sandy Downs homer, another of Bob's, and another, and another, a P.J. strikeout, Lefty blowing a bubble in the dugout, a Jeff Carter catch against the right field wall, a Dixon dinger, another Louise steal, et cetera, et cetera, and so on, ad elation.

With every high point of the season cut to and between Bob's sixty home runs—the Sinatra tune faded into Springsteen's "Glory Days" and that into Queen's "We Are the Champions"—it was a nine-minute opus dedicated to the grandness of the game and the greatness of the team. And after it was through, the South Field fans cheered, they screamed, they yelled and shrieked. It sounded to Louise and her teammates as if the cheering would never end—cheering for them, for what they had accomplished. But it did end, only to be replaced by chanting. A chant that set those goose bumps a-marchin'.

"Beat the Braves!"

"Beat the Braves!"

"Beat the Braves!"

⊕ **29** ⊕

Vincent Van Tombstone

Over in the American League East, things weren't such a piece of cake for Cole Robinson and the Yankees. Going into the final three games of the season, the Yankees were locked in a dead heat tie with the archrival Red Sox—with each team having ninety-two wins on the year versus sixty-seven losses. And though Fenway Park had been historically kind to the Bombers, in recent seasons the New Jersey squad had seemed clueless in Beantown. The Green Monster was most definitely not on their side.

Cole was pitching the first of the games, a Friday night, prime-time affair. It was his thirty-third game start—a win would give him twenty-three on the year versus six losses. And with an ERA well under 2.00 and some 217 strikeouts, the AL Cy Young seemed a virtual lock. Roy Henna with the Rangers was the only other twenty-game winner in the league (his record: 21–8), but his ERA was pushing 3.00, and his strikeout total wasn't even in the league's top ten.

Baseball fans everywhere were tuned into Boston—the only remaining pennant drive. It was the summer of '49, the summer of '78, the summer of '99 all over again. Even Louise and her teammates seemed more interested in watching the scoreboard than in their now meaningless game at Shea. And in Bob's hospital room, there was no doubt as to which game he and Margaret would watch.

"What happens to Louise and Cole if their teams make it to the World Series?" Bob asked.

"It makes them both play a little harder," Margaret explained.

"Could make for some exciting baseball," he said, suddenly becoming quiet and withdrawn.

"I'm sorry," Margaret whispered.

He shook his head. "My fault. At the start of the season I told myself I was going to try and break the Maris record. It was a bad business decision, that's all." He smiled at her. "A hostile takeover that didn't work."

Margaret nudged his arm. "You didn't have a clue you'd hit sixty home runs."

"I most certainly did," he said, clearing his throat and straightening out an imaginary tie. "Right after number fifty-nine sailed out of the park, I thought to myself, Hey, I've got a week. Maybe I can hit one more."

"Watch the game," she said in fake annoyance.

"Yes, ma'am."

⚾   ⚾   ⚾

The Yankees won the Friday night game by the narrowest margin allowable by baseball law—final score: New Jersey 2, Boston 1. Cole pitched a complete game, and afterward, at the Yankees' postgame press conference in Fenway's visiting clubhouse, he dedicated it to Bob Dixon. "In Yankee eyes, Bob," he said, "the record is yours."

On Saturday afternoon, the tide turned back to the Red Sox, who pelted hit after hit off the Yankees' starting pitcher, Greg Maddux, who lasted only three and a third innings before being pulled by skipper Dave Winfield.

But the damage was done—six runs for the Red Sox, then another two in the seventh inning, and another in the eighth. And the game was theirs, 9–4. The American League East once again had two teams reigning supreme. And it would all come down to one game, with Boston having the home field edge.

⨷ ⨷ ⨷

On Sunday afternoon, Louise and her teammates won their third in a row from the New York Mets—their fourth in a row overall—and finished their premiere season with a record of 98–63. One hundred sixty-one games, with one not played—one not necessary—because of a lunatic in a Yankees shirt who felt intent on executing his supposed Second Amendment rights.

The Mets finished the season in second place, six games back, with a record of 92–69—a most comfortable position for the team since the mid-eighties. No one else in the division was even close.

That night, Louise celebrated with her mother and Bob in his hospital room. They celebrated the end of her first regular season in the big leagues by watching the one regular season game that mattered: the Yankees versus the Red Sox in Fenway Park.

⨷ ⨷ ⨷

Over in his makeshift South Field office, Special Agent Wesley Selden was also tuned in to the game. He was working a Sunday, and working late, and the green grass of Fenway looked a little off-color on the small file cabinet–top TV. Selden looked up every time the crowd screamed. A Yankee run. Then another. He laughed to himself and looked at the stacks of papers on his desk. Three stacks. The largest pile, the one to the left, contained each and every one of the first Tombstone letters, these with the original single stone drawing. The next largest pile, positioned to the right, contained the copies of the second Tombstone letter—the double-wide stone for Louise and Cole.

He shook his head and took a sip from the coffee mug half filled with bourbon that waited patiently on the corner of the desk. A loud groan blurted from the tinny TV speaker. The Red Sox had blown a bases-loaded opportunity, and going into the eighth inning the Yanks were winning 2–0.

The third stack, the smallest of them all, sat in the middle of his desk. It was Tombstone's latest incarnation. But where the first was plain, and the second ominous, this rendering was startlingly alive. It was almost as if the son of a bitch was taking art lessons—Vincent Van Tombstone. Maybe he should recheck all the art schools. Like anyone in art school gives a good goddamn about baseball.

On the TV, the announcer called out the familiar "going, going, gone" as one of the New Jersey hitters belted one out and over the Green Monster. Selden looked up to see how many of his pin-striped teammates were on base. Two. He shook his head slightly and grinned. "Fucking Boston," he muttered.

Fucking Tombstone, he thought, slapping his hand down on the third pile. Enough. His head hurt. He couldn't think. And tomorrow morning he had a meeting with Matt Stern to discuss heightened security measures for the playoff games against the Braves. For six months he'd been working on virtually nothing but baseball, working on nothing but Louise Gehrig. The American taxpayer's money at work.

A resounding *clack!* from the small TV.

Selden choked back a satisfied smile and took one last look at pile number three. The double tombstone, but behind it, off to the side—like the plot across the street—was a fresh grave, and another tombstone, marked only with the initials B.D. He sighed loudly, then downed the remaining bourbon. He shut the game off with a half inning left to play and the Red Sox down 5–0. "Good night Boston," he said to the TV, silencing it. "Have a nice winter."

He slammed the door to the office and headed home, the image—Tombstone's ghastly threat—lingering in his head.

30

No Excuses

Two thousand, five hundred ninety-one games later—with one game canceled due to what *New York Newsday* dubbed "Statistical Warfare!"—and the regular baseball season was history. Time for twenty-eight teams to go home. Time for seven hundred players to go fishing, or hunting, or golfing, or maybe time they started shopping for Christmas. Time they caught up on their reading, or maybe the writing of their memoirs. Time to test the free-agency waters—at least for some. Time to play a little guitar, watch a little TV, see a few movies, spend some time with the girlfriend and/or the boyfriend and/or the wife and kids. Time to become a lounge chair quarterback. Or basketball. Yeah, some courtside seats. Hockey? Don't think so. It was time for a little much-deserved R and R.

The season was a bust after all, though they'd tried their damnedest. Really, they'd sweated their butts off. It just wasn't their year—even though they most definitely took it *one game at a time*. Ask the manager—that was the game plan: one game at a time. If only they could have won a few more of those single games. If only . . .

And sure, there were the postseason awards: Cy Young, MVP, Rookie of the Year, Gold Gloves, et alia. But most of those were usually won by players on teams that won, on teams that finished first, or were at least in contention.

Oh, well.

No run support. That was it, at least in the minds of some 280 or so pitchers. Or errors. My goddamn teammates can't even catch an easy pop fly. Or speed and the lack thereof. If only our leadoff hitter could run as well as he renegotiates contracts.

The infielders and outfielders and catchers all agreed to disagree. It was the pitchers. They all sucked, giving up hit after hit after hit. And did they ever listen to their catchers? Not a chance. And then the ball if over the fence, gone and good-bye.

But hey. It's only a game, they all collectively thought. Right? We're rich. We're young. We're healthy—well, mostly healthy. We're shining stars. And, what the hell, there's always next season.

⚾   ⚾   ⚾

But for four teams, for ninety-nine players—with one absent because of what the *Los Angeles Times* called an "Error of Humanity"—there was the power and the glory of a postseason life. The League Championship Series, and of course, the October Classic: the World Series. It was their chance to prove that their 162-game serving from the 2,591-game pot was not a fluke, was not in vain, was not, as their detractors might reason, a mistake. They were there to demonstrate their talent, their ability, their ego. They were there to prove they deserved to be ranked alongside baseball's elite: the Yankee teams of the twenties, thirties, fifties, sixties and late seventies, the Big Red Machine, the Oakland A's with Reggie Jackson, the Chicago Nationals of Tinker to Evers to Chance fame, or even the early-seventies Orioles and the late-seventies Phillies—even they'd do. They were there because those most recent on- and off-season acquisitions were brilliant. Those salaries justified. They were there because they kicked everyone else's butt and took no prisoners. Damn the torpedoes! Full steam ahead! We're going to the World Series! We're going to Disneyland. We're going to the fucking moon!

Then again, maybe it was luck. Maybe it was just their year. The gears connected, the wheels turned, and some higher power in some higher place smiled down a cheshire cat grin of baseball teeth, pointed impolitely, and screamed, "Hey, you! Yeah, you! I think it's time you won some games."

2000 FINAL STANDINGS

AMERICAN LEAGUE

East	W	L	Pct.	GB
New Jersey	96	66	.593	—
Boston	95	67	.586	1
Toronto	86	76	.531	10
Milwaukee	81	81	.500	15
Baltimore	80	82	.494	16
Atlanta	77	85	.475	19
Detroit	71	91	.438	25
Memphis	52	110	.321	44

West	W	L	Pct.	GB
Texas	103	59	.636	—
Chicago	94	68	.580	9
Seattle	91	71	.562	12
Minnesota	89	73	.549	14
Kansas City	87	75	.537	16
California	79	83	.488	24
Oakland	77	85	.475	26
San Francisco	38	124	.235	65

NATIONAL LEAGUE

East	W	L	Pct.	GB
Manhattan	98	63	.609	—
New York	92	69	.571	6
Chicago	86	76	.531	11.5
Florida	82	80	.506	15.5
Buffalo	79	83	.488	18.5
Pittsburgh	78	84	.481	19.5
St. Louis	75	87	.463	22.5
Philadelphia	69	93	.426	28.5

West	W	L	Pct.	GB
Atlanta	110	52	.679	—
Cincinnati	95	67	.586	15
Arkansas	88	74	.543	22
St. Petersburg	81	81	.500	29
Colorado	75	87	.463	35
San Diego	70	92	.432	40
New Orleans	68	94	.420	42
Los Angeles	49	113	.302	61

MANHATTAN METEORITES STATISTICS
2000 Season

POS	Player	Games	AB	BA	H	2B	3B	HR	HR%	R	RBI	BB	SO	SB	PO	A	E	DP	TC/G	FA
1B	L. Gehrig	158	622	.301	187	42	13	15	2.4	119	85	96	32	136	1293	82	4	112	8.7	.996
2B	E. Jones	157	534	.263	140	11	2	3	0.6	51	32	46	57	32	220	232	14	110	2.9	.969
SS	J. Maldonado	159	596	.310	185	41	20	34	5.7	104	119	58	75	7	298	400	17	107	4.4	.976
3B	D. White	161	579	.287	166	19	1	28	4.8	98	112	74	127	1	122	257	17	30	2.6	.957
RF	J. Carter	146	520	.292	152	29	9	19	3.7	74	81	29	94	5	290	14	2	2	2.1	.993
CF	J. Young	161	627	.319	200	37	11	9	1.4	146	51	103	58	102	439	11	12	0	2.9	.974
LF	S. Downs	156	547	.266	145	10	0	11	2.0	48	57	46	91	2	367	16	7	1	2.5	.982
C	B. Dixon	151	598	.342	204	21	3	60	9.9	130	163	88	67	3	753	69	9	11	5.5	.989
UT	P. Benson	36	103	.254	26	0	0	1	1.0	12	14	8	10	0	162	11	7	12	5.0	.960
C	J.J. Manzi	21	62	.219	14	0	0	1	1.6	9	6	1	12	0	68	8	0	1	3.6	1.000
OF	A. Capodanno	36	41	.195	8	1	0	0	0.0	6	3	1	9	0	67	2	7	1	2.1	.907
OF	D. Matz	64	172	.245	42	5	1	7	4.1	21	17	14	35	8	112	5	10	0	2.0	.921

PITCHER	W	L	PCT	ERA	G	GS	CG	IP	H	BB	SO	ShO	Relief Pitching			Batting			
													W	L	SV	AB	H	HR	BA
R. Borders	23	6	.793	1.41	32	32	19	252	113	34	328	11	0	0	0	99	23	1	.232
D. Gaston	18	7	.720	2.57	33	33	3	237	185	53	212	4	0	0	0	86	13	0	.151
S. McKnight	14	11	.560	3.05	34	33	1	214	188	90	168	1	0	0	0	71	8	0	.113
R. Garcia	11	10	.523	4.23	33	32	0	198	180	86	114	0	0	0	0	69	10	0	.145
T. Stewart	13	8	.619	3.89	30	30	0	195	167	64	189	0	0	0	0	66	4	0	.061
A. King	5	10	.333	5.01	59	1	0	109	106	35	75	0	5	10	13	11	1	0	.091
P. Coleman	3	7	.300	4.67	76	0	0	96	91	37	42	0	3	7	6	2	0	0	.000
L. Scheer	1	2	.333	3.81	57	0	0	62	40	28	12	0	1	2	9	0	0	0	.000
P.J. Strykes	10	2	.833	1.23	68	0	0	74	32	4	106	0	10	2	39	6	3	0	.500

Overnight with Howie

"Go ahead, Joey."

"No. You go, Howie. Get it out of the way. Just say it."

"Say what? Ahh . . . I told you so, maybe?"

"Yeah, well. I have just one thing to say about that. The Mets choked."

"Oh, c'mon. They were outplayed in every category. Just look at the Meteorites' stats. That is one great team."

"On paper."

"What do you mean, on paper? They won the division, didn't they?"

"Right. And after four games with Atlanta, they'll be sent home packing."

"Hey, don't count the Meteorites out just yet."

"Are you saying they can beat Atlanta without Dixon in the lineup?"

"Maybe."

"The Braves have the home field advantage."

"I still say, maybe."

"You're crazy."

"And you just hate Louise Gehrig. If the Meteorites had a man at first base, you'd be their biggest fan."

"They be a kick-ass team."

"Right. But they suck because of Louise."

"You said it."

"Joey. Have you looked at what she did this year? A hundred and thirty-six steals. A batting average of .301, with forty-two doubles, thirteen triples, and fifteen homers. Plus she got eighty-five ribbies. C'mon. Give the woman credit. That's one hell of a year. A career year."

"Next thing, you'll be saying she deserves Rookie of the Year."

"She'd get my vote. And I'm tell you, it's a toss-up between her and Dixon for MVP."

"How can you even say that? Dixon won the Triple Crown."

"But Gehrig is the catalyst on the team."

"You're just blinded by the way she looks."

"What she looks like has nothing to do with it. Louise Gehrig is a damn good baseball player. By any standards."

"By your standards, Howie. By your standards."

"Joey, what is it going to take to get you to admit you're dead wrong? If they take Atlanta?"

"They won't."

"But what if they do?"

"They'd have to win the World Series."

"Okay. Louise and her teammates win the World Series. Then will you admit that you've been wrong? That Louise Gehrig deserves to be playing pro ball?"

"I don't know."

"Well, think about it. In the meantime, we've got to take a break. But when we come back, we'll be joined by Atlanta Journal-Courier *baseball beat writer Arnold Loiten, who's down in Atlanta. He'll tell us how they're preparing for the Meteorites down in the land of peaches."* ·

◉ PART SIX ◉

The Postseason

One of the beautiful things about baseball is that every once in a while you come into a situation where you want to, and where you have to, reach down and prove something.

—Nolan Ryan

⊕ 31 ⊕

Late

"*Aaaaahhhh! Raaaalf wra aaahhh cau cau wra raaaalf, ptt ptt ptt, aaahhh wra cau cau cau.*"

Those were the sounds to which Margaret awoke on the first Monday morning following the end of baseball's regular season. They were rushing out from Louise's master bedroom, banging into walls, slam-dancing, hip-hopping, juvenile delinquent sounds. They were accented with spittle and pain, mucus and the lining of a throat. And they were loud.

Margaret hurried to her daughter's aid, finding her kneeling before the toilet, seemingly retching her guts into the porcelain bowl. She walked over silently, pulled a towel from the rack of many, and dabbed at Louise's forehead.

"You're going to wake the sunglassed one," she said, in reference to Louise's FBI-appointed bodyguard, then, in that soothing motherly tone that always seemed to help, added, "Are you okay?"

Louise shook her head, then nodded. Taking the towel from Margaret, she wiped off her face, then tried to stand.

"Here," Margaret said, helping Louise up to at least a perching position on the edge of the toilet bowl.

"Thanks."

"Was it something you ate?"

"I don't know. I've been feeling like shit ever since ..." Louise took a deep breath, then ripped off a strip of toilet paper and blew her nose.

Margaret filled a glass with tap water, then handed it to her daughter.

After taking a small sip, Louise cleared her throat. "Y'know, since Bob got shot."

Margaret was dumbfounded. She just stared at her daughter.

"It's nerves, or something." Another deep breath. "I'll be okay."

"You been throwing up for a week?" Margaret asked, the tone now more circumspect than soothing.

"Something like that." Another sip. "Why?"

"Oh, no reason," Margaret said, not meaning it. "Are you late?"

"Late?"

"Your period?"

"I've never been all that regular to begin with."

"But are you late?"

"Maybe a few days."

"Just a few days?"

"I don't know." Louise was suddenly defensive. "I was due early last week. Monday or Tuesday. But I'm always a little late when I'm stressed out."

Margaret nodded, rather unconvincingly, or so it seemed to Louise.

"What?" she said. "I mean, Bob getting shot. The whole Tombstone shit. I've got a federal agent following me around day and night. My team made the playoffs. I'd say I've had more than my usual share of stress lately."

"When you were with Cole, how long ago was that?"

"With him?"

"Sexually speaking."

"The first time?"

"Uh-huh."

"Three weeks ago."

"Oh."

"What?"

"Were you . . . careful."

Louise exhaled loudly, and answered truthfully, against her better judgment. "For the most part."

"For the most part? What exactly does "for the most part" mean?"

"It means, *for the most part.*"

"Oh, God. Louise. No."

"No, what?"

"I think you better take a test."

"What are you talking about?"

"An HPT."

"Mom." Louise attempted to stand, then quickly thought better of it, and sat right back down, crossing her legs as if that was what was planned all along. "I'm not pregnant," she said. "I can't be pregnant."

"And why not?"

"I've got the NLCS to win," she said, adding softly, "I've got to get to the World Series."

"Dear, I hate to have to break this to you, but nature doesn't stand still for baseball. Nature doesn't give a hoot about the national pastime. It don't know batting averages from a hole in the wall. It don't know homers from weak pop flies. It don't know the Mets from the Boston Red Sox. It don't—"

"I get your point, Mom."

"Do you?"

"Yes. And I'm not pregnant."

"You're just a week late."

"Right."

"And throwing up every morning."

"Something like that."

"Three weeks after some *for the most part* protected sex."

"You got it."

"Baby," Margaret said, her own life history lessons flashing before her eyes, "I hope to hell you're right."

32

Biblical Proportions

The Braves had home field advantage. Just as it should be, really. With their record of 110–52, they certainly deserved the privilege. But their record actually had nothing to do with it. It was an even-numbered year, and on even-numbered years, the NL Championship Series began on the Tuesday following the end of the regular season in the home park of the Western Division champ.

In the American League, the Yankees had the home field edge, despite their inferior winning percentage of .592 versus the Rangers' .636. Their series would begin on the Wednesday following the end of the regular season.

And, again, because of the even-numbered year, the World Series would begin at the home of the National League champ—either Atlanta or Manhattan—on Saturday, October 14.

⚾   ⚾   ⚾

On the Monday afternoon following the end of the regular season, Louise took a taxi to South Field, where she packed up her gear and then, together with her teammates and coaches, boarded a bus that took them to John F. Kennedy International Airport, where a private jet was waiting to whisk them south.

There was a buzz in the air, a ring-a-ling-a-ding-dong, electric, excited, Gatorade acid test of triumph, guts, and glory. Could an expansion team perform a miracle? In a way, they already had. Never before had one come so far, so soon, so goddamn furiously. But the Braves were a dynasty of a sort—a modern dynasty. No team played harder, no team was more intimidating.

DAVID VS. GOLIATH was what the *New York Post* headline screamed. Posing as many *could they*'s, *would they*'s, and *what-if*'s as was legally allowed by journalistic law.

Most analysts were predicting the Braves in five games, a few, the Braves in six. Only one of any note, Mike Lupica, was going with his heart and not with his head.

In his *Newsday* column, Lupica wrote, "The Meteorites will beat the Braves. I don't know if they'll accomplish this in four games, five, six, or if it'll take all seven. But they will prevail. I'm sure of this. Absolutely. Not because they are a better team than the Atlanta Braves. Not by a long shot. The Braves are the best team in baseball, the best team we've seen quite possibly since the '86 Mets—and like the '86 Mets, they are too confident in that knowledge. So confident, in fact, that Rocky Goetz and his teammates don't even realize that they are the ones who are intimidated.

"Knowledge that *Yes, we are great!* is all that the Atlanta Braves have going for them at this point in time. And it is all they are going to get. Aside from the opportunity to go home a week and a half early to watch Louise and company beat up on either the Rangers or the Yankees. Aside from the opportunity to watch their latest hated rivals collect those World Series rings.

"The Meteorites will win because this is their time, this is their year, the first year of a new century. A century full of promise and hope and expectations fulfilled. Louise Gehrig's year. Louise Gehrig's century. She, her teammates, her manager, and Matt Stern have forced baseball to the next level. Hardly a willing participant, baseball kicked and screamed, and said, 'Hell, no, I won't go!' It's fans shouted obscenities and made threats. But baseball and baseball fans didn't have a choice. The Supreme Court, led by the late Chief Justice

Norven Dougherty, saw to that. So the participants and fanatics shut up and reluctantly swallowed the bitter pill. And like a spoiled child unwilling to see the other side—a sickly child unwilling to take the medicine necessary to get well—they went along grudgingly, for the ride. And one hell of a ride it was. Entertaining—the most invigorating baseball season in years. Exciting—watching Bob Dixon chase and almost break Roger Maris's unbreakable single-season home run record was as good as this sport gets, seeing Louise break Rickey Henderson's steal record was even better. When it was through, baseball looked around, and, hey, what do you know? It survived Louise Gehrig with record ticket sales and the highest overnight television ratings in the history of the sport. Revenues up. Interest up. Respect up. Wow! That wasn't so bad, now was it?"

Louise and her teammates walked out onto the manicured grass of Fulton County Stadium to begin their stretching and warm-up exercises. She looked around, trying to get some bearings. A few too many non-baseball-related thoughts were swirling through her head. Butterflies were flying loop-the-loops in her stomach. And the press was everywhere, outnumbering the players by about four to one.

"They're here because of you," P. J. Strykes told her.

"I hope not," she said.

"Remember, I made it to the World Series three years ago. There weren't half as many of them then. And this is only the NLCS."

"Yeah," Louise said. "Only the NLCS." Extra emphasis on the *only*.

P.J. smiled. "You nervous, Balls?"

"Yeah," she said, exhaling through the word. "More so than I'd ever admit to you."

"Just try and think about something other than baseball."

"Like what? Tombstone?" She hooked a thumb over in the direction of her sunglassed FBI guard, who kept an eye peeled from the top dugout step. He reminded Louise of a superhero, with that bulging chest and those chiseled features, and she never saw his eyes—not even at night. Or maybe one of the World Wrestling Federation's superstars. Except that his hair wasn't long enough to be a wrestler. No, her bodyguard was just a plain ol' superhero. BureauMan, she thought, laughing just a little at such nonsense. "Or maybe I can strike up a conversation about the weather with my shadow."

"Okay," P.J. said. "How 'bout a good book? What are you reading right now?"

Louise shrugged indifferently. "P.J., I haven't picked up a book in weeks."

"There you go. Me, I'm just finishing up the fifth book in the Vampire Chronicles and I'm wondering what's going to happen to Louis and Lestat in book six. That takes my mind off the game, calms me right down. Next thing you know, I open my eyes, and I'm on the mound. I don't have time to worry about losing. I just set, wind up, and throw strikes."

"So, what you're saying is . . . ?"

"What I'm saying, Balls, is that you don't read enough."

She nodded just slightly, and watched as P.J., a shit-eating grin playing with the corners of his mouth, ran to the outfield to begin working out with Reggie Borders, game one's starting pitcher. A book, or something other than baseball. Hmm. Nothing came immediately to mind. Except for maybe her morning sickness, which had somehow accompanied her to Atlanta. She didn't remember packing it. In fact she purposely tried leaving it behind. But no, there is was. First thing. Good morning. God damn it!

"Hey! Gehrig!" Jesus Maldonado called, whipping a ball her way from the other side of the outfield.

Louise reflexively moved her mitt up and over. The ball made a soft *thud* as its leather hit more leather. That sound. The slight snap back of her hand. She inhaled deeply. The freshly cut grass—how she loved the smell of freshly cut baseball grass. She rolled her head from side to side, rolled her shoulders as well.

What the hell was I thinking, she thought, pulling the ball from her glove and rocketing it back to the shortstop. In a few hours she'd be facing the Atlanta Braves for a chance to go to the World Series. This was the stuff of dreams and prayers. This was a sandlot fantasy come true. This was what her grandfather must have talked about in his sleep—are you watching Joe? Do you and Norven have those field box seats?

Hell, nothing else should matter.

"Top of the seventh here at Atlanta's Fulton County Stadium, and if the term *pitching duel* ever applied, I'd say it did tonight."

"True enough. Reggie Borders and Rocky Goetz have shut the hitters down. They've both faced the minimum and are both working on perfect games."

"We could be in for a long night."

"But something's got to give."

"Young steps up to the plate. He struck out his first at bat, then hit a weak grounder to short to lead off the fourth inning."

"Sacker sends his sign. Rocky set, winds up, and . . ."

"Strike one."

"He's throwing heat tonight."

"I've never seen Rocky Goetz this cool against the Meteorites. Usually he's rattled."

"Well, Louise is in the on-deck circle. Maybe she'll get to him this time."

"Young hits a blooper over to shallow center field. Lawrence backpedals. Easy out."

"And here comes the war chant."

"The most annoying sound in all of professional sports."

"You gotta love it."

"Love it? I hate it."

"Louise steps in. She's oh for two, hitting a weak grounder to third in the first, then a tremendous fly ball to right field in the fourth inning."

"Braves right fielder Shane Brown made a remarkable leap up against the right field wall, robbing Louise of at least a double. With her speed, maybe a triple."

"Sacker's calling for the fastball. That's a switch."

"He knows Louise never swings at the first pitch."

"And strike one."

"It certainly would be interesting if both the Eastern Division teams win and Louise has to face Cole Robinson in the World Series."

"You're not suggesting an asterisk for the history books, are you?"

"Absolutely not."

"It just would be interesting. That's all."

"There are plenty of interesting aspects already."

"Rocky lets it fly. A curve, down and away. Just outside. Ball one."

"I'm wondering how I'd feel if I were facing my lover in a similar situation."

"They're both professionals. I don't believe for a minute that either would compromise the integrity of the game."

"Another curve. Ball two."

"That's only the second time tonight that Rocky's been behind in the count."

"And I agree. They've both great ballplayers. I think they'd sweat blood to get their hands on a World Series ring."

"You have such a way with words."

"Thank you. But really, the fact that they date won't have anything to do with the outcome of the game."

"I agree. But it will give journalists a lot to write about."

"If anything, I think the added pressure will only make them play harder."

"If that were actually possible."

"Louise connects. A ground ball to third. Wilson handles it easily, throws it to Varga—two down."

"Right now I'll bet Lefty Johnson is wishing he had Bob Dixon in the lineup."

"It's the pitching. The Braves have matched the Meteorites goose egg for goose egg. And they've got their dream lineup."

"True enough. Hernandez doesn't have any excuses."

"Maldonado steps in."

"Goetz lets fly with the heater, and whoa. He hits him."

"That was obviously unintentional."

"Jesus is steaming."

"Looks like he got him on the upper arm."

"Goetz isn't saying a word. It's a different man out on the

mound from the pitcher who plunked Louise Gehrig earlier this season."

"I'd say Louise taught him a lesson."

"I'd say he doesn't want to get tossed from this game."

"Maldonado goes to first, and Darryl White steps in. This is the first time this game four players have come to bat in an inning."

"The pitching has been truly spectacular."

"White asks for time. Those are some big shoes he's been asked to fill, hitting cleanup after what Dixon accomplished this season."

"He hit twenty-eight balls out of the park this season, batting .287. Those aren't bad numbers."

"Granted. But he also led the team in strikeouts with 127."

"And he's got one already in this, the first game of the NLCS."

"Rocky looks over at Jesus on first."

"Jesus really isn't much of a threat to steal."

"Rocky sets. Here comes the windup."

"Strike one."

"According to the radar gun, that ball was traveling at ninety-nine miles per hour."

"White steps out, adjusts the Velcro straps on his batting gloves, then steps back in."

"Sacker sends the sign."

"They're going with smoke all the way."

"Can you blame them? Rocky's a human flamethrower to-night."

"And White fouls it back."

"Matt Stern announced today that if the team made it to the World Series, Bob Dixon would be throwing out the first pitch."

"It'll be great to see him. I hear he's doing quite well."

"Unfortunately he won't be well enough to make an appearance at one of the League Championship games this weekend."

"He'll still be in a wheelchair."

"Yes. That knee'll take some time to heal properly. White fouls another ball back. The count remains at oh and two."

"Y'know, they say the two most painful places to get shot are in the stomach and the knees."

"I think it probably painful no matter where you get shot."

"True enough. Did you know that the man who shot Dixon is pleading temporary insanity and that the National Rifle Association has set up a fund for his defense? You can call and make a donation."

"Yeah. 1-800-ASSHOLE. Can I say that on TV?"

"This is cable, remember? Anything goes."

"I wonder if anyone's called in yet."

"I'm sure there's some nut out there who feels the Second Amendment needs protecting."

"Great. So this goofball'll get off and gun down some other player."

"No. I think he'll be spending the rest of his years in Bellevue."

"Exactly where he belongs."

"I can think of a few others who should be locked away with him."

"Tombstone, perhaps?"

"That's got to be eating away at Louise."

"She seems to be holding up pretty well."

"On the surface anyway."

"Rocky sets. Here comes the pitch."

"A called third strike."

"White just watched it sail by."

"Look at the look on his face. He's just standing there."

"Seventh-inning stretch time. And at the end of six and a half innings, it's the Manhattan Meteorites nothing, the Atlanta Braves nothing."

"We'll be right back after this commercial break."

THE BASEBALL BEAT

by Arnold Loiten

I would have never expected it to come down to this. One game. ONE GAME will decide whether the Atlanta Braves or the Manhattan Meteorites represent the National League in the first World Series of the twenty-first century. Someone, please. Pinch me, slap me, shake me, for goodness sake. Tell me I've been dreaming, that I've been having the most horrific six-month nightmare of all time.

Please.

No ... didn't think so. It's real. But I still need to hear it again ... to believe it.

I'll begin with the first game of the NLCS. The ace of the Braves' staff, Rocky Goetz, one-hit the expansion team. But then, the ace of the Meteorites' staff, Reggie Borders, one-hit the world champs. The difference: a bottom-of-the-ninth dinger from pinch hitter Rufus Perry. It was a classic example of the most unlikely of heroes coming to the rescue. It was as classic a pitchers' duel as I, in my fifteen years plus of covering this game, have ever seen. Twenty-three Ks in all. Beautiful, just beautiful.

The following evening's game, played only a few short hours after the Texas Rangers beat the New Jersey Yankees in the first game of the ALCS, was neither beautiful nor classic. Braves starter Brent Costello gave up five earned runs in three and a third innings. And Louise Gehrig went four for five, with two stolen bases. Enough said.

Watching the Yankees win the second game of their series must have inspired the Braves, because the third game of the NLCS was a laughter. Final score up in the Big Apple: Atlanta 11, Manhattan 2.

The next day, the third game of the ALCS took place in Arlington, Texas. The Yanks again won, and like the Braves they led their series two games to one.

Then came the rematch: Goetz versus Borders, this time with Reggie having the home field advantage. This time home field advantage actually meant something. The ace of the Braves' pitching staff gave up six earned runs in two thirds of an inning while Borders gave up only two hits and no runs. Beautiful, just beautiful, at least for Manhattan fans.

The next afternoon, the Yankees won their third in a row, while up in Manhattan, it was the Meteorites' turn to laugh. David Gaston won his second game of the series, and Louise Gehrig had her second four-hit performance.

Then the Yankees finished off the Rangers in front of a stunned Arlington crowd, while the Braves headed back home with their tails between their legs.

Game six was do or die for Keith Hernandez's team, as would be game seven if they could manage a win. And while I wouldn't call it the most awe-inspiring baseball I've ever seen, they did just squeak by, beating the Meteorites by a run, 4–3.

Which brings us to tonight. The seventh and final game. I still don't believe it. The Braves should have been able to plow through the Meteorites. Just as the Rangers were predicted to sweep the Yankees. But as we all know, there are no certainties in baseball. And predictions are about as valuable as that deed in your safe-deposit box claiming you own a piece of the Brooklyn Bridge. That's what makes the game great. That's what makes baseball special.

Which is why the Braves must win tonight. Not for Atlanta. Not for the bonuses and incentive clauses. Not for all those poor vendors who invested in preprinted-shirts. But for history. For the integrity of the game. Because baseball *is* about integrity. It's about morals, and America, and my mom and her delicious apple pie. And if the Yankees and the Meteorites face off in the October Classic, that Series will be marred. In future editions of *The Baseball Encyclopedia* a giant asterisk will appear over the line scores of the games. And when readers look toward the bottom of the page to see what the giant asterisk represents, they will read the following: Manhattan first baseperson Louise Gehrig and New Jersey pitcher Cole Robinson were having an affair at the time the games were played.

And I don't care what anyone says, when you're involved with someone, it changes everything. To which I, as one of the thousands of sport columnists across the world, must say, "Shame on you, Louise Gehrig. Shame on you, Cole Robinson. Shame on you both for what you've done."

NATIONAL LEAGUE CHAMPIONSHIP SERIES

LINE & BOX SCORES

Game One—October 3

Manhattan	000	000	000		0	1	0
Atlanta	000	000	001		1	1	0

Manhattan	AB	R	H	BI	BB	SO	SB	AVG
Young, cf	4	0	0	0	0	2	0	.000
Gehrig, 1b	4	0	0	0	0	1	0	.000
Maldonado, SS	2	0	0	0	1	1	0	.000
White, 3b	4	0	0	0	0	2	0	.000
Carter, rf	4	0	1	0	0	1	0	.250
Downs, 1f	3	0	0	0	0	1	0	.000
Jones, 2b	3	0	0	0	0	0	0	.000
Manzi, c	3	0	0	0	0	1	0	.000
Borders, p	2	0	0	0	1	0	0	.000
TOTALS	**29**	**0**	**1**	**0**	**2**	**9**	**0**	

Atlanta	AB	R	H	BI	BB	SO	SB	AVG
Lawrence, ss	3	0	0	0	0	2	0	.000
Kravitz, cf	3	0	0	0	0	1	0	.000
Varga, 1b	3	0	0	0	0	1	0	.000
Brown, rf	3	0	0	0	0	2	0	.000
Wilson, 3b	3	0	0	0	0	0	0	.000
Sacker, c	3	0	0	0	0	2	0	.000
Lillywhite, lf	3	0	0	0	0	2	0	.000
Cara, 2b	3	0	0	0	0	1	0	.000
Goetz, p	2	0	0	0	0	3	0	.000
Perry, ph	1	1	1	1	0	0	0	1.000
TOTALS	**27**	**1**	**1**	**1**	**0**	**14**	**0**	

Pitching		IP	H	R	ER	BB	SO	ERA
MANHATTAN								
Borders		9	1	1	1	0	14	1.00
	l, 0–1							
ATLANTA								
Goetz		9	1	0	0	2	9	0.00
	w, 1–0							

Game Two—October 4

Manhattan	201	103	010	8	14	0
Atlanta	000	000	020	2	5	1

Manhattan	AB	R	H	BI	BB	SO	SB	AVG
Young, cf	4	2	1	0	1	0	1	.125
Gehrig, 1b	5	2	4	2	0	0	2	.444
Maldonado, ss	4	1	2	3	1	0	0	.333
White, 3b	4	0	1	1	1	1	0	.125
Carter, rf	5	1	2	1	0	0	0	.333
Downs, lf	4	0	1	0	1	1	0	.143
Jones, 2b	4	1	0	0	1	1	0	.000
Manzi, c	5	0	2	1	0	0	0	.250
Gaston, p	3	0	0	0	1	1	0	.000
Benson, ph	1	1	1	0	0	0	1	1.000
Matz, ph	1	0	0	0	0	0	0	.000
TOTALS	**41**	**8**	**14**	**8**	**6**	**5**	**4**	

Atlanta	AB	R	H	BI	BB	SO	SB	AVG
Lawrence, ss	3	1	1	0	1	0	1	.166
Kravitz, cf	4	0	1	1	0	2	0	.143
Varga, 1b	4	0	0	0	0	2	0	.000
Brown, rf	3	0	2	1	1	0	0	.333
Wilson, 3b	4	0	1	0	0	1	0	.143
Sacker, c	4	0	0	0	0	1	0	.000
Lillywhite, lf	4	0	0	0	0	2	0	.000
Cara, 2b	4	0	0	0	0	1	0	.000
Costello, p	1	0	0	0	0	1	0	.000
Martinez, p	1	0	0	0	0	1	0	.000
Perry, ph	0	1	0	0	1	0	0	1.000
TOTALS	**32**	**2**	**5**	**2**	**3**	**11**	**1**	

Pitching	IP	H	R	ER	BB	SO	ERA
MANHATTAN							
Gaston	7	3	1	1	2	8	1.29
w, 1–0							
Garcia	⅔	2	1	1	1	0	13.51
Strykes	1⅓	0	0	0	0	3	0.00

ATLANTA

Costello		3⅓	9	5	5	3	2	1.50
	I, 0–1							
Martinez		2⅔	2	1	1	1	2	3.38
Sweeney		1	1	1	1	0	0	9.00
Black		⅓	2	1	1	1	0	27.03
Murphy		1⅔	0	0	0	1	1	0.00

Game Three—October 6

Atlanta	006	003	020		11	16	0
Manhattan	000	000	020		2	7	1

Atlanta	AB	R	H	BI	BB	SO	SB	AVG
Lawrence, ss	5	3	3	1	1	0	2	.364
Kravitz, cf	5	2	2	0	1	0	1	.250
Varga, 1b	5	3	3	6	0	0	0	.250
Brown, rf	4	1	2	1	1	1	0	.400
Wilson, 3b	5	0	1	0	0	2	0	.167
Sacker, c	5	1	2	2	0	0	0	.167
Lillywhite, lf	4	0	1	0	1	0	0	.091
Cara, 2b	4	0	0	0	0	1	0	.000
Traube, 2b	1	1	1	1	0	0	0	1.000
Decker, p	4	0	1	0	0	1	0	.250
Perry, ph	1	0	0	0	0	0	0	.500
TOTALS	**43**	**11**	**16**	**11**	**4**	**5**	**3**	

Manhattan	AB	R	H	BI	BB	SO	SB	AVG
Young, cf	4	1	1	0	1	0	1	.167
Gehrig, 1b	3	1	1	0	2	0	1	.417
Maldonado, ss	5	0	2	2	0	1	0	.364
White, 3b	4	0	1	0	0	2	0	.167
Carter, rf	4	0	0	0	0	1	0	.231
Downs, lf	4	0	1	0	1	1	0	.143
Jones, 2b	3	0	0	0	0	2	0	.000
Benson, 2b	1	0	0	0	0	1	0	.500
Manzi, c	4	0	0	0	0	2	0	.167
King, p	2	0	0	0	0	2	0	.000
Matz, ph	1	0	1	0	0	0	0	.500
Capodanno, ph	1	0	0	0	0	0	0	.000
TOTALS	**36**	**2**	**7**	**2**	**4**	**12**	**2**	

Pitching		IP	H	R	ER	BB	SO	ERA
ATLANTA								
Decker		8	6	2	2	4	10	2.25
	w, 1–0							
Murphy		1	1	0	0	0	2	0.00
MANHATTAN								
McKnight		2⅓	8	6	6	2	0	23.15
	l, 0–1							
King		3⅔	1	3	3	2	1	8.10
Coleman		1	0	0	0	0	2	0.00
Scheer		⅓	4	2	2	0	0	54.05
Garcia		1⅔	3	0	0	0	2	3.86

Game Four—October 7

						R	H	E
Atlanta	000	000	000			0	2	0
Manhattan	600	000	00			6	12	0

Atlanta	AB	R	H	BI	BB	SO	SB	AVG
Lawrence, ss	4	0	0	0	0	2	0	.286
Kravitz, cf	4	0	1	0	0	1	0	.250
Varga, 1b	4	0	0	0	0	3	0	.188
Brown, rf	3	0	1	0	0	0	0	.385
Wilson, 3b	3	0	0	0	0	2	0	.133
Sacker, c	2	0	0	0	1	0	0	.143
Lillywhite, lf	3	0	0	0	0	2	0	.071
Cara, 2b	2	0	0	0	0	1	0	.000
Traube, 2b	1	0	0	0	0	1	0	.500
Martinez, p	1	0	0	0	0	1	0	.000
Perry, ph	1	0	0	0	0	1	0	.333
Willis, ph	1	0	0	0	0	1	0	.000
TOTALS	29	0	2	0	1	15	0	

Manhattan	AB	R	H	BI	BB	SO	SB	AVG
Young, cf	4	1	0	0	2	0	2	.125
Gehrig, 1b	3	1	2	0	2	0	3	.467
Maldonado, ss	4	1	3	2	1	0	0	.467
White, 3b	5	1	2	1	0	1	1	.235
Carter, rf	4	0	1	0	1	0	0	.235
Downs, lf	5	0	1	0	1	1	0	.188

Jones, 2b	4	1	1	0	1	2	0	.071
Manzi, c	4	1	2	3	1	0	0	.250
Borders, p	5	0	0	0	0	1	0	.000
TOTALS	**38**	**6**	**12**	**6**	**9**	**5**	**6**	

Pitching	IP	H	R	ER	BB	SO	ERA
ATLANTA							
Goetz	⅔	5	6	6	3	1	5.57
l, 1–1							
Martinez	4⅓	5	0	0	2	2	1.29
Heffernan	1	1	0	0	0	0	0.00
Sweeney	⅔	0	0	0	2	0	5.40
Black	⅓	0	0	0	1	1	13.51
Murphy	1	1	0	0	1	2	0.00
MANHATTAN							
Borders	9	2	0	0	1	15	0.50
w, 1–1							

Game Five—October 8

Atlanta	010	100	100		3	7	2
Manhattan	001	108	54		19	24	1

Atlanta	AB	R	H	BI	BB	SO	SB	AVG
Lawrence, ss	4	0	1	0	1	0	1	.263
Kravitz, cf	4	1	2	0	0	1	0	.300
Varga, 1b	4	0	1	1	1	0	0	.200
Brown, rf	4	1	1	1	0	1	0	.353
Wilson, 3b	4	0	1	0	0	1	0	.158
Sacker, c	3	1	0	0	1	0	1	.118
Lillywhite, lf	4	0	1	1	0	2	0	.111
Cara, 2b	3	0	0	0	0	2	0	.000
Traube, 2b	1	0	0	0	0	0	0	.333
Costello, p	2	0	0	0	0	1	0	.000
Perry, ph	1	0	0	0	0	1	0	.250
Willis, ph	0	0	0	0	1	0	0	.000
TOTALS	**35**	**3**	**7**	**3**	**4**	**9**	**2**	

Manhattan	AB	R	H	BI	BB	SO	SB	AVG
Young, cf	6	3	3	2	1	0	2	.227
Gehrig, 1b	5	4	4	3	2	0	2	.550
Maldonado, ss	6	2	4	4	1	1	1	.524
White, 3b	7	2	3	3	0	0	0	.416
Carter, rf	6	1	2	2	1	1	0	.261
Manzi, c	5	3	4	2	1	0	1	.381
Downs, lf	6	1	1	1	0	1	0	.182
Jones, 2b	3	0	0	0	0	2	0	.059
Benson, 2b	1	1	1	0	1	0	1	.666
Gaston, p	5	2	2	2	1	1	1	.250
TOTALS	**51**	**19**	**24**	**19**	**7**	**6**	**8**	

Pitching		IP	H	R	ER	BB	SO	ERA
ATLANTA								
Costello		5⅓	15	10	9	5	4	12.46
	l, 0–2							
Black		⅔	1	0	0	0	0	6.75
Martinez		⅓	4	4	4	1	0	6.14
Heffernan		⅔	1	1	1	0	1	5.40
Sweeney		⅔	3	4	4	1	0	19.29
Murphy		⅓	0	0	0	0	1	0.00
MANHATTAN								
Gaston		9	7	3	3	4	0	2.25
	w, 2–0							

Game Six—October 10

Manhattan	000	100	020		3	8	0
Atlanta	010	020	01		4	6	0

Manhattan	AB	R	H	BI	BB	SO	SB	AVG
Young, cf	4	0	1	0	1	0	1	.231
Gehrig, 1b	3	1	1	0	2	1	1	.522
Maldonado, ss	5	1	2	2	0	1	0	.500
White, 3b	5	0	1	0	0	1	0	.276
Manzi, c	4	1	3	1	1	0	0	.440
Carter, rf	4	0	0	0	0	3	0	.222
Downs, lf	4	0	0	0	0	1	0	.154
Jones, 2b	4	0	0	0	0	1	0	.048

	AB	R	H	BI	BB	SO	SB	AVG
McKnight, p	3	0	0	0	0	1	0	.000
Matz, ph	1	0	0	0	0	1	0	.333
TOTALS	**37**	**3**	**8**	**3**	**4**	**10**	**2**	

Atlanta	AB	R	H	BI	BB	SO	SB	AVG
Lawrence, ss	3	0	0	0	1	0	1	.227
Kravitz, cf	4	1	1	1	0	1	0	.292
Varga, 1b	4	1	2	1	0	0	0	.250
Brown, rf	3	1	1	0	1	0	0	.350
Wilson, 3b	4	1	1	1	0	1	0	.174
Sacker, c	3	0	1	1	1	0	0	.150
Lillywhite, lf	4	0	0	0	0	3	0	.091
Cara, 2b	3	0	0	0	0	2	0	.000
Decker, p	3	0	0	0	0	1	0	.143
TOTALS	**31**	**4**	**6**	**4**	**3**	**8**	**1**	

Pitching		IP	H	R	ER	BB	SO	ERA
MANHATTAN								
McKnight		7	5	3	3	3	5	8.68
Stewart		0	1	1	1	0	1	9.00
	l, 0–1							
Strykes		1	0	0	0	0	2	0.00
ATLANTA								
Decker		7⅔	8	3	3	4	6	2.87
	w, 2–0							
Murphy		1⅓	0	0	0	0	4	0.00
	s,1							

◉ **33** ◉

Have a Drink on Me

One game. Nine innings. A total of fifty-four outs. That's what it all came down to. A win, and it was on to the World Series. A loss, and it was better luck next year.

Las Vegas oddsmakers—who had originally made the Braves even-money favorites to take the series in four games—suddenly were leaning in favor of the Meteorites. Louise and company were seven-to-five favorites to win the seventh and deciding game, while the Atlanta team was pushing long-shot status. A ten-dollar bet on Atlanta would bring the bettor forty bucks, provided, of course, the Braves won.

Even the analysts were changing their tunes, proclaiming the miracle of Manhattan and other such easily memorable clichés. Mike Lupica wrote *I told you so* column after *I told you so* column—including one devoted to the sudden and timely emergence of Jo Jo Manzi's usually misguided bat. he was bathing in the afterglow of being so very right.

But many others were still holding strong. "The Braves are teasing us," many, the Arnold Loiten protégés of the beat reporter's world, proclaimed. "They're just too damn good to lose."

⊕   ⊕   ⊕

With Reggie Borders and Rocky Goetz—each with an NLCS win and a loss to his credit—again ready to do battle for their respective teams, game seven looked, at least on paper, like one of those classic matchups. One of historic baseball proportions, and all that. Forget David versus Goliath—this was Goliath versus Goliath.

Louise was relatively calm. That morning she took a long and very hot bath in her Atlanta hotel suite. And from the private confines of her bath, she spoke via telephone with Cole, who was back in New Jersey, preparing to face either Louise and her mates, or the Braves, in the October Classic.

"I can't tell you how badly I want to see you," he said.

"You can tell me," she said.

He laughed. "You know what I mean."

"I guess. But it's better this way. If we lose tonight."

"Which you won't."

"Which we won't. I'll be in your arms tomorrow night."

"And if you win?"

"If?"

"Did I say if? When, I meant, when."

"You'll be seeing more than enough of me come Saturday night."

"That's not exactly what I had in mind."

"But it's for the best. You know that. We can't be sleeping together at night, then facing each other in the World Series the next day."

"Will you still love me if the Yankees win?"

"Yes. Will you still love me if the Meteorites win?"

"I think so."

"Think so?"

"Know so. I know so."

"That's better."

A little silence.

"I want you so bad right now," he said.

"How bad?"

"You don't know."

"Why don't you tell me."

"Hmmm?"

"Go on. I'm lying here alone in a Jacuzzi built for about six. The water is very hot."

"Where's SunglassMan?"

"SunglassMan is staking out the hallway. Why? You want me to invite him in?"

"Are you naked?"

"I don't usually wear clothes in the bath."

"Then, no. Let him stay in the hall."

"I think he can see through walls anyway."

"Well, that's as close as he's going to get."

"That's as close as I want him to get. I've never been into steroid experiments."

"Hmmm. So, you're naked, huh?"

"Very naked."

He lowered his voice to an Imus-like growl. "Touch yourself."

She lowered hers. "Where?"

"You know."

Louise laughed. "I am."

Cole gulped hard. "I've never done this before."

"You might like it."

"I feel strange."

"Take it or leave it. If we win tonight, it's all you'll get for a while."

"Go Braves!"

"Thanks a lot."

"What do I do?"

"If I have to tell you . . ."

"No, I mean. Jeez. You start."

"Do you always leave everything to the woman?"

"If I can get away with it."

"Umm."

"And I kind of like it when you take charge."

"I'll bet you do."

After the shower that followed the nap that followed the desire for a cigarette that followed the orgasm that followed a late-morning wake-up call of nausea and sweats, Louise dressed, locked up, then, accompanied by her bodyguard, met her team-mates in the hotel lobby for the bus ride over to Fulton County Stadium.

The media troop was out in full play—everyone from Loiten to Lupica, with swings to both ends of the alphabet.

"Are you nervous?"

"Are you ready?"

"What are your plans if you lose?"

"And what if you win?"

"Can you beat the Yanks?"

"Will you play against Cole?"

"How can you get a hit off of someone you're sleeping with?"

Microphones were shoved at Louise mainly, but also at Jesus, at Reggie, at Jo Jo, at Lefty on her side, at Rocky, at Pete, at Lenny, at Keith on the other, all while the participants were try-ing to stretch, or run, or take BP, or just plain warm up.

"I'll sure be glad when these assholes finally leave us alone," one Atlanta player was heard to have said.

"No you won't," came the response from one of his team-mates.

⚾   ⚾   ⚾

"I'll sure be glad when this baseball season is over," Special Agent Wesley Selden said to Joseph Billings, one of the more than two dozen assistants assigned to help him secure the Ful-ton County Stadium site.

It had already been a long game for Selden. It had begun when he arrived at the stadium a little after 10:00 A.M. and found a package waiting. It was addressed not to Louise Gehrig, but to Special Agent Wesley Selden, FBI, in care of Fulton County Stadium. As per usual, the return address portion of the label was blank, but this time around the shipping company responsible for delivering the parcel was not the U.S. Postal Ser-vice, but UPS—United Parcel Service. The box, though shirt-box size, weighed virtually nothing. And when he shook it, nothing seemed to move around inside. So, using a small Swiss Army blade he kept on his key chain for just such purposes, he sliced away at the packaging tape, then pulled at the flaps to reveal the latest masterpiece inside. It was an exact replica of the Manhattan Meteorites away uniform. The smallest Meteorites uniform. The number 4 prominent on the back. And over the number, the name Gehrig. But what made this uniform much different from the one Louise would soon be wearing was that it was riddled with gunshots. Throughout the chest and pelvic area were bullet holes caked with what Selden guessed to be pig's blood, a dozen of them in all. He turned the uniform around and over and inside out, looking for the telltale signature. A Tombstone, spelled out in some more of that blood. But there was no signature to be found. Strange, Selden thought, nodding a few times to himself, wondering, Could there be another nut out there? Or was Tombstone just getting careless? His gut told him it was the latter. He hoped his gut was right as he jumbled up the uniform into a tight little ball and placed it back in the box. Then he placed that box on the desk he was using and went to work making sure that the son of a bitch didn't even come close.

"I heard you loved baseball," Billings said. "It was why you wanted to work this case."

"I do love baseball. But I didn't get to watch one game this year. Not in its entirety."

"You missed one hell of a season."

"So I've heard."

The agents were in the Braves' clubhouse. On the oversize television monitor, opera star Cecilia Bartoli could be seen singing the national anthem. They stared for a moment at the set—mentally removing the hats they weren't wearing, unconsciously placing their right hands over their hearts.

". . . and the home of the brave."

The 52,007 in attendance roared their support as the Atlanta Braves took to the field.

A walkie-talkie clipped to Billings,'s belt chirped. He lifted it to his face and began speaking.

"Billings."

"Williams here. The perimeter of the stadium is clear. Every-one's inside."

"Ten-four." He turned to Selden, "Everything's clear here. How about watching a little of the game?"

But Selden was already doing just that. His eyes were glued to the monitor as Jamaine Young approached the plate.

Tickets to the seventh and final game of the NLCS were the only ones Geraldine Willard could afford. Good tickets. Close to the first base bag. Very close. Field level, three rows back close. Game one would have run a thousand per—and scalpers were only selling them in pairs. Game two—same thing. Game six, down to 750. Game seven, "Gimme a grand for the pair." But only if she bought them prior to the first game. Bought them on a nonrefundable basis. If the series didn't go the distance, she was out one thousand bucks. But one thousand bucks was all she could really afford—and she was not about to blow her easiest opportunity to enact a little sweet revenge. Even if it meant paying for two tickets when only one would be used—she certainly couldn't risk bringing one of her daughters, or a friend—while the other would be nothing more than a lonely pocketbook social center.

Louise was in the on-deck circle, swinging the fungo bat over her head, when Rocky Goetz let loose his first pitch.

"Ball one!" the ump barked.

Louise smiled slightly, and aimed that smile's warmth back toward the dugout—at Jesus and Lefty. A first-pitch ball from Rocky was always a good sign.

She waved the fungo over her head. A number of banners in the park caught her attention as she spun around. One read: Go, Rocky, Go! Another read: Louise Gehrig for President! An-other: ROCKY—Women and Family Jewels First! One read: At-lanta Braves—World Champs Two Years in a Row! Another: Have a Good Winter, Balls! Then there was: We Know Ted

Turner, and Matt Stern Is No Ted Turner! And, of course, a John 3:3.

And while Barefoot & Pregnant! bothered the hell out of her, Rocky—Get Back in the Kitchen, Where You Belong! made her smile.

But is was a sign that read Real Ballplayers Wear Panties! that made Louise laugh, laugh heartily and out loud, as Jamaine fouled off the next pitch.

"Strike one."

⚾　　⚾　　⚾

A loud bang snapped their attention away from the monitor.

"Isn't that a little premature?" Selden asked the man unloading a few cases of iced Dom Pérignon from a hand truck.

"Just doing my job," the man said. "Three cases for the Braves, three for the Meteorites."

"Do the losers get to open their bottles anyway?" Billings asked.

"Might as well," the man said. "It's a long off-season."

On the monitor, Young fouled back another pitch.

"Let's go watch some baseball," Selden said.

"I was hoping you'd say that."

The two agents excused themselves from the champagne delivery man and headed toward the exit of the Braves' clubhouse. Passing a wall of lockers, Billings gave a harder-than-he-expected shove at one of the slightly open metal doors. But instead of slamming shut, the door bounced back and rattled loudly against the adjoining locker, the shock knocking the contents off its top shelf and onto the clubhouse floor.

"Don't know my own strength," Billings joked disconcertedly as Selden, shaking his head, kneeled to pick up the fallen items.

"Holy shit!" the champagne delivery man said. He was watching the monitor. He shot a quick glance toward the agents. "Young just got a hit off Rocky," he explained, adding, "Damnit!"

"How 'bout that?" Billings said, smiling at the TV screen.

But Selden didn't answer.

Billings turned away from the televised action, back to face his boss. "What's up?"

Selden didn't look up, he couldn't even breath. He was too busy examining the disrupted contents of the locker. Contents that included, among other items, a baseball glove, the current issue of *Swank* magazine, a Beavis & Butthead key chain, a Sony Walkman with headphones, the latest Metallica tape, some double-A batteries, a bottle of generic ibuprofen, a hairbrush, some hair gel, and a medium-size leather portfolio.

"Here comes Louise," said the champagne delivery man, his eyes still fixed on the monitor.

Selden didn't blink. He didn't say a word. Billings knelt by his side and gazed downward. Then they both turned and locked eyes—their question burning holes in the air-conditioned room—Do you see what I see?

Slow nods.

The leather portfolio sat in Selden's hands. Opened, it revealed a few number six drawing pencils perched in their little looped holders, three blank priority mail mailing labels, a mostly blank sketch pad—a few pages haphazardly torn out—and all three original Tombstone drawings, each meticulously encased in a clear plastic sheath, as if waiting innocently, patiently, to be copied.

⚾   ⚾   ⚾

One step. Her first step out of the on-deck circle that had been stepped so many times before. It all suddenly seemed so old, the on-deck circle, her uniform, this stadium, the grass, even the freshly painted lines—foul and otherwise. It was too familiar, a let's-get-this-over-with kind of feeling.

Another step. And another. And a few more. And Louise was in the batter's box. She looked first at the umpire, then at Pete Sacker; then, digging in, raising her bat to its familiar position over her shoulder, she turned and glared at Rocky Goetz.

He was looking right at her, through her. Waiting to see which pitch his catcher would call, he spit out a glob of tobacco, then smiled.

And Louise couldn't help but think the most familiar of thoughts: You're still an ugly son of a bitch, Rocky Goetz. And you always will be.

"Who's locker is this?" Selden asked of the man delivering the champagne.

The man turned from the television and shrugged. "Don't know," he said after less than a split second of thought. "What's the number on the uniform?" he asked, motioning toward the Braves jersey hanging in the open locker.

Billings stood and pulled the jersey from its hook. "Twenty-seven," he said, reading the back.

"That's easy, then," the champagne delivery man said, pointing toward the monitor. "That's number twenty-seven right there."

Sacker wasn't quite as worried about Rocky's first pitch to Louise as he was the second, third, fourth, and however many others it took before she was either out or on base. The first could be whatever the hell Rocky wanted—a fastball, a slider, a change-up. Pete didn't care and he wasn't about to argue. Louise would never swing at it. She'd just watch it fly by and adjust. So if Rocky was in his fastball mode—which Pete assumed he was—let him get it out of his system on this first pitch.

Pete looked over to first. Jamaine Young was taking a considerable lead off the bag. He had thrown Jamaine out once earlier in the season, but was late on three other occasions. Three out of four successful steals during the regular season. But Sacker knew as well as anyone that the regular season didn't mean squat during the playoffs—just ask the '88 Mets.

Rocky caught his catcher's gaze, spun around, and rocketed the ball to Lenny Varga at first. It was close, but Young dove back in and the ump spread his arms out wide.

"Safe."

In the clubhouse, Selden and Billings stared at the monitor—a huge close-up of Rocky on the mound, then a reverse angle shot—the number twenty-seven looming larger than life on his back.

"Jesus Christ!" Selden said.

"Should I radio the others?"

Selden watched the TV for a moment. Now the close-up was of Rocky's face—he had turned back to face the batter. Cut to a close-up of Louise. She glared at the pitcher, then—Hold on, Selden thought to himself, did I just see her wink? He shook his head slightly to himself. On the tube, Rocky received the sign from his catcher, set, then glanced once over her shoulder toward the first base bag.

"Sir?"

"In a minute," Selden said, seemingly transfixed by the baseball images.

"But—"

Selden held up his hand to silence Billings. "I said in a minute."

The underling gulped, nodded, then turned his attention toward the game.

Rocky wound up and delivered. The ball shot out of his hand, Jamaine took off from first—a tremendous jump, and Louise swung away.

Clack!

Seemingly a fraction of a second later, Louise was standing on first, Jamaine was crossing home plate, and Rocky was circling the mound—around and around and around—muttering obscenities to himself.

The champagne deliveryman's jaw dropped. "Jesus Christ!" he grumbled. "That girl never swings at the first pitch." He turned to face the agents. "Never."

Billings looked from the deliveryman's face back to Selden's. A question mark distorted the junior agent's features.

"No, Billings," Selden said, finally, grinning ear to ear. "Let's wait."

"Wait, sir?"

"To call the others."

"But . . ."

"Let's let Louise get even with the son of a bitch on her own terms."

⊕   ⊕   ⊕

Geraldine took a deep breath. There was Louise, standing not thirty feet from where she sat. She reached down toward her ankle and tapped the handle of the .38-caliber automatic pistol lodged in the top of her right boot. The shiny blue metallic pistol was easily concealed by her oversize pants—baggy and brightly flowered. No one—not even the numerous cops and undercover agents patrolling the stadium—could tell.

She watched Louise take a lead off the bag. Now or later, she thought to herself. Now! No, not now. Louise would be stealing—that much was obvious. Later, the bottom of the first, or the bottom of the second, or, hell, she had nine bottom-of-the's from which to shoot her right, to shoot her dead. Then Louise would just be playing her position—no real running around—just a lot of concentration on the batter, and maybe a man on base. Yeah, Geraldine thought, patting the gun one last time. Not yet. But soon. Soon Louise Gehrig's uniform will look just like the one I sent that FBI guy.

Soon.

⊕   ⊕   ⊕

In Bob Dixon's private room in St. Noah of the Divine Roman Catholic Hospital, he and Margaret cheered when Louise took off on Rocky's first pitch to Jesus Maldonado. An uncontested steal—Sacker didn't even throw to second. Louise had such a lead and jump, he figured it wasn't even worth the effort.

The soon-to-be-married pair high-fived each other.

"Way to go!" Bob yelled.

"That's my little girl out there."

"Yeah, well if you think you're proud now, just wait till she gets into the World Series."

⊕   ⊕   ⊕

At the plate, Jesus began to laugh. He could see the look in Rocky's eyes. "Your man's rattled," he muttered to Sacker. "He's got those Louise Gehrig jitters."

Sacker didn't say a word, but deep down he couldn't disagree. Ricky *was* rattled. He had seen the symptoms before, not often, but on a few very memorable occasions. He looked out at the mound and flashed the sign for a slider.

Rocky nodded, set, thought about taking a glance toward second, thought better of it, then let loose.

"Shit!" he screamed as the ball sailed over Lenny Varga's head, stayed fair, and ended up out in the far corner of right field. "God damn it!"

"Gotta bring some over to the visitors' clubhouse now," the champagne deliveryman said to the two FBI agents.

"I think they'll be needing theirs more," Selden said, grinning at the monitor as the score was flashed at the bottom of the screen—Manhattan 2, Atlanta 0.

They watched the deliveryman exit the clubhouse before turning back to business.

"Want to arrest him at the end of this inning?" Billings asked.

Selden shook his head. "Wait till the end of the game."

"You sure?"

A nod. "Unless the Braves somehow start winning. Then we'll throw them the bone. Otherwise, I'm enjoying his suffering."

After Rocky walked the next batter, third baseman Darryl White, Geraldine figured it was time for her to take a walk around. She was restless and nervous, sitting still and waiting for Louise to make a defensive appearance at first. Maybe she'd grab a beer or a hot dog, or some peanuts even. With the teams hottest hitter, Jo Jo Manzi, coming up to bat, the top of this first inning was far from over.

During the time it took Geraldine to get to the nearest Fulton County Stadium field level concession stand, wait in line, and order and pay for a kosher hot dog, a small box of popcorn, and a medium-size diet cola, Rocky had walked Jo Jo Manzi on four straight pitches and now had the bases loaded with Jeff Carter coming to the plate.

Geraldine loaded up the dog with mustard, hot relish, and, even after some second thoughts, freshly chopped onions. Moving her cardboard tray over to a counter area, she took one large bite of the dog, then another. Then a sip. Carter had worked the count full—three balls and two strikes. Don't, Geraldine thought. Please don't walk him.

She took another bite of the dog, a large bite—too large. Bits of mustard-covered meat squished out of the right corner of her mouth. She chewed slowly, awkwardly, but had yet to swallow when she heard the familiar voice call her name.

"Geraldine," that familiar voice called again. "Is that you?"

She turned, forced a hard swallow, then wiped at both sides of her mouth with a napkin emblazoned with the Braves logo. "Kevin?" she asked softly.

"How are you?" he asked, stepping forward, himself carrying a cardboard tray containing a hot dog—likewise smothered in mustard, hot relish, and freshly chopped onions—some peanuts and a large beer.

"I'm fine," she said, wiping again at her mouth, in the fear that some of the mustard might have lingered. "I . . . ahh . . . yeah. You look good."

"Thanks," he said. "So do you." He placed his cardboard tray on the countertop next to hers, then took a small sip of beer. "I've been meaning to call you."

"Really?" she said, suddenly so confused. Her anger, her absolute rage, ran screaming from her head, knocking over plans and justifications, leaving her head in turmoil, leaving her heart beating abnormally fast, leaving her privates in a hopeful little world all their own.

"Uh-huh." He picked up his hot dog, shrugged, laughed at his own overabundance of toppings, then took a bite.

"Mine too," she said, motioning toward her dog. She took a sip of her soda, then another bite. And though she secretly worried that mustard was once again congregating on the corners of her mouth, that thought was secondary to the sudden yearning for her husband that was flooding every important part of her anatomy.

Bob shook his head sadly when, after fouling back a half dozen balls, Jeff Carter watched one sail over the outer corner of the plate, belt high, for strike three.

The look on the right fielder's face said it all—*fuck!*—one hit could have put the game away, and he had struck out looking.

Left fielder Sandy Downs was up next. Going into the seventh game, he was batting a dismal .154—second lowest batting average for a nonpitcher on the team, to second baseman Elvis Jones's pathetic .048.

"Sandy's had a tough series," Bob said.

"Maybe now's the time he breaks out," Margaret suggested.

"Rocky just got a strikeout. The confidence is in his corner."

"Meaning?"

"A double play."

"How can he make someone hit into a double play?"

"A chest-high pitch over the outside corner of the plate. Sandy reaches, makes contact, belts it right to the shortstop." He snapped his fingers. "To second." He snapped them again. "To first. He's out of the inning with only two men coming home."

"One man and one woman," Margaret said.

But Bob just nodded. Nodded and watched as Rocky pitched and Sandy hit, and like he predicted, it was time for a commercial break.

Reggie Borders had already struck out Braves leadoff man Joey Lawrence for the first out in the bottom half of the first inning by the time Geraldine and Kevin finished their hot dogs and decided it was time to return to the game.

"Where are you sitting?" she asked.

"Oh, way up," he said. "I was just taking a walk down here to see how the other half lived."

"You alone?"

He nodded. "You?"

"I've got an extra seat."

He smiled.

Geraldine felt herself get all tingly. She even thought she felt her knees go weak.

"Would you like some company?"

"I'd like that a lot."

"You sure? I mean . . ."

She lifted an index finger up high and placed it against his lips. "I'm sure," she said, feeling a slight electrical shock.

Carrying their drinks and snacks, they made their way back to Geraldine's shooting distance from Louise seats.

"I've really been thinking a lot about you," Kevin said. "About us."

"Me too."

"How're the girls?"

"They miss you."

They talked and reminisced, almost as if nothing had happened, almost as if the first baseperson standing so close had never affected their lives. They talked through Reggie's striking out of center fielder Kravitz. They talked through Varga's easily caught foul pop fly. And when they next remembered to look up at the scoreboard, what they saw was that the first inning was over, and the Meteorites were winning, 2–0.

"Elvis is having a dreadful series."

"True enough. Only one hit in twenty-one at bats."

"Rocky needs to get his bearings and shut the Meteorite batters down. He needs to forget about Louise swinging at the first pitch."

"Which he won't."

"Tell me about it. I'm still in shock."

"Then he needs to pray that his teammates can get three runs off Reggie Borders."

"Borders has given up more than two runs only twice this past season. Once in late May, when he gave up four to the Phillies, and again in August, when he gave up five to the Cards."

"Rocky lets loose with a fastball. Strike one."

"Elvis wasn't even close with that swing."

"He batted .263 during the regular season. But as everyone knows . . ."

"Right. Rocky sets. Another fastball. Strike two."

"Y'know, Elvis is another member of Louise's book club."

"I've heard that."

"In fact, this afternoon, during a pregame interview, a reporter from the Atlanta station asked him if he was nervous. Y'know what he said? He said yes, because he didn't know if Mitch would make it out alive. The reporter was obviously confused, so he asked Elvis, who's Mitch? And Elvis explained that Mitch is the lead character of *The Firm*. And that he had something like twenty-five pages to go in the book, but wouldn't be able to finish it until after the game. He said it was driving him nuts."

"Maybe Elvis should spend a little more time worrying about his hitting right now and less about fictional characters."

"Here comes the pitch. Elvis connects with a little looper into the gap which might just drop."

"It does drop! And Elvis Jones is standing on first base with a hit."

"Man, I don't think I've ever seen him happier."

"He's got a Louise Gehrig smile plastered to his face."

"And here comes Reggie Borders to the plate."

"Though Reggie doesn't have a hit in this series, he batted .232 on the year—twenty-three hits in the ninety-nine times at bat, with one homer. That's second in the National League for pitchers."

"If he gets a hit here, we'll definitely see Rocky fall apart."

Billings radioed the other Fibbies, and as Rocky Goetz walked his opposing pitcher on four straight pitches, they began gathering in the Braves' clubhouse.

"So what are we waiting for?" one of the agents asked after viewing the evidence that had very conveniently dropped out of Goetz's locker.

"For Hernandez to pull him from the game," Billings explained.

"I don't get it," another of the agents said.

"Something tells me he's going to fall apart on his own," Selden explained. "Without any help from us."

"A hunch?"

"Something like that."

"But aren't hunches usually about the guilt or innocence of a suspect?"

"Yeah," Selden said.

"But this one's about whether or not Goetz will win this game?"

"Exactly. It's a baseball hunch."

The agent nodded and did everything to avoid Selden's eyes and wild smile. He looked at the other agents, then around the clubhouse. "Guess they won't have much use for the champagne," he said finally. "I mean, if your hunch is right."

"Exactly what I was thinking," Selden said, the grin turning to a laugh.

"Sir?"

"Pop open a bottle."

"But . . ."

"What are you waiting for? Someone might as well enjoy the stuff."

Jamaine Young stepped up to the plate, Louise into the on-deck circle. Elvis was on second, Reggie on first. There were no outs.

Pete Sacker gave Rocky the sign for the curveball. Taking a deep breath, the pitcher nodded and set. He shot a quick glance back at second, then began his windup. Elvis and Reggie took off before the ball was out of Rocky's hand. Seeing his teammates run, Jamaine swung sloppily through the pitch, knocking himself almost to the ground in the process. Sacker caught the ball, stood to get a clear view over the stumbling batter, and rocketed the ball to third in an attempt to get out the lead runner. The throw was perfect, but just the slightest bit late. Elvis was safe, as was Reggie. A double steal. Two Meteorites—the very bottom of the team's batting order—were in scoring position with no outs.

"These really are amazing seats," Kevin said. "How'd you get them."

"Oh, you know," Geraldine said, searching for a lie. "A friend of a friend at work."

"Where was this friend before?" Kevin asked with a huge smile.

She shrugged it off and he dropped the subject.

"I never even knew you liked baseball," he said, shaking his head when Jamaine swung through an obvious ball to get fanned by Rocky. One out.

Geraldine watched her husband as he watched Louise Gehrig walk to the plate. There was that look in his eyes. That . . . that . . . oh, God. She suddenly felt nauseous. She suddenly felt dead again.

"She's one hell of a ballplayer," Kevin said, turning to face his wife, reaching out, placing his hand warmly on top of hers.

"You think so?" Geraldine forced out the words as she swallowed back some vomit.

"Absolutely."

They watched for a moment as Louise took the first pitch, a curveball, low and outside, for ball one.

"Have you ever seen a sweeter swing?" Kevin asked.

"I don't know."

"Last February, I thought my life was over."

"Then you found her," Geraldine said. Her eyes were beginning to water. She hated herself for it, but she couldn't stop it. God damn it. God damn her!

"No," Kevin said. "Because of her. I thought Louise Gehrig was the worst thing that ever happened to baseball. I hated her. I wanted to kill her."

"You hated her?" The tears suddenly stopped themselves short.

"Uh-huh." He watched for a moment as Rocky let loose and Louise fouled the ball back. "Then, the more I watched her, watched what she was doing, the more I realized how wrong I was. I realized that she was one of the best things to ever happen to the game."

"You don't love her?"

"Love her?" Kevin turned to look at his wife. He spotted the on-hold tears. "Honey," he said, touching her face. "I don't love Louise Gehrig. I love you."

"But."

"I just like watching her play the game."

"Oh," Geraldine said. She would have said a lot more if suddenly the dam hadn't broken, setting free a tidal wave of instability and homicidal tendencies.

Kevin put his arms around his wife and pulled her close, while over her shoulder he watched Louise work the count full, then take a borderline pitch, which the ump called in her favor. The bases were loaded. Time to put the game away, he thought as he gently stroked his wife's hair.

⚾   ⚾   ⚾

"Okay, Mr. You-Don't-Catch-In-The-Big-Leagues-As-Long-As-I-Did-And-Not-Know-A-Thing-Or-Two-About-Pitchers," Margaret said. "Call it."

Bob smiled. "Maldonado hits a double and clears the bases."

"This time put your money where your mouth is."

"Fine. A hundred bucks says he hits a double."

"Not money."

"You said, put your money—"

"I know what I said."

"Okay, what then?"

"The loser has to be the winner's slave for a twenty-four hour period."

"I couldn't live through a twenty-four-hour period as your slave."

"I'd go easy on you."

Bob exhaled loudly. "Okay. But on one condition. If I lose, I don't have to pay up until after the knee is healed."

"Deal."

A handshake.

Rocky set and delivered, and Maldonado ripped a line drive into the gap between center and left field. Elvis scored, Reggie scored, but Louise stopped at third, held up by Reggie's lack of base speed. Braves center fielder Charlie Kravitz got the ball to shortstop Joey Lawrence so quickly that Jesus was held to a single. A single and two more RBI's—he'd take it.

"Remember," Bob said. *After* the knee heals."

"Uh-huh," Margaret said with a huge smile. "Whatever you say."

From Louise's third base vantage point, the world seemed to be swirling—the night lights of Fulton County Stadium, the flashes, the scoreboard, all were fusing into a northern lights special effect complete with end-of-the-world sound effects, in Georgia, of all places. She knew that with four runs on their side and Reggie on the mound, the game was more or less in the bag, though an insurance run or two or three definitely wouldn't hurt.

Darryl White was at the plate. He was the least patient hitter on the team—127 strikeouts on the year proved it. But maybe he could just work out a walk, she thought, as he had in the first inning. Or, if he hit a sac fly to extreme right, then it'd be 5–0.

She looked into the stands, wishing Cole were there, or at least her mother. But no one. Louise had brought no one with her to Atlanta. Just her bat and glove, and her teammates. Right now baseball was all that mattered. Baseball was all that could matter.

Rocky set and let loose.

"Strike one!" the ump yelled.

Louise turned, touched the bag, then leaned off. I've done it before, she thought—stealing home that is.

Rocky turned her way, and she trotted back and again tagged

up. Meteorites third base coach Sam Cox leaned close and said, "Patience."

She nodded her understanding.

Sacker sent Rocky a sign he could live with. The pitcher set, wound, and delivered.

The ball caught the handle of Darryl's bat and popped up and back foul. Sacker stood, threw off his mask, backpedaled, and easily put the ball away.

Two outs.

"Shit!" Louise muttered.

      ⑪   ⑪   ⑪

"And here comes Jo Jo."

"Batting .440 coming into this game, he's got to be considered one of the offensive heroes of this series."

"Along with Jesus and Louise."

"True enough."

"Sacker's going out to the mound. Do they walk him and give a bases-loaded opportunity to Jeff Carter? Or do ,they pitch to him?"

"Carter hit nineteen homers this year. Three of those were grand slams."

"What would you do?"

"I'd pitch to him."

"Why's that?"

"It's a half dozen of one, six of the other."

"Sacker goes back to the plate and takes his position."

"And it looks like they're going to pitch to Jo Jo."

"Good. I was never a fan of the intentional walk."

"Sacker calls for a curve, inside and low. Louise has a pretty big lead off third, Jesus' lead off first is marginal at best."

"He was never known for his speed."

"Here comes the pitch."

"And Jo Jo hits it a ton!"

"Oh, my! It's going, going . . ."

"This feels good. This feels real good."

"That ball has left the building! That ball has left the state!"

"Gone and good-bye. And the Meteorites take a seven to nothing lead in this, the deciding game of the NLCS."

"And here comes Keith Hernandez, out to stop the bleeding."

"It's a little too late for that."

"Rocky doesn't say a word. He knows his time is up."

"Listen to the crowd boo."

"It's gonna be a long off-season for Rocky Goetz."

⑩   ⑩   ⑩

"Y'know, I've always wanted to see New York," Kevin said, sitting back down after giving Jo Jo Manzi a standing ovation.

"What are you saying?" Geraldine asked.

"Well, maybe we could go to New York, get some tickets for the World Series. Have some fun. I don't know. We could use some time alone, don't you think?"

She nodded.

"Call it a second honeymoon, if you like. It'd be fun."

"Really?"

"Sure."

"But can we afford it?"

"We'll make do. It'd be nice to get away—just the two of us. I mean"—and here the words stuck in Kevin's throat—"if you'll take me back."

"Oh, Kevin," she said, throwing her arms around his neck, the past six months of her miserable existence suddenly vanishing into the repression zone of her mind. "I've missed you so much."

"Is that a yes?"

"Yes, yes, yes. Absolutely it's a yes."

⑩   ⑩   ⑩

Rocky Goetz was muttering obscenities to himself as he entered the Braves' clubhouse and came face to face with a large number of champagne-drinking men dressed in dark blue suits.

"Rocky," Selden said, raising his glass high. "Good game."

"Who the fuck are you?" Rocky said. "And what the fuck are you doing in here?"

Billings stepped up, whipped out his badge, and pressed it forward, inches from Rocky's face.

"FBI, Rocky."

"Big fucking deal. You gonna arrest me for pitching like shit? Is that a federal offense now?"

Selden laughed, then slapped a glass of champagne into the pitcher's hand.

"What the fuck is going on?" Rocky asked.

"Have a drink first," Selden said, grinning from ear to ear. "I think you're going to need one."

Game Seven—October 11

Manhattan	250	000	000			7	12	0
Atlanta	000	000	000			0	5	2

Manhattan	AB	R	H	BI	BB	SO	SB	AVG
Young, cf	5	1	2	0	1	0	2	.258
Gehrig, 1b	4	2	2	1	2	0	2	.519
Maldonado, ss	4	1	3	3	2	0	0	.533
White, 3b	4	0	1	0	1	1	0	.273
Manzi, c	4	1	2	3	1	0	0	.448
Carter, rf	5	0	0	0	0	2	0	.188
Downs, lf	5	0	0	0	0	1	0	.097
Jones, 2b	4	1	1	0	1	1	1	.080
Borders, p	3	1	1	0	1	0	1	.100
TOTALS	38	7	12	7	9	5	6	

Atlanta	AB	R	H	BI	BB	SO	SB	AVG
Lawrence, ss	4	0	0	0	0	3	0	.192
Kravitz, cf	4	0	1	0	0	1	0	.286
Varga, 1b	3	0	2	0	1	0	1	.296
Brown, rf	4	0	0	0	0	2	0	.280
Wilson, 3b	3	0	0	0	0	3	0	.154
Zitser, 3b	1	0	0	0	0	1	0	.000
Sacker, c	4	0	1	0	0	1	0	.166
Lillywhite, lf	2	0	0	0	0	2	0	.091
Fay, lf	1	0	0	0	0	1	0	.000
Cara, 2b	3	0	1	0	0	0	0	.045
Martinez, p	1	0	0	0	0	1	0	.000
Perry, ph	1	0	0	0	0	1	0	.200
Traube, ph	1	0	0	0	0	1	0	.250
TOTALS	32	0	5	0	1	17	1	

Pitching	IP	H	R	ER	BB	SO	ERA
MANHATTAN							
Borders	9	5	0	0	1	17	0.33
w, 2–1							
ATLANTA							
Goetz	1⅔	6	7	7	4	1	10.03
l, 1–2							
Martinez	4⅓	3	0	0	3	1	3.86
Gaston	2	2	0	0	1	2	2.00
Murphy	1	1	0	0	1	1	0.00

Overnight with Howie

"Joey, I'm hearing violins."

"Yeah, but they're playing my song, Howie."

"What's that? 'Achy Breaky Heart'?"

"Very funny. But we'll see who's laughing after the Yanks sweep the Series."

"Oh! Oh! Oh! Another grand prediction. Man, you're giving Bensonhurst a bad name."

"That's why my girlfriend told me."

"She sounds like a smart lady."

"She's going out with me, ain't she?"

"Yeah, well. That notwithstanding."

"Mark my words, Howie. Next week I'll finally be able to say, I told you so."

"Believe me, I'll be the one saying, I told you so."

"No way. Louise had the Braves hexed. It's as simple as that. But that won't happen with the mighty Yanks."

"From what I hear, Louise has one Yankee permanently under her spell."

"Cole Robinson is too smart. He knows that if he loses, he'll never get any again."

"How do you figure?"

"Women don't have sex with men they don't respect."

"I see. So, what's your girlfriend's excuse?"

 # PART SEVEN

They say the first World Series is the one you remember most. No, no, no! I guarantee you don't remember that one because that fantasy world you always dreamed about is suddenly real. And the thing has ten thousand legs and it simply eats you up.

—Sparky Anderson

34

No Simple Answers

The Meteorites arrived back in New York early Thursday afternoon. Throngs awaited—throngs of friends, throngs of fans, throngs of media, throngs of throngs.

While many of the local newspapers were busy dubbing the first World Series of the twenty-first century "The bridge and tunnel Series," others were busy theorizing as to whether the Cole-Louise affair would have an impact and whether they would attempt a rendezvous prior to and/or during the possibly seven-game contest, while all wondered what would become of Rocky Goetz, aka Tombstone, while all wondered, Why? Rocky, why?

Margaret met her daughter at the airport. She had a limo waiting that would take them first to St. Noah's for a quick hello to Bob, then home.

They walked through the airport, Louise smiling and waving and even signing a few autographs. Then, once locked safely away in the backseat of the limo, she took a few long deep breaths and tried to relax.

"Your grandfather would have been proud," Margaret said.

Louise nodded, but her mind was elsewhere. "I need your help, Mom."

"When?"

"Tomorrow morning."

"Okay."

⑪   ⑪   ⑪

"Hey, Balls."

"Hi, Bob."

"You got robbed."

"Of what?"

"The series MVP."

"Naw. Reggie deserved it."

"Pitchers never deserve it. I should know, I've worked with enough of them."

"Besides, if they gave it for offense, it'd have been split three ways between Jesus, Jo Jo, and me."

"Yeah. Can you believe Jo Jo?"

"No one can."

Bob smiled. "At least the team doesn't have to go digging for my replacement for next season."

"I don't even want to think about next season."

"This one's almost over. All you've got to do is win four more games."

"Hey, no problem."

"It might not be as big a problem as you think."

"How's that?"

"The Cub factor is swinging in your favor."

"Cub factor?"

"Yeah," Margaret explained. "The team with the most ex-Cubbies always loses the World Series."

"I've never heard that," Louise said.

"It's true."

"So, who were the ex-Cubs in '86?"

Margaret smiled. "Guess."

"No way."

"Uh-huh."

"Bill Buckner?"

"Ding, ding, ding, ding, ding," Bob said. "Good answer."

Louise thought for a moment. "We don't have any ex-Cubs on our team."

Bob nodded. "Tomlin's real superstitious. When Stern told him he wanted to win it all the first year, he took no chances in putting together the roster. No ex-Cubbies."

"What about the Yankees?"

"That's the good part," Margaret explained.

"They've got four."

"Convenient."

"And if history proves correct . . . ," Bob said.

"As it rarely ever does," Louise countered.

". . . you should come out ahead."

"Was it everything you dreamed?" Bob asked.

Louise thought for a moment, then answered, "No. Most of the time it seemed like just any other ball game."

"Hmm. Really?"

She shrugged. "For me anyway. It had less to do with winning the pennant than it did with beating the crap out of the Braves. It was personal, more personal than even I realized. I tuned out the deluge and focused on Goetz. I had something to prove. Not to anyone else, but to myself. I had to prove that I was a better baseball player than he was."

"I think you proved that."

"For this season."

"Next season you're not going to have to worry about Rocky Goetz."

"So, it'll be someone else."

"Maybe," Bob shrugged. "Maybe not."

"But like I said . . ."

"You don't even want to think about next season."

That night, Louise ate a quiet dinner at home. Alone. She had been thinking a lot about Rocky Goetz. To finally have a face for the name Tombstone. Somehow it all fit, yet somehow it didn't. She just couldn't picture Rocky as an artist, not even a bad one—though somehow the image of him painting genitalia on a Louise Gehrig doll, or painting Cole's face on the head of a dildo, well, that fit. That fit her image of the sick son of a bitch perfectly. But the gunshot-riddled uniform was another story. Goetz steadfastly denied sending it, despite admitting to everyone else.

"Then who the fuck sent it?" Selden demanded during the interrogation.

"Someone else, I guess," Goetz insisted. "Someone who feels just like me."

"Great," Selden said. The thought that there was another fruit loop with a hard-on for Louise Gehrig made the special agent want to just pack it in, give it up, and move away. Far away.

But the notion didn't really surprise Louise, not after everything. She was used to it all by now, the good, the bad, and the extremely ugly.

She was even used to the reporters and photographers who had set up camp on the sidewalk in front of the entrance to her apartment building, waiting, just waiting. A few had even tried to gain access to her apartment, or at least the lobby, but Ziggy was vigilant, and even had one particularly obnoxious scribe arrested.

"Yeah," Cole said during an after-dinner, after-meditation phone conversation. "Here, too."

"Can you fucking believe it?"

"We're news."

"Great."

"How are you feeling?"

"Ask me in about ten days."

"Think you'll be feeling better then?"

"I certainly hope so."

"Then what?"

"Well, let's see. I'll vote in the election."

"For Rush?"

"Like us, like you . . . like now."

"Right. And then?"

"My mother's wedding."

"That's it?"

"Basically."

"So, you've got some free time on your hands."

"I've got some free months on my hands. Why? What do you have in mind?"

"A vacation."

"Go on."

"I've never been to the Keys."

"Christmas in the Keys."

"And Thanksgiving and New Year."

"How about Valentine's Day."

"Pitchers have to report to camp early, remember?"

"We can always celebrate it early."

"If we're still talking."

"We'll still be talking."

"Promise."

"I'd bet on it."

◍ ◍ ◍

The next morning, Margaret arrived at Louise's apartment with a veritable shopping bag of home pregnancy tests. Louise greeted her at the door. "C'mon in," she said, eying the bag.

They headed toward the kitchen, by way of the living room. Billie Holiday was playing softly on Louise's stereo, "Good Morning Heartache," her soul permeating the room, a friend offering support.

Margaret emptied the shopping bag onto the kitchen table. Then she opened her purse and pulled out an antique silver cigarette case which Louise hadn't seen in quite some time.

"What's that doing here?" she asked her mom.

"Thought it might relax you," Margaret said, opening the case and pulling out a meticulously rolled joint.

"I can't believe you," Louise said.

Margaret fished around in her purse for a moment. "Damn it!"

"What?"

"You got a lighter?"

Louise retrieved a battered old Zippo from one of her

kitchen drawers and handed it to her mom. "I just want you to know I don't approve of this."

"Be quiet." Margaret lit the joint and took an exceedingly long drag. After finally exhaling, she passed it to her daughter.

Louise held it aloft for a moment, staring at its glowing tip.

"Go on."

"I don't know."

"It'll relax you."

"It'll make me horny."

"That's a side effect you can live with."

She nodded and brought the joint to her lips. She took a small drag at first, then another, much longer one. Then exhaling, she passed it back to her mom.

"That's wasn't so bad now, was it?"

Sipping a glass of ice water, an awfully relaxed, extremely buzzed, and genuinely horny Louise read the back panel instructions of HPT box after HPT box, then asked, "Aren't there any where I don't have to pee into a little cup?"

"Sorry," Margaret said.

"They can put a man on the moon . . ."

"Too bad they can't put them all there."

Louise laughed. "I thought you were happy with your man."

"I am. But it felt like the right thing to say."

Louise held up one of the boxes. "Okay," she said. "So this one turns pink"—she picked up another—"this one displays a plus sign"—another—"this one turns pink *and* displays a little check sign"—another—"this one shows two lines for 'knocked up' versus one line for 'ya lucked out.' "

"Is that what it says?"

"I wish they had the balls to be so honest." Another, "This one turns blue."

"Yeah," Margaret said, motioning toward one final box, "and that one?"

Louise scanned the instructions. "Turns blue *and* displays a plus sign."

"Okay. Which one?"

"Might as well do them all."

"All six?"

"Why not."

"That's a lot of pee."

She hoisted her glass and took another sip. "I've been drinking water all morning."

"Good girl."

Within fifteen minutes, Louise had her answer.

"This one's pretty blue," Margaret said.

"Definitely blue. A pretty shade."

"Yeah. Sort of matches your eyes."

"Here's a plus sign."

"No arguing that."

"Pink with a check."

"Yup."

"Two lines."

"One, two."

"This one's pink."

"I like the blue better."

"Me, too."

"And that one?"

"Blue with a plus sign." She turned it over a few times. "It's sort of neat looking actually. Maybe I'll have it coated in Lucite and made into a refrigerator magnet."

Margaret shot her daughter a cockeyed look. She wasn't sure if Louise was joking.

"Maybe not."

A shrug. "It's pretty damn unanimous."

"I'd say so," Louise said. "Guess it wasn't nerves after all."

"Like you ever believed it was."

"Not really."

Louise pulled out an empty trash bag from one of her kitchen cabinets and swept the half dozen HPTs, their boxes, and instructions into the bag, tied it tightly, and tossed it aside.

"Are you going to tell Cole?" Margaret asked.

"One of these years." She looked at her mom. "I don't think he could handle it."

"You might be surprised."

"I don't want to risk it. Things are good."

"And?"

"And nothing. Things are good. That's enough."

"Right."

Louise stood, said, "I've got to take a shower. The team's got an afternoon workout at the park." She walked her mother to the door. "Tell Bob I said hi."

"I will."

A small kiss on the cheek.

"Are you gonna be okay?"

"Are you kidding? I've made it to the World Series. Of course I'll be okay."

"Yeah. All right then. See you tomorrow night."

"Right."

"Love you."

"Love you, too."

⚏   ⚏   ⚏

The shower was never-ending—Billie up full blast, just like the water. Hot, so very hot, Louise let it pound her, beat her, scald her. She let it cleanse her very soul.

Her mind was flooded—the possibilities and doubts contorting into the monster of her worst nightmares—a werewolf, a zombie, Rocky Goetz, and Rush Limbaugh, all morphed into one. She thought about next April. Would she be at first base, making as if nothing had happened? Or would she be seven months pregnant, watching the games on TV, rooting her teammates on while she painted a nursery and shopped for strollers? Or what if Rush Limbaugh was elected president, would she even be allowed to play? He was threatening to ban her and all women from the game. Could he carry out his threat? Or would the owners come to her defense? They'd realize she'd been good for the game, wouldn't they? Or what about the Supreme Court—could it protect her right to play? With Justice Dougherty gone, could the other judges even care?

She placed her hand on her stomach and pressed delicately. Is it a boy? she wondered. Or maybe a girl? And did it have Cole's fastball and her speed? Or maybe Cole's speed and her fastball. No, impossible. That was a phenom there in her belly. The hair would be dark—definitely dark—that much she knew. But the eyes, her blue or his gray? And would it be tall or short? Fat or thin? Would it be smart? Would it have freckles? Would it get picked on in school? Would it be a jock, or a computer nerd? Or maybe a cheerleader, heaven forbid? And names. Max for a boy. No, Evan. Or maybe, Shane. And Chanel for a girl. Definitely Chanel. Chanel Gabrielle Gehrig. Or Chanel Gabrielle Robinson?

"I'm sorry, Chanel," she whispered. "I really, really am."

And when there were no questions left, when the pain seemed unbearable, Louise broke down and cried. She cried for Bob, and for Norven Dougherty. She cried for her mom and for her granddad Joe. She cried for P.J. and Jesus and Lefty. She cried for baseball, and even for Rocky Goetz. But mostly she cried for herself and for Cole and for this child they most likely would never see.

"Hey, Saint Jude," she said. "It's me again. Yeah, I know. I've asked for a lot this year. I've been a real pain in the butt. Just let me play. Just let me get one more hit. One more steal. Yeah, yeah, I know. And, well, you"—she lowered her voice—"someone, certainly delivered. And you're probably sick of hearing from me. All my little lost causes. But, ya see, I've got one more favor to ask. Not so much a favor really, as it is a question. What should I do, Jude? What the fuck should I do?"

◐ **35** ◑

Fly Me to the Moon

Liz Phair performed the national anthem, Bob Dixon threw out the first ball, and at 7:45 P.M. on Saturday, October 14, in the year 2000, Louise Gehrig, Reggie Borders, Jesus Maldonado, and their fellow teammates took to the exquisitely manicured grass of South Field, while the Yankee batters waited patiently for their turn to come to the plate.

Watching the historic event live and oh so in person, the 38,710 in attendance cheered. Watching history via satellite, a billion baseball fans the world over did likewise.

In the safety and comfort of his living room, Special Agent Wesley Selden placed his slippered feet up on his coffee table, sipped at some good bourbon, and smiled.

In his private executive box, Matt Stern, his lawyer, Ronald Manelli, Yankee owner George Steinbrenner, baseball commissioner J. Danforth Quayle, National League president Henry Aaron, American League president Yogi Berra, and their dates and/or wives, laughed and partied to the splendor of the game.

From their two mezzanine seats, Kevin and Geraldine Willard, already stuffed to the gills on hot dogs and beer, cuddled in anticipation.

And in two specially reserved seats, just off to the right of the

Meteorites' dugout, Bob Dixon and Margaret Gehrig roared their approval.

While over at first base, Louise Gehrig was turning cartwheels in her head, genuflecting to the great god Louisville and the goddess Slugger. Deep down in her soul, she sang hallelujahs and amens. Hell, as she looked around at the flashbulb-lit shrine of leather and sweat and large men in black suits who lived to scream "Yer out!" it all of a sudden hit—hit hard, hit low, hit right, left, and center. It hit her in the head and knocked her on her ass. It tickled her earlobes and plucked at her pubic hair. It made her mouth dry, her nipples hard, and her toes tingle. It set off little nuclear bombs in her subconscious and depleted her ozone layer. It was bigger than an orgasm, mightier than birth. This was it, the '86 Mets, and she was Mookie. She was Ray Knight. She was the first woman in space. The first   o race. She was the first woman on the fucking moon.

Yeah, she thought, just *yeah!* over and over and over again.

That's when she noticed the banner. There were hundreds of them all over the stadium, most urging the Manhattan team on—**Sweep!** seemed to be the most popular phrase—but one in particular stood out. It read: **Lou Gehrig Would Be Proud!**

"I hope so," Louise said quietly, nodding to herself as she slipped two fingers into her back pocket. Checking, double-checking, just in case. It was there. Her prevention, her medication, her little good-luck charm. The first refrigerator magnet to ever take part in a World Series game. And why not? she figured. It had been good to her so far. And though she didn't for a minute believe these games to be a lost cause, Louise was playing the odds. And at that moment, with that magnet in her back pocket, the odds were most definitely in Louise's favor.

⑪   ⑪   ⑪

Up in heaven, Joe Gehrig turned to Norven Dougherty. "Can you believe she's still carrying around that old magnet?"

The old justice shrugged. "There are worse things for a girl to believe in."

"I guess," Joe said, with a shrug of his own.

They were quiet for a moment, as down behind South Field's home plate, an umpire yelled, "Play ball!"

"Y'know," Joe said, "that still gives me tingles, to this day. Every time I hear it."

"I know what you mean," Dougherty said. "That and the crack of the bat."

"Especially when someone connects for a dinger."

"Especially," Dougherty agreed.

Sitting to the other side of Joe was Lou Gehrig, who, clearing his throat, turned to address Louise's grandfather. "Hey, Joe," he said.

"Yeah, Lou. What can I do you for?"

"I just wanna know," the old Yankee great said, a beaming smile aimed Joe's way. "You guys gonna talk all night, or are you gonna watch the game?"

Joe smiled back, his pride contagious, is love bountiful. "We're gonna watch the game, Lou. You can bet on it. We're gonna watch the game."

Epilogue

Just prior to the start of the seventh game of the World Series, Special Agent WESLEY SELDEN received an urgent call from the director of the FBI. He was told that a plane was waiting for him at JFK. The plane would take him to Tokyo, where a near national security disaster needed his complete and immediate attention. The next afternoon, SUNGLASSMAN, who was also assigned to the Japanese case, purchased a copy of the international edition of *USA Today* and presented it to his superior, who then finally got to at least read about what happened in game seven of the October Classic.

In late November, while standing on the sidelines during the Thanksgiving Day Atlanta Falcon football game, ARNOLD LOITEN was injured by the Dallas Cowboys' Emmett Smith when the running back plowed into the reporter, knocking him unconscious and breaking three of his ribs and his left arm. Wanting some time off anyway, and now needing some to recuperate, Loiten took an indefinite leave of absence from his post at the *Atlanta Journal-Courier*, and is now hard at work on an un-

authorized biography of Louise Gehrig, which will be published
in the spring. The book is tentatively titled *Shame on You.*

In early December ROCKY GOETZ was found guilty of aggravated harassment and sentenced to eighteen months in a
minimum-security prison. After only a few weeks in prison, he
became a born-again Christian and legally changed his named
to Jesus H. Christ. He spends all of his free time painting
portraits of his new namesake, then trading them to equally religious prisoners for wads of chewing tobacco. He has subsequently been released from his contract with the Atlanta Braves,
and is looking forward to an early parole so he can test the free
agency waters . . . in Japan.

During the winter baseball meetings, DAN QUAYLE resigned
from his post as commissioner of baseball to pursue a life in private practice. Though HANK AARON seemed his most likely
successor, the owners committee was said to be carefully mull-
ing over the choices, and would most likely make its decision in
time for spring training. According to DAVID LETTERMAN,
The Owners Committee Number One Choice to Replace Dan
Quayle as Baseball's Commissioner: Schottzie.

MATT STERN, having turned a considerable profit from his
not-risky-after-all baseball venture, began moving away from
speculative investments and considered settling down. Within a
month of his baseball team winning the World Series, he proposed to his latest girlfriend, supermodel JENNIFER HANSEN,
telling her, "I want to have lots of babies." And though they had
been dating for only two weeks, Hansen, a seven-caret diamond
engagement ring weighing down her left hand, was said to be
seriously thinking it over.

⑪   ⑪   ⑪

During the postgame press conference, DAVE WINFIELD was publicly admonished, then fired, by GEORGE STEINBRENNER, only moments after their Yankees lost the seventh game of the World Series. The owner is reportedly negotiating with RICKEY HENDERSON about the vacant managerial position. According to Henderson, "The money's right, but I need some time to think it over."

⑪   ⑪   ⑪

Following an appearance at the Democratic National Committee celebratory bash, where he got to meet President-elect Al Gore, World Series MVP P.J. Strykes, on the advice of a first base–playing friend, spent a few relaxing weeks in the Key West sun. One evening, while working on a Duval Street crawl, P.J. met and fell quite immediately in love with the man of his dreams, runner-up American League Rookie of the Year Daniel Hoffman. The next morning, they rented a seventy-eight-foot yacht named *Hedonism* and took off on a cruise of the Caribbean, where they can be spotted searching for private beaches and worrying about nothing more than the perfect margarita.

⑪   ⑪   ⑪

After trading in her .38-caliber automatic pistol to the local authorities for a pair of front-row Michael Bolton concert tickets, GERALDINE WILLARD and her husband, KEVIN, packed up their four daughters and all of their belongings and cruised north to Edison, New Jersey, where he, because of his vast knowledge of the genre, immediately found work as the day manager of the local Porn 'N' Stuff adult bookstore. Geraldine, who to this day worries that the FBI will one day discover that she sent Agent Selden that gunshot-riddled Louise Gehrig uniform, subsequently got a job at a phone sex company, where

she is known as the Dominatrix Cassandra, and can be reached
by calling 1-900-ABUSE-ME. (A $2.75 per minute service charge
always applies.) The couple is currently at the end of a very
long waiting list for Manhattan Meteorites season tickets.

Minor league umpire BOBBY WIELECHOWSKA was promoted
to the majors at the conclusion of the 2000 season. He was assigned to the National League. His opening day assignment was
to be in Atlanta, where the Braves would be playing their newest
archrivals, the Manhattan Meteorites.

While accepting the National League's Most Valuable Player
Award, BOB DIXON hinted that there was no need to wait, that
he was most definitely interested in managing a major league
team. And though he and MARGARET are on an extended
honeymoon somewhere in Europe, he is, via those overseas
fiber-optic phone lines, presently in hot negotiations with numerous general managers. George Steinbrenner is not among
them.

LOUISE GEHRIG purchased a vintage Victorian house in the
old town district of Key West and spent much of the off-season
painting, decorating, and refurnishing. When not working on
the house, the National League's Rookie of the Year read,
swam, cultivated the old magnet collection, and made wildly
passionate love to COLE ROBINSON. And though it had been
a miraculous year by most any account, Louise knew she had
made mistakes—both on and off the field—mistakes that she'd
never repeat. Never. She'd practice harder, she'd practice
longer, she'd be ready come spring training. And as penance
for the big one, she anonymously donated her entire $287,000
share of the World Series Championship pot to the Planned

Parenthood organization, then invested a little petty cash in a lifetime's supply of condoms.

⚾   ⚾   ⚾

JOEY FROM BENSONHURST never did call WFAN again.